How to Save a Life

How to Save

A NOVEL

a Life

Eva Carter

BALLANTINE BOOKS / NEW YORK

2022 Ballantine Books Trade Paperback Edition

Copyright © 2021 by Eva Carter
Book club guide copyright © 2022 by Penguin Random House LLC

Published in the United States by Ballantine Books, an imprint of Random House, a division of Penguin Random House LLC, New York.

BALLANTINE and the HOUSE colophon are registered trademarks of Penguin Random House LLC.
RANDOM HOUSE BOOK CLUB and colophon are trademarks of Penguin Random House LLC.

Originally published in hardcover in the United States by Ballantine Books, an imprint of Random House, a division of Penguin Random House LLC, in 2021.

Published in the United Kingdom by Mantle, an imprint of Pan Macmillan, London.

Library of Congress Cataloging-in-Publication Data
Names: Carter, Eva, author. Title: How to save a life: a novel / Eva Carter.
Description: First edition. | New York: Ballantine Books, [2021]
Identifiers: LCCN 2020018546 (print) | LCCN 2020018547 (ebook) |
ISBN 9780593158883 (paperback) |
ISBN 9780593158890 (ebook)
Classification: LCC PR6108.A78 H69 2021 (print) | LCC PR6108.A78
(ebook) | DDC 823/.92—dc23
LC record available at https://lccn.loc.gov/2020018546
LC ebook record available at https://lccn.loc.gov/2020018547

Printed in the United States of America on acid-free paper

randomhousebooks.com
randomhousebookclub.com

1st Printing

Book design by Susan Turner

This book is dedicated to first responders everywhere,
who go toward danger to help the people who need them most.

How to Save a Life

THIS IS HOW TO SAVE A LIFE.

Imagine a room with a hundred people in it: a packed pub, maybe, full of people you know and care about.

One by one, without warning, your friends and family members begin falling to the floor. Eventually, only six or seven are left standing.

That's the truth about cardiac arrest. Without immediate help, fewer than one in ten people will survive.

It can happen to anyone, anywhere.

And the moment it does, the clock starts ticking. The heart no longer pumps blood to the brain and the body, starving them of oxygen.

But with the help of someone like you, many more patients could survive. Imagine thirty of those people you care about standing back up and dusting themselves down, alive and ready for their second chance.

It's ordinary people like us, not doctors, who are most likely to be there when the worst happens. At work, in the park, at home, even in the pub.

A person's chance of recovery depends on what happens next—starting with you.

This is the chain of survival. And the first link in the chain is both the easiest and the most important.

It's simply recognizing that someone has had a cardiac arrest—and calling for help.

If you see someone unresponsive and not breathing properly, call 999. Every single second counts.

Kerry

Six minutes.

I have six minutes left to be kissed.

Three hundred seconds and counting, if I don't want to end another year—let's face it, an entire millennium—as the only seventeen-year-old in Brighton who has never snogged another human being.

Most of the girls in the sixth form have gone all the way. You can tell from the way they move: dancing wildly on the shingle beach, wearing heels that keep sinking into the gaps between the pebbles, unsteady and sexy and—

"Which do you think will implode first, the National Grid or air traffic control?" Tim says, passing me the can of Diamond White cider. When I raise it to my lips, all that's left is apple froth.

I look up at the sky. "You probably shouldn't be quite so excited about the idea of the world ending."

He grins. "I can't help it if I crave a bit of drama sometimes."

You and me both.

"We don't have long to wait to get our share of it."

This time next December, I'll be at Manchester Uni. And, impossible as it seems now, the odds are that by then I *will* have been kissed—and hopefully a lot more. But the prospect of finally losing my virginity isn't even the most exciting thing about the year 2000 because in a year's time, I'll be training as a doctor. With a bit of luck, and the right questions on his physics exam paper, Tim will be doing the same.

"If Y2K doesn't wipe us out . . ."—he looks at his Swatch—"five minutes from now. Makes me feel quite reckless, being on the brink of disaster."

Reckless isn't Tim's style, but his eyes are bright: I can see the beach fires the hippies have lit reflected in them. Except it's not just the flames. There's something else in his face, an intensity . . .

Oh shit.

He's going to try to kiss me.

He mustn't.

Maybe it wouldn't be the absolute worst thing, if we did it in private. We've rehearsed slings and burn dressings on each other, so why not kissing? Both of us want to be prepared for when it really matters.

Except I don't think he's thinking of it as a rehearsal . . .

I move backward and break eye contact, staring resolutely over Tim's shoulder to where Joel and his mates are having a knockabout on the lawns, lit by the Victorian lamps that line the prom. The frost has set the earth like concrete but the boys don't seem to notice. They're too busy trying to outrun Joel, even though they know they never will.

He moves twice as fast as the others, the football always at his feet. He was in the same class as me until we were sixteen. While Tim and I stayed on at school, Joel hit the big time, starting a professional football apprenticeship with our city club, the Dolphins. He's one in a million. Everyone either wants to *be* him or be *with* him, me included. I think Tim might be the only person I know who doesn't care about Joel one way or the other.

". . . Perhaps we can blame the Pagans. You know, for deciding New Year should happen in December," Tim says, embarking on a new lecture. I let the words float toward me, without taking them in. "Or I suppose it might have been the Romans."

"Maybe." I stay far enough away that he can't reach. Everything has to be clear for Tim: he's one of the smartest kids in the sixth form but sometimes he's also the densest, and I can't let him convince himself it's a good idea to kiss me.

Kiss me.

I imagine saying those words to Joel. Let myself believe for a moment that instead of laughing in my face, he might do as I ask.

On the lawns, Ant makes a clumsy attempt to tackle Joel but falls over his own big feet, and Joel vaults across his best friend's legs to score again.

The ball flies over the two Gap sweatshirts laid as goalposts.

Six–nil to Joel. I've been counting.

". . . but why didn't they choose the summer solstice to mark a new year?" A speck of cider foam sits on Tim's top lip, and I'm about to lean over and brush it away. Except . . . what if he thinks I'm flirting?

I want it to go back to how it's been since we were seven: in and out of his garden and ours; every Tuesday, checking each other's vital signs in the Scout Hall. I hate the new us: how he guffaws at my jokes when they're not funny and gives me sideways looks as though he's only just noticed that I'm female.

"Summer solstice would make for a better party. Sacrificing virgins, roasting pigs. Or the other way around."

I get so twitchy now listening to his meandering monologues. I imagine walking away from him and heading onto the playing field, the icy blades of grass spiky through my tights.

In this other reality, I would easily score a goal.

Joel would embrace me in a victorious hug.

Louise Norman's jaw—newly braced but sadly not wired shut—would drop, astonished at my grace.

Maybe grace is too improbable. I'd settle for being surprising. For being *noticed*. At school, at home, here. Anywhere would do.

At the edge of my vision, Joel is running.

And then he's not.

He doesn't trip, or throw out an arm to right himself or break his fall. Instead, he drops, facedown, legs outstretched. The boy who fell to earth.

The others play on: Fat Matt does a double take when he gets possession of the ball and propels it toward the neglected goal.

I wait for Joel to get up. What's he playing at? He's not a joker the way Ant is, and I can't believe he's risked injury by falling so clumsily. In his last year at school, before he got his big break with the Dolphins, Joel was the only one of the popular kids never to smoke or drink. Even tonight he's stuck to orange juice.

Ant pivots back, calling out, "Come on, Joel, you knob," and when he reaches his friend, he nudges him with his big black shoe. Once. Twice. The third time is more of a kick.

Still Joel doesn't move.

Certainty strikes me like lightning. I drop the can of cider—Tim is still waffling on about the satanic origin of Christian rituals—and though I fully intended to *walk* toward Joel, my legs have other ideas.

Even as I run across the lawns, I'm cursing myself for being so obvious, but I can't stop. After keeping my crush secret for nearly seven years I'm about to blow it.

Almost there.

Joel's stillness makes me catch my breath. The other boys circle around him, catcalling. Ant frowns and as I step into the circle, our eyes meet. I brace myself for mockery—Ant has teased me on and off all through school—but instead, I glimpse panic.

"What's wrong with him?" Ant asks.

"He's messing about," one of the lads says. I'm already kneeling down beside Joel, the grass sharp against my shins.

"No," I say, "he's not." My loud voice surprises all of us. "Be quiet. I need to listen, check how often he's breathing."

If he's breathing.

ABC. The first aider's alphabet flashes through my mind, anchoring me. I've trained for this.

I lean in, close to Joel's face. If he's only blacked out, I should be able to feel the warmth of his breath. But apart from the sweet smell of orange juice, there is nothing.

Airway. I tilt his chin, feeling the slight prickle of stubble under my fingertips. I part his lips with my fingers, seeing him no longer as the boy I fancy but as a puzzle to be solved. Nothing seems to be blocking his throat.

He should be breathing.

"Ant. We need to move him, onto his back."

Joel is heavy, a dead weight. But as we wrestle with him, Ant and me, I feel powerful. Joel's on his side for a moment, before he flops down onto the grass with an obscene smack.

"Watch it!" Fat Matt says. "His legs are insured for ten grand each!"

They're worth nothing if he's dead.

Breathing. His chest isn't moving. *Nothing* is moving. Time has slowed, but my thoughts are faster, clearer than they've ever been.

I glance up. "One of you needs to run to the call box and phone 999. Ask for an ambulance. Tell them he's not breathing. Tell them to come fast."

The five boys stand there, mouths gold-fishing, as though I'm speaking a foreign language. "Paddy, you go."

He shrugs and kicks at the earth, as though he's unsure whether to obey me and risk having the piss taken for the next year.

"I'm serious. Go *now*." I get back to work, pulling Joel's long, lean arms to his sides. "*Run.* And, Matt—go and stand by the road. Try to flag down a police car."

When they do what I say, we're all equally gobsmacked.

"Tim!" I call out.

He's pushed his way to the front. As I pull Joel's sweatshirt up to reveal his chest, I wait for Tim to kneel down at my side, to take over. In drills, he's always the one fighting to step in.

But when I look up, he's just staring at me. I don't have time to work out why.

C is for . . . *circulation.*

Am I really going to do this?

There is no one else.

"Get everyone to move away," I tell Ant as I shuffle closer to Joel, my knees touching his arms.

His dark-gold skin is covered with a film of sweat. I'm trying to find the right spot between his ribs: my pale hands look like a little girl's, and my nails are ragged and bitten.

Doubt fills me. He *cannot* be dying. Any moment now he'll sit bolt upright, laugh in my face. I'll be known forever as the idiot girl who fell for Joel's windup.

But as I glance down past his torso, I see a dark patch around his groin. And then I smell the sharp tang of urine and I know this is not a joke.

"Please, Ant, nobody needs to see this. Move them away."

"You lot, move. Give the girl some room."

I place my right hand over my left and push down for the first time.

No. Too cautious. The plastic training dummy always popped up and down jauntily. Joel's ribs and muscles fight me.

I do it again. Harder. There's nothing jaunty about this.

The third time feels right. I do what I was taught to, tuning in to my own voice as I count out loud.

one and two and three and four and five and six and—

They taught us the right, rapid rhythm using the old kids' song "Nellie the Elephant," but right now, the nursery rhyme pace feels wrong. Jaunty, again. The jokers in our branch of the ambulance cadets used to try to find the most inappropriate songs with the same tempo.

"Stayin' Alive."

I repeat the lyrics in my head to time what I am doing but they're so inappropriate, they sicken me. My hands feel too weak for the violence needed to force the blood around Joel's athletic body. Was that a rib buckling? He will be so badly bruised when he wakes.

If he wakes.

It's not the movies. Hardly anyone survives in real life.

I mustn't think like that. Push harder. Try a different song.

"Another One Bites the Dust."

But the lyrics to that one are even harsher.

fourteen fifteen sixteen seventeen

I realize I've been holding my breath. I try to take in as much air as I can, to give to Joel.

twenty-eight, twenty-nine, thirty

I tilt his head back, the smooth skin of his throat taut and still warm. Pinch his nose hard to stop precious oxygen escaping.

Lower my head. Seal his lips against mine.

Close by I hear one cheer, then a volley of them. Somewhere in Brighton, fireworks explode.

It's the year 2000.

I taste orange juice. I look left, down Joel's body, waiting for his chest to rise, for his lungs to inflate.

And I pray—though Tim and I have discussed this at length and are unsure God could exist—that this horrible primitive thing I'm doing might, against the odds, be enough.

Tim

JANUARY 1, 2000

I cannot move.

I stare at Kerry, kneeling on the grass next to Joel, and I know she needs me, they both need me, but *I cannot move.*

Do *not* panic. Perform a primary assessment: Danger? There is none. Responsiveness?

I am responsive, I can breathe, I am uninjured. But I can't bloody move.

What's wrong with me?

Not syncope, because if I had fainted, I would be lying next to Joel. But I am still upright.

Around me, the world is in motion, exactly as it was before midnight. The traffic lights are still in sequence, the music still blares from the clubs, the sky is still free of burning airplane debris.

And Kerry is giving Joel CPR.

But I cannot move.

Why? Think, Tim.

This is not full paralysis because I can breathe, and swallow, and feel my body, from the tips of my fingers to the ends of my toes. So probably not a stroke or spinal injury . . .

The Millennium Bug was meant to bring Armageddon, but instead, I am the glitch.

It should be *me* doing the compressions and rescue breaths. Kerry might be cleverer at school, but she always comes second to me in ambulance cadet competitions. She's too impetuous, which can lead to catastrophic errors, while I always analyze with clearheaded efficiency. It's why she takes silver when I take gold. I even made it to the national finals.

But my body won't let me act. My legs are leaden, as if I'm in a nightmare. Sweat prickles in my armpits, my groin. I don't think I can smell worse. Have I pissed myself or is the stink coming from Joel?

Even when I try to open my mouth, to call out for help, my jaw seems to be locked in position.

But perhaps this is a good thing. I can't draw attention to myself, and no one should see me frozen like this, least of all Kerry. Plus she must not be interrupted. Nothing is as important as what she's doing now.

3

Kerry

As I prepare for the next rescue breaths, a horrible gagging noise comes out of Joel's mouth. Animal, not human.

"Joel. Joel, are you waking up? Can you hear me?"

I stop the compressions, willing his rib cage to inflate on its own. Nothing happens.

I remember something the resus instructor said. *Agonal breaths are a sign that the brain is dying from oxygen starvation.*

I restart the compressions.

Some of the girls crowded around are crying. Farther along the prom, the hippies are drumming and singing, and the fireworks keep filling the sky with sparks of color.

"What's Kerry doing to him? Not a doctor yet, is she?" I hear Louise Norman lisping to someone.

"Is Joel dead?" another girl asks.

"Don't be stupid," Ant says. "He was running with the ball just now. Of course he's not dead."

Except Ant might be wrong. Joel doesn't *look* dead, yet. But if I'm right, and his heart *has* stopped, then my hands are the only things keeping his blood flowing, my breath his only source of oxygen.

It can't possibly be enough.

I don't hear a siren but the grass around me changes color: blue, orange, blue, orange. The rhythm of the flashing light confuses me, breaks my own pattern, and I replay "Stayin' Alive" in my head, matching its pace, *pushing, pushing, pushing* . . .

For the first time, my arms are tired. When I reach thirty compressions and dip down to give Joel another rescue breath, I realize how ragged my own has become.

I seal my lips against Joel's again. Exhale. Is it my imagination, or is his face colder now?

"Kerry. Listen. I'll take over the compressions after your two breaths." Tim's voice. *Where the hell have you been?*

I don't look up. Can't break the cycle. Every beat counts.

As I raise my head from the rescue breath, our hands touch, and Tim slips into position.

Like me, he looks surprised at how much force it takes to push down the rib cage. He pumps once.

That's not hard enough.

Have I done the wrong thing, letting Tim take my place?

He pumps a second time.

"Lads, come on. Let us through." A man's voice, world-weary. The edge of my vision fills with the lemon brightness of the first responder's fluorescent jacket.

"What have we got here? One too many to see in the New Year or—" The paramedic stops abruptly. I look up just as his frown turns to understanding. "Jeff," he shouts out, "I think we've got an arrest. Get the defib."

He understands.

"All right, mate," the paramedic is saying to Tim. "You've been doing a grand job. First-aid trained, are you?"

When Tim doesn't answer, I speak for him. "He's a St. John's Ambulance cadet . . . So am I. The patient . . . we think . . . he's in cardiac arrest." I sound as though I've been running cross-country. "He collapsed . . ." I remember the fireworks. "Just before midnight. We've been giving . . . two rescue breaths every . . . thirty compressions."

The paramedic nods. "All right, love, give us some space to do our work now."

I have no strength left to move.

"The patient's name is Joel." Tim speaks now, his voice imitating the calm tones the paramedic used. "He's seventeen. On his way to being a pro footballer. Or at least, he was."

The paramedic flinches. "Right. My name's Roger. Who are you?"

"Tim."

"All right then, Tim. I will take over after the next fifteen compressions. My colleague Jeff is coming with a defibrillator from the ambulance. You've done a brilliant job."

Roger shoots me an impatient glance as he pushes in between me and Tim. I scoot backward as the paramedic takes over. Tim looks shell-shocked, even though he's done less than a minute of CPR. I did ten, or longer.

A hand reaches for mine, steadying, pulling me up.

"Is he going to be all right?" Ant's hand is strong but his voice is small. "Kerry?"

I'm surprised he remembers my real name, after years of calling me nasty nicknames. "I hope so."

Ant is still looking at me, but his hand has dropped to his side. "Were you doing CPR? I feel like we're in an episode of *ER*."

"I was . . ." It seems unbelievable already, what I just did. "I was making sure Joel's blood kept circulating. To keep the oxygen reaching his brain."

Ant nods. "On telly, they wake up. Why hasn't he woken up?"

My hands are starting to shake. The paramedic continues CPR. A second crew member runs toward Joel's prone body, carrying a bulky bag.

"The cardiopulmonary resuscitation can't wake anyone on its own." Tim brushes his hands against his jeans. "They need to shock his heart back into the correct rhythm, using a defibrillator."

I don't think Ant will have understood Tim's answer.

"Everyone move back, please," one of the ambulance men calls out.

"You heard them!" Tim shouts, shooing the other kids away.

"How did you know to how to do that?" Ant asks me, shaking his head.

"I know first aid. Tim and I both do."

I hear an electronic beeping, followed by a robotic female voice. There's a gap where the other kids have broken the circle and I move so I can see Joel again.

Analyzing . . . analyzing. Shock advised.

Stand clear.

It's impossible not to look. Will this work? If it doesn't, am I to blame?

Joel's body buckles upward from the grass as the shock is delivered. As he crashes back down to the ground, I hold my breath.

Analyzing, analyzing.

Shock advised.

It hasn't worked. Joel is still dead.

For the first time, I hear sirens. They must have sounded before, but I was too preoccupied to hear them. A second ambulance and a police car mount the pavement and drive across the grass toward us.

Stand clear.

A couple of the lads are hiding cans under their coats and shuffling off, a reflex response to approaching police.

Joel's body bucks and crashes down a second time.

I hold my breath.

Analyzing, analyzing.

"We've got a pulse," one of the paramedics calls out.

Ant's eyes widen. "He's gonna be OK?"

It is eighteen minutes past midnight: that's how long Joel's brain and body have been deprived of oxygen. Even if his body is responding, the odds are that what I did wasn't enough.

Ant stares at me, his face fierce. "A pulse means his heart is beating, right?"

The second ambulance crew is setting up kit on the lawns, like a mini–field hospital. Tim is talking to the police; the officers frown as Ant and I approach.

"Keep back, lad, give the ambulance crew some space to do their job," the policeman says.

"He's the patient's best friend," Tim tells the female officer. She's skinny with gray wiry hair under her cap, but her colleague has a huge belly and his face is slick with sweat, as though even the walk from the car has been too much for him.

Yet it's Joel–the fittest kid I know–lying on the cold earth.

The policewoman leads us toward the car, but Tim holds back. I see the determination on his face: I think he's hoping to cadge a lift in the ambulance.

Let him.

"Bet this is your first time in the back of a cop car," Ant says, as we climb in.

I manage a weak smile: he's trying to help us both feel better. "This definitely wasn't how I thought tonight would go."

It feels like years ago I was *that girl* worrying about whether Tim would kiss me.

"We'll follow the ambulance," the policewoman says. We look out the windows and it's when the lights of the Palace Pier blur that I realize I'm crying. Why?

I'm nothing to Joel. He barely recognizes me, even though we walked the same route home from school for five years. But I still want to be at the hospital when he wakes up.

If he wakes up.

$$\sim\!\!\wedge\!\!\wedge\!\!\wedge\!\!\wedge\quad 4$$

Tim

People worship heroes, but it's all down to the amygdala. We think we make rational choices, but it's this almond of cells, buried deep in the brain, that determines whether we're courageous or cowardly, if we fight or if we freeze.

So it wasn't my fault. *Right?*

"Are you all right, there, Tim?" asks Jeff or Roger, keeping his eyes on the road. He's told me his name twice now but I'm no good at remembering and I can't see his badge. Roger or Jeff is in the back with Joel. "Big thing you did for your mate. He's got the best chance, thanks to you."

"Yeah."

I know that less than one in ten patients who suffer out-of-hospital cardiac arrests survive. Will Joel be the lucky one?

"And the girl who was hanging around? Was she the lad's girlfriend?"

Kerry. What was it about *her* amygdala that made her able to act while I froze? She's always been more impulsive than me, but even so, we should both have been prepared.

"No, definitely not his type. Kerry and I are first aiders. We've both applied to study medicine if we get high enough grades in our exams."

"Doctors-in-waiting, eh? At least you're not afraid to get hands-on when it counts, which is more than I can say for some."

It was the siren that snapped me out of my paralysis. By then, Kerry must have been exhausted, her compressions becoming inefficient, reducing Joel's chances. Taking turns was the best way to maximize the chances of a good outcome. When I took over, I brought fresh energy.

Who am I kidding? I screwed up. I failed.

We turn up toward the hospital, and Jeff/Roger puts his foot down.

"How's he doing, Roger?" The driver—Jeff, I must remember that—calls over his shoulder.

"Stable. Hanging on in there."

I wish I was in the back with Joel, where everything needed to preserve life is stored, neatly shelved, ready for use. After the unbearable chaos of that scene on the lawns I crave order.

"You know, whatever the outcome," the driver says, glancing at me briefly, "whatever happens to the lad in the end, you mustn't feel guilty. You must tell yourself, *I stepped in.* When everyone else was standing around gawping, I was the one who tried."

I open my mouth to confess to my paralysis, those shameful minutes when I left Kerry to work on Joel alone. This man will absolve me, reassure me that it doesn't matter who gave the CPR, all that matters is *someone* did.

My failure to act could even help Mum accept that becoming a doctor might be beyond my capabilities. She's in denial about the rejections I've already had from three of the four university medical programs I applied to. *It only takes one, Tim.*

"Tim . . . ? Will you promise me that, Tim?" the driver continues.

As I try to form the words to explain what really happened, I picture my mother's face.

She can't know what a pathetic failure I am: it would kill her.

Next time I'll be better.

I close my mouth.

The lights of Sussex Hospital's A & E are ahead. This place represents Joel's only hope of coming back from the dead. *And* my only remaining hope of becoming a doctor. I get a guaranteed interview for the medical degree program here in my home city because I'm Mum's caregiver.

It's all I've ever worked for, all she's has ever wanted. My mother knows me better than anybody else in the world—except Kerry—and if she believes I can do it, I should believe it too.

She'll certainly never forgive me if I don't do it.

I should see what's just happened as a lesson. I can learn from my mistakes. And I *did* step in, eventually. I can talk about that at my interview, make my strategic thinking a positive. It will be the five years of training that make me the doctor I was born to be, not a few minutes of indecision.

"I promise, Roger."

"It's Jeff," he says, "but under the circumstances, I think you can be forgiven."

5

Kerry

A & E is deserted. The twitchiness I felt in the back of the police car turns into full-blown panic.

Where is Joel?

"Hello? Is anyone there?"

My hands and arms ache and tingle from the CPR. But the feeling of powerlessness is worse. I *need* to do more.

I bang on the screen at reception but no one appears. I bang again, beyond caring whether I smash the glass. At least that'd attract attention. The policewoman gently pulls my arm away.

"We don't need you slashing yourself, on top of everything, do we? It's quiet because this is the calm before the storm. Your friend was lucky to get here before the New Year punch-ups start."

Lucky.

A & E has never scared me before. The opposite, actually: I've been here three times, thanks to various scrapes, and each time I've liked the buzz more.

I even mentioned my experiences as a patient at one of my med school interviews. The first time was after I fell out of a tree in Tim's garden—I'd ignored him when he told me not to climb too high. The agony after my shoulder hit the earth was all-consuming.

But when I came into the hospital, and they took me beyond those swishy double doors, a young woman—the most junior of junior doctors—took one look at me and warned me it would be excruciating for three seconds as she reset my shoulder but then everything would be OK again.

I told the interview panel: *She was right. It was like magic, the way she knew what to do. I want to be able to do that for people too.*

"Kerry?"

I look up and Tim is walking toward Ant and me. When Tim hugs me, I remember how close we came to kissing, and I pull away.

"They said we're allowed to use the family room over here; it's more private."

And more claustrophobic: two rows of five chairs each, facing each other. I sit next to Ant, who has finally stopped jabbering about everything and nothing.

Tim sits down opposite us. "So Joel has been taken to resus. He was stable in the ambulance. What Kerry and I did helped keep him alive but now it's up to the doctors."

"Has he woken up yet?" Ant asks.

Tim and I exchange a look.

"He probably won't wake up for a while," Tim explains. If at all.

"I could talk to him, like they do in the films." Ant steps toward the door. "Anyone got a Walkman? He hates 'N Sync, so if I play 'Music of My Heart' or something, he'll definitely wake up."

"He won't, because he's sedated, so the doctors can do tests, work out what caused the problem with his heart," Tim says.

I want to say something to make Ant feel better. But my mind is blank.

"Your hands are shaking," Ant says.

I look down. He's right. I grip my knees through the sequined material of my dress, but still my hands tremble. Ant reaches across to hold them with his so mine can't shake anymore.

"Joel Greenaway? Where *are* you?"

The voice comes from the corridor. We head back out into the main waiting area, where Fat Matt is shrugging off a policeman.

"Matt, we're over here." Ant goes to embrace his friend and the sound of their backslapping reverberates around the space. I see tears in Ant's eyes, which he hastily wipes away, disguising the movement by running a hand through his hair. "Is Joel's dad with you?"

Fat Matt shakes his head. I realize he's not even fat anymore, just sturdy and muscular. I wonder if the nickname will stick forever, a lifelong reminder of a brief chubby phase aged fourteen. "The doctors took him straight in to see Joel."

"That's good news, ain't it?" Ant says. "So how come you look like you've seen a ghost?"

"Not a ghost. A *woman*," Matt says. "Mr. Greenaway was with a woman who was *definitely* not Mrs. Greenaway. The copper had to bang on the door loads of times and eventually when Joel's dad opened it, I could see her behind him. Not much older than us. In a dressing gown!"

Ant tuts loudly. "Enough, OK? You don't mention this to anyone, especially Joel. Hear me?"

Matt looks pissed off not to have had a chance to tell the full story. I tune out while Tim plays the grown-up again, explaining what's what, and I am suddenly so tired I could lie down on the lino now and sleep for twenty-four hours.

But I won't leave until I know if Joel has made it.

As A & E fills up, the volume increases too: shrieks of laughter, singing, sobbing. Two more of Joel's mates have found their way to the hospital and we're crammed into the smaller waiting room. One of the lads asks what I'm doing there, but Ant silences him with a warning look.

At two-ish, I try to call home from the pay phone but there's no answer. They'll all still be at the Pier Players' Christmas Bash. My big sister, Marilyn, tried to persuade me to go—"Come on, there's costumes and everything," she said—and the fact she thought dressing up might be a clincher just proves how little she knows me.

What if I *had* gone with them? I catch my breath and my palms tingle again. No one else would have known what to do . . . Except Tim, of course.

But he froze.

A nurse finally tells us there's no point waiting, that Joel has a long night ahead and only family will be allowed in to see him. The others slope off, but Ant and Tim and I huddle under the porch outside, the cold like a slap in the face.

"I don't want to go home," I say. "Not when he's here."

Ant lights a cigarette. "You could come to my parents' café. They'll still be up. They were catering for a big party tonight."

"My mum will be wanting me home," Tim says.

"She's got lupus," I add, before Ant starts calling him a mummy's boy. "She needs a wheelchair sometimes and Tim looks after her because his dad's not around."

Ant shrugs and takes another drag on his cigarette. If he already knew, he doesn't let on.

The doors to the hospital slide open and a man stumbles outside. It takes me a moment to realize why he's so familiar. When Joel got signed to the Dolphins as an apprentice at sixteen, they printed a picture of him in *The Argus* with his parents. All the girls in our class agreed Joel's dad was cute for an old guy, that he'd passed on his looks to his son.

The man is Joel's dad, except now he looks at least a hundred years old.

His hand reaches into his jeans pocket, but when he removes a packet of cigarettes he just stares at them, as if he's forgotten what they're for.

The electric doors begin to close again but then stop because Mr.

Greenaway is still in the way. It happens twice more before Ant walks toward him. He takes a cigarette from the packet, lights it, and hands it back.

"Come stand with me, Graham," Ant says, and it's weird to hear him use a first name for someone's father. But Mr. Greenaway does as he's told and we stand there in a huddle.

The cigarette burns down to its tip and Ant takes it, stubbing it out under his trainer. I see grass in the grooves of his sole from the kickabout on Hove Lawns.

"What if he doesn't make it?" Mr. Greenaway says. "What if Lynette doesn't get home in time?"

Ant frowns. "You're not allowed to say that, Graham. None of us can give up on him. Not now. Not ever. These guys didn't." He points at Tim and me.

Mr. Greenaway looks up: I don't think he noticed us before. A brief, automatic smile appears on his face and I see Joel in his features.

"You're friends of Joel's?" he asks, his voice hoarse.

"These guys saved his life!" Ant announces and I wait for Tim to clarify what really happened.

"We're first-aid trained," Tim says to Joel's dad. "We happened to be in the right place at the right time. And now he's in the right hands." When I try to catch his eye, he stares into space. Does he even realize he's lied by omission?

"Joel's a fighter, OK? Everything's going to be fine," Ant says.

I want to speak up, because I don't think it's fair to give Mr. Greenaway false hope. Joel might not be Joel anymore.

But instead I stay silent. Sometimes it's kinder to let people work out the truth for themselves.

6

Joel

You don't really want to hear too much about waking up from a coma because it'll stop you believing in happy endings.

Spoiler alert: I lived. According to the tabloids, I am the Millennium Miracle.

But coming back from the dead is nothing like the movies. No stepping toward a heavenly light, before a soppy voice tells you *it's not your time.* No opening your eyes to find your loved ones weeping with happiness by your bed and Sarah fucking McLachlan singing "Angel" in the background. Definitely no pretty nurse mopping your brow.

Instead it's this nightmare of buzzers and beeps and gloom interrupted now and then by harsh lights. It's a cycle of waking and falling and waking. Like being in a dodgy old computer game, but instead of Lara Croft holding you down, it's a gang of killer medics.

They tell me I woke up twice before I actually spoke. I don't remember that. There is *so much* that's been wiped from my memory.

But the first time I really remember waking up, *she* was there.

"Joel?"

At first, her features were blurred, like I had snow in my eyes.

"Joel!" She was shouting now. "Stay awake. OK? I'm Kerry. Kerry Smith. From school."

She said it like she didn't expect me to recognize her or even know her name. But I knew plenty about Kerry Smith. When we were eleven, in our first year at senior school, I followed her and Tim bloody Palmer home every day.

Sometimes, instead of heading up toward the Avenue and my own house with its electronic gates and triple garage, I'd hang back and watch Kerry instead. I thought her house, with its plastic hanging baskets and that yellow Fiesta parked badly on the narrow drive, was the definition of *normal*. And normal was what I wanted.

On Tuesdays and Wednesdays, her mum didn't work, so she'd greet Kerry with a hug and a glass of OJ. The other days, Kerry would watch medical shows: *Casualty* and *ER*. One time, there was this massive row between Kerry and her big sister, Marilyn: cushions, magazines, and a bright red shoe sped past the window. I couldn't hear what they said through the double-glazing but they made up within minutes. I envied them. I had no one at home to argue with, though the fridge was always full and we had Sky Sports years before anyone else I knew.

"Joel?" Kerry repeated. Behind her, zombies in white moved so quietly I thought they must have been floating. Was this heaven or hell or something else completely?

"What's happened?" My throat felt like someone had sandpapered it but I couldn't feel the rest of my body. Except my hand, which throbbed as if I'd been stung by a bee.

"I should get your dad; he's only in the waiting room."

Dad was here? This was serious.

"And your mum will be here in the early hours. She's been desperate to get home but the flights from Australia were booked solid."

Mum was going to leave a live broadcast, her first presenting gig in ages, to be with me? It didn't get more serious than that.

"What time is it?"

Kerry glanced up above me. I tried to move my head but it didn't budge.

"It's ten-thirty. At night."

Why was she was lying to me? There hadn't been more than a few minutes until midnight when I was playing football near the West Pier.

And Dad? Dad was at home, drinking champagne, probably shagging some girl who wasn't Mum. Because Mum was on the other side of the world on live TV . . .

My brain felt as slow as dial-up Internet, trying to make sense of where I was, pixel by pixel, waiting for the full picture to load.

I reached toward Kerry, but something stopped my hand going any farther. I was in the hospital, but why? "Did someone jump me?"

Yobs sometimes pick fights with me because I'm in the football squad, or because I drive a nice car, or just to look macho in front of their girlfriends.

She leaned forward: her cheeks were pink but under her eyes, the skin was blue-black, as if she hadn't slept for days. "No. You had a problem with your heart. You were playing football, do you remember?"

"'Course I do. How much time before the fireworks?"

Kerry blinked. "Joel, you . . . missed them. It's January the second now. Nighttime. You've been asleep."

"For two *days*? Don't wind me up."

"OK. Not sleep, exactly; they kept you in a coma, to protect your brain." She looked around for someone to rescue her. "I can get the doctor. He'll explain it better than I can—"

But I'd heard enough. I tried to swing my legs off the bed. But instead of my feet hitting the floor, my upper body lurched forward while everything else stayed where it was.

A sharp pain at the crook of my elbow made me gasp. I was falling toward the floor, a meter below me, and I braced myself for it to hurt like hell when my face smashed onto the shiny gray lino—

"Nurse! He's trying to get out of bed!"

The white-uniformed zombies were on me. The enemy! Loads of them. I punched and kicked and tried to bite myself free, but nothing was working properly; my arms and legs were flailing and—

Dad.

I smelled my father before I saw him, espresso and Aramis, and his body broke my fall, my head wedged against his chest, his strong arms trapping me in a hug, mumbling soft words into the top of my skull.

Joel, Joel, Joel, like a football chant, *my son, my boy, my Joel.*

I'd been stronger than my dad since the age of thirteen. Probably hadn't hugged him since then either. The shock of that hug made all the remaining fight drain away.

My body had *never* let me down before. My whole life, it had done what I asked, made me faster and stronger than anyone else.

And now, suddenly, it was a traitor.

7

Kerry

"Have I got toothpaste on my face? Or seagull poo in my hair?"

Tim checks me over as we cross the playground. "You look fine."

"Then why is everyone staring at us?"

As he looks around, one of the younger students is actually *pointing* at me, as though I've grown an extra head.

"You're right. How . . ." I can see him searching for precisely the right word. *"Peculiar."*

This attention is freaking me out. The last thing I want is to be indoors after four days at that stuffy hospital, but we run up the steps to the stinky Portakabin that serves as the Sixth Form Common Room to escape the stares.

The temperature inside is colder than outside, but at least we're out of sight. I empty the kettle of water that's sat there since we broke up for Christmas, watch the beige flakes of limescale disappear down the plughole. Could it have been hard water that made Joel's heart malfunction?

I can't seem to stop asking myself the same questions, over and over again. Why did it happen to him; why then; why was I there? And the big one: did I get the CPR wrong? Is *that* why Joel is consumed by terrifying rages since he woke up—because I failed to get enough oxygen to his brain?

The answers aren't clear; as the doctors keep saying, all we can do is *wait and see.*

I focus on spooning coffee granules into two mugs, pouring over boiling water, adding sugar.

As I hold out the coffees, the last drops of water in the kettle come back to a boil. The guttural sound is chillingly familiar. My heart pounds, and I close my eyes as I realize what it's like: Joel, lying on the grass, his mouth opening, gasping for breath, that same agonal gurgling . . .

I hear the mugs smashing before I register scalding coffee splashing against my legs.

"Watch out, butterfingers!" Tim calls, but it's too late; the liquid has soaked through my tights, trapping the heat against my skin.

Despite the pain, I crouch down to pick up the shards of china.

"Kerry, you're hurt!" He's at the sink, filling the washing-up bowl with water. My shins prickle as blisters begin to form, but I keep going.

"For God's sake, Kerry, stop doing that."

I straighten up, holding the broken mugs in my coffee-sticky palms. Without warning, Tim tips the bowl toward me. A wave of icy water splashes over my knees, my legs, down into the new Doc Martens I got for Christmas.

"What the *hell* did you do that for?" My boots are flooded, but my scalds don't hurt any less.

"I . . ." He blinks, as though he's as mystified by his behavior as I am. "It's what you're meant to do with burns. I couldn't just stand there and do nothing."

It's on the tip of my tongue: *what, like you did on New Year's Eve?* We stare at each other.

Should I tell him, finally, how dreadful it was for me? How alone

I felt as I pushed and puffed and knew I had someone's life, literally, in my hands. I want to ask him too, why he's taking equal credit for the resuscitation when it was almost all me.

As the liquid puddles on the floor, I decide it has to be said. I see him flinch, as if he knows what's coming.

"Tim, about that night—"

"Please, Kerry. I've learned my lesson, it'll be different next time."

I stare at him. I have to tread carefully. "It's nothing to be ashamed of. And it doesn't mean you're not suited to be a doctor or anything like that. But maybe it's better we clear it up, especially as we don't even know if I did it right or whether Joel is going to recover properly—"

His eyes widen. He looks as scared as he did on the lawns. "Mum can't know," he whispers. "It'd destroy her if she knew what really happened. That's the only reason I've not explained—"

The bell rings for class. Like Pavlov's dogs, we respond as we've been trained to. Our conversation can wait.

As we go toward science block, my wet feet chafe against new leather. After class, I'll talk to Tim again, before things get even more out of hand. I understand why he doesn't want people to know. Elaine Palmer isn't quite the sweet, brave single mother everyone else sees. She will be upset. Angry.

But still, the truth matters more. I *did* step in. Whether Joel's rages are permanent or not, if I hadn't acted, he wouldn't have stood a chance.

I've never seen myself as vain. But perhaps I am, because there's a part of me that also wants people to know it was mousy Kerry Smith who saved the day.

As I squelch into Chemistry, the familiarity of the lab makes me feel normal for the first time in five days. Our classmates *are* staring at us, but I tell myself it's because my skirt and legs are drenched.

Mr. Sykes emerges from the store cupboard and blinks at us as though he's spent the last fortnight guarding the petri dishes and Bunsen burners.

"Well, here we all are. You will recall that I was skeptical about the idea that the so-called Millennium Bug would lead to the end of the world. My delight at being proved right is tempered by the fact that rather than picking over a post-Armageddon landscape for scraps, I am fated to spend the morning with you lot, attempting to explain the nucleophilic addition mechanism as it relates to aldehydes."

He twists his face into something that resembles a smile.

"However, before we embark on that doomed quest, there is something else." He reaches underneath his desk and retrieves an old Marks & Spencer carrier bag: he pulls out a rectangular box and presents it to us as though it's a momentous breakthrough in organic chemistry. In fact, it's a battered-looking chocolate Yule log.

"The elephant in the room needs to be addressed. Because two of our number did rather an extraordinary thing on New Year's Eve, and I took the liberty of buying cake—half price for cosmetic reasons and now only two days past its sell-by date. I propose we spend twenty minutes dissecting the log and bombarding Mr. Palmer and Miss Smith with questions, and then nothing more will be said. Agreed?"

When I look at my six classmates—most of whom have never paid me any attention before—there's the same hunger I saw in the eyes of the younger students when I walked across the playground. They *want* to talk to me.

Is this what school life might have been like if Tim and I had never been neighbors? I wasn't always the nerdy girl. At primary school, I was invited to parties, even Louise Norman's seventh birthday at Chessington World of Adventures. I never won a Barbie lookalike contest—unlike my sister—but I was passably pretty. When I was seven, I got two Valentine's cards from boys in my class.

But just as my Calico Critters phase ended, Tim moved into the bungalow opposite. His dad was still around at first, but he left within a year of moving into Hazelmere Crescent and Tim turned from a shy boy into a mini-adult. At first, I hung around with him because I felt sorry for him, but then we bonded over first aid and chemistry sets, no longer ashamed of being different from our peers and our families.

When people judge Tim, they don't see what his life is really like. It's not just the drudgery of constant caring, which involves things no kid should have to do for a parent. It's also riding the roller coaster of his mother's moods.

Her obsession with him being a doctor was the reason we joined St. John's Ambulance Cadets together. Though we both love it. He's hardworking and eager to take medals home, while I like the disaster-movie rehearsals for a compound fracture or a catastrophic bleed. We're as weird as each other.

Mostly I am OK with being a nerd, though sometimes I wish I was "allowed" to flirt with Ant and Fat Matt and Joel—especially Joel. Or go to a party as Ginger Spice to Louise Norman's pigtailed Baby.

As Mr. Sykes passes out precisely calibrated slices of cake on hospital green paper towels, the questions begin.

"How did you know he was dying?"

"What was it like to kiss Joel Greenaway?"

"Will you be getting a medal?"

"One question at a time, you rowdy lot," Mr. Sykes says, but he really is smiling now. "Why don't you start at the beginning, Miss Smith?"

Tim glances at me nervously. This is my chance to tell the truth: the new version would be around the school by the final bell.

Except Tim's mum has never been prouder of him than she is now. Does telling the truth matter more than their happiness? He might have failed once, but when I think of what he does, day in, day out, he's the bravest person I know.

I can't punish him for a few minutes of weakness. So I begin to tell a new version of our story that is not the truth but is believable. If I focus hard enough, it'll replace what really happened in my head.

"We were down on the lawns, waiting for midnight, with a bunch of people from our old tutor group. And, like always happens when Joel Greenaway is around, there was a kickabout . . ."

8

Joel

JANUARY 5, 2000

I call them *bastard liars* when they tell me I died.

The doctors, nurses, pharmacists, Dad, Mum, even Ant. They're all in on this conspiracy to keep me in hospital by making up stuff about what happened to me. They say I "died" for eighteen minutes, and that it was only Tim pounding on my chest that kept me going.

Bullshit.

Sure, my ribs are knackered and every breath hurts like hell. And there are times when I can't control my body, so my limbs spasm at random, jerking and lurching with all the power of my best kicks.

It's bad, yeah, but I can't have died. Even a dumb footballer knows that's a one-way street.

Out in the real world, Sunday turns into Monday which turns into Tuesday and now it's Wednesday and I'm already being left behind. My parents have given up their round-the-clock vigil, and when they come in at lunchtime, they're all over each other, like my trauma has made them fall in love again or something.

Ant's gone back to catering college and Kerry's back at school so there's been no one to protect me from the staff who keep coming to prod or poke or scan the body that doesn't look or feel like mine anymore.

But now it's dusk. She's here. Kerry, I recognize her footsteps. I feel safe as long as she's nearby.

"How are the jerks?" she asks, when she reaches my bed.

"Driving me mad," I reply.

"Oh no." Her forehead creases with worry. "I thought you looked a lot less juddery?"

"I was talking about the *doctors.* The jerks. Get it?"

It takes her a moment. But now she's grinning so broadly she looks about five years old. "A joke! Joel, you made a joke."

"Yeah, and?"

"Jokes are hard. They take wordplay and understanding and a sense of humor. It means . . . well, it means you're still *you.*"

Every time she comes in, she repeats the jerks question and I give the same answer: it's our in-joke. She's the only one I trust not to be part of the conspiracy.

"They're going to move me," I tell her on Friday. Or is it Saturday? No, I'd know in my bones if it was match day.

"About time. You don't belong in here with this lot." She looks over her shoulder at the other patients, who are mostly out of it. "I mean, they're not great conversationalists."

"Neither am I, Kerry. I kick a ball and grunt occasionally, and I didn't pass a single exam." Not that I've ever cared about exams. All that matters to me is football.

Kerry laughs. "You never needed qualifications to be a megastar and the nearest our school had to a pinup."

I realize she's blushing. Why would she blush when she's paying *me* a compliment? My brain feels foggy as I try to work out what I should say next. Am I meant to say *No, I'm not that good*? Because that would be a lie. I am good. I really bloody am.

The silence has gone on a bit too long and I'm in danger of saying something that proves what a dickhead I am. Since I woke up from the coma, I can't always control what comes out of my mouth. Before, I found it easy to get on with people, have a laugh. Kerry is wrong: I'm not *still me*. The new me is unpredictable and rude. A *stranger*.

I hate it.

My nurse, a dark-humored blond-haired giant from the Czech Republic, comes into view. I turn to him. "I'm hoping it'll be livelier on the cardiology ward. That's where I'm going, right, Vaclav? Can't wait."

"You'll miss us when you're gone. This place is like first class on the airplane. Downstairs it's economy. And the view is not five-star."

The view is the one thing I like about ICU: I feel like I'm in a helicopter that hovers over the city. Vaclav has moved my bed so I can see the beach and two piers floating on top of the gray water.

"The main thing is, it means they think you're getting better," Kerry says.

I shrug, which bloody hurts. When Tim visited me, he explained that he must have bruised my ribs when he gave CPR. I banned him from visiting again because he's to blame for the pain that comes when I breathe or twist or laugh. "I don't think there was anything wrong with me in the first place."

She leans in and I can smell the flowery perfume my first girl-friend used to wear. Weird. I've never seen Kerry as a girlie girl. Or, even, as a *girl* at all. "There must have been. People our age don't drop dead for no reason, there has to be a cause and they need to find it, we've talked about this, Joel—"

Have we? People keep telling me we've already discussed all kinds of stuff, and when I tell them I don't remember, they blame the drugs that put me in the coma.

But what if it's not the drugs? What if my brain was wrecked by the eighteen minutes when I wasn't breathing properly?

"So you think I died as well, do you?"

"Well . . ." Kerry picks at the nail on the ring finger of her left hand. All the other nails are short, but this one is red raw and almost down to the quick, as if she's chosen to take all her stress out on it. "Only technically."

My foot begins to shake under the bedsheet. We both watch it—Vaclav looks up from paperwork, always vigilant. After a few embarrassing seconds, the movement stops of its own accord. "People can't come back from the dead, except in Stephen King books."

"It wasn't like that."

"What *was* it like? Tim told me some of the details but . . . I forgot."

Only three people saw the whole thing close up: Ant, Tim, and Kerry. Ant won't talk to me about it because it's "too mental" and if I ever see Tim again, it'll be too bloody soon.

"Are you sure you want to hear it again?"

I don't want to, but Kerry is the only person I can trust. "Go on then."

"It was nearly midnight and I . . . happened to be looking across the grass when you fell." She blushes again. "I ran over and you didn't seem to be breathing so Fat Matt went off to get an ambulance while I"—she stops—"while I did rescue breaths to put oxygen into your blood and . . . Tim . . . did CPR because your heart had stopped beating."

"And broke my bloody ribs, yeah, he told me. But what made you think I was dead?"

"There were signs."

"What signs? Some bloke with a tail and fire coming out of his arse trying to carry me off to hell?" I'm shouting but I can't seem to stop. This keeps happening.

She sighs. "Your eyes were blank. You made a funny noise. And the other thing is . . . you wet yourself."

"I pissed myself? In front of *everyone*?"

Kerry nods glumly. "It was only me that noticed. I tried to stop anyone getting close enough to see. Don't be embarrassed, it's just the muscles relax when someone . . ."

When someone dies. I close my eyes. The others are bastard liars. But Kerry? If Kerry says it, it has to be true.

"We kept doing the CPR and rescue breaths till the ambulance arrived."

"You mean the kiss of life?" A horrible thought occurs to me. "*Tim* did the kiss of life on me?"

"No. I did." Her cheeks are bright red now. "It's not actually a kiss. It's just transferring air from my lungs into your lungs using my . . ." She hesitates. "Well, using my mouth."

This new detail is overwhelming. "I can't stand this."

"Sorry, I wouldn't have done it if there'd been any other—"

"Go home, Kerry."

"Joel, I've only just got here. Dad's not picking me up till seven."

"Then walk. You need the exercise; you're chubby." She's not chubby, she's just right. But I *want* to hurt her, like she hurt me telling me about me wetting myself like some wino passed out on a bench at the Level. "At least you *can* leave. I fucking can't."

"If you're embarrassed, don't be," Kerry says flatly. "Everyone knows you were out cold. No one thinks you'd ever kiss a girl like me if you had the choice—"

My brain zaps like it's shutting down. "Just go."

Something slaps onto the bed: a sports magazine. She always brings me a present. "I was wrong about you being the same, Joel. You might have ignored me before but you were never deliberately *mean*."

I close my eyes. She zips up her coat and her steps fade away.

"She's gone now," Vaclav says. When I open my eyes, he's by the bed, shaking his head, his massive eyebrows meeting in the middle as he frowns. "You want to say sorry the next time you see her; you're going to need all the friends you can get."

Vaclav is an idiot. I've never had a problem making friends. If anything, I've got too many. I sigh. The moods, the tiredness, the pain—the *difference*—it's got to get better, if I try hard enough. The real me will be back before you can say *Joel Greenaway is the Dolphins' greatest hope.*

The day after I move wards, Coley, the club coach, and Murray, the under-23s team captain, show up at my bedside carrying what looks like Tesco's entire fruit aisle.

"All right, Bananaman? Brought you some supplies."

I got my nickname because I'm the only football trainee to take nutrition seriously, eating fruit instead of chocolate, drinking OJ instead of beer. Now I wonder: why did I bother?

In my tartan Granddad pajamas, I feel like a sick person and I can tell from the pity in Murray's eyes that I look like one too.

Screw him. I'm the better player and the rumors say he's going to be dropped this season anyway.

"We lost the match without you, sunshine," Coley says. He's the one I have to impress. His own career ended after injury, and I've always felt sorry for him, because it's my worst nightmare. "Taylor got stretchered off after a nasty tackle."

I grin. "You wanna see a really nasty tackle?" Even as I start to unbutton my pajama top, I'm beginning to regret it. But I'm committed now. I pull the two sides apart to show them my chest. "I woke up thinking I'd done ten rounds with Tyson."

But they don't laugh, they cringe. My torso is black and blue and purple and green, like Joseph's Technicolor dream coat.

Murray pulls a face. "That must have hurt."

I'm about to tell him I didn't feel a thing because I'd been dead at the time, but I stop the words coming out. "No big deal. I'll be back on the pitch before you know it."

Coley is still staring at my chest. "You can't rush getting fit again, all right, Joel?"

He's never used my first name before. At the club, apprentices are hazed mercilessly. In our first year, they broke us down—cleaning the lavatories, skivvying for the adult players. This year, they're building us back up again as footballing automata. We put up with it because *nothing* in the world feels as incredible as playing.

Coley's eyes meet mine, and a flash of understanding passes between us.

I put on my best determined face. "Sure, Coach. But I won't let you down. The game is everything to me."

"All right, Greenaway. However long it takes, we'll wait for you."

9

Kerry

JANUARY 12, 2000

"No one is looking. But you've got to hurry!"

Blood rushes in my ears as Joel scuttles out of the bay behind me, toward the double doors.

I don't want him to leave the safety of the ward, but if I don't help, he's threatened to sneak out alone. Plus, I need him to trust me tonight.

The nurses are distracted by undertaking painstaking surgery on a lemon drizzle cake brought in by someone's relative. They don't see us dash along the corridor and into the emergency stairwell. We're planning to walk down to the hospital cafeteria together.

Except now he's panting like a pensioner on eighty fags a day. "Maybe we should take the lift after all," I say.

He doesn't even have the puff to argue so we wait for him to get his breath back. We're on the fifth floor and I stand guard next to the top step, so if Joel does collapse, at least he won't tumble down the stairs.

This is the new me: ready for action. In the dinner queue, on the bus, at Churchill Square shopping center, I scan the people nearby for signs of imminent cardiac arrest. The muscles in my arms have finally stopped aching but they're primed to pump and pummel someone else's chest, to the beat of "Nellie the Elephant Packed Her Trunk . . ."

"Kerry, I'll need to . . . borrow your coat."

I am halfway through taking it off before I realize what he means. "Oh no. No way are you going outside. It's below zero."

Joel shrugs, and the movement makes him wince: the cartilage between his ribs could take another month to mend, the doctors say. "All I've smelled for the last twelve days is hospital food, bedpans, and antiseptic. I need fresh air."

"You won't be told, will you?"

"I usually get my own way because I'm so charming."

Charming is the last thing Joel has been over the last few days.

We both hear the lift ding as it arrives on our floor.

"Act normal," he says and straightens up, but I see the pain in his face as he pulls open the fire door. There are several patients, plus a nurse, in the lift already. She looks at us suspiciously. We're out of place in hospital: too young, too alive.

"Lovely afternoon for a stroll," Joel says and the nurse glances pointedly at his slippers.

He waits until everyone has left the lift before shuffling out. "Please, Kerry? I haven't even breathed year 2000 air yet, have I?" He fixes me with deep amber puppy dog eyes.

I make a decision I could come to regret. "Are you hungry?"

Joel shrugs. "I've forgotten what real food is like."

The fish and chip shop is empty except for us. The windows are steamed up; and while we wait for our order, I clear a patch of glass with the palm of my hand, so I can see the hospital's lights just up the hill: I'm already worried Joel won't manage the incline heading back. He's taken ages to catch his breath after the walk downhill.

"You see, the air's exactly the same as it was last century."

He shrugs. "Yeah, but the smell of those chips beats the farts from the old guys in my bay."

His jokes give me hope that the old Joel might gradually win the battle against the new nasty version. He's still beautiful—ordinary words like *good-looking* or *fanciable* aren't up to the job. But his skin is grayish and his eyes sink into their sockets.

The guy who took our order comes out from behind the counter with the warm parcel. "Not gonna die on us, is he?" he asks me.

Joel and I exchange another look: a shared knowledge. *If only you knew, mate.*

I start giggling and so does Joel, and it's turning into one of those back-row-of-assembly laughs, the ones you try to contain but just can't, because the hilariousness grows out of proportion and has to find a way out.

He laughs and coughs, laughs and coughs, and the chippie man brings over a mugful of water.

"What's so funny?"

"My sides are splitting," Joel says and that pushes us over the edge again.

Eventually he runs out of energy. I unwrap the chips: the trapped steam has made them soggy and delicious. This is the smell of our hometown.

We eat. Or rather, I watch Joel eat. I'm not hungry. It's partly the stress of being responsible for him, but mostly because I've already had a traitor's afternoon tea.

His parents picked me up from school earlier, took me to the Grand. I thought it was a thank-you treat, but the scones stuck in my throat when I realized what they wanted. *Joel has to have the operation,* Lynette kept repeating, and it felt strange to hear that persuasive voice, so familiar from TV shows and adverts, directed at me.

I don't think she's used to people saying no.

Water dribbles down the pane in droplets, Joel is still stuffing his face.

"Don't eat so fast," I say. "I'm not so confident about my Heimlich maneuver."

"Is it not as good as your kiss of life?"

His eyes are questioning. If I didn't know better, I'd say he was flirting. But *no one* flirts with Kerry Smith, especially not Joel Greenaway. "You're not nearly dead enough for that."

He looks away, eats another handful of chips. "You're really gonna be a doctor, then?"

"So long as I get the grades."

"Once they let me out, I won't be caught dead in a hospital again." He grins.

"Have they said when you might be discharged?" I stare ahead so he can't read my face. I already know the answer. His parents told me everything.

"Soon. They've run out of tests to do on me."

"Have they found what caused it?"

He sniffs. "No. Just bad luck. But lightning doesn't strike twice."

"Except if they haven't found the problem, what's to stop your heart stopping again, Joel? Next time someone might not be there to help."

Next time I might not be there.

"Fuck's sake. You sound like my mum. They're sending me home with pills, it'll be fine."

I take a deep breath, taste bile and strawberry jam in my throat. "Only . . . isn't there some operation they can do? I read about it. Some gadget they can implant that'll fix your heart if it *does* misbehave again."

Joel's mum had held up a cigarette packet to show how *tiny* the implant would be. But I've seen Joel's body. Forcing a metal box into his toned torso would be like painting a mustache on the Mona Lisa.

"They got to you," Joel says. "My parents."

I can't deny it. "They did mention it. But that's not why I'm saying this. Ever since it happened," I say very quietly, "I wake up every night from the same nightmare. We're on the lawns. You fall but I can't run. The fireworks go off and you're there, lying on the ground, and nobody sees you except me."

"Get over it, Kerry. It's only a pathetic dream."

A flash of anger lights me up inside. "You know, they'll never let you play again if there's the slightest risk you could drop dead on the pitch."

He gawps at me.

"Face it, Joel. Without the operation, you're done as a footballer."

His jaw drops farther. I want to take my words back, even though they're true. "Fuck you, Kerry. If I can't ever play again, there's no fucking point to anything."

Now he's stumbling toward the door, but he doesn't even have the strength to open it. I do it for him, hating the helpless expression on his face.

"Joel, I'm sorry, I shouldn't have said it like that—"

He stares at me. "They'll let me play, with the box thing?"

I didn't dare ask his parents that question. Joel plays an elegant game, but football is a rough sport. Would any team field a player with an implant that's vulnerable to the smash of a ball or even a deliberate tackle?

I don't know for sure. What I do know is that the metal box is the only guarantee he'll stay alive. So I smile as I reach for his elbow to help haul him back uphill. "I think it's got to be your best shot."

10

Tim

"Just pop in here and we'll dab on a bit of makeup, stop you going all shiny on camera."

Joel hesitates in the doorway.

"Come on, Joel," I say. "After broken ribs and cardiac surgery, I'm sure you can handle going on TV."

He gives me a dirty look but steps into the room. Bulbs surround a giant mirror, and our reflections are pale, Joel's most of all.

The researcher drapes a towel over the front of Kerry's red velvet dress, which makes her breasts look even bigger. I look away. They *torture* me, make me forget we're meant to be friends. I must find out which part of the brain is responsible. It might help me feel less dirty.

The powder smells of vanilla and musk, though the musk might be caused by other people's sebum. Kerry's face is now tangerine, but she looks older, more together.

If only I could go back to how I felt about her before we started sixth form. Finding her attractive is inconvenient. No, it's *agonizing*. Sometimes I think we'd make an excellent couple, in the future, but other times, I catch her looking at me as though she can't stand the sight of me.

"You next."

"Don't you have professionals to do this?" I ask.

"The presenters do. And the famous people. But you're kids," the researcher says. She's only a few years older than we are. "This is your fifteen minutes of fame. Enjoy it while it lasts."

I close my eyes as the powder rains down on my face, trying not to inhale. When I open my eyes again, my skin is matte in the mirror, like the corpses in my Edwardian anatomy book. It's not surprising no one fancies me.

"Now you . . . ah." The researcher looks down at the orangey shade of the makeup and back up at Joel's ghostly face. She's only just realized how ridiculous the shade will look on him. "You can probably go without."

I bet the TV people will like that. The sicker he looks, the better the story.

Joel shrugs. He doesn't seem to care about anything, certainly not about being in a TV studio to talk about being the Millennium Miracle.

They've put in an implantable cardioverter defibrillator, which will give him an instant shock if he suffers another arrhythmia. It's incredible technology, and I've been trying to talk Kerry into asking Joel to let me take a look, but she says I'm being ghoulish. Which is not true: surely it'd only be ghoulish if he was actually dead.

I talked about the ICD when I went for my interview with Sussex's medical program. That, and the resuscitation, and my involvement, and how it had confirmed how strongly I feel about becoming a doctor. I'm pretty sure it tipped the balance. But I still have to get the grades, and while hard work gets you Bs, only brilliant students like Kerry get the triple As medical programs prefer.

"Once we get onto the studio floor, keep as quiet as possible because we're broadcasting live," the researcher says.

Inside the studio it's smaller than I expected. Camera rigs slide around on wheels, circling the set. There's an L-shaped sofa in front of a fake window that lets in fake sunshine. To the side, I see a raised circular podium where a moonfaced chef is showing two presenters how to use a blowtorch to caramelize custard in a heart-shaped dish.

The burned sugar fumes catch in my throat.

". . . and we'll be back after the break, with a review of *Toy Story 2,* plus the incredible story of how a teenager's kiss helped to save the life of a brilliant young footballer."

I catch Kerry's eye. Where did they get *that* from? For the first time in weeks, I remember that the story we've been telling about what happened that night is just that: a story.

No. It's worse than that. A collection of lies.

"And we're off-air, reset please. Get rid of all this bloody smoke? We have three minutes sixteen."

Staff with headsets and clipboards appear from nowhere. The researcher tells us where to sit on the yellow sofa. "Kerry in the middle, please, Joel nearest the presenters, Tom at the end."

"My name is Tim," I say, but quietly.

While the female presenter's makeup is retouched—no universal orange powder for her—her husband greets us with presidential handshakes.

"Guys, it's great to have you here. And especially you, Joel. What a story. We've worked with your mother over the years; we couldn't believe you'd got sick, but now you're looking in great shape, really great."

Joel does *not* look in great shape. It's only six weeks since his heart stopped, and four since they implanted the box.

The female presenter joins us. My mum loves them, though Joel's mother—"call me *Lynette!*"—was less complimentary on the ride up. "They cater to the lowest common denominator, but at least it'll get the first aid message out to the widest possible audience."

"I couldn't have done what you two did," the woman gushes, giving each of us a hug in turn. Her cheek glances against mine, the skin damp.

"It'll be over before you know it," the male presenter is saying, as he smooths down his hair with his fingers. "You'll forget the cameras are even there."

The man with the biggest headset is counting down with his fingers.

"Off we go," the woman presenter whispers out of the side of her mouth, so as not to affect her rictus smile.

"Welcome back to our Valentine's special! We have the most incredible story for you now; one to restore your faith in teenagers, the NHS, and the power of a kiss."

A red light appears on the top of a camera facing us. Someone should have told us whether to look joyful or deadly serious.

"Yes, while the rest of us were celebrating the millennium, talented teenage footballer Joel Greenaway was literally fighting for his life—and, astonishingly, it was two of his old school pals who came to his rescue. Kerry Smith was the first to notice something was wrong, right, Kerry?"

I can't breathe. She's stuck to my story since I begged her to, and so have all the witnesses: they saw us both working on Tim, and memory is malleable. But it's one thing Kerry telling a white lie for my sake. It's another repeating it to millions of people . . .

"Tim and I spotted it at the same time. We all used to go to the same secondary school. The lads were playing football and I just . . ."—she's blushing now, from the studio lights—"I happened to be watching when Joel collapsed."

"No warning, nothing?" the man asks.

"One minute he was running and the next . . ."

"Do you remember that moment, Joel?"

"No. No, I don't."

They wait for more but he's already answered their question. You'd think they would ask better ones, all the years they've been interviewing people.

"Now what probably saved your life was that both Kerry and Tim here are first aiders, right?"

I nod. "St. John's Ambulance Cadets, yes. We're going to be doctors. We both have offers from university medical programs, so long as we pass our end-of-school exams."

The woman beams at me. "Amazing. So which of you two made the diagnosis?"

Kerry shoots me a terrified look. I answer for her. "First aid isn't about diagnosis; it's about assessing vital signs and stabilizing the patient so he or she can get to hospital. Joel was in the worst state possible, not breathing or responding. He was effectively dead."

"Gosh, you know your stuff, Tim," the woman says, leaning forward. "Which means the only way to bring him back to life was with mouth to mouth, am I right?"

No. I am about to correct them, because this kind of misinformation could endanger patients, not help them. But Kerry is finally talking.

"Well, that and chest compressions, to keep the blood going to his brain."

"But you did give him the kiss of life too?" the man insists.

Kerry blushes. "We call them rescue breaths. It's not . . . not like a normal kiss—"

"Unless a normal kiss involves pinching your partner's nostrils and blowing hard enough to make their lungs inflate," I say, to help her out. A joke, on national TV. Mum will be proud.

The hosts laugh, then the guy continues, "And all this is going on literally while the new millennium is starting?"

"There were fireworks going off," Kerry says, "though we hardly noticed them."

"I gather, Kerry, you were also at this young man's bedside when he opened his eyes? Would you like to tell us about that, Joel?"

Joel frowns. "I'd no idea where I was or what had happened. It was horrible."

After another slight pause, the woman leans forward. "And you've had a pacemaker fitted to make sure your heart won't play up again?"

I have to correct her. "Actually, it's a defibrillator—"

The presenter's eyes are stony as she ignores me. "And, *Joel,* are you back on the pitch again yet?"

Silence.

"Joel?" Kerry says softly.

"I'm getting my fitness back. I'll be playing again by spring."

If he believes that, he's even dimmer than I thought.

"Now," says the man, "this is our Valentine's Day special, and our viewers will be wondering if this *heart*-warming Millennium Miracle has a happy ending. A little bird told me that what happened on New Year's Eve might *just* have been Kerry's very first kiss . . . ?"

No. *Oh no.*

"You're a very bad man, Alastair, to ask a girl a question like that." The woman slaps his knee. "But I *will* ask a more delicate version. Is there any romance in the air? After all, this is the girl who helped to save your life."

What are they playing at?

Joel sighs. "I've got football, I'm too busy for a girlfriend."

A disembodied hand passes the biggest bouquet of roses I have ever seen to the male presenter. "Ah well, football comes first. But we did think you might like to thank Kerry with *these*?" He hands them to Joel, who looks as though someone has just put a baby alligator in his arms.

He almost throws them at Kerry. "Thanks for doing what you did."

The woman presenter claps her hands in delight. "Now, how about a little peck on the cheek? I think it's the *least* this girl deserves."

If he kisses her now, I don't know if I will be able to stop myself knocking him out . . .

Kerry shakes her head. "The flowers are enough, thanks."

She doesn't want Joel to kiss her. I grin at her over the top of the bouquet.

Maybe it's a sign that Kerry *does* feel the same way about me.

A sign that all is not lost.

11

Joel

The show is the most humiliating experience of my life aside from pissing myself on the lawns when I died.

Three million people watched me make a tit of myself on TV today.

Afterward, my mother drags me to the control room so she can network. I need to sit down like an invalid while she air-kisses the producer and director—"Sweetheart, I still haven't forgotten our close shave with the Mafia when we were filming *Holidaymaking* in Sicily in 'ninety-seven, but what fun!"—and congratulates the interviewers on their latest BAFTA.

The cab pulls up outside the Ivy, and the driver tries to maneuver Mrs. Palmer's wheelchair out, but Tim has to take over. He's strong and I'm weak and I hate it.

I've only been out of hospital for three weeks. The doctors said I was young and otherwise healthy so I should get my fitness back superfast. Their idea of fitness must be different from mine. The box is the worst thing of all. I see its hard edge every time I shower, like an alien under the flesh of my belly.

"You all right?" Kerry asks as we wait to go into the restaurant, behind my mum and Kerry's, who is buzzing at the idea of going somewhere so *showbiz*.

"Looking forward to going home. You?"

She shrugs. "I want to emigrate. All that stuff about never kissing anyone before? I don't think I can *ever* go back to school after this."

That bit did surprise me. Like everyone at school, I always thought that Kerry and Tim were together. What surprised me even more was how knowing they're not an item felt like . . . well, something good.

It must have been Mum who made the presenters ask that question. There's nothing she won't do to get in with the right people. We're only at the Ivy now so she can *be seen*. Neither Dad nor I like showing off his wealth, but I guess that's because we've both always had money. His family bankrolled the TV production company he started when he was twenty-two, never doubting that he'd be a success.

When they fell in love—and I think they *did* love each other once—my parents were the golden couple, and Mum created an on-brand life. She dressed them both in the right clothes, decorated and sold their Camden flat, then oversaw the refurb of Curlews, our ridiculous gated house, while she was eight months pregnant with me. I was another project. She even tried to persuade my dad I should go to private school instead of the local primary, but he was having none of it: thought I needed something to keep my feet on the ground.

It was the right decision. The only time I didn't feel lonely was kicking a football around the playground or Dyke Road Park. And that's where I was scouted and the rest is history . . .

"Dom Pérignon, I think," Mum tells the waiter, and I see Mrs. Palmer clock the price and her skin goes from off-white to blue. But my mother insists it's her treat.

"To our three extraordinary children!" Mum raises her glass and we all follow suit.

"You got that right," Kerry's mother says. "For years, I've been convinced they gave me the wrong baby to take home from hospital, with the rest of us such noisy gobshites. Turns out she had her own special talents. She's our star!"

Kerry looks as if she wants to hide under the table. I know that feeling.

"I see star quality in my boy too." Mum nudges me. "A footballer's career is short, but he'll make a brilliant commentator when the time comes. He's got the looks, right, Kerry?"

Kerry's face turns red and she stares down at the shepherd's pie Mum ordered for all of us because *it's what you have at the Ivy.*

Does that mean Kerry *fancies* me? I really want to know.

"Handsome is fine, but you want a man to have a brain," Mrs. Palmer says, winking at Tim.

OK. That means I'm not Kerry's type and she's definitely not mine.

My mother scowls. "Joel is extremely bright. If it hadn't been for his Dolphins apprenticeship, he'd be off to university."

This is news to me. I never took school seriously. I already knew what I was born to do. "Stop embarrassing me, Mum!"

"Oh dear, they never change, do they?" She laughs but her eyes look . . . what is that? Afraid? Hurt? It's harder for me, now, to read faces or say the right thing. Sometimes it's like some of the kinder bits of the old me didn't come back when the rest of me did.

But I do know she and Dad went through hell when I got sick. I can't imagine how it'd feel to have your kid lying there, not knowing if he's ever going to wake up or not.

The doctors still can't say what made my heart stop, but they're leaning toward some faulty gene I might have inherited from Mum or Dad.

They say it doesn't change anything right now, but told us I could see a genetic specialist when I'm older and want kids of my own.

I may not know what my future holds, but I'm certain about one thing: I will *never* be a dad, because I wouldn't wish what's happened to me on my worst enemy, never mind a kid.

12

Kerry

Eighteen.

It sounds so grown-up. I can vote, get legally smashed on vodka in a pub, die for my country. Not that I'm interested in doing any of those things. But there is one new experience I *do* want to try.

I'm throwing a party. Well, Tim is organizing it, on my behalf. Nothing on the scale of Marilyn's, four years ago, which featured a Spice Girls fancy dress theme, a vodka bar, and my sister bursting out of a birthday cake, like her namesake, singing "Happy Birthday to me." (It wasn't even ironic.)

Now she rushes into my room, wielding a curling iron and a fistful of hair products. "That's perfect on you," she says, surveying my dress, a fifties design with a red mermaid print, which Mum bought me from a shop in the Lanes. "A great fit. It even makes you look like your boobs are as big as mine. Tim's not going to know where to look."

"We're mates. Not all men are obsessed with . . ."

"Sex? For a doctor-to-be, you have a lot to learn about biology, dear sister."

Marilyn yanks me onto my stool by my hair and, without ceremony, begins to curl a section of it. I've been her model since I was a toddler and she back-combed my fuzzy baby hair so roughly half of it fell out. I had the last laugh: my hair is now chestnut-colored, glossy, and possibly the one thing about me she envies.

"He's probably organized a Harry Potter read-in at the library," Marilyn says. Tim hasn't invited her.

"You're just jealous."

"Yeah, clearly I'm missing out on the party of the century."

It is *my* party of the century. Maybe the best one I'll ever have. I'm not stupid. I know none of this would have happened if it hadn't been for *that night*. Before that, I didn't have enough friends in my year group to fill a Mini.

Tim isn't as keen on making new friends, but if I'm on my own now, other kids ask to sit with me at lunch or in the common room. And after they've got the cringe-worthy stuff about me kissing Joel out of the way, we move on to chatting about normal things too.

"Ouch." The curling iron sizzles against my neck. "Watch out, Marilyn."

"Who is coming? Will *Joel* be guest of honor?" she asks, in a sing-song voice.

"I've no idea."

I want him there, obviously. But Tim is in charge of invitations and he's not exactly Joel's biggest fan.

Which is why I haven't told Tim how often I still check in on Joel. Nothing's *happening* between us—I am *not* Joel's type—but I can't bear to think of him and his dad rattling around that huge house alone, Lynette off filming a property program in Spain.

At first Joel's teammates would show up, trying to talk him into a night on the town, but he's said no every time and they've stopped asking. So all he has to break up his week are visits from Ant and me, hospital appointments, and sessions with the private physical therapist helping him get his fitness back.

I worry about his rages. Once, he got so mad I thought it might set his ICD off, but it abated as soon as it started, leaving him as sleepy as a toddler who'd overdone it. As I walked home, the guilt came again, and the fear he might be in better shape if only I'd stepped in thirty seconds faster, or done CPR more firmly . . .

There's no way of knowing. But he's no longer Joel Greenaway, Local Hero. He *looks* the same, but he seems a lot less confident and laid-back, more snappy and stressed. I've researched it, and behavior change can affect people who've been resuscitated after several minutes "down." It might get better but there are no guarantees.

The doorbell rings. Dad calls up the stairs, "Your carriage awaits, Kerry!"

"I'd better go."

Marilyn unplugs the curling iron and gives my head a quick blast of hairspray. "Don't want to keep Prince Charmless waiting, I suppose."

I smile. "He's gone to a lot of trouble."

My sister surveys me. "You scrub up well. You could have anyone, the way you look tonight."

I think of Joel and blush.

Marilyn winks at me. *Has she read my mind?*

I hurry down the stairs. My dad does a comedy wolf whistle, and Mum is grinning. "Look at my baby girl!"

As I get into the cab, Mrs. Palmer waves at me excitedly from her window across the road. She must know where the taxi is taking me.

The driver pulls away and I look out the back, as our house—and Tim's bungalow—get smaller and smaller. It feels like I'm finally leaving shy schoolgirl Kerry behind.

Long live the new me.

As the taxi pulls up outside Ant's parents' café, the fizzy feeling grows. The idea of the party being here had crossed my mind, though I tried not to get my hopes up. All the best parties have happened after hours at the Girasol—a.k.a. the Arsehole—over the years. It's just I've never been cool enough to be invited to one before.

The string lights between the lampposts sway and creak in the dusk light. Ahead, the Palace Pier sign seems to be flashing just for me.

This is my night.

"Have the best birthday, beautiful girl," the driver calls after me as I get out. Beautiful? No. But perhaps the stuff that's changed *inside* has created some kind of optical illusion.

Before, I'd have done anything to avoid walking into a roomful of people. Now, whoever I meet, there's this kernel of knowledge inside me, a rabbit I could pull out of the hat if I am feeling shy. *Hello, my name is Kerry, I'm eighteen today, I'm doing A levels in biology, chemistry, and physics and—oh, did I mention, I helped to save somebody's life?*

The lights are turned down in the Girasol, though I think I can see the flicker of candlelight. At the door, I hesitate, suddenly afraid that this is the best bit, this anticipation.

When I think of what disappointment would look like, the image of a packed room, with no Joel, flashes through my mind.

As I push the door open, a cheer deafens me. It looks like the whole sixth form is in here and I take in the medical-themed decorations: red crosses and bunting made from bandages and "Dr. Beat" blasting out of the speakers. I see Tim straightaway, dressed in blue scrubs, his sweet, hopeful face seeking confirmation that he's got this right.

But even as I head toward him, I am scanning the other faces, my fixed grin faltering, until . . .

There. Joel leans on the bar, a distance between him and the others.

My smile turns goofy and my heart changes rhythm, a blush spreading from my cheeks and the warmth traveling all the way through my body. And for a split second, his face changes and I wonder: could he fancy me back?

Now Tim is embracing me, his herbal aftershave making me want to sneeze, but I can't break eye contact with Joel.

"Is this OK?" Tim whispers in my ear. "Did I get it right?"

"God, yeah. You know me so well. It's *everything* I wanted."

13

Joel

I've got to get the hell out of here.

Away from all the smart, smug kids who can only talk about exams and college interviews.

Away from Tim, who looks like the cat who got the bloody cream as he snakes his arm around Kerry's waist. Whenever my ribs ache or my scar itches, I blame him. The idea of him pawing at my body as I lay dead on the grass makes me want to hit him, and I've never hit anyone in my life.

But mostly I need to get away from *her.* Until she walked into the Arsehole tonight, I thought she would only ever be a mate, yet the minute I saw how beautiful she looks, I realized . . . it's nowhere near as simple as that. And it's scrambling my crappy brain.

I spin back toward the bar and look for Ant. He grins and grabs another bottle of Sol beer for me. I shake my head and mouth, "No, I'm going home."

"You lightweight, you only just got here—" he calls out, the way he always does when I drink OJ or leave a club early the night before a match, and it's like the old days when we took the piss out of each other all the time. But his face changes, suddenly fearful. "Are you sick?"

"Nah. This isn't my scene."

"Mine neither, but once they've got through a few crates, it'll be . . . friendlier." Ant winks at me. It's not even eight weeks since I had that *thing* put in, but I'm meant to be getting back to normal, being the old Joel, the one who pulls girls without trying, and has random Dolphins fans buy me drinks in clubs and tell me I'm the future of the team.

Mostly, I feel like *that* Joel is dead. Except when Kerry walked in, my body responded like it used to. I *wanted* her.

She's not mine to want. I've already had too much from her. She visits me, with Ant, and makes jokes and makes me do my exercises and eat healthy food. I *know* I ought to be working even harder at building myself up, but it's hard to see the point of the protein and veg I used to mainline because my perfect diet didn't protect me.

"Want me to come out, Bananaman, help you get a cab?" Ant asks, even though he's the only one behind the bar.

Fury rises from nowhere. *What, I can't even be trusted to get a fucking taxi now?* I close my eyes. *Don't hate him, he's your best mate, he only wants you to be OK.*

"I'm not an invalid," I say. Still rude, but nowhere near as nasty as what I wanted to say.

The music changes. That bloody awful 'N Sync song, "Music of My Heart." Enough.

Out on the blustery seafront, the anger is whipped away with my breath, and I look for the lights of a taxi.

It's past two, and I'm making toast in the kitchen to take back to the guesthouse when someone knocks on the door.

In the porch light, Kerry looks like the dancer on the top of my mother's musical jewelry box.

"You left," she says.

"Sorry. Tired." It's my get-out lie. No one challenges someone who died for eighteen minutes.

Her forehead wrinkles in a cute frown. "You don't look tired. Can I come in? I'm not ready to go to bed."

Bed. A flash of her in *my* bed, naked.

She stumbles on the doorstep, falling toward me, and when I catch her, I feel the strength in my arms, the sharp reflex that helps me stop her hurting herself. Her face is so close to mine, and I want to kiss her but . . .

She pirouettes away from me, across the checkerboard tiles in the hall, into the kitchen. Her feet look impossibly tiny in silver high heels.

"Where is everyone?"

"Mum's in Magaluf filming a Scottish family finding their forever home and Dad is out with *a friend.*"

She nods sympathetically. I've never told her outright about his affairs, but I've come closer than I have with any of my mates. "Is he coming back tonight?"

"Probably not. Quite often he stays over with his friends." With *her.* A different *her* every few months. They never last. My parents don't seem to like each other, but they're still wedded to the idea of being a Power Couple.

"Home alone, then?" she asks, mischief making her voice all husky.

"I was in the guesthouse, watching telly. Do you want to join me?"

Before now, we've always chatted in the kitchen.

She blinks.

I hold my breath.

"Why not?" she says.

The guesthouse was built as Mum's swanky garden office, but when I got my football apprenticeship, I moved in because I wanted more independence and she didn't want me to leave home. I slept out there, brought a few girls back. But mostly it was mates I had around, playing Resident Evil and GTA. They'd drink beer and smoke weed, though I never did.

Now I do. Why *wouldn't I?* It's temporary, though. As soon as I'm back at the club, I'll have a reason to look after myself again.

I flick a switch and the pathway lights up, a dozen spotlights leading the way to the guesthouse, a hundred meters from the house. The design is feminine, with mullioned windowpanes and a blue-slate roof with a real chimney for the log burner.

"Oh, that looks adorable."

And so does Kerry, standing there in her puffy dress, eyes wide from drinking, hair shining like the chestnuts in Stanmer Park.

Without thinking, I take her hand to lead her inside.

After admiring the wood burner and the soft green walls and the mint velvet daybed—all my mother's choices—Kerry plonks herself down on the sofa with a sigh.

I get her a beer. "What's it like being eighteen? My birthday's not till August."

Kerry laughs. "The same, except my feet hurt more than they did yesterday." She stretches out her legs.

I try to look only at her shoes but my eyes travel past her slim ankles to her calves, her thighs . . . I blink, thinking of Tim's arm around her waist. My fists clench. "Did you do a lot of dancing?"

"Yeah. I'm a terrible dancer. But it was my party so I thought I should give it a go. And anyway, it didn't matter after you . . ." She stops suddenly, swigs her beer. "Why did you go so early?"

"Tired, like I said. Did I miss any gossip? Any punch-ups, anyone get off with anyone else?"

"No. Unfair, right? I'm the birthday girl. I should have been kissed, at least. But I guess the entire population knowing I've never kissed anyone means it's not a tempting prospect. I might be as bad at kissing as I am at dancing."

I say nothing. *Nothing happened with Tim.* It's stupid but it feels like a tiny victory.

"You've kissed a lot of girls, Joel."

"Not *that* many." It's a lie, but suddenly it matters to me that Kerry doesn't think I'm some cliché footballer who shags a different woman every weekend.

"Are some girls no good at it? Like some people can't sing in tune or draw a straight line?"

It crosses my mind that this might be her way of *asking* me to kiss her and let her know if she's any good.

No. I'm being an idiot. Clever people have always done my head in, but since my cardiac arrest, it's much worse. Everything they say is a riddle my brain can't unravel. Does she want to kiss me or not?

I want to kiss her.

My bottle is empty so I go to the mini-fridge and take a fresh beer to her end of the sofa.

I still want to kiss her.

I set the bottle down on the Moroccan brass table. I've wanted to kiss her since I saw her walk into the Girasol tonight.

Would she be here, be saying these things, if she didn't want the same?

Slowly, I sit on the sofa next to her and turn her face toward mine. "No one is crap at kissing with the *right* person."

I lean in toward her, smelling the yeasty beer on her breath, and our lips meet for the second time ever.

At least this time I'm awake.

Her face gives off heat, like a bonfire. I part her lips with my tongue, gently, wanting it to be right for her. She sighs and begins to kiss me back. I run my hands through her thick hair and I can smell coconut.

I move away for a moment. "OK?" I whisper, looking into her eyes.

"Yes. Except . . . tell me. Am I a crap kisser?"

"I think you already know the answer to that one."

This time *she* kisses *me*. I haven't touched a girl since 1999. Ant says I'll want to when I'm "on the mend." But what if I brought a girl home and she was revolted by the raw scar under my ribcage and the freakish bulge where the metal edge of my implant pushes out the skin?

Plus, what will happen to my heart when I finish? I haven't even dared to have a wank, I'm so scared of my defib going off.

But with Kerry, it's a nonissue. She's a virgin, so nothing more is going to happen. This is just about making her feel amazing. I relax into the kiss and I feel like I'm thirteen or something. No pressure, no expectations.

Except she's moving my hand toward her breast, slipping her dress off her shoulders . . .

"Kerry. You've had too much to drink. The kissing is fine."

"No. I've been waiting so bloody long." Her voice is a whisper. She reaches toward my jeans and tries to undo the top button.

"You should wait until you're really sure, or at least sober." I'm not the kind of guy who takes advantage of a girl who has had too much to drink, but I don't know if I can keep protesting much longer.

"I fancied you since the first time I saw you, Joel." She takes my other hand and pulls her knickers aside so I can touch her. The look on her face makes me feel like a god, not a tragic cardiac patient. Like the old Joel.

She won't be shocked by the box: the night after my operation, I showed her the line of stitches and the bump where the implant sticks out.

Kerry wants me despite all of it.

And I want her too.

I take her hands to help her raise herself off the sofa. She stumbles slightly.

"Are you sure you won't regret this?"

She kisses me again, and I reach behind her to unzip her dress, which falls to the floor with a sigh. Underneath, she's wearing a light pink bra with a rosebud at the center between her breasts, and matching knickers. I want her *now* but I try to take everything slowly. I take off my jeans and lay the sofa throw over the wooden floor and draw her down, so we're kneeling, facing each other.

I kiss her lips, her neck, her collarbone, as I unclasp her bra. My lips move toward her nipples. I hear her heartbeat and my own.

I take her hand and guide it across my rib cage, tracing the line of the wires along to the defibrillator. The skin is still sore most days but not now.

"Is it going to be OK?" she asks me. "Is it safe?"

"I hope so," I say. But I don't actually care.

I move her hand away from the box, past my belly and farther. She touches me. Will being this hard put pressure on my heart?

Fuck it. I reach over to the drawer where I keep condoms.

"You're so beautiful, Kerry. I won't hurt you. I promise."

She smiles back. "And I promise I won't hurt you either."

14

Kerry

One second, I'm a virgin and the next I'm not, and the sharpness lasts for the briefest time, like when you pull off a plaster, before revealing new skin underneath.

I gasp.

"Are you all right, Kerry? Did I hurt you?"

Now my body feels unfamiliar. He is me and I am him and this is *right*.

"You didn't hurt me."

"Should I stop?"

I murmur a no because I definitely don't want *that*. Joel starts to move faster, finding his rhythm and I move against him, finding mine. In his neck, a blood vessel pulses and I think, *Without me that wouldn't have happened ever again.* None of this would.

His body feels strange next to mine but also familiar. The muscles of his back are smooth under my hands but I don't grip too hard. I don't want to hurt him or put pressure on the implant. He shimmers in the light of the wood burner and I know this is how I will remember him when I am old and this is a distant memory. This glorious glow, rather than the gray pallor underneath my outstretched palms on Hove Lawns.

A night breeze rattles the window. The feeling that's building up between me and him begins to grow, like another pulse circulating between us, the look of concentration on his face deepens and

I know what this is

What it's called

But I hadn't expected

Hadn't realized

Hadn't guessed

it

would

feel

this

incredible . . .

"Kerry!"

His voice seems to come from somewhere a long way off. I open my eyes. I am no longer Kerry but just sensation.

The noise I make doesn't sound like me.

Joel's eyes flicker and for a moment I remember how he looked when he wasn't breathing.

"Joel?"

His eyes snap open but I still don't think he's seeing me and he comes and all the tension goes and he kisses me and I think:

I love you, Joel Greenaway.

Instantly the thought changes to *I am an idiot.* That wasn't love.

He reaches down to move a strand of damp hair away from my eyes, kisses my forehead. "You are not the girl I thought you were, Kerry Smith." He's still slightly out of breath.

"I'm not the girl I thought I was either."

I hear Tim's voice in my head. *Postcoital contentment is not the same as love. Oxytocin, the bonding hormone, helps mammals pair up for long enough to reduce the death rate in their offspring.*

I don't care.

Joel sits up and his arm around me pulls me up too. There's beer left in his bottle and we share it. He kisses me, gets up, fetches two more bottles, and lays them against my back, the glass deliciously cold.

"Was everything OK for you?" I ask, even though I know I shouldn't because it sounds needy.

He smiles but instead of taking the piss, he says, "I wasn't sure I'd ever have the nerve to do that again, but everything still seems to be in working order."

"I'm no expert but I'd say it is. Were you really worried?"

He seems to be about to say something but instead he hands me my beer and takes a sip from his own. "Nah. And so long as I can still score goals too, it'll be as if I never died in the first place."

Before my own doubts about his future spoil the moment, I put down my bottle. "How many condoms do you have?"

Joel grins. "Why would you ask a question like that?"

Don't chicken out now. Be cool. Be wild.

"Well . . . we're both here. I've been a late starter and you've been out of action for too long."

"I'm definitely back in the game tonight but at least give me a minute to get my breath back." He puts down his beer too and reaches over to pull me close enough to kiss. "Happy birthday, Kerry Smith."

I sneak home around four-thirty. When I undress, my underwear looks like it belongs to a younger girl, not the woman I am now. As I climb into bed, I'm sure I won't sleep but I do, deeply.

In the morning, I shower and I touch my body tentatively under the flow of water. My muscles ache in new places.

Why didn't I slow down last night? It's pretty extreme to go from first kiss to sex in under an hour. I remember seeing shock cross Joel's face before desire replaced it . . .

I've always wanted more adventure, but this urge to act on my desires has only begun since I saved Joel's life. That night changed us so much. He doesn't feel like the old Joel since then—and I almost don't recognize myself either.

"Kerry, do you want a cuppa?" my sister calls up the stairs.

I make my way down to the kitchen.

"Not like you to start the day singing, Kerry."

I hadn't realized I was.

"Young love is so adorable," Marilyn says. "Did Prince Charmless finally get into your knickers last night?"

I shake my head but I'm blushing.

"Aha, did you get your hands in his?"

I'd love to tell my sister what happened, but it would be the big news around all her mates before midday. I might as well take an ad out in *The Argus*.

"Some things should stay strictly between a man and a woman," I say.

"Ha! I knew it!" she says, and as she takes me in her arms to waltz around the kitchen, I smile to myself. Last night was perfect. Joel was so different from what I expected: careful and sweet and . . . well, loving, I suppose.

As I dressed before I left, I was already rationalizing it as a one-off, even as a kind of favor, him sleeping with me in exchange for me saving his life.

Except when he walked me home, we stopped on the corner and he kissed me like he *really* meant it and whispered, *"How soon can I see you again?"*

The answer to Joel's question is eleven hours.

I only wait that long because the thought of leaving the house and bumping into Tim is so horrifying. After all the trouble he went to organizing my party, I don't want to hurt his feelings.

So I stare at his bungalow and wait until he and his mum leave, her pushing the shopping trolley that helps her walk, on the days she's strong enough to venture outside. The second he's out of sight, I sprint to Curlews and the security gates open before I have to buzz. Joel has been watching out for me too.

"Dad's in London for a meeting," he calls from the doorway.

I almost have another orgasm in anticipation. I definitely have another two before we finally lie down on the sofa in his guesthouse to quench our thirst with more beer.

"You know, I remember the very first time I saw you," Joel says. I'm nestled against him, careful not to lean on his left side so I don't put pressure on his scar or the box underneath. "The day we started at secondary school."

I twist my head up to look at his face. "I never thought you noticed me at all."

"Even though we walked home the same way most days?"

"That's just because you live *here* so of course you'd come through the estate . . . Hang on, are you saying you *stalked* me, Joel Greenaway?" Saying his name makes me tingle.

"Well it wasn't love at first sight or anything—"

The word *love* sends a warm wave through me. *He said it* wasn't *love, Kerry, get a grip.*

"—but I was in the tutor group room with Ant, and you came in, with Tim trailing behind you like a puppy. You caught my eye and I knew you were . . . different."

"Nerdy, you mean!"

"Not like that. You looked around like you were sizing us all up. When you got to me, your eyes seemed to see everything about me. Like you were some wise owl or something."

I remember that day. I stood outside the classroom for ten minutes, trying to persuade Tim that it was all going to be OK even though I was scared too.

I did walk in ahead of Tim. Joel was sitting on a desk, already the center of attention. When he looked up at me, it freaked me out. We'd never met, but there was such a strong recognition between us. As soon as I looked away, I felt ashamed, as though I had no right to look at someone so special, never mind think we had a connection. I understood, without question, that throughout school, he and I were going to move in different worlds.

I trace my hand along his arm, sensing the power in his muscles, despite everything that's happened to him. "Twit-twoo. I am a wise owl!"

"Not like *that*."

"You're making it up, Joel. If you noticed me at all, it was because you knew I was the kind of girl you'd never talk to in case it damaged your street cred."

He pulls a face. "Fair point. But it was my loss."

I close my eyes and let myself imagine what it would have been like if he *had* climbed off that desk and come over to me and asked my name. If we'd been friends, first loves . . .

It's so ridiculous that it makes me giggle.

"Worth the wait," Joel says and when he reaches down to kiss my forehead, I think he might mean it.

Falling in love is not what I expected it to be. Yes, it's intense and sexy and like being on a drug that makes you want everyone to be as happy as you are.

But love is also farcical: I have to creep out of the house because I don't want to hurt Tim's feelings. Love is frustrating. I want to be spending all my time with Joel, touching him, leaning against his chest, listening to that magical heartbeat. Instead, I am meant to be studying for my A levels. Even when I force myself to come home, I can't focus on my work because I am replaying our time together.

Love is troublesome. Whenever we touch on what happened to Joel, I hate myself for the lies Tim and I told. One day, soon, I have to explain to Joel what really happened, that it was me who did the CPR as well as the rescue breaths. Not because I want credit, but because now we're so close, it feels wrong to keep any secrets about the night when everything changed.

Most of all, love is scary.

Because the rational part of me knows this cannot last. Even if we stay together till I go to medical school, some other girl will pounce on him the instant I board the train to Manchester.

But for now, my brain refuses to admit that inevitably Joel will hurt me one day.

15

Joel

MAY 9, 2000

She makes me stronger.

Is it the way she looks at me? Like I'm the old Joel, the one with all the strength and the talent? When I see myself through her eyes, I can believe I haven't lost everything.

"What will we do to celebrate on Friday?" she asks.

We're in the guesthouse—we spend most of our time here, because Kerry gets jittery when we're out in case we're spotted together—and we're trying not to have sex, because it's my team physical tomorrow.

If we manage not to, it'll be the first time since we got together on her birthday.

One of Dad's mates gets him pirated videos so we've tried to distract ourselves watching *Final Destination,* though every time someone dies, Kerry gives me a weird look, like she's expecting me to burst into tears.

But keeping my hands off her is so tough. Maybe we *should* do it, get it out of the way, because the afterward is good too. Listening to her talking about her dreams, telling her mine. They couldn't be more different but she tries to imagine how it feels to be on the pitch, and I try to get my head around the fact she likes gore so much she wants to make a career out of it.

"What would you do with that?" I ask her, every time one of the actors loses a limb or ends up with a gatepost through their skull.

"A tourniquet." She slaps my hand, which I swear has started creeping up her top without me knowing. "Not till the weekend, OK?" She wants to focus on revision for her first exam on Thursday.

I sigh. "The weekend. Might as well be ten years away." But I sit on my hands to stop them misbehaving. "How about I take you to . . . I dunno, Concorde, to show you off? The lads always take their girlfriends there on Fridays, we'll get into the VIP lounge, show I'm back in the game?"

She raises her eyebrows. "When the exams are over." She's convinced Tim will freak out and fail them all if he finds out we're together.

"Are you sure you're not ashamed of being with a knucklehead who didn't scrape a single C grade?"

"You're as smart as me."

"Bollocks, Kerry. If I didn't have football, I'd struggle to get a job pulling pints or sweeping up on the seafront."

"Well, if you had to, you could do resits."

If you had to. The implication behind those words chills me: if the football doesn't work out, I could sit in a classroom again, with all the other losers.

"I'd rather die than go back to school."

She frowns and I feel like shit. "You don't mean that, Joel."

I do. "You're right. I'm nervous about tomorrow. I tell you what would take my mind off it, though."

She gives me *that* look. Not some fake pout that my other girl-friends have copied from Page 3 pinups, but a steady gaze that makes me want to see inside her head, even though it'd probably terrify me, because she's so clever and she understands me more than anyone ever has, more than I understand myself.

I'm kissing her and I stop caring about tomorrow and so does she.

The next day Dad drives me to the training ground. Funny how he never had time to do this when I was a kid.

"Stop here," I say, before we turn the corner. I've had to surrender my driver's license for six months because of my heart—but I don't want anyone on the team to know *that*.

Cold rain drips down my collar as I walk the last stretch, and I try not to shiver. The beta-blockers mean I feel the cold like I never did before, but once I've warmed up in the gym with Coach Coley, I won't notice it as much.

Today's a half day so the field is empty but I wonder if any of my teammates will have hung around.

The green plastic cones are stacked tall next to the goals. I know every centimeter of that field: the swampy parts where Coley makes us do push-ups in the mud if he thinks we're not trying hard enough. The spots where I've scored some of my most dazzling practice goals.

I'm ready for my trial. That field will tell them if I'm still Joel Greenaway, the homegrown Dolphins hotshot.

Or if I'm a nobody.

As I walk into the drab building, Coley comes out of nowhere.

"Let me look at you, Millennium Miracle! How are the ribs, Joel?"

Joel. I wish he hadn't used my first name.

"All healed up, Coach. Dying to get back to it. Even the chores. My pros will have the cleanest boots, and the toilets will never have been so clean."

He leads me into the boardroom. I'm expecting to see the physio, or a medic, but instead, Lance Rossiter stands next to the trophy cabinet. No one likes the chairman, but the money he made from telecoms is helping us climb steadily back up the league. I've never so much as spoken to him before.

"Mr. Rossiter!"

He shakes my hand, his skin cool and shiny, like leatherette. "Good to see you back, kid. Had us all worried for a bit. And you might have come across Diane from public relations?"

A skinny blond woman reaches across the table to shake my hand. "Sit yourself down," Rossiter says, pulling out a chair. "Biscuit?" The plate is piled high with the posh kind, wrapped in gold foil.

"Not for me. I'm upping the protein at the moment, to build my muscles ready for training again."

When I turn to Coley, he gives me a weak smile.

Rossiter slaps his hands together. "So, now, Joel, we wanted to talk to you about something a bit special. Coley's idea, so I'll hand over to him." He gestures with one hand toward the coach.

"We want a campaign to roll out defibrillators at grounds. When you got . . . sick, I looked it up and I couldn't believe the survival rates were so low. Only five in a hundred people make it in some parts of the country."

"That's why I'm the Millennium Miracle," I say.

"But more defibrillators could change everything," Coley says, like this is news to me. *Yeah, that's why I've got my own personal one.*

Rossiter and the PR woman nod like the Muppets.

"We thought we could start installing one at the ground, with you as our figurehead. How does that sound?" Coley smiles expectantly, as though I should be whooping, like I've been picked for the main squad.

"Great. Yeah, I mean, anything to save lives, right?"

Rossiter stands up. "Excellent. I'll leave you guys to thrash out the details. Diane will do a press release, how thrilled you are to stay involved with the club you loved, et cetera. We'll cover all expenses . . ."

His voice seemed to fade out as my brain processed the previous sentence. *Stay involved.*

"Mr. Rossiter, I'll be happy to be part of that, so long as it doesn't get in the way of getting my fitness back."

"Sure, sure. It needn't clash with hospital visits, and whatever it is you do next. Do you have plans? We could chip in for a course or something . . . ?"

He's putting on his coat. I stand up too. "I'm coming back to join the team. That's what I'm doing next."

People are let go all the time. Ninety-nine percent of apprentices don't make the grade because of injuries or attitude or lack of talent. But *not* me. I am the one percent. Everyone knows it.

Rossiter stares at me for a moment. "With a metal box in your belly? Even if we wanted to get you back out there, our insurers would go ape."

I shake my head. "I'm indestructible now. I'll outlive the rest of you." A doctor told me that when I'm ninety and at death's door, someone will have to turn the thing off, or it'd keep shocking me back to life. I'm about to explain when Rossiter sighs and puts his hand on my arm.

"Son, do you know what pace a football travels at? Over seventy miles per hour. The top speed recorded is one hundred and fourteen miles per hour. That'd catapult your bloody pacemaker through your rib cage and halfway across the stadium."

"The doctors must have told you, Joel," Coley says.

I feel something hot as lava building inside me. *Rage*: rage at what they've said, rage at the decision being made without me, rage at this whole thing that's happened to me . . .

"Told me what?"

"That what you've had put in is not compatible with professional sport."

"No. I wouldn't have had the operation if they had."

"Maybe you've forgotten," Coley adds. "Your dad told us you were having trouble with your memory."

I want to rip the stitches apart and yank the fucking ICD out. I'll do anything for one last chance.

Rossiter pulls on his leather gloves, the wanky kind with holes on top. "Joel, I'm as disappointed as you are. You were one of the most talented players I've ever seen. But chin up, lad. Give the campaign some thought. You don't have to be playing to keep football in your life."

I don't move as he leaves and Coley follows him out of the room.

"They never told me, I swear," I say to Diane. "Nobody told me."

She shrugs. "The doctors never told my auntie she was dying either. Nobody wanted to be the one to say it out loud."

My scar burns, my head throbs. Am I really the only person who didn't understand? My life *did* end in 1999. Tim and Kerry should have walked away and let me die on the lawns . . .

That would be better than this.

It's Kerry's face I see, her voice I hear, that afternoon in the chippie, when we talked about the operation. I can almost smell stale fat and feel the vinegar stinging my fingers as she says, *It's got to be your best shot.*

Did *she* know it was a lie?

Would she have done that to me?

Whether she did or she didn't, she must know *now,* but she's not said a fucking word. And there's another thing she must know, after all the time we've spent together: that for me, life without football in it feels more like death.

No one else will understand. I can hear them now: *You're so lucky to be here, focus on that.*

No one knows what it's like to have a gift that makes sense of your whole existence. When I was on the pitch, I was better than good—I was a star. I was alive. What am I if you take the football away? A nobody.

Last night, Kerry said I could do resits. *Resits.* She must have been trying to prepare me, but instead it's another bloody betrayal, the idea she thinks I could settle for a life like everyone else's. I thought she *knew* me.

They must have called my dad because he's come to pick me up, lifting my head off the table, taking my hands, walking me across the car park. I can't look at Coley as we leave. When I get home, I don't go to the guesthouse but into my old bedroom, with my squad posters and signed programs Blu-tacked to the wall.

Kerry comes around but I tell Dad not to let her in. "Tell her I'm tired. Tell her I'll call her in the morning."

I hear them on the doorstep, her protesting, him repeating the same lines.

When he finally shuts the door, I am almost relieved. She wasn't who I thought she was, and I will never be Joel Greenaway again.

16

Kerry

I go home but I don't sleep.

What if it's over?

No. It can't be over, because that means it's the end of the world.

His dad was kind but firm. *Joel's had a knockback,* he kept repeating. *I'm sure it'll look better in the morning.*

But I know Joel, I understand what this means.

Of course, I knew what would happen at the club. A braver person would have tried to warn him, but I couldn't take away his hope like that. It would have been like performing an amputation.

I kept telling myself he already knew, at some deep level, that his career was over. How could it *not* be?

Instead of imagining his reaction when they told him, I try to fill my head with physics, ready for my exam tomorrow. But all I see is him.

———

I take my exam in a trance, somehow manage to fill pages in the exam booklet, though when I close it at the end, for all I know I've written *Joel Greenaway* over and over again.

Mr. Greenaway turns me away again tonight and the heavy dread grows inside me. I phone Joel's mobile from our landline, but it rings and rings and then goes dead.

I can't settle, so I walk toward the seafront, faster, faster, but as I pass all the secret places we've been together, the hurt grows. The overgrown railway line above the viaduct where we'd kissed and I made us go further because I'd never had sex outdoors. My new wildness made it seem like the best idea ever.

The bikers' pub opposite the station—the one we knew we'd never be spotted in—where we drank cider to toast our one-month "anniversary" and a woman with the worst tattoos I'd ever seen bought us whiskey chasers because she could tell we were in love.

Last week, when it was *very* late, we went back to the spot on the lawns where he—technically—died. We crossed the prom to where the sea lapped against the shore and we paddled out and stared at the red-black horizon and the old pier and it felt like we were looking into our future.

Tonight I watch the sunset again but I don't feel the warmth and my brain can't process the color. It's as if someone has dimmed the world, to the very lowest setting. There is just enough light to navigate by, but all the landmarks and objects I know are reduced to gray, shapeless things.

Is this it? I count the days we've been together. *Sixty-seven*. Is this all the happiness I get?

The third time I go to Curlews, an empty taxi is leaving, the automatic gates closing behind it. Mrs. Greenaway is still in her coat when she answers the door. I can see her suitcases behind her in their giant hallway and her skin has a Costa del Sol glow.

"Hello, love." There's sympathy in her voice. That scares me:

what's happened between me and her son is obviously significant enough for her to know already.

"Please tell Joel I'm not leaving until he comes to talk to me."

She narrows her eyes and I feel like I'm being scanned at an airport. "Wait there," she says, eventually.

The door closes gently in my face.

I look up at the house to distract myself. It's soft and inviting inside, all expensive sofas and deep carpets. But outside, the dark brown bricks are too uniform and cold, the double-glazed windows designed to shut out the noise and grime that makes Brighton what it is.

When the door opens, Joel stands in front of me and my heart expands, too big for my rib cage.

But he doesn't ask me in, or kiss me, and every part of my body feels that rejection, my arms empty, my lips bereft. He steps onto the limestone chippings, pulling the front door closed behind him. I take him in: the unshaven chin, the wary eyes, the sour smell of alcohol, even though it's still morning.

"Are you all right?" I ask. Stupid question.

He doesn't bother to answer.

"Why won't you see me?"

"Have a guess."

"Please, talk to me. Whatever happened, it's going to be OK."

"You think I'm fucking stupid—"

"No I don't."

"Yes you do. *It's going to be OK.* No. It's not. Football was all I had to live for and it's gone and I might as well have died and you and fucking Timmy should have left me there, all right?"

I flinch. "We can get through this, together. You're in shock—"

"I'm not. I'm totally calm. I didn't want to see you because it's over. It was fun, but we were never gonna last."

His voice has a hard quality I've never heard before. He sounds like his dad.

"That's it, then?" I hear the catch of tears in my throat and hope he hasn't.

Joel shrugs. "Look, you're not my type, Kerry. You knew that, right?"

"So . . . why then?"

He smiles, but his eyes are cold. "I felt sorry for you. Wanted to road-test my new gadget. Thanks for helping me give it a workout. You saved my life, I saved you going to university a virgin. We're quits."

He turns around before I can find any words. This time the door slams and the chippings blur as I run toward the gates, determined he won't see me cry.

17

Kerry

ABC

I close my eyes but the letters are burned into my brain.

The waiting is over and my grades are in: A for biology, B for chemistry, C for physics. It might as well be three Fs.

Around me, I hear squeals of delight. Everyone else is off to uni. I am not.

"Kerry? What does yours say?" Tim's hand is on my shoulder, anchoring me. I open my eyes and try to read his face, because he's opened his envelope too.

"You first." I hold out my hand and he passes me his results slip and I brace myself to cope with his disappointment as well as my own. If I've failed, he must have done too.

A. A. A.

Wow. He did it. His hard work paid off. Thank God: one of us is going to be a doctor.

"Bloody hell, Tim, you pulled it out of the bag." I reach my arms around him so he can't see my face. Even a few seconds will give me time to recover so I can celebrate with him. He deserves this. He's such a decent person—he's forgiven me completely for the weeks when I avoided him, though he has no idea it was because I had been seeing Joel.

"Hold on." He breaks away. "What about you?"

"Don't spoil the moment."

But he snatches the slip from me and stares at it.

Even though I half-expected failure, it's still shocking to see it in writing.

"This is a mistake." Tim's face is the picture of righteous indignation.

"It's not. If anything, they're better than I feared. I did warn you."

"But you weren't being serious. Everyone says they did worse than they actually did." He stares intently at the paper, as though he can change the letters by willpower alone.

"Nope. I really did fuck them up."

He starts pacing the playground like one of those polar bears cooped up for too long in the zoo. "We'll appeal . . ." When I don't respond, he tries something else. "Or call the university and see if they'd take these grades. Or you can resit, apply for next year . . ."

I shake my head. "I needed three As, nothing less. And they won't consider resits for medicine, you know that. I'm OK, though, Tim. It's OK."

"No. It's not OK!"

I hate seeing him so distressed. "Tim, there's more to life than being a doctor."

"For other people, Kerry. But not for you. There's no *reason* for you to fail."

Except there is a reason; it's just not one I can ever tell him, or anyone else.

"We can't let it spoil *your* celebrations. Come on. Let's get to the Arsehole before they run out of booze."

We follow the swarm of sixth formers toward the seafront.

Tim still hasn't called his mum about his results, though she'll be on edge waiting to find out.

I make him use a call box by the pier to phone her, and while I wait outside, I imagine what this day would have been like if I'd got the right grades too. The alternate reality, where I didn't go to Hove Lawns on Millennium Night, so Joel would have died and we would never have slept together and he would never have broken my heart.

And the results slip tucked into my jeans would read A. A. A . . .

"All done," Tim says, coming out of the call box.

"What did she say?" I ask.

"She was thrilled."

But he seems down. "What's the matter, Tim? If this is about *my* results, that'll make me very cross. You deserve your grades."

He hesitates. "I . . . I don't know. I didn't expect to get these results. I thought I'd be calling the universities to see what last-minutes spaces they had on other courses. It'll take me a while to adjust."

You and me both.

Except there's something in his tone that makes me wonder if there's more to this.

"But in a good way, right?" I give him *that* look, the raised-eyebrows, tight-lipped expression that always makes him tell me the truth. "I mean, do you still want to do medicine?"

Tim seems frozen, exactly as he was on the lawns eight months ago. If he's having doubts, it's better that he faces them now. "You know, nothing's set in stone. You still could do biochemistry. Your mum'll get over it. It's not the end of the world. Tell me what you want."

He says nothing. A gull is swooping toward us, as though it's about to dive-bomb, and we both duck, sensing the air moving as it passes only inches from the tops of our heads.

"I want to get drunk, Kerry. Because we both need to! But before that, I want to do this . . ." For a moment I wonder if he's going to kiss me.

And I wonder what that might be like. "What's that?"

But now he's frowning. "It can wait." He links his arm in mine and we cross over to the Girasol café. We haven't been here since my birthday and I cling on tighter to Tim.

We have to fight to get inside and up to the counter. Ant is serving, throwing bottles in the air like he's a cocktail barman, nodding his head along to Eminem.

"We're out of Estrella!" he shouts toward the kitchen. "Oi, Joel, did you hear me, we need more Estrella!"

Joel.

I need to leave. I twist around but more people are already backing up behind me. I push but the wall of drunk sixth formers doesn't budge.

He steps through the door with a crate of beer, and it's as if he knew I was there all along: he looks directly at me. Despite everything, I can't take my eyes from his.

You made me fail. I saved your life and you *ruined* mine.

He drops the crate at Ant's feet with a clatter and rushes back into the kitchen. *Did he ever love me?*

"Stop," I say aloud and Tim turns to me, concerned.

"What's up?"

I reach for his hand: solid in mine. My best friend, the person I can always rely on.

"We're never going to get served in here," I call out over the music and the clamor. "Let's go to the beach and celebrate on our own. *You're going to be a doctor!*"

"I've got something to tell you," Tim says, hours later, when we're lying on the beach at dusk, bloated by too much beer and tiny under the clear lilac sky above. "I don't think I am going to be a doctor."

I turn onto my side to look at him. Is this a joke? I can usually guess his punch lines but not this time. Maybe my instinct was right and he's only now plucked up the courage to admit to his doubts. "Go on."

He sighs. "We're broke."

It's the last thing I expected him to say. I sit up quickly and regret it, as the whole beach spins.

Tim sits up too. "I can't afford to go to medical school, Kerry. The builders came to look at the cracks in the roof I spotted a few weeks ago and they think it's subsidence, which is going to cost thousands to fix, and the place is worthless without it. Plus, we haven't been able to pay the mortgage for three months and I can't go to university if we're homeless."

The beach continues to whirl around me. "Three *months*? Has your dad stopped paying maintenance?"

"The minute I hit eighteen last October."

"OK, so you get a student loan."

"It wouldn't be anywhere near enough."

"What does your mum say? She'd live in a cardboard box if it meant you could still study medicine."

Tim stares out to sea. "I haven't told her about the arrears. I never thought I'd get the grades for medicine, so why worry her? I do have a plan, though I know she won't like it."

From the sideways glance he gives me, I have a hunch I won't like it either. "Selling your body?"

He scoffs. "Yeah, that'd barely pay for fixing the bath tap. No. I need to earn some money and get on top of the repairs before the whole place falls down. Try doing the plastering and decorating myself. Then sell the bungalow, buy a flat somewhere farther out."

"A flat? How would that work with your mum's wheelchair?"

"Flats have lifts. Or we could move up to Scotland, where Mum's family are, it's cheaper up there." He exhales. "Once I've started work, got on top of the debts, things will be clearer."

It feels like we're on a listing ship. "You've already got a job?"

"No, but . . . There was an ad in the cadets newsletter, for ambulance control call-handlers. It's not bad money once you're trained up, plus my first-aid training will be useful. Shift work, too, so I can be around a lot for Mum during the day. I've got an interview next week."

"How long have you been planning all this?"

"A while."

"And this is the first time you mention it? The point of being best mates is you tell me *everything*." Although the moment the words are out of my mouth, I feel like a total hypocrite.

"You've been preoccupied."

Guilt consumes me. I should have realized he was in this mess. Should have done something to help. Instead, I was too busy feeling sad about Joel to see that my oldest friend was struggling.

"I'm sorry."

"Why? It's not your fault, Kerry. Or your responsibility." He pushes his hands onto the pebbles, trying to get up, but the alcohol has affected his balance and he keeps falling back down.

As I reach out to steady him, I try to imagine Tim dealing with 999 calls. He *hates* talking on the phone, and I know he'd struggle to process garbled or inconsistent information.

There must be a solution, if only I can figure it out. Money shouldn't stop Tim becoming a doctor if it's what he wants.

Tim grabs my hand and we pull each other upright. "Tim, listen. *I* will find a way to fix this." Doubt crosses his face, so I punch his arm, hard, and he winces. "Don't you dare give up."

He's smiling again. "You're drunk, Kerry Smith. And I've been through it a thousand times already. But even so, I'd never put it past you to achieve the impossible."

18

Tim

Nowhere in the application process for medical school did they assess the liver's ability to process alcohol. Tonight, more than ever, this seems a dangerous omission.

"Come on, Palmer, get it down you!"

A blue flame dances on top of the sambuca, and even though I've seen the others drink it without sustaining burns, my instinct for self-preservation stops me following suit.

"Oh sod that, if he's not having it, I will!" Harry Wilcox snatches the shot glass from me and I am no longer the center of attention.

I estimate that my liver's processing power is about average within my cohort. In the fourteen weeks since term began, five people have been incapacitated by booze, in various ways, mostly involving vomit. Perhaps we're simply acclimatizing to the noxious bodily fluids we're going to come across in the years to come.

"Smart move with the sambuca," says Laura. "I had a friend in sixth form who breathed at the wrong time and ended up with singed nostrils and zero nasal hair."

"Now that I *would* like to see," I say, thinking of Wilcox specifically. A moment later, I realize how bad that must have sounded, but she's laughing.

Laughing *at* me or with me?

"Fancy a dance?" She grins at me.

I try to weigh up whether this is a joke at my expense. "I don't dance."

"Everyone can dance. Come on, Palmer! Throw some shapes!"

Is she coming on to me? Laura is clever and pretty, but not *too* pretty, so perhaps there isn't a huge mismatch in our relative attractiveness. Statistically, relationships where one partner is far uglier than the other never work.

But a woman who was coming on to me wouldn't use my surname, would she? Or maybe she would. My mother's unconditional adoration hasn't equipped me to comprehend women I am not related to.

Even Kerry baffles me in countless ways. Since she's moved into the spare room, I can study her behavior in even more detail, as a field biologist might, but it makes less sense than ever. She shops, cooks, washes up illogically. And she's reckless too. Since she passed her test, she drives everywhere as though she is catastrophically late.

But it's her kindness and bravery that baffle me more. How she keeps smiling even when my mum's jibes are so perfectly targeted. How she gave up on medicine and took the ambulance job and moved into the bungalow so I could come to medical school.

I still wonder what made her screw up her exams. She has always been so much smarter than me . . .

Laura is pulling me onto the dance floor and I sense the others looking our way again.

She grins at me as the next song starts—"If This Ain't Love," not bad—and I try to forget that anyone is watching. Because if I can get over my self-consciousness, I'm better at dancing than people would expect. Could the same apply to kissing?

"Bloody hell, Palmer," Laura shouts above the music, "you're a dark horse."

"What can I say? Hidden talents."

"I wonder what else you can do?" When she smiles wolfishly, I wonder: is this where the physical side of my life begins? It's developmentally long overdue.

I'm in the bathroom when the clock strikes midnight. New Year is meaningless as far as I am concerned. When I return, the dancefloor is sticky and striped with party-popper streamers and Laura looks disappointed that I wasn't there for Big Ben's bongs.

When everyone goes back to Wilcox's flat, I plan to head home, but she drags me with her. Chateau Wilcox—he has a kitsch painted sign on the door—is a big basement flat a couple of minutes' walk from the hospital. Wilcox's parents bought it for him, and he's taken on a couple of flatmates who're already on their clinical years "so they're hardly here, which suits me as I get the place to myself."

We're only two streets up from the sea, and the patio garden smells of ozone and the wind tastes of salt, but it's stopped raining for a bit. We're warmed by more booze and the temporary bonhomie it's generated. There's a big box at the far end of the patio, next to the flint wall, and Wilcox strides over to it and claps his hands to make sure he has everyone's attention.

"We made it, you guys. Only one term in, but we're here, the next generation of doctors. Medics for the new millennium. Bone-saws, anesthetists, slashers. Some of us are going to make history, invent cool stuff. Some of us will have to content ourselves with getting filthy rich by removing wrinkles from ladies of a certain age."

Everyone laughs. I have to admit, he's pompous but funny.

"But I know from my dad, and my uncle, and their dad before them, that the mates we make now will stay with us for decades. The chums forged over our cadavers always last. So drink, be merry, and *bang.*"

He takes a box of matches from his pocket and lights the edge of the box, then races back to the rest of us on the patio. We wait. Wilcox looks pissed off.

"That cost over three hundred quid, it'd better . . ."

The first firework tears out of the box, exploding in the sky like a giant white chrysanthemum, as though it's testing the air for the others. They follow—three show-off minutes of color and noise. I wonder if the patients in hospital are seeing it.

And whether Kerry is seeing it, or whether she's too focused on the flashing lights on her screen, less than a mile away, in ambulance control.

"Gorgeous, aren't they?" Laura says, snuggling up to me, pretending it's colder than it is.

Even *I* can tell she wants me to kiss her. "Yes. Not sure they're worth three hundred quid though. Excuse me, I need another drink." As I walk away, relief is tempered by regret.

Every sofa in the living room is occupied by snogging couples, but the kitchen is quiet. I help myself to a vodka and Coke.

"All right, Palmer?" Wilcox stands in the doorway. "Has the luscious Laura got her teeth into you yet?"

It's odd to see him on his own: he's always surrounded by acolytes. His money, I could take or leave. What I crave is his confidence. Time to leave, before my envy uncoils into something darker. "I'm heading off now."

He slaps me on the shoulder. "Hey, if you're sleepy, I might have a little something to perk you up." He taps the side of his nose.

We all know Wilcox does cocaine. I've never "done" anything, not even the weed and E the cool kids did in sixth form. I never got offered either.

But now I wonder: *could* coke make me more like Wilcox? "All right."

His bedroom is tidy, his king-size bed neatly made for when he tires of being the host.

Wilcox opens a drawer in the oak desk. The tin box he takes out used to hold toffees but now contains a bag of powder, which he tips onto the inlaid writing surface and divides into two lines with a credit card.

"You first?"

"No, you," I say, because I have no idea what to do.

He sits on the leather chair and rolls up a slip of paper he takes from a pile in the drawer—I was half-expecting a fifty-pound note—and pokes one end into his nostril. He leans down and snorts, sucking up the line of powder like a mini-Hoover.

He sits up, sniffs, blinks, smiles. "Whoa. Never get bored of that."

He passes me a new piece of paper. I think of our introductory course in communicable diseases, wonder if that's why he doesn't use banknotes. The paper is hard to roll and he takes it from me. "First time, Palmer? Watch." He positions it by my nostril so I can push it in, guides my face toward the cocaine. There's a gentleness about him, the bedside manner in his genes.

As I snort, I feel the powder travel up my nasal cavity, the experience faintly medicinal. *All gone.* I sit up. Where is the coke now? I picture my anatomy book. Perhaps somewhere between my inferior and superior turbinates.

How long will it take to reach my brain? Perhaps I will feel nothing at all.

But now it's happening, a rush of something I can't quite name. I am still myself but unapologetically so. Not the scared schoolboy who froze on the lawns this time last year, but a man who can act, can take control. I feel my face breaking into a wide grin.

I glance up at Wilcox, who is also grinning. "Good, right?" he says. "There's more where that comes from. You scratch my back, I'll scratch yours."

"Right." I don't know what he means but I don't care. For now, I feel like his equal.

I go out into the garden and find Laura and kiss her full on the lips before either of us has a chance to change our minds.

I walk back because there are no cabs and I don't have enough cash for the New Year tariff anyway. The last hit of coke has worn off and it's late. Or early? It's 5:00 A.M. Where did the time go?

A lot of it was spent kissing Laura. It felt better than the cocaine and she wanted to go further but . . . well, I like her so I didn't want to rush. I wonder if we could *date*.

A girlfriend, a vocation, a future.

As I walk, guilt starts to harden like the frost: Mum has been alone for ten hours and Kerry has been working the dreaded New Year shift while I have been partying.

The lights are still on in Kerry's parents' house but our bungalow is dark. There's a note stuck to the front door. DON'T FORGET FIRST FOOTING.

We don't do much to mark my mother's Scottish heritage, but this weird tradition is sacrosanct, to avoid bad luck for the whole of 2001. On the ledge, Mum has laid a lump of coal—always the same one, shrinking over the years—plus a piece of bread, a teaspoon of salt, and a crystal sherry glass half-full of whiskey. I hold my breath as I put my key in the door, hoping I won't wake her. But as I carry the items over the threshold, I hear her voice.

"Tim?"

I go into her bedroom, fearful. Will she be able to sense what I've done? Her eyes are bright from the reading lamp. "Happy New Year, Mum."

She reaches out for the gifts and I place them on the table. "You never forget. You're a good boy."

Relief washes over me. "Ah, I don't know about that."

"How was your party?"

"Brilliant." I say no more because I'm too tired to process the difference between the things she'd want to know, and things I should keep to myself.

"That's nice, Son. I was worried when it got late and you weren't home but I told myself: he's with a bunch of doctors, what harm could come to him?"

I lean in to kiss her dry cheek. "That's right, Mum. Everything is fine; 2001 is going to be our year."

19

Joel

After the bongs, and "Auld Lang Syne," my bloody mother has another surprise in store.

"Let's sing 'Happy Birthday.'"

I look around the roomful of neighbors and London production people she's invited to her soiree. For the first time in a decade, she's turned down a live outside broadcast somewhere on the other side of the world to spend the New Year with her family—and, I realized too late, with all the people she wants to impress.

I wait for her to single out the poor sod who was born on New Year's Day.

"Today my gorgeous son Joel is one year old."

No.

She's beckoning me over and I look for an escape route but there is none.

Mum puts her arm around me. "Now, I know he *looks* eighteen, but this time last year, my baby boy was floating somewhere between life and death. Fortunately for him, he came back to us, and so I like to think that every New Year, he'll be celebrating an additional rebirthday.

"Happy rebirthday to you . . ." she starts to sing, and the guests join in. *Awkward* is not the word. Ant gives me a sympathetic look, but even he mouths along.

When it's over—I never knew a single verse of "Happy Birthday" could last so long—Ant has already grabbed a bottle of Grey Goose. "I thought you might need this."

"I need more than that," I say. "Let's go to the guesthouse."

"Fuck, telly people are full of themselves," Ant says, as I shut the door behind us and he starts rolling a joint. He should have been working at the Arsehole but laid it on thick with his dad about being with me as I relived my trauma, so he was allowed to escape before midnight.

"That's why I could never work in TV." I'd been offered a couple of runner's jobs through Dad's production connections, but instead I help out at the café, shooting the shit with Ant, drinking espresso to try to cancel out the slo-mo effects of my daily dose of bisoprolol.

"You gotta find something. You're bored. And you're getting fat. Like a great big baby." He lifts my T-shirt to reveal a softness there and I pull it back down, ashamed. "Not so much Bananaman as *donut* man these days."

"Leave it."

Ant shrugs, lights the joint. "Worry about you. Hard not to when I saw you half-dead on the ground twelve months ago."

"Get it right. I was fully dead, according to the papers. Mr. Millennium Miracle, the second coming."

Yeah." He takes a deep drag and smiles. "I saw her the other day, you know. In the supermarket."

He doesn't need to say her name.

I hate myself for what I did to Kerry but she deserves better than me, a failed footballer with no future. The final time she tried to persuade me to change my mind, I wanted to say yes, because she was the only thing I still cared about.

But as she stood in front of me, telling me everything would be OK, I knew she'd never give up on me and that would only drag both of us down.

So I had to say things I didn't mean. *Cruel to be kind,* like the song.

"Did she say how uni is going?" I gesture for Ant to hand the joint over. I never smoked before but now it's the only way I can sleep.

"She never went! Dunno why not but she's working for the ambulance service now, answering 999 calls. Oh, and even bigger breaking news? She's living with Tim."

Sourness fills my mouth, so sharp I might throw up. *"Tim?"*

"She swore they're just flatmates, but that's weird, right, her parents only live over the road. Has to be something going on. Nerd-on-nerd action!"

I can't speak.

Ant hasn't noticed. "You know, when Kerry kept visiting hospital, I did wonder if she had a thing for *you.*"

"She's not my type."

"Yeah. Way too clever for you!" Ant laughs. "But you need to get in the saddle again. Otherwise, what's the point in being alive?"

I don't tell him that I wonder about that every single day.

THE CHAIN OF SURVIVAL: PART TWO

The moment someone has a cardiac arrest, the clock starts ticking.

Every minute that passes without help increases a person's chance of dying by 10 percent or more.

But you can do something and the only equipment needed is your hands. You've seen it on TV, on hospital shows or disaster movies. CPR, that crazy pounding on someone's chest, is simple and anyone can do it. Kids, pensioners, *you*.

CPR stands for cardiopulmonary resuscitation. Pushing down on the chest means you've taken over the job of the stopped heart: sending blood and oxygen around the person's body and especially to their brain, which needs it most for survival.

You need to use enough force to bruise or even break a rib. You might be worried you're going to do more harm than good. But if someone has had a cardiac arrest, they are effectively already dead. You cannot make things worse. But you can make things a hell of a lot better.

Remember the chain of survival? The second link in the chain takes courage.

Begin CPR as soon as possible and don't stop till expert medical help arrives and can take over.

20

Kerry

"Ambulance service, is the patient breathing?"

"No. No! It's my dad, he was making tea literally just now, and I heard this thump and—Dad, Dad, wake up!"

A Category 1 call. This is why we exist.

"OK, I need you to stay calm for me. Help is on its way. What's your father's name and how old is he?"

"Mike. Mike Purcell. He's sixty-seven. Come soon, please! Dad!"

As I take her details, I hear the hiss of the kettle in her kitchen, a late-night local radio discussion about parking permit zones. "And what's your name?"

"Jane."

Jane is the first link in the chain.

"Listen to me, Jane, an ambulance is coming but I need you to help your father by giving him chest compressions. He's on the floor already, right? He needs to be on his back, on a flat surface."

The instructions appear on the screen, though I know them by heart. On the map next to them, a little moving dot shows the progress of the ambulance my colleague has dispatched. Six minutes away.

Jane is panting. "He's on his side. I can't . . . He's a big man."

"Is there anyone there to help you?"

"No. Oh shit, Dad . . ."

"All right, get him flat on his back as quickly as you can."

"But what if he hits his head?"

This part is hard: how do you tell the caller that the person they love is beyond pain, as far as we know?

"Please do as I say."

She groans, her mouth right by the receiver: I picture her, the phone tucked into the crook of her neck. I hear a slap as the patient falls. "Is he in the right position now, Jane?"

"Yeah, I think so. But why isn't he breathing?"

"You need to help him. Kneel down next to him and move his clothes out of the way so you can see his chest properly."

A flashback: the sight of Joel's perfect torso as I pulled up his T-shirt to do what I am asking Jane to do. I replace my mental image with one of this older man, with more fragile ribs and looser skin, but so much life still ahead.

My current patient's collapse was witnessed. Like Joel, but unlike many others, he does have a chance.

"Now place your palm right in the center of his chest, below the nipples. OK so far?"

"I think so."

"Now place the other hand over the first one and begin to push down, hard, by at least two inches, at the pace I'm going to give you: one and two and three and four. Keep your arms straight, one and two and three and four . . . Are you doing that now, Jane?"

"It's going to hurt him. Dad, wake up!"

I've lost count of the number of times I've read this script in eleven months with the service. It hasn't worked once. The crews have never been able to restore spontaneous circulation. My first death almost broke me, because saving Joel had convinced me I was invincible.

I got over it. You just do.

A colleague stands close by, both of us staring at the screen, willing the crew to get there faster.

"My arms are getting tired . . ."

"I know, Jane. Help is nearly there but don't stop. Keep that rhythm going, good hard pushes."

"But what about . . . When they arrive?" She's panting now. "How do I open the front door?"

I remember how lonely it feels, to know you're the only one keeping someone alive.

"Run—safely—to the door then go back to your dad to restart compressions immediately. They're pulling up outside. One and two and three and four . . ."

A musical doorbell rings in the background: an Abba song. "Take a Chance on Me."

Jane takes the phone with her and I hear her tell the crew "Please. Don't let him die," before she resumes her counting—*one and two and three and four*—and then one of the crew says, "We'll take over CPR, love."

"Jane?" I say, softer now that I don't have to help pace her compressions. "I'll leave you with the crew, OK?"

"But . . . what am I meant to do now?"

"You've done brilliantly. You've given your father the very best chance. Take care."

"Bye . . ." Even though there are now two people with her, and more on the way, she sounds more alone than before.

I end the call, and exhale. My colleague nods: he knows about the comedown. "Textbook, Kerry. Nice work. We're not that manic, so take a couple of minutes."

I shake my head. "I'd rather get on to the next thing."

He shrugs. "Your call."

An hour later, the dispatcher comes over to my station. She's smiling. "They got return of spontaneous circulation on your arrest, second time with the defib."

"Mr. Purcell?"

She nods. "Woke up too. Looks like he's fully compos mentis. You did it."

Jane did it. "That's my first ROSC."

"You know how rare it is. Girl done well. He's gone straight into the cath lab, ECG showing suspected heart attack."

The rest of the shift flashes by. The feeling is back, the one from after Joel woke up, that euphoria. Even though I never touched Mr. Purcell, will almost certainly never see his face, I helped his daughter to save his life.

I can smell bacon frying as I walk up the path. When I let myself in, Tim appears in the joke apron my mum bought him for Christmas, with a six-pack torso and skimpy lifeguard shorts printed on the plastic. The radio is on; Kylie sings "Can't get you out of my head."

"One egg or two?"

"Two. I helped get someone back tonight, Tim. ROSC in under ten minutes."

He comes closer, and gives me a bear hug. I can smell fresh coffee on his breath. "You're getting an extra rasher of bacon for that."

It's a ritual we've adopted at the end of a run of nights. Tim'll do a cooked breakfast for two, and we'll sit and chat. This morning it's warm enough to eat in the garden, which also means we won't risk waking Elaine as we talk. It looks a lot better out here: I talked the builders who fixed the subsidence to throw in some patio slabs for free.

He brings out the plates and I tell him the story, though I leave out the part about it reminding me of Joel. I know how Kylie feels.

"It's incredible that you're saving lives while I've barely scratched the surface of a cadaver."

"Not when I'm about to eat." It's a joke, because I'm not actually squeamish. As I cut into my first egg, the perfect runny yolk pours onto my toast. He gets it right every time now, even though he couldn't cook at all when I moved in.

He hasn't learned for my sake. His girlfriend, Laura, probably gets breakfast in bed when he stays in her student room. She never stays overnight here. His mother approves of her because she's a med student, too, but Tim tells me he couldn't bear to do *that* under her roof.

"Is Laura back from the States on Saturday?"

He shrugs. "Sunday, I think. If I get up in time, I might fetch her from the airport or something. Though Heathrow is a bit of a trek."

"You old romantic."

He blushes. It's weird, us both dating. Nice weird. We've had great chats about Laura, and about Andy the paramedic—until he dumped me last month, that is. It didn't hurt, which was a relief but also . . . I dunno, I'm worried I'll never feel that intensity again, the way I felt about—

"I should pick her up, I guess. I think she'd be very grateful . . ." he peters off, grinning. Is he imagining *how* grateful? For all our discussions about life, death, medicine, and the nitty-gritty of us both dealing with his mum's personal care, we don't discuss our sex lives.

"I'm sure she'll have missed you." I hear something barbed in my voice. It's been strange, ceding territory to this girl I am not sure deserves my best friend.

We sit and eat and all seems well with the world: the birds sing and the clouds pass across the autumn-blue sky and I think, *I am happy again.* My life here is good, in a way I couldn't have imagined a year ago.

My family worried that moving in with Tim was me punishing myself for failing to get my grades. But right now I can't think of a place I'd rather be than this scrappy patio, with my belly full of fried food, my arms tingling in the sun, knowing I have saved another life.

"Kerry! *Kerry,* wake up. You have to come."

Before I can open my eyes, Tim is in my room, and I'm instantly on high alert because he always respects my privacy, so it must be something bad—

Elaine. A fall, a stroke, a heart attack like Mr. Purcell?

"Your mum?"

I push the duvet off and remember belatedly that when I couldn't sleep, I took off my T-shirt.

Tim stares for a split second before turning away embarrassed, and I pull the duvet back over while I grope for my top under the covers. "Have you called an ambulance?"

Still he doesn't seem to hear me. I'm about to slap him when he says, "No. Why would I do that?"

My hand closes around the cotton of my T-shirt and I pull it over my head and jump out of bed, toward Elaine's bedroom. But the lounge door is open and she's there, sitting upright on the sofa and clearly no worse than usual.

The TV is on, some disaster movie. I can't even tell how long I've been asleep, but I do know I'm pissed off that he's woken me for *this*.

He puts his hand on my arm and nods at the TV. "It's an accident or—or something worse. It's New York."

I stare at the screen and realize this same scene—a plane hitting a skyscraper—keeps playing on a loop, while a smaller image of the building on fire is superimposed. "Where Laura is?"

He nods. I'm awake now but I have no idea what to say or do, and as the three of us watch the same unreal footage while a news presenter vocalizes our own bewilderment, the only thing I know for sure is that I want to be with the people I love.

It takes two hours to get news of Laura: two hours during which both towers fall and my parents and Marilyn come home from work to join us in the bungalow, unable to stop watching. Even though there is nothing we can do, I almost feel culpable. We're not responsible for the act—who knows *who* is behind this?—but witnessing hundreds, maybe thousands, losing their lives as the buildings collapse makes me wish I could be doing something. Anything.

Laura manages to call from the hotel and when Tim answers the phone and his face changes and he gives us a thumbs-up, we all burst into tears. It's not real relief, though. How could it be?

It goes dark and we're still watching. Eventually my dad starts saying we must eat, because it's not going to help anyone if we don't. They go back across to their side of Hazelmere Crescent. Elaine refuses to go to bed but falls asleep for long enough for us to carry her into her bedroom.

When we're alone again, Tim breathes heavily. "Jesus, Kerry. Why would anyone do this?"

I shake my head. I am imagining the American equivalents of me and the paramedics and the firefighters and the police and the doctors and the nurses.

"You must have been beside yourself about Laura."

He nods and takes a gulp of the brandy he's poured. "The thing is, though, Kerry, all the time I was ringing around, trying to find out where she was . . ." He closes his eyes. "Don't get me wrong. I'm relieved she's OK. But I knew there was only one person I wanted to have here with me, safe, in this room, where no one can get us. And that's you."

"Well, of course, I—"

Before I can finish, he's kissing me, tasting of sweet brandy, but the real sweetness is how tender it is, this kiss, and how much I want to kiss him back. It is not only desire, though that is there too.

Most of all, it's safety.

21

Tim

MAY 15, 2002

It feels strange to be saying goodbye to Christine. We never spoke, she knew nothing about my life, and—aside from what I could surmise from the state of her liver and arteries—I knew nothing about hers.

Yet, in her silence, she's taught me almost everything. And today, in the university chapel, we're thanking her and the other cadavers donated to our medical school this year, for letting us take them apart.

"The generosity of this gift will be felt for decades, as the doctors-to-be in this room use the knowledge and skills they have gained to treat many thousands of patients in the course of their careers," the dean intones.

Even Wilcox has allowed his permanently arched eyebrow to drop, and without that sardonic touch, he looks younger. Laura sits between us. There were no recriminations when I told her about me and Kerry after she was finally allowed to fly back from New York. She just said, *I always thought it'd be you and her.*

Wilcox thinks she'd shagged someone during the summer break anyway and was probably relieved she didn't have to dump me first.

"It takes a special person, and special families, to choose this type of donation . . ."

The first time we met Christine, there was laughter, but that was mostly to cover up the fear we all felt at seeing a dead body for the first time. It was like being plunged into a horror film: the sting-y, suffocating smell of the formalin, the chill of the room, and then the reality of *it*—or should it be *her*, we didn't know the correct way to think of a cadaver—this former human, ready to reveal her secrets.

After that first session, we went to the pub and ate two-for-one meals, mistaking our sudden appetite for something metaphysical, till Wilcox told us it was well known that the smell of the chemicals made you hungry.

I wonder if Christine will stay my favorite patient. In the dissection room, working through the layers and labyrinthine complexities of a body, I could almost believe in God.

When the service is over, we drink weak coffee and eat petticoat tails of shortbread with family members. Small talk is never my forte, and as I try to dredge some up, it's hard not to look for traits that might tell us if Christine's relatives are here: a double-jointed thumb clasped around a pale green teacup, a rather prominent supraorbital ridge.

"Pub?" Wilcox says, when the last of the guests have gone and we're helping to clear the meeting room. Even he has found this tough.

"Pub!" Laura confirms.

It's tempting. "A quick one?"

"More like a full-on bender." Wilcox taps his suit pocket. "I have everything we need."

The thought of what I already owe him for more essential supplies changes my mind instantly. We've gone beyond coke: Wilcox offers an extensive range of pharmaceutical solutions, a pill for every ill. I never give him *cash*—he's not short of that—but he expects payment in kind. I struggle enough with my own essays, without having to do his too. Which then means I need more meds to help me focus, and more to help me sleep.

Even the most devious street dealer couldn't have come up with such a perfect vicious circle.

"On second thought, I might head off . . ."

"Back to your 999 girl? So *sweet,*" Wilcox says. The raised eyebrow is back.

I turn to Laura in time to see a brief flash of what looks like hurt in her eyes. "Not even a quick toast to Christine and her perky liver?" she says.

It does feel disloyal to go now. The strange camaraderie that medical school generates must be like what soldiers experience at boot camp. In the anatomy lab, we face the messy brutality of the body. We bond over our mistakes.

But the strongest bond I have is not with these people. Kerry covered up the worst mistake I've ever made, and then her generosity made sure it wouldn't ruin my life.

Right now *this* soldier wants to be home.

She's sleeping before her night shift, but I can't resist getting into bed next to her: luckily, Mum is asleep too so I don't have to make small talk with her first. The first time I had sex with Kerry, pure need overcame my reluctance to do *that* under my mother's roof.

Now we share a room but we're well practiced at making love in gleeful, conspiratorial silence.

Kerry turns toward me, kisses me with a toothpaste mouth.

"How was it?"

"Strange but uplifting." I run my hand down her naked back. Laura taught me many things and that paramedic boyfriend of Kerry's did the same. For a long time in sixth form, I thought we were destined to be each other's firsts, but that might have been mortifying.

As it is, we are devastatingly compatible. Making Kerry come makes me feel more capable than anything else in my life. Correction: it is possibly the *only* time I feel capable.

"You're always horny after anatomy."

She's reciprocating, running her hand down my chest and farther.

"It's the carpe diem thing."

Her body is warm and her ribcage expands as she laughs. "It's not *life* that you want me to seize, though, is it, Tim?"

This time last year, I wouldn't have dared dream that Kerry Smith would be in my bed, that we'd be about to make love.

Do I deserve her? It's not normal to keep secrets from the person you love. But the drugs are only temporary, till the exams are over. Or just into the start of next term, because already I am having sleepless nights at the thought of breathing, talking patients who might confirm my fear that I am not cut out for this.

STOP. NOW.

She kisses me again and I let the biological response overwhelm my thinking.

22

Kerry

SEPTEMBER 7, 2002

"Kerry, are you sure I can't use these pesetas anymore?"

"Kerry, what's this funny thing on my tapas? I ordered scampi but it's got *tentacles*." "Kerry, I can't find my purse, do you think I've been robbed? Oh, shit, and my driving license has gone too."

I'm meant to be on holiday, the first since an all-inclusive family holiday to Greece, age fourteen. Mostly that time I hid in my room, rather than be forced to conga or enter into some cringey talent show.

My sister's Barcelona or Bust hen weekend is a stretch for me financially, but Tim insisted I come and "have as much fun as humanly possible." The trouble is, even though I'm the youngest here, I seem to have become the default parent.

By the time I've helped Naomi, Marilyn's maid of honor, to report the theft of a purse stuffed with shiny new euros, everyone else is steaming drunk at a beachside bar. I lean over to kiss Mum, and squeeze in alongside her on the white leather sofa. "Started without me?"

She grabs a waiter. "Let me help you catch up."

The mojito royale goes down very easily, the bubbles sending the alcohol to my brain at warp speed. I decide to get so drunk that Marilyn's hens will have to fend for themselves.

I wish I was here with Tim instead. It's been a dreamy summer, though he's turned a bit tetchy now he's started doing more placements.

". . . it's mainly birthdays and special occasions now. Oh, and when the Dolphins win. But when we put our minds to it, we can still be pretty imaginative," my mum is saying. Please don't let her be talking about sex.

One glimpse at Marilyn's face confirms my fears. My parents have always been more touchy-feely than most, and part of me is proud that they still love each other deeply. But I don't want to know the details.

"Mum, do you have to?"

"Oh, Kerry. You're turning into such a prude."

Am I? "You wouldn't think that if you'd heard the calls I take about people's genitals, or how they claim they've lost items up their orifices."

They demand I share the stories then, involving people "falling" onto brooms and bottles and toilet brushes. "What's even more amazing is that sometimes they fall on these objects after they've accidentally popped a condom on the end of them. Still doesn't make it safe sex!"

The excitement of my job might have worn off, but it can't be beaten for hen night entertainment.

Inevitably, the more we drink, the lewder people get. Naomi had what she's called a "starter marriage" followed by a "quickie divorce." "But now I'm single, I see more action than I did when I was married. It's how it goes. Even you two will do it less once you've got a ring on your finger, Marilyn."

"Never! Neil is like the Energizer Bunny." My sister's fiancé is a plumber, rugged and handsome but quiet, so she can take center stage.

"You and Tim will be next, will you?" Naomi says to me.

"We're not even engaged."

Although I *can* imagine us married. We already act that way, referring to each other as Mr. and Mrs., doing the gardening and chores in an ironic way, teasing each other as though we're in an episode of *The Good Life,* and having nonironic sex afterward.

"Promise me, Sis. Don't. Marry. Tedious. Tim!" Marilyn says, her face stern. When I told her Tim might not be able to make the wedding because they're already starting placements, she began plotting which single men to seat at my table.

She's always been pretty enough to get what—or who—she wants without too much effort, and that includes her husband-to-be. She'd never believe me if I told her it's not like that for everyone. Though I feel a little more glamorous here, now I've caught the sun. A couple of Spanish guys have even tried to chat me up.

Naomi shakes her head. "Isn't there some cute paramedic who'd sweep you off your feet and put the adventure in your life?"

"I had a cute paramedic. They're overrated, as is adventure."

"Everyone wants adventure!"

I shrug. "I've done a bungee jump. That was exciting." *Surprisingly exciting:* as I plunged, I felt like the old me, for a few milliseconds. "I've booked a charity sky-dive next month too."

Marilyn laughs. "If I lived with Tim, I'd ask them not to give me a parachute."

"Kerry is a very different person from you," my mum says, putting a protective arm around me and breathing biscuity cava fumes into my face. "Chalk and cheese. Tim is a lovely lad, and personality is the most important thing. If Kerry doesn't want the fireworks, that's up to her!"

I want to tell her that there *are* fireworks with Tim, but not the out-of-control, exam-ruining kind. That he's a surprising lover: sweeter than Andy the paramedic, more patient than Joel ever was.

Joel. He almost ruined my life, so why does my body still jolt at the thought of him?

Nostalgia for first love, that's all it is. The future is so much better. My whole life is ahead of me, with Tim at my side. Isn't that the most reassuring feeling of all? Us against the world!

Mum is nudging me, pointing at her watch. "Drink up, Kerry. We don't want to be late for Topless Tapas! Apparently, the men are hot stuff."

My sister's wedding day comes three weeks after the hen weekend, in the middle of a heat wave: perfect for her sleeveless dress, but shitty for me and Naomi, sweltering in our floor-length aqua silk sheaths. I look like the Little Mermaid who forgot to apply her antiperspirant.

Everything else is beautiful: Marilyn, the church, the flowers, my parents' outfits, and the posed photos under the bandstand, with the faded West Pier in the background, still glamorous despite the decay. And now I'm hiding in the sunlit front parlor of the regency-era house she's hired for the reception, all chandeliers and gilded coving.

But I can't relax. My only qualification for being a bridesmaid is my shared genes. Give me a grand mal seizure and I'm happy, but I am clueless about reception etiquette.

"Does she need her hair redoing? It's gone a bit frizzy."

Naomi has it sussed. "This is her postceremony relaxed beach-wave style, as detailed in the manual, page seven." It's not a joke. Marilyn had a whole "look book" printed up and distributed to key personnel. It's not *entirely* about vanity. She wants to become a wedding stylist, "because weddings are the best fun ever."

There isn't a single cell of my body that could regard this as fun. Tim feels the same, but he's got the perfect excuse, with a day's shadowing at the community hospital in Worthing. He pretended it was accidental, but I saw his forms. He *volunteered*.

"Kerry?"

It's like seeing a ghost.

Joel is wearing an old-school bartender's outfit—white shirt, waistcoat, black tie—and it makes me wish we'd both been born in the 1920s. Maybe it's the cut of the outfit, but he looks as though he's just strolled out of an underground jazz bar. It's only seeing him now that I realize how his brush with death dulled his beauty.

Now he's back to how he was before.

My pulse is racing, but this is *anger* I am feeling, not attraction.

"What the hell are you doing here?"

"I . . ." He gestures at the uniform. "Working. Ant's in charge of the bar and he asked me. He never mentioned it was Marilyn's wedding; if I'd known, I'd never have come."

"Why the fuck would Ant do that?"

Joel shrugs. "He doesn't know about what we were. I guess he didn't think it was relevant. When I realized, I was gonna leave but then I saw you and . . ." He exhales. "Look. Do you want me to head off? Ant will hate me for leaving him in the lurch, but I don't want to spoil your day."

I glower at him. "How thoughtful of you."

"Kerry—"

"Stay, go, whatever you want. It's nothing to do with me. Stay, probably, I can't be responsible for people going thirsty at my sister's wedding."

"Are you sure?"

I try to stare him out, shame him into looking away. But he doesn't. I need to say something to end this moment because the longer it goes on the harder it is to dam this flood of memories.

"*Whatever,* Joel. Stay. It'd be a shame to waste your costume."

He pulls a face. "Embarrassing, right? Your sister was very specific about how we should look, according to Ant. She made a better choice with your dress."

Self-consciousness makes me prickle with sweat. "The other bridesmaid picked the style because she's a leggy waif. Unlike me."

A flicker of something crosses his face. "I think it suits you better."

"Yeah, well, I'm counting the hours till it comes off."

He runs his eyes up and down my body. "Right." When he smiles at me, he looks like the *old* Joel Greenaway, the prodigy, the pinup, the boy who couldn't help being a charmer.

I turn away from him because I can't get my head around any of this.

Easy, sexy jazz drifts through from the garden and I know it must be time for Marilyn and Neil's first dance. They've been rehearsing a slinky show-stopper.

The parlor is empty now, except for us.

"Look, Kerry . . . I'm sorry."

I wave him away. *Not now.* Not today. Not *ever.*

"You'll never forgive me and that's OK. I behaved like the world's biggest shit, but I did it for you."

I spin back around to face him. "You what?"

"I'm a loser, Kerry. Look at me. Dressed up to the nines to pour drinks at someone else's party. This is as good as it's gonna get for me. As soon as they told me I was off the team for good, I had to end it between us. For *your* sake."

"Bullshit. You only thought about yourself, you bloody coward. I didn't care if you never kicked a ball again in your life. I love . . . *loved* you for what I thought you were. Not because I thought you were going to play for England or earn a million quid a week."

He opens his mouth to respond but I'm not finished yet.

"And what did I get back for loving you? I screwed up my exams, which nearly ruined my whole life. I've ended up with no degree and a job going nowhere and you have the nerve to tell me this was all for me? You're a user and a—"

He catches hold of my wrist mid-rant and pulls me toward him.

"You said you *love* me . . . even a thicko like me knows the difference between the past and present tense."

Did I? *Do I?*

No. I love Tim. I really do. And this *stuff* I'm feeling now is muscle memory. "I said I *loved* you. Before you screwed everything up."

"Kerry, I am so, so sorry for the way I behaved. Seeing you now, I wish . . ."

My rage is turning into something else. His lips are on mine and despite everything, I want this . . .

Over his shoulder, through the bay window, I can see the Peace Statue and the lawns to the right of it and the sea beyond.

We pull apart. Who made that kiss happen?

Farther away, I hear "Unchained Melody" begin and the applause outside as my sister and her new husband take to the floor. "I'm meant to be watching their first dance . . ."

But instead of letting me go, Joel kisses me again, this time properly, and that music doesn't seem anywhere near passionate enough to express how it feels to be here, in the moment, with the first boy I ever kissed, the only man I've ever felt this way with—

No. I *love* Tim. He's my best friend. If the passion with him is more *controllable,* that's better. *Safer.*

Isn't it? But this kiss, this *kiss* . . .

The house bell rings, loud and self-important. I break away to see a shape where the porch meets the bay window.

Tim.

He's staring through the glass, frozen. What did he see?

Someone in stiletto heels is bulleting across the tiles to let him in.

Joel and I have jumped apart but Tim is thundering into the parlor. Rushing at Joel.

"No, stop."

I'm trying to get between them but even though Joel is fitter and bigger, whatever Tim saw has given him the strength of a man twice his size.

I am breathless, still reeling from *that kiss.*

Tim's fist strikes the side of Joel's cheek. Joel doesn't cry out. He's not even fighting back. I don't want him to hurt Tim, but why isn't he defending himself?

It seems to make Tim even more furious.

"Tim! We can talk about it. Don't punch him again, please—"

I picture bruises blooming on Joel's body and I know how to stop my boyfriend hurting my ex. "Tim, please stop, you might set off his ICD."

Tim's arm drops, his fist slackens, and when he looks at me, the hurt in his face makes me wish I could take back my words.

23

Joel

I deserve the pain.

For kissing Tim's girlfriend—because that's what she is, Ant has seen them together. But I deserve it more for breaking Kerry's heart.

When he stops punching me, I want to tell him to keep going, to smash me up properly. Then Kerry can walk away from him. Come back to me. The way she kissed me just then, the one thing I know is that she still feels like she did two summers ago and—

"How long has this been going on?" Tim asks, between gasps.

I glance at Kerry—already my left eye is swelling up. The kiss lasted, what, twenty seconds? Two minutes?

But "this" really started the night of the millennium. Just because we haven't been together doesn't mean I haven't thought of her most days.

What do you want me to say, Kerry? I ask her with my eyes.

Tim sees the look she gives me and raises his fist. Out of instinct, I block the punch with my forearm.

"Tim, please, it's my sister's wedding, don't make a scene . . ." Kerry sounds like she did that time on the driveway at Curlews, when she begged me to let her help me and I shut her out. "It's not worth it."

She wants him, doesn't she? I don't blame her. *He* has a future, and that's what Kerry needs.

Decision made.

"Come on, mate, you don't want to do this, we were only talking."

"I'm not your *mate*. I know what I saw."

"You didn't see anything, Tim. I haven't seen Kerry in years and we hugged to say hello, she's glad I'm doing so well."

There's doubt in Tim's eyes. I'm getting somewhere. I reach into my waistcoat for my Silk Cut. "Do you smoke? Looks like you could use one."

He glances at Kerry. Yeah, I reckon goody-two-shoes Tim *does* smoke but he thinks she doesn't know. I play along.

"Breath of fresh air while I have one, then? Clear your head. You've been working, right? I can smell antiseptic. Respect, man. I couldn't do your job for all the money in the world." I don't usually talk like this, but it'll help him feel superior.

"They don't pay me anything while I'm training."

He wants to back down too, so it's easy to lead him out, down a side street.

"Yeah, Tim, but soon you'll be loaded. I've seen the motors in the hospital car park when I go in for appointments. The specialists rake it in."

"That's a long way off," he says grimly.

As I get my lighter out of my pocket, my fingers touch the joint I saved for after. Weed switches off the bad thoughts. I take it out and see him clock it. "Wanna share this instead of a cigarette?"

He shrugs but takes the joint, lights it casually, takes a long drag. *Interesting.*

"Not your first time, then."

Tim shrugs. "Doctors and drugs. The clichés are true. I prefer the prescription kind but . . . it's been a long day."

I smile. "We all need something to get us through."

He inhales the weed and the tension seems to leave as he exhales. "How've you been?"

I don't want to tell him, but the more I reveal about my own shitty existence, the less of a threat I'll seem. "I'm . . . still working stuff out. Been through my Elvis phase, eating like a pig, feeling sorry for myself. But I'm trying to come out of it. Ant is helping me."

He nods. Offers me the joint and I take it back unwillingly. I don't want to lose the taste of Kerry on my lips.

"Ant's a decent bloke. Did he get the weed?"

"Good shit, right?" I take a drag and hand it back to Tim. "No, not Ant's scene. Keep the rest of it if you want."

He shrugs again but pinches the half-smoked joint out between his fingers and pockets it. "Cheers. But I was hoping you might know where to find other stuff."

Seriously? "Like what?"

"Speed? Ritalin at a push. Nothing heavy."

"Thought you guys got pills for free. Perk of the job."

"That's higher up the food chain. I'd be lucky to score a free incontinence pad."

I shake my head. "Sorry. I don't deal."

"No. Shit. I'm sorry, I didn't mean to imply—" He stops. "It's not a big thing for me. Just exam time or when the long hours are a struggle."

Who are you, Tim Palmer? Because you're not the bloke I thought you were.

"All the other med students do it too," he adds; he knows he's revealed more than he meant to.

"Sure," I say, but what I want to do is pin him against the wall and ask him what the *fuck* he thinks he's doing, when he has a brain and a future and *most of all* when he has Kerry.

I watch his lips as he justifies himself, but I don't hear a word he says because there's this rushing in my ears, like I used to get in the months after I died, this big tsunami of noise and feelings: guilt, rage, hatred, sucking me under . . .

Is this really what Kerry deserves? Tim, with a secret habit? Or me, with nothing to offer except the way it feels when we kiss?

What if neither of us deserve her.

"Stop!" I say out loud.

Tim stares at me. I hate him and pity him. But if Kerry cares about him, maybe the one thing I can do is protect them both.

And there's something else: I like the idea of having one over on him. Tim was the one who brought me back to a life I hate. This feels like turning the tables, regaining a tiny bit of control.

"I'll ask around," I'm saying, without planning to. "The chefs usually have something. Same problem. Late nights, long hours. You got a mobile? Let's swap numbers and I'll text you if I get lucky."

When we meet in the same spot later and I hand over a little bag, he looks so relieved it almost feels like I'm doing something good.

I'm not a dealer.

I've only got one client and selling to Tim doesn't count, because I don't make any money out of the odd upper or downer. I know Kerry's the only one earning so she's paying, indirectly. If he's going to take pills, at least I can make sure they're safe and cheap. That feels like I'm helping in my own way.

We have a regular bench, two blocks down from the hospital, overlooking the sea. Since I sold him a few pills on the day of Marilyn's wedding, it's become a routine. He texts me what he wants and I get hold of it from some OK guys I know who hang out on the Level. Not like I have much else to do.

"All right?" I say when he arrives with his polystyrene cup of hospital coffee and his homemade sandwich.

Did Kerry make that for him?

"Yeah. We're sound. Especially my mum; she's on some new medication that Kerry researched," he says. Tim seems to have forgotten what he saw at the wedding. He almost treats me like a mate.

But we're not *mates*. Meeting him is like picking a scab: hearing about Kerry, staying involved in her life, means that wound never has a chance to heal . . . if Tim's got his bad habit, this is mine. I'm not ready to break it.

"Listen, I don't suppose you could get hold of fentanyl?"

"That's a bit of a step up. Why do you need it?"

"As a painkiller, nothing sinister . . . I was moving a patient and hurt my back."

"So go to the doctor." I can't help sneering.

He shrugs. "I never get time. My back's a bit weak from when I used to have to haul Mum in and out of the bath as a kid. I hadn't finished growing."

Did he do that on purpose? No, he wouldn't want me to pity him. But I do. When I turn to look at him now, I don't see the weasel who condemned me to this crappy life or the idiot who lies to Kerry instead of facing his fears.

I see a little Tim looking after his sick mother, trying to do his best.

I'm no soft touch, but that feeling of power is back. What's the harm? Kerry wants him to become a doctor, so this would be helping her. "I'll ask around."

Happy, balanced people probably think that getting into drugs is a cliff-edge decision you make, a single choice to jump out of real life.

But it's really not. Or at least, it wasn't for me.

It started when I began to spend more time with guys on the Level. One afternoon, I got chatting to a guy in a trilby—Spike—and he introduced me to his mates, red-bearded Ham and a pixie-faced girl called Zoë. And even though it was November, we stayed there till long after dark, even after the cider and the weed had run out. Despite my beta-blockers, that night I didn't even feel the cold.

As I wandered home, drunk and stoned and loose and light, I tried to work out why I felt so good, but my brain was too scrambled. Next morning, I worked it out. The spliffs helped but it wasn't that. With my new mates, I didn't have to explain myself. They'd never known Joel Greenaway, superstar.

The next morning I went straight back there, and they greeted me like an old friend. And suddenly it didn't feel like any big deal to move on from weed to the other stuff they shared, which depended on what they could get their hands on. The old Joel would have been horrified by the damage drugs could do.

The new Joel doesn't give a shit, so long as it feels good *now*.

What keeps me going back, day after day, isn't the drugs. It's the sense of belonging. I've only felt that twice before: in the team, and with Kerry. I've missed it. Of course, when we do ecstasy, I love my new friends even more. Speed always makes me nervous, because of my heart, but it's hard to resist, when they're all off their heads and I want to be too.

I'll never be as bad as them. Ham does crack and heroin, and I think Zoë does too. She once told us this "funny" story about giving her dealer a blow job in return for drugs.

"All women turn tricks, one way or another," she said, and I wondered what had happened in her life to make her believe something so shocking. But everyone else was laughing and I ended up joining in. We laugh a lot.

Sure, when Ant's dad sacked me for missing three Christmas party shifts at the Arsehole, I knew I'd let him down. But after the crap I've had to deal with, I deserve some fun, right?

I don't even remember New Year's Eve, which is fine by me—2003 feels no different from 2002.

We have a loose routine. On cold days, and dole days, we go to the Caroline of Brunswick and make a pint last all day, nipping out or to the bogs to do whatever pills we've chipped in to buy. On sunny afternoons, we go to the beach instead. The three of them take the piss out of me for being a tourist, because I don't smoke crack, plus I have somewhere comfortable to sleep, and parents who will bail me out.

Except, as the weeks go by, comfort stops mattering so much.

Spring is coming and with the warmer nights there'll be no need to go home at all . . .

Tim and I still meet on the bench, and I sell him what he needs. The fentanyl was a temporary thing, he's back to speed and sleeping pills now; he knows what he likes. Perhaps we aren't so different after all. Except that he's studying, acting normal.

Me? Not so much.

Mum and Dad have tried to talk to me a couple of times, but now they've given up, and so has Ant. Fine with me. It's easier that way . . .

My eyes snap open. I'm in my bed in the guesthouse, hungover, hungry, dry-mouthed. The spring sunshine coming through my window is too bright. Normal. Except this morning smells of autumn: bonfires and decay.

Even I can't have slept through an entire summer.

I turn my head to look for the source of the smell.

Nothing's burning, nothing's smoking.

Not in here. But what if the main house is on fire?

I leap out of bed to check. No. But that smell gets stronger. Without changing—slept in my jeans last night anyway—I pull on my parka and follow my nose. Out of the house, down Dyke Road.

Smoke rises from somewhere on the seafront. Has a plane crashed on the beach? Or is it something to do with us invading Iraq? Has Saddam Hussein launched a WMD aimed at London and missed?

As I'm crossing Seven Dials, there are other people going the same way, following the smell.

"What's going on?" I ask a bloke my age, in an estate agent suit.

"It's the pier. It's on fire."

"Which pier?"

Soon enough, I can see for myself. The Old Lady. The prettier West Pier, the one that belongs to Brighton, lit from the inside. There are hundreds of us, maybe thousands, watching from the shore. But where are the helicopters and the boats trying to put the fire out?

People are red-eyed from tears or smoke. I pick my way in between them, heading for the place where my mates usually hang out, next to the sea wall. I can't look away from the burning shape for more than a few seconds: the orange flames licking through the black-and-white pavilion that sits majestically on the water.

"Someone saw a speedboat there beforehand."

"Gotta be deliberate. How else would a fire start in the middle of the bloody sea?"

"Oh, I dunno, one of the gulls might have dropped a lit cigarette . . ."

I see Spike's trilby above the crowd. Zoë is crying and it makes her look even more wrecked than usual. Ham is strumming something melancholy on his guitar.

We've wandered across the sand to the pier a couple of times, when the tide's been low and we've been high. You can stand underneath, and though the ironwork's covered in bird shit, and it stinks, you can see glimpses of what it used to be through the gaps: faded signs advertising sticks of Brighton Candy Rock and BEST STOUTS AND ALES, and old theater tickets blowing around like a snowstorm. All that paper must be fueling the fire.

I sense someone watching me.

Turning, I see a woman in uniform. My face arranges itself into a *whadyoulookingat* sneer before I recognize her.

Kerry.

It's too late to get away. As she walks toward me, I'm conscious of how filthy my parka is, and grateful that at least the smoke should drown out the smell of my friends.

There've been half a dozen times since her sister's wedding when I've thought I've seen her: turning a corner in the Lanes, or through a shop window. I've always hidden in a doorway, rather than face her. Now the shock in her face is worse than any mirror.

"Hello, Joel. Isn't it awful?" She looks beautiful, even in the unflattering green jumpsuit, even with no makeup.

"Can't believe it," I say. "Bastards."

She smiles nervously at the others then back at me. "So how've you been? You working?"

Zoë laughs. "Joel doesn't need to work. He's got the Bank of Mum and Dad with their endless cash machine."

Kerry frowns at her. Zoë's only three years older than us, but she could be the poster girl for how drugs fuck up your complexion.

"I'm between jobs."

Spike stands up. "If you're not gonna introduce us, I guess I'll have to do it for you, you rude wanker. I'm Spike," he says, raising his trilby and holding out his other hand.

I cringe when I see her small clean hand take Spike's, with dirt and tobacco embedded under his nails.

"This is Ham, and you've already met Zoë."

"With two dots," Zoë says.

"Don't forget the dots." I laugh, feeling protective of both women, somehow. "This is Kerry, we . . . went to school together. Works for the ambulance service now. She's cool."

No one speaks and eventually Kerry says, "Right, better go. Nice to meet you all."

We all regard the pier for a moment.

Kerry frowns at them, then turns to me. "You know where I am if you ever want to talk, Joel."

This big, empty part of me wants to follow her, beg for help. But she's done more than enough for me and look where it got her.

"Good to know," I say, wanting to sound smart. "Just call 999, right?"

Spike and Ham and Zoë laugh and I join in.

Kerry blinks. I've hurt her again because that's my only bloody talent.

As she walks away, I track her green-lapeled shoulders till she's lost in the crowd. The fancy café with the glass doors starts to play Pavarotti's "Nessun dorma," and I hate myself even more than I hate whoever started that fire.

$$\text{--}\Lambda\Lambda\text{--} 24$$

Tim

July 1, 2003

I expect my mother to sob at the departure gate but instead, she leans stoically against Kerry's mum and waves goodbye, as though the two of us are off to war, not India.

There've been so many times in the last weeks when I've wanted to cancel: to go back to the Northumbrian cottage hospital I originally picked, where I could have observed day cases, taken long walks in clear air, and tried to regain a handle on the parts of this year's curriculum that are a blur, like stations passed on an intercity train.

But this trip is not about me. It's about us.

I promised Kerry an adventure, a thank-you for all the support she's given me so far.

"Make sure you always sleep under your nets and don't pet *any* dogs; they all have rabies. And watch out for people who might have SARS," Mum calls out, when we're about to go through security. We found a charity that gives grants for short-term respite care, so Mum will be properly looked after. I wave one last time and turn away.

"I need to stock up on vodka," Kerry announces as soon as our cabin bags have been X-rayed. Mine has been packed and repacked countless times over the last month. I have a change of underwear, a small mosquito net, sunscreen, repellent, analgesics, vaccination record, hydrocortisone cream, and alcohol gel in my little bag of liquids.

Kerry packed this morning: a Stephen King paperback as thick as a brick, a T-shirt and shorts to change into as soon as we land, sunglasses on her head, and a bottle of her favorite shampoo, "because it's the only one that tames my mad hair." Oh, and the iPod her control room buddies bought her; barely bigger than a cigarette packet, with four thousand tracks loaded onto it.

She didn't think her boss would agree to a month's unpaid sabbatical, but she's wasted in that job and he's clearly willing to do what it takes to keep her.

As am I.

"I'm proud of you, Tim," she says, once we're settled into our cramped midrow seats on the plane. "You're pushing yourself beyond your comfort zone."

"You know me, Kerry. Adventure is my middle name."

We both laugh. Wilcox and his mates are off to high-end hospitals in exciting places, ideally by the beach. They'll scrub in to assist surgeons on cutting-edge procedures, in between trips to Niagara Falls or Ayers Rock.

The ones without the right pedigree—like Laura—are aiming to max out on hands-on experience in remote African villages. A few have stayed home, mostly the GPs-in-waiting who get turned on taking blood pressures without supervision.

India is somewhere in the middle. I've picked one of the least deprived states, Kerala, with beaches where Kerry can sip chai and find herself, and a well-equipped teaching hospital where I can observe surgeries without having to treat actual patients.

Even so, I keep asking myself, *What have I done?* I haven't flown since I was six, and that was only to Marbella when Dad was still around. I like things to stay the same. Just as the body is desperate for homeostasis, people need external stability too.

Or, at least, *I* do.

But there's one enormous positive. India is five thousand miles from Joel and his supplies and that smug look he gets whenever I buy from him. Cold turkey scares me but it's the only way, especially as I can't rely on Joel anyway. I think he might be sampling the wares.

Maybe spending four weeks with Kerry will help me feel more secure. Lately, everything Kerry does has seemed like a sign she's about to leave me, from the eyebrow raises when I ask her how she is, to the moans about how frustrating her job has become, and the dangerous charity stunts she's started to do in her spare time. Does jumping out of a plane mean she *wants* to jump out of our relationship? Does rappelling down a cliff mean she's desperate to escape?

"Penny for them?" Kerry asks.

"I can't believe it's really happening."

"I know! Perhaps you'll find your specialty at long last."

Most of my cohort already have plans for the future, but I'm paralyzed by indecision. *Not for the first time.* However hard I try to put it out of my head, my failure that night on the lawns seems to follow me like a ghost.

Pathology is one option: I loved lab work at school, and samples are hard to kill. But to qualify, I'll still have to go through two grim foundation years as the most junior doctor there is, right at the bottom of the pile. I've seen what it's like on placements: met a guy only three years older than me who was in charge of fifty surgical patients overnight. I don't know that I'll ever be ready . . .

Do all med students feel like this, deep down? Certainly, we can't admit to nerves. The pills have been the only thing to mute my self-doubt but I need to change that.

Kerry is waiting for my answer. I laugh and say, "I've already decided what to do. I'm going to run away and join the circus."

She nods. "So, we're talking animal bites, spinal injuries, eye trauma from juggling balls, allergic reaction to clown paint? I'd say that makes you an ED doctor."

That's the most terrifying specialty of all. "Yeah, that's me, Brighton's answer to George Clooney."

But as the plane taxis, I can't help thinking that A & E or even a circus ring teeming with tigers might be preferable to what lies ahead at the end of the flight. I've spent years clinging onto the status quo. What the hell have I signed up for?

We step out of the airport into hot, multicolored chaos. Kerry slept on the flight, but I didn't, which is adding to my trancelike state. My body floats on waves of soggy warmth, as we step between people and cars and cows and potholes full of rainwater the color of strong tea.

Monsoon season.

The hospital has arranged a driver, so we follow him to his car, and Kerry sits in the front, chatting away. I pretend to sleep in the back, shivering from the fierce air-con in here.

Yet I can't keep my eyes closed: there is too much to see. I had feared I would hate it, but instead, the world beyond the cab window fills me with an unfamiliar feeling. *Excitement.* Everything is unknown, and so am I. Perhaps this can really be a fresh start.

Energy pulses through me, as powerful as any drug. For the last few years, I've thought that I needed pills to avoid burning out. But what if the opposite is true? That I needed drugs not because life was too much, but because I need more of it. More than Brighton and Hazelmere Crescent and my mother's bluebell-scented living room have to offer?

"What exactly are you doing here?" the surgical director asks, peering over his spectacles.

Jet lag means I can't quite process the question.

"Sorry, I thought we had an appointment?" I compare my watch to the clock on the wall, wondering if I set my watch wrong, but they both say ten o'clock.

Mr. Mukherjee shakes his head impatiently. "No. What are you hoping to achieve at our hospital?" He is a small, plump man with incongruously long and slender fingers. Surgeon's hands. I wonder if this physiological advantage sits somewhere on the same DNA strand as the icy egotism most surgeons possess.

"A different perspective on healthcare?" I blurt out, feeling sweat bloom again under my arms.

"And your first impressions of our hospital suggest it will be very different from the British National Health Service?"

It feels like a trick question. "I don't like to judge anything on first impressions."

"Hmm." His eyebrows arch above his glasses. "We don't need unqualified British students to save our patients' lives." His accent has traces of Manchester vowels—I read his bio and he worked there for a decade before returning to India.

"Of course not, I never—"

He talks over me. ". . . and if you wanted the chance to live out your savior fantasies, you should have gone somewhere a lot less developed."

I almost want to tell him that I came here in an attempt to prove to my girlfriend that I am interesting and adventurous. "This isn't poverty tourism. I promise that's not why I'm here."

"That is *something*. Although I note that on your application, you don't even have a specialty in mind yet." Mr. Mukherjee clearly sees this as another failing.

Should I invent an enthusiasm or a vocation? My mind has gone blank. I cast around the room, looking for something I could latch on to: as my eyes race over the spines of the books on his shelf, I notice a desk calendar showing beaming schoolchildren playing on a beach.

He's shaking his head. "It's irrelevant anyway, Tim Palmer. The electives were organized by a colleague who left and the last thing I need is an underwhelming British medical student who can't even string a—"

"Public health!" I blurt out. The desk calendar has been sponsored by the public health department.

Mr. Mukherjee raises his eyebrows. "So you applied for a surgical elective in a teaching hospital because your interest lies in public health?"

"It's a recent development." *Very,* very recent.

He is about to call me out on the lie. Except, as I wait to be put in my place, I wonder if it *is* a lie. Public health has barely been mentioned in my training, but isn't it about analysis and logic?

"This hospital is the wrong place for you, young man."

I go to rise from my chair, wondering how I am going to tell Kerry we've flown around the world to be told I'm not wanted.

"But . . . I do have an idea. A former colleague has a project a little north of here, involving maternal and child health in rural areas. You *might* be able to do something useful there." He sounds skeptical. "There is one caveat, however. How do you feel about working in a conflict zone?"

It takes a week to sort, a week in which the doctors deign to let me watch a few minor surgeries while Kerry goes to the beach on local buses and comes back sunburned and full of stories. She makes friends with families in the relatives' block where we're staying, plays cricket with the kids in the corridor, and we share their meals in the evening: freshly made curries loaded with coconut and spice. I develop a taste for the heat. It helps to conceal the metallic taste in my mouth that I suspect is caused by drug withdrawal.

Some nights I sleep badly, too, but I know I must see this through.

"You've changed, Kerry," I say, as we queue to be given the extra shots we need for a rural placement. My med school knows I'm changing locations but we've had to tell a few white lies to get the OK. "When we were at school, you would never have chatted to all those strangers."

"True. My job has cured me of being shy." She smiles. "But you're exactly the same as you were then."

Ouch. "Come on. Would the old Tim be preparing for a dangerous mission in the jungle?"

She laughs, but we both know I'd have been on the next plane home if she hadn't been here. She makes me a better person. But what do I do for *her*? "I'm not thrilled at the opportunity to get murdered in a tribal conflict I've never heard of."

"It can't be *that* dangerous or no one would go there," she says, "and as for the jungle, I bet they're exaggerating . . ."

It *is* the jungle. It feels dangerous. And far from being "a little north," as Mr. Mukherjee suggested, our new base is a five-hour flight and a railway journey to the nearest town, then a couple more hours in a battered jeep.

Everything here is red or green: dry earth and dense forest. The heat and humidity are as intense as Kerala, though judging from the parched-looking bamboo and teak trees, the monsoon hasn't yet arrived.

We pass villages and rice paddies, women in short saris and, sometimes, children running after our jeep and waving. Kerry suggests stopping to hand out some of the pens and stickers we brought as gifts, but the driver shakes his head.

"Not here."

I start to see the signs that this is not a peaceful place. Our driver stops twice when commanded to by baby-faced soldiers, younger than Kerry and me. They ask questions, rifles hanging from their shoulders, and seem bemused by our decision to come here. I can't imagine theirs is a desirable posting. I never realized there were conflicts like this in India.

When we arrive, it doesn't resemble any hospital I've ever visited before, though a modern block would have seemed bizarre at the end of a rough track that's fighting a losing battle with nature. Instead, it's more like a large village. Inside a perimeter fence are dozens of buildings, some grander than others, with plastered mustard-colored walls and tiled roofs. Other structures are simpler huts. People—staff and patients—walk between the buildings or sit on verandas, listless in the heat. Signs in English and another script point to the outpatients and the pharmacy.

We get a guarded welcome from Siya, the postgrad who has been given the job of settling us in. She's our age, dressed in a T-shirt and long combats, and is beautiful enough to be the sixth member of the Spice Girls, though she's actually a research student.

"Someone pulled strings to get you in here," she says. "We're mostly Indian-staffed and we don't welcome foreigners gawping at our patients."

She leads us past a refectory—"Vegetarian food only, and there's no smoking or drinking here, plus you will help with manual labor to keep the campus clean. And as for your girlfriend, I hope you have a good book with you because there is *nothing* for someone unqualified to do here."

I glance at Kerry and see an expression I know too well: determination. The last thing she intends to do here is read.

Before I get a chance to settle into our cottage, Siya wants to take me to meet the Boss.

"Can't I shower?"

She doesn't even bother to answer.

"What's the boss's name? Is he scary?"

"*Her* name," Siya snaps. "It's Dr. Murty, but everyone calls her the Boss."

The Boss scrutinizes me as I step into her office, the fan whirring above her desk. She is wiry but powerful, with thick tortoiseshell glasses that obscure any sense of her age. "What can you do for us?" she asks, without preamble. "We don't need average people. What is the one thing you are better at than anybody else?"

Even if I weren't exhausted and sweatier than I've ever been in my life, I'd struggle to answer. When I was a kid, it was easy: physics, first aid, talking my mum into getting up even when she felt there was no point anymore . . .

"I'm quite proficient at basic patient care. Feeding. Bathing."

"That is what families do here. Come on, boy. You are studying medicine. You must be made of *something* more than your appearance suggests."

As I did in Mr. Mukherjee's office, I look around for inspiration, but this space is almost monastic.

On the Boss's desk, I see a pile of unused, headed stationery. I read the title upside down: RURAL MEDICINE CAMPUS AND RESEARCH CENTER.

Research.

"I am logical. I see patterns in data. I like Excel."

"Interesting." The Boss's mouth twitches: not quite a smile, but something closer to the expression of a wolf who's caught sight of Little Red Riding Hood. "How hands-on do you wish to be while you're here? If you are in any doubt about the correct answer, let me give you a clue. There will be *very* few opportunities to treat patients, I value them and our reputation too much to hand them over to a clumsy boy."

"I . . . I am happy to help wherever you think I might be most useful."

"And that is the *right* answer." She stands up and sweeps out of the office, her buoyant sari adding to the feeling I have of being pulled along on the slipstream of a speedboat. "Let me introduce you to our resident computer genius. You two might be able to make the most beautiful formulae together."

25

Kerry

I came to India to find myself, but two weeks in, I'm as lost as ever.

The country is even more beguiling than I expected—the extremes of landscape, the smells, the chance to get to know people whose lives are so different from mine. Kerala was beautiful, but it's here in the forest that I feel most alive.

Except, every day, my frustration grows. When Siya told me I wasn't allowed to get involved in anything, I convinced myself I'd soon find a way in. In reality, progress is painfully slow—at first, no one would even let me help in the kitchen, or sweep up outside the clinic buildings. I was so frustrated I was tempted to head out alone, but Siya was full of dire warnings about the dangers lurking *outside*.

So we've made a deal—I won't risk it provided she finds a way to let me go out one single time. I've had to give her all my hair products *and* lend her my iPod as a bribe. So today I'm leaving the project, to head out into the villages. Tim doesn't know, and neither does the Boss.

"You are crazy," Siya says, as I climb into the truck that'll follow the bigger mobile medical unit. I've feigned illness so Tim won't disturb me during the day and even arranged pillows in my bed to resemble a person, as though I'm a teenager sneaking out to an illicit disco.

I learned that trick from Marilyn.

"So, will you and Timothy get married soon?" Siya asks after a few miles sitting in silence. She's driving, turning the massive steering wheel with the strength of an ambulance driver twice her size.

"He hasn't asked." The thought of a proposal sends an icy feeling down my spine, almost welcome in the humidity. The rains we encountered in Kerala have finally reached this region, turning the landscape darker and, well, *junglier*. But the downpours never provide much respite from the stickiness.

"Maybe he doesn't think you want to marry him. Maybe he'll find someone else. A doctor has value, and he is quite handsome."

I smile. Does she fancy Tim? I picture him in full Bollywood Indian wedding regalia, trying to follow a complicated dance routine and messing it up . . .

Except Tim *can* dance. I'd forgotten that and it gives me a jolt far more unsettling than the potholes on the track. What else have I forgotten about this man I love? I've been in a funk for months and none of it is his fault.

We enter the first village and I stay in the van as Siya goes in to chat with the women and their babies. The scene is charming, with chickens and pigs and cows wandering at will. But what I know from Tim's work in the research office has made it clear the reality is the opposite of idyllic.

Ten million people here go without basic primary care, and while the villages seem safe during the day, at night it's rebel country. Most ordinary people try to straddle a line between the state and the Maoists, but when violence erupts, it's bloody, with mass killings by both the rebels and the police.

After forty minutes, I'm allowed into the garden of a bungalow, where the mobile medics set up scales and vaccination supplies in the shade.

"This is the home of the local health worker," Siya tells me. "You can only watch, OK? Do not touch."

So I do watch, as the babies are weighed, their chests listened to. They are chubby and sweet—I'm not broody, but even so, part of me would like to reach for one of the infants, feel the solid warmth in my lap.

Siya comes back over to me. "You know, we used to have babies die every year from exposure. Mum and baby were made by the elders to sleep open to the elements, till the village could afford to buy food for the baby's naming ceremony."

Tim's told me about the other dangers the women face. Many suffer domestic violence or sexually transmitted diseases passed on by their husbands. Even "everyday" problems like TB or snakebites can be fatal here.

On the way to the next place, Siya asks about me. I tell her about taking calls in the underground control room we call *the pit,* and explain the technology that lets me track an ambulance as it heads toward a caller's address, knowing that occasionally it's only my voice keeping someone alive.

Those calls where I made a difference used to be enough, but over the last year—longer, if I'm really honest—the rest of it has been getting to me: the hoaxers, the time wasters, the mental health patients whose voices I recognize because they call so often and never get the help they need.

"And that's enough for you? It sounds so . . . removed."

Her question stays in my mind as we stop at the second village and I watch the children being checked. It won't leave me even after we get back to base. I don't own up to Tim about where I've been. It's better for him not to worry about me.

"I love this work," he says as we sit on the steps of our shared dorm building, sipping chai. "People are bored by statistics, but it's where the nuggets of wisdom are hidden. You can see from the figures that analysis can save more lives than individual doctors."

"And you don't mind not having the patient contact?" I think of the yearning I felt to hold a child.

He shakes his head. "What if I could help hundreds, thousands of people, instead of one? I know it's not as sexy. You don't get grateful relatives buying you chocolates. But if it works, then who cares?"

Tim looks different tonight. His eyes are brighter and he smiles more, his hands swooping as he explains the improvements they've made here, the work there's still to do.

I feel different myself: traveling, experiencing how other people live, even seeing Tim lit up for the first time in . . . well, months.

I realize something as he talks. At home, I've stopped seeing him as Tim, my funny, eccentric first aider and best friend. Instead, I've been blaming him for the decisions I've made. Yes, I made sacrifices to help him, but that was *my* choice.

When did my negativity begin?

Marilyn's wedding. After that kiss with Joel. I've allowed a man who betrayed me to poison my future, as well as my past.

What a spoiled brat I am, holding Tim responsible for how disappointing my life feels right now. I am twenty-one years old. It's about time I got my shit together.

"What?" Tim says. "Have I got a spider in my hair or something? You're looking at me very strangely."

I don't plan it, but I find myself leaning over to kiss Tim, his lips still hot and sweet from his tea.

He kisses me back.

Next morning, my head is all over the place. Tim and I didn't have sex last night—there's nowhere private enough, and his fear of cobras meant he refused to sneak off-site. Still, I felt closer to him than I have in months.

"You're very quiet, Kerry. Not alarmed by my driving?"

I've talked Siya into letting me go out with her again, heading out to drop supplies off to some of the women workers. We've been on the road for an hour and she's a little more relaxed today.

"No. You drive well. It's more . . . what you said yesterday, about

being distanced from the callers, the people who needed help? It *does*
frustrate me. I didn't realize till yesterday, watching your colleagues
with the kids, and I craved that . . ."

"A baby with Timothy?"

"God, no. Not yet, anyway. I mean real contact with actual
patients." I shrug. "We're all different of course. Tim is the opposite,
he's loving the public health work, which—"

Siya brakes suddenly and I shoot forward toward the windscreen
before the seatbelt tightens across my body.

Ahead of us, a moped lies on its side, along with a carpet of
dried-out leaves, the kind they use for the horrible beedi roll-ups
they call *poor man's cigarettes*." Flies are already gathering.

I reach for my door handle, sure there must be a casualty nearby,
but Siya stops me. "No! It could be a setup. An ambush."

The words sound melodramatic, but she's right to hold back. The
first responder's acronym DRABC was drilled into me at ambulance
cadets and *D* stands for danger, though even back then, I found it
hard to hold back.

I peer through the window. "We can't just drive past, can we?"

Siya stares through the glass. "I . . . I don't know. Perhaps the
person on the bike has gone for help. Can you see anybody?"

There's a ditch to the side of the track, which separates us from a
rice paddy. I scan it. Poking out at the far edge, I can see something
rounded, browny pink. "Is that a foot?"

Siya edges forward in first gear, and even though she keeps the
revs down, it sounds as loud as a jet engine. If rebels are waiting in
the trees, they could jump out at any time. We have supplies on
board, but no phone to get help: there's no signal this far into the
jungle.

The scooter lies diagonally across the track, so we can't get past
even if we decide not to get out. Siya's knuckles have paled where she
grips the steering wheel.

The foot—or whatever it is—moves.

"Look. It's definitely a person, Siya."

"I'll back up, turn around. We can go back and get help."

"If the rider is badly hurt, he needs help now, not in two hours!"

Before she can start reversing, I grab the door handle and this time I *do* clamber out, though I'm half-expecting a bullet to thump through my back, or unseen hands to grasp my ankles and pull me into the forest.

When that doesn't happen I keep going, and I hear Siya's door open behind me. I reach the ditch, and I see a boy of fourteen or so, lying on his back, eyes flickering in a face covered in blood. His chest moves up and down and his hands clutch at his leg. The bright white bone of a fractured femur pokes out of his thigh, surrounded by raw, bloody tissue.

Shit, that must hurt.

But that's all the emotion I allow myself before trying to think of a way Siya and I could get him out of the ditch without doing more damage.

"Siya, what kit do we have in the truck? Is there anything flat we could use as a stretcher?"

I climb down into the ditch, and the boy opens his eyes and tries to move away, terrified. A *good* sign. He's conscious. "It's OK," I say in my calmest voice, not knowing if he's likely to speak any English but hoping my tone will convey reassurance. "We're going to help you."

"Here's what we've got for first aid," Siya says, passing down a green bag that contains the basics. "And don't get your hopes too high, but I have an idea for the stretcher."

I dress the head wound. I can't see any spinal injury, but that doesn't mean there isn't one. I *do* know that if he stays here, he'll die.

"How about this?" Siya stands over us, holding up a large oblong piece of plastic. "It's the shelf from the back of the truck. The Boss will kill both of us if we get blood on it, but I think it's worth a try."

Screw the consequences. The casualty needs me and I know exactly what I must do to fix this.

———

The boy survives, but halfway through the verbal lashing Siya and I get from Dr. Murty, I wonder if we will.

"Siya! How could you put at risk all the trust we have built? This stranger could have destroyed it all with one ignorant word or deed."

"I didn't think it through, Boss. Ma'am."

The office is spartan but for a teak grandfather-style clock. The pendulum swings back and forth, and I can hear the strong, regular beat.

"That is obvious, Siya. Imagine if she'd been hurt in a vehicle or even ambushed, the damage it could have done to our reputation."

"You're right. I am so sorry."

"Enough. I will decide your fate tomorrow. And as for you, Miss . . ."—she checks her papers—"Miss *Smith,* I am shocked to see that you work in your own country's health service. How about we send a few *curious* tourists into your hospitals? Shall we let them operate instead of your surgeons?"

"I . . . it was an emergency, he needed treatment."

"And you—a girl with zero medical training—were the right person to provide it?"

"I was the person on scene. I know I shouldn't have been there but the thing is . . . honestly, I would do the same again."

And not for purely selfless motives either. The buzz was incredible. Better than jumping out of a plane.

The Boss scoffs. She has gray hair and a soft face, but now it's terrifying. "Untrained, you are useless to me. You will make arrangements to leave as soon as possible."

"But my boyfriend—"

"He will stay," she says, as though it's her decision and not his. But as I leave the office, my own heartbeat outpacing the clock's, I realize I *have* to let Tim stay, because this place could be the making of him.

I've almost packed by the time he learns what the Boss has decided.

"But it's not fair, Kerry, you did the right thing!"

I shrug. "The only reason I was there in the first place was because I broke the rules. And it's true, I *could* have put the project, myself, the villagers in danger."

He reaches for my hand. "You can't help helping. It's one of the things that makes you *you*. And you saved the kid. I'm proud of you."

I return the grip. "I'm cross with myself for jumping in, but I'm a bit proud of myself too. And Siya. She made a great partner."

"Well, no way am I staying behind while you go home."

I laugh and let go of his hand. "I'm not going home, yet, Tim. I'll head back to Kerala, cruise the rivers, even learn to meditate so I stop rushing into situations like a bull in a china shop."

"Without me?" He looks freaked out.

"I'm a big girl now."

"But we were meant to be here *together*. That was the whole point!"

Before I can answer, he storms off. As I finish packing, I try to work out why he's taking this so hard while I am relatively calm. The trip *has* changed things for the better. I've stopped blaming him for my own screwups. I fancy him again. The two are almost certainly connected. But will these feelings last once we're back home?

I zip up my case. The car to take me to the nearest station is due in three hours. Being alone in India is the kind of adventure I've been craving. So why don't I feel happier?

Tim walks back into the room, eyes blazing.

"You're staying," he blurts. "If you want to, that is. I talked to the Boss. Told her she was being too harsh, that if she insisted you leave, I would too. That we come as a team, or not at all."

I don't think he's ever stuck up for me before.

No. I'm wrong. I remember another night, when we were little, a cold evening back in his mum's bungalow when the two of us were dressing up in old clothes. We found two men's shirts—I suppose they must have been his father's. Maybe his mum had kept them in case he came back.

Mine was white and Tim's blue, and we put them on backward,

like surgeons, and we were looking for underpants to wear as surgical masks when his mother walked in.

We froze, expecting a telling-off. Instead, she started to laugh.

"Oh, hens, look at the pair of you. Dr. Tim and Nurse Kerry. Aren't you both adorable? Let me get my camera."

"I'm not a nurse, I'm a doctor!" I shouted.

Poor Tim looked from me to his mother and back again. I knew he was afraid of her moods and her tongue. But he folded his arms across his chest and nodded. *"That's right, Mum. Kerry and me are both doctors. We're going to make everyone better!"*

"So will you stay?" Tim asks. "I need you with me."

I have never been able to say no to someone who needs me. But what about *my* needs? I've realized I can't make someone else happy unless I am happy myself. "Of course I'll stay. But when we get home, I want things to change. I'm going to need your help."

"Anything you need. It's the least I can do."

And as we hug each other, I plan how to tell him what it's going to take for me to be happy again.

It is the last night of our stay. We eat our meal with the others—a modest feast in our honor, with my favorite dal and the mango and jaggery drink Tim likes. The Boss has already said goodbye to us in private, praising his analysis of the consequences of illegal payments demanded of women in labor. She thanked me, with a pained expression, for my strictly policed menial work in the clinic.

Siya has almost forgiven me for landing her in it, and she's the one doling out handmade cardboard medals.

"This is for you, Timothy, for being a very cute nerd!" She blushes as she pins the square "medal" to his shirt. It reads EXCELS AT EXCEL.

Mine is circular and made from tinfoil, with letters scored through to reveal the white card behind it: CLEAN GENIE.

I smile as I pin it on myself. "Surely, SHIT SHOVELER would have been a more accurate description. Along with vomit, blood, wee, and the rest." This place has taught me much more than how many colors and consistencies of bodily fluids there are.

The Kerry who arrived here was so stuck in a rut she couldn't work out why. Siya saw it straightaway: I've had enough of being hands-off. I want a second chance to become a doctor.

When I told Tim on the night I decided to stay, I worried he'd laugh. But instead he kissed me and immediately promised to do everything he can. *Payback time,* he said.

There are no guarantees. I'll have to retake chemistry and physics, get more volunteering experience, build up my application. I can't wait to get home and begin.

Now Tim and I stand alone on the veranda, sheltered from the rain.

"I want to go for one last walk," he says. It has become a nightly ritual for us over the past few weeks.

"Sure."

We take our usual route around the edge of the campus, listening to the kids in their dance class, and the singing coming from the mess kitchen. Tim slips his hand into mine. It fits perfectly. I never noticed that before.

"I'll miss this place," he says.

"The work?"

"Partly. But also, I'm not looking forward to being a clueless medical student again."

The sounds of the forest get louder the farther we get from the buildings. I won't tell him how much I envy him, that I'd swap in an instant, even though his next two years will be the toughest yet.

"You won't always feel clueless, Tim. In a way it's better to be unsure of yourself; you're less likely to make mistakes."

He stops, next to our favorite tendu tree, with foliage so dense you can stand underneath it in the heaviest monsoon rain and barely get wet. "The other thing I'm going to miss is being here, with you—"

I laugh. "We're going to be together back home."

"Hear me out, Kerry."

I nod.

"This is the wildest thing I've ever done, coming here. And it worked, didn't it? Not only for me but for . . . well, us." He turns to face me and takes my other hand. "I couldn't be the person I am without you, and I don't want to be without you . . . Perhaps it's the wrong thing to do. Probably is . . ."

"What is?"

"I know I'm shit at this stuff but . . . Kerry Smith, would you . . . not now but soon, maybe, if you could bear it. Would you consider marrying me?"

26

Joel

Tim summons me to our bench as soon as he gets back from India. His face is tanned and he pulses with self-satisfaction.

I can barely look at him. I wonder what pills he needs from me this time.

"Kerry and I are getting married," he announces, studying my reaction.

"Wow," I manage. After a few seconds, I add, "Congratulations, I guess."

"We're waiting till after my finals. July 2005. Save the date." He laughs. "Actually, *don't* save the date. I don't think you'll be invited. Though the final guest list will be Kerry's department. She's already planning it all."

I can't imagine *my* Kerry getting excited about bouquets or dresses. But I can't imagine her saying yes to marrying Tim either.

"Anyway, Joel, that's not why I came. I did without . . . help while I was in India, despite being in the middle of a conflict zone. So I've realized I don't need pills anymore."

"Seriously? It's not easy to come off some of the stuff you've been taking." *And if he quits so easily, what does it say about me?*

"It was tough at first. But my body is now a temple."

He could have told me that by text. The *only* reason he wants to meet is to see my face when I find out he's won and I've lost.

I try to smile, but my heart—my bloody heart—isn't in it. He slaps me on the arm, a victor's gesture wrapped up as friendliness—and walks away.

The tide is all the way out and a heat haze rises under the remorse-less sun. I ache from loss and missed chances. I want to stop feeling this way.

I go down to the narrow sandy strip and I run and run and run. This heat wave is killing people and they're telling the elderly and infirm to stay indoors. To me, it sounds like a challenge. How much farther before I set the ICD off? I crave a flash of pain, or oblivion.

I collapse from exhaustion, but somehow my heart keeps on beating.

When I get home, I throw my fucking heart pills down the toilet. Let's see how my traitor body likes *that*.

Two weeks after meeting Tim at the bench, and eight days after my twenty-first birthday, I die for the second time in my life.

I've just bought cider for Spike and Zoë. We're coming down from coke and I need booze the way other people need ibuprofen, to dull the pain of normal. The heat and the bright blue sky make my head throb.

Two bull terriers are tearing around the Level in front of our bench. I light a fag.

The world darkens and the scorched grass horizon is now diagonal.

I take a breath, but there's no oxygen in the air. My chest is tight. A memory: this is how it felt in training, after sprints.

Again, I try to suck in breath. Nothing. Not like training, then.

As I topple onto the grass, I picture a goldfish, plucked out of its bowl by a cat, lying on the carpet, gasping. Will the cat slice it open with a claw, or will the end come more slowly, from suffocation . . . ?

Flash.

Kick.

Which comes first? They're both ferocious.

Current stops my useless heart. Electricity ricochets through every cell, followed by oxygen. Sweet, sweet oxygen.

I'm back.

I understand, suddenly, what happened. The doctors told me the ICD firing would feel like a kick from a donkey. *That* was a juggernaut.

"Greenie, what's up?" Zoë's shrill voice, from a long way away. I try to answer her, but nothing comes out. "Greenie . . ."

Another shock. Just as painful. My eyes spring open but all I can see is the striped plastic bag from the off-license, right next to my face, rustling in the breeze.

Is this going to be the last thing I see?

Darkness falls again and there is a big terrier drooling onto my face and I don't know if it's trying to revive me or savage me and I close my eyes and picture Kerry. In my head, I apologize to her for wasting the chance she gave me.

Sorry for messing everything up. . . .

I am not bloody dead.

I spend two days back in the cardiology ward on the seventh floor. My dad comes, eyes red, asks me why I stopped taking my pills. I can't talk to him, or to the good-cop/bad-cop cardiologist, pacing team, and physio. They even bring in a shrink, who tries to talk me into trying antidepressants, but is too uptight to prescribe me the Valium I'd really like.

The minute I get out, I look for Ham and Spike and Zoë again. I find them in the puddles under the Palace Pier, smoking crack.

Until now, I've been playing at being a junkie. But I'm sick of games. For the first time, I join in.

Oh, it's perfect. Better than I could have imagined . . . before it's even worn off, I know I will want to do it again and again.

Weeks pass in a blur even though every single day lasts a lifetime. A few days stand out, like the night that Wayne Rooney becomes the youngest football player ever to score for England during their match in Macedonia. I celebrate with heroin. My parents threaten to stop paying my allowance but don't have the guts to cut me off completely.

When autumn comes, Tim slopes back, saying he needs a *little pick-me-up* to help him cope, and I don't feel smug because what's the odd Ritalin compared to what I'm using?

On an icy November morning, Ham dies.

I'm not there—it's one of the few nights I've bothered to go home, for warmth and for another handout. Spike finds him and I get nightmares imagining what Ham's face looked like, that red beard surrounding bloodless blue lips. We hold our own funeral service, decorating a bench on the prom with flowers we nick from Tesco. Then we get high to take away the pain and by the end of the night I can't picture him anymore. Death isn't that unusual on the streets but it's enough to freak Zoë out and she disappears from Brighton to get clean.

So now it's only Spike and me. We can't bear to go to the prom because it reminds us of Ham, so we mostly hang out on our favorite tomb behind St. Nick's church, chasing oblivion.

Today is no different. Till I realize I'm dying, for the third time.

Except this time it's not on purpose.

"Spike . . . I'm crashing . . ."

He's out of it. Snoring.

Christmas shoppers are walking past, scowling and tutting, like we've walked into a church in the middle of a funeral and started swearing.

My funeral?

They are my only hope, the tutting people. I know my ICD
should protect me again. But the wave of fear that's traveling through
me convinces me I can't survive this. That whatever shocks my black
box might generate, they won't be enough.

That without help, I will die.

Unexpectedly, I don't want to.

My limbs won't coordinate and my mouth is spouting gibberish.
Come on, come on. Shout, scream, *anything.*

"Help me! I'm fucking dying here!"

I come around in the ambulance, more sober than I've been in months.

"Back with us, then, lovey?" A paramedic older than my mother
pats my hand. "Don't worry. You're going to be fine, now. Till the
next time, at least."

Narcan. It has to be. Other junkies talk in awed tones about the
miracles it creates: about dead men walking again, blue-faced corpses
pinking up within seconds of receiving the Lazarus drug.

"Can you tell me who you are?"

"Joel. My name's Joel."

"Good lad, Joel. And can you tell me the date?"

"December. 2003. Is it the twelfth? Fourteenth?"

"The twenty-first but you're near enough. How do you feel?"

"I feel . . ." Relieved. And very nauseous. "I want to be . . ."

"All right, lovey," she says, managing to get a cardboard dish
under my mouth in time to stop any vomit hitting the floor of the
ambulance, though some runs down my chest.

I claw at my stinking T-shirt, trying to pull it off. The paramedic
does it for me, raising my arms and rolling the fabric up. She has tinsel wrapped around her neck. I hadn't even realized it was so close to
Christmas.

When she sees the raised bump on my body, her eyes widen.

"What's that?"

"ICD."

"You get arrhythmias?"

Before I can answer, she's shouting through the hatch, telling her colleague that we need to get to casualty on blues and twos, swearing under her breath.

"I'm fine," I say, though really I'm desperate for another fix: that's the downside of Narcan. "Seriously, I'm good to go."

"You're not. The medication we gave you can cause . . ." Her voice is reassuring but the calmness doesn't extend to her eyes. "Problems."

The vehicle speeds up. The siren sounds. I sense death in here, circling.

I am seeing my funeral again: a room full of people I know. My parents, Ant. *Kerry.* Though I have used up all the sympathy I deserve.

My hand grips the paramedic's until we reach the hospital. The doctors stabilize me, and for the first time, when I see the impatience in their eyes, I feel shame.

Someone finds a hoodie from lost property to replace my vomit-stained T-shirt. I am about to start the walk back to St. Nick's to score again, but something stops me.

Another first: *I don't want to die.* Or at least, not like this.

I'd like to go and see Ant, but his dad has had the kind of stroke that's made his mum stop believing in God, and Ant is trying to run the café single-handed. The last thing he needs is me and my self-pity.

So I go home.

Dad is in the kitchen when I let myself in. He takes in the state of me but says nothing and the weariness in his expression looks like defeat.

"I'm going to try harder this time," I say.

He smiles sadly but he doesn't believe me.

I go back to the guesthouse and I drink a pint of water instead of helping myself to beer. I turn on the heating and within seconds, my shivering stops. I climb under the thick throw on my sofa.

For years, I've had the same words looping around my head: *I didn't deserve what happened to me.*

But the same is true of the good stuff. I don't deserve my parents or the wealth that cushions me. I did nothing to deserve the talent I was born with or the cute face that the drugs have destroyed.

I *did* deserve to lose Kerry. It's time to accept that and move on.

I make no promises out loud. But I start to eat regularly, and I stop drinking, go to bed early on December 31, wake up ready for 2004 to be the year I finally sort my shit out and stop hurting everyone.

One day, when I look in the mirror, I see myself instead of a cadaverous junkie, and that's the morning I call Ant and ask if I can work a few shifts for him again. He takes some convincing, but when someone lets him down for a Burns Night ceilidh at the end of January, I fill in and work harder than I have in years. Gradually the shifts get more regular. Busy, busy, busy. The less time I have to think, the more likely I am to stay clean.

I'm walking home from a St. Patrick's Day party shift, my hair sprayed shamrock green, when I get a text.

GREENIE! Am back in Hove. Call me. Luv Zoë.

I haven't heard from her since Ham died and she took off, saying she was going to get clean. Should I ignore her? Probably. But the fact she has a phone—and credit to text me—is positive. Life has been tough for Zoë but maybe she's going to be OK.

I call because I want to know how she's doing. "Hey, Zee, I thought you'd disappeared for good."

"Could say the same about you, Greenie. You well?"

"Yeah. I'm . . . not using anymore."

She laughs. "Snap. Boring, innit? Fancy meeting up for some herbal tea?"

I know ex-users are the worst people to help each other, but even so, I'm desperate to talk to someone who understands how hard this is.

When she arrives at our house, her eyes are clear and bright as they widen in amazement. "I knew you had money, but this is fucking incredible."

"Yeah, I was born with a silver spoon . . ."

"Nothing better for someone who likes heroin as much as you did." She laughs and the lines at the corners of her eyes crease with wickedness. "Kidding. Ha, look, you've got green hair!" Her laugh sounds different from when she's high: more childlike.

When we get to my guesthouse, I make coffee. As I hand it over, I can smell alcohol on her breath. Not completely *clean* then, but booze is an improvement on what she was doing before.

"So where did you go?" I ask her, after she's stopped stroking the furniture and cooing over the window boxes. The daffodils Mum plants every year are starting to come through.

"Back to my home town, it wasn't all that," she says, grimly. I wait for her to say more, but instead, she points to the flowers. "That's a Martinette. They bloom earlier down here."

I try to imagine where Zoë learned the names of daffodils. But before I can come up with a reply, she's reaching for me, touching my neck.

"Hold on, Zoë."

"Shhh. You like me, don't you? And I've always fancied you. Let's have fun. Where's the harm?"

Where *is* the harm?

She's not Kerry.

But I can't have Kerry, because she's chosen Tim.

Zoë's lips touch mine.

Afterward, we lie sweating on the floor. She's naked but I'm not: I stopped her taking off my T-shirt because I didn't want her to see my ICD. None of them know about my heart. After the big drama when I was arrested on the Level last year, I told them I'd had a fit after overdoing the pills.

Zoë's body is as slight and pale as I expected. But now I see her skin is covered in scars: faded track marks, crisscrossed self-harm lines, and a nasty pink slash across her stomach. Surgery, or self-inflicted? Clearly, we both have secrets.

I pull the throw off the sofa to cover her up, as much to stop me having to see her pain as to keep her warm. But she beams at me for the trivial kindness, as though I've presented her with a giant bunch of flowers.

"Why fank you, you are a gent and no mistake."

It's a perfect music hall Cockney accent. "Where did you learn to do all your voices?"

"We moved a lot when I was a kid, so I adapted my accent to fit in. Then when I went into care, it was handy to be able to make people laugh by doing impressions."

I want to look after her, show her she's worth more than she's been given. I want to help her.

Maybe this is *my* turn to save a life.

27

Tim

"So what's the goriest thing you've seen so far?" Marilyn asks, her knife slicing through lamb so pink that blood is pooling on her plate. Easter Sunday lunch with the in-laws-to-be, and already the interrogation is in full swing.

"Depends a bit how you define gory? I could offer cysts, tumors, hemorrhages . . ."

I could tell her about how blood clots after it's left the body, darker than the red currant jelly on her plate. Or describe the dermoid cyst we all pored over in the lab, with its own teeth and nails and impossibly long strands of blond hair that reminded me a lot of hers.

"Yeah, but have you treated any actual patients?" Marilyn's voice is mildly contemptuous. "I mean, it's been, what, four years since you started? I was dealing with clients from day one."

"It's not quite four years yet. And I have helped to diagnose people, done tests. But because it's slightly higher risk than filing people's nails, they want to make sure we know what we're doing."

Marilyn doesn't laugh, but everyone else does, even her husband, Neil, who usually falls into line, however outrageous her pronouncements.

She pouts. "Well, we do *medical* enhancements too and my Botox training only took a weekend, and it's a well-known fact beauty therapists do injectables *way* better than doctors."

One reversible, trivial procedure compared to the entire canvas of the human body and all its frightening possibilities: a bucket of chardonnay has made Marilyn even more full of herself than usual.

But she's closer to the truth than she knows. Because right now, anything seems preferable to a lifetime of doctoring. If that's even an option for me anymore, after the nightmare of last week's exams.

"With respect, Marilyn," my mother says, in the sarcastic tone she usually reserves for me, "I wouldn't trust you with anything sharper than a pair of tweezers, hen. Whereas my son is going to change the world."

Oh, *Mum,* if only you knew.

Every year, I tell myself it'll get better. My first two years were bearable. The third was tough, but after India, I thought I could stop taking the pills, be the doctor my mum wants me to be, the fiancé Kerry deserves.

I was wrong. It's like running on a treadmill operated by a sadist. I'm keeping up with the academic side, but now working with patients . . . Venipuncture is the ultimate humiliation, reducing my poor victims to tears in my doomed missions to find a decent vein.

My contemporaries laugh about their own incompetence, but they are all more capable than I am. Laura has a mosquito's ability to find blood, while Wilcox charms everyone, even the matrons, into doing his dirty work. Plus he always seems to find *the* question that unravels a patient's condition, however mysterious or obscure.

But I can't be too hard on Wilcox, because if he'd never introduced me to the uppers and the sleeping pills, I would have crashed out in year one.

". . . but I'd love him to be a cardiac surgeon. Or a wonderful, warm GP, the kind of man who takes care of generations of families, and always has time for someone in need." My mother is talking, and even though I zoned out of the beginning, I see pride in her eyes as she shares her ambitions for me.

My only ambition is not to kill anyone.

Mum is tipsy as we support her crossing the road back to the bungalow, her soft Scottish accent suddenly more muscular. She goes straight to bed.

Kerry pours us both a glass of white wine and we sit next to each other on the sofa. My hand hovers over the remote control and I am so close to turning on the telly, to emulate the loud chatter and disagreement that filled the Smith family dining room.

No. Stop being a coward. She deserves advance warning of what is coming.

"Kerry. I don't know if I can do this."

"Hmm? Do what?" She's picked up the *Radio Times,* scanning the columns for something to watch. Her brow furrows, trying to focus despite being a bit drunk. She looks adorable, and I want to kiss her, not hurt her.

But I must, for both our sakes.

"I don't know if I'll ever be a good enough doctor." My deepest fear, expressed in one sentence. Other people might have forgotten what really happened on Millennium Night, but I haven't. I don't think Kerry has either.

My words hang in the room like the stench of blood-darkened melena stools, and I wait to see if she'll choose to ignore them. The Easter bunny in Mum's homemade nest decoration stares at me with its crossed button eyes. *Strabismus: caused by vision problems or, occasionally, retinoblastoma. Always investigate. Rarely gets better on its own . . .*

She doesn't move for a very long time. Her answer could change everything or nothing, and I am sure she senses that.

"Don't be daft, Tim. You'll be great."

Denial.

"But what if I'm not?"

"We all get low moments. You're tired, after your exams."

I *am* tired, though I can't sleep without the fuzzy embrace of Wilcox's benzos. I had to go back to him for supplies in January, partly because Joel got a lot less reliable, but also because I couldn't bear to see how far he'd fallen. A proper junkie now.

Compared to him, I am functioning. At least now I only use *medicines,* the kind that come in boxes and blister packs.

Maybe the Adderall has worked and I have passed. I've got it wrong before. I was sure I'd failed my A levels but got three As. Though in retrospect, was predicting my failure a case of wishful thinking? If I'd got lower grades, I wouldn't be in this mess now.

Kerry is still smiling at me. An evening like this, where she's not working, and I'm not studying, and we're both a bit merry, is so rare. If I let this go, we might even end up in bed for the first time in months. (My problem, not hers. The only reason I haven't asked Wilcox for Viagra is because he would *never* let me forget it.)

"You're right, Kerry."

She takes a sip of her wine. "Look, you'll be OK. We've always been there for each other. Right from the first day we met."

I close my eyes and see it so clearly: my mother dragging me into the Smiths' garden, Kerry smiling, leading me toward the table, where a pile of chocolate biscuits was melting in the sun.

Within seconds, her sister had turned a hose on us both, soaking us from head to toe. "Bloody Marilyn."

Kerry smiles. "But we dried each other off *and* we got extra Wagon Wheels. We always work things out. Nothing's changed."

She's wrong. Everything's changed. She just doesn't know it yet.

I lean across to kiss her, wishing I could relive the last four years, do all of it differently. All of it, except for this bit.

28

Joel

I feed Zoë up, like the baby bird she reminds me of. I tell her she's cute, which she is. Even though she's three years older than me, she makes me feel like the grown-up.

After almost seven weeks of TLC, she's a different person. Her skin has cleared up and she's stopped drinking and, with the money I've loaned her, she's moved into a nicer hostel.

I won't lie. Seeing her blossom makes me feel good too. I needed a project to keep me on the straight and narrow. We have sex sometimes, but only because it's easy. We're not in a relationship.

What she needs now is work, so I take her to the Girasol before the bank holiday, to see if Ant might give her a trial shift. If she worked alongside me, I could keep an eye on her. She chats to him for a while, then gobbles up his Full Spanish Breakfast, followed by a Creme Egg brownie, and I feel proud. When she goes to the loo, Ant comes over.

"You know she's in love with you, don't you?"

"Don't be stupid, we're friends."

But when she comes back, I see her through his eyes. My mouth goes dry. Her glow isn't only about better nutrition and laying off the hard stuff. She's reapplied her lipstick in the toilets and if Ant is right, that's for my benefit. The sounds of the café—Britney singing "Toxic" on the radio, kids squealing, the hiss of sausages in the pan—grow louder and more menacing.

How do I pull back from this without destroying her?

"You OK, Greenie?" she says, her head cocked to one side.

"Let's go back to my house."

She winks, as though she knows exactly what I'm after. She couldn't be more wrong. The moment we're in the guesthouse and I've closed the door, she's pawing at me and trying to kiss me and I feel revolted, not with her but with myself.

"Zoë, stop, please. Sit down. I need to say something."

"Am I in trouble?"

I stand in front of her. "Look. I really care about you. But I think we should cool it a bit."

Zoë looks puzzled. "But . . . you love me, don't you?"

"I do love you. As a friend."

"No. No. It's more than that."

"I meant it when I said you were beautiful, Zoë. And the sex was amazing, but we're both too fragile to commit, right?"

She says nothing.

I plow on. "We can still support each other but I don't think we should be in each other's pockets. We need to work out what we want to do with our lives and—"

"I'm pregnant."

My sympathy wanes: it's a low blow to lie about that. "No you're not. We always use something."

"If you don't believe me, go buy a test. I'll pee on a stick in front of you."

There's a note of triumph in her tone that makes my stomach turn over. "You've done a test already?"

Zoë nods. "Yesterday. My period hasn't come and my boobs hurt so I went to the family planning. I was going to tell you tonight. Look, I bought this." She reaches into the new bag I got for her and pulls out a cheap teddy, smaller than her hand. "Only from Woolworth's and I got it in yellow because that way it won't matter if it's a girl or a boy—"

I snatch it out of her hand. "You can't have a baby, Zoë. You can't even look after yourself."

"We look after each other, don't we? And it's not like we're going to struggle for money. It's a bit soon, but accidents happen." She grins cheekily but her eyes won't meet mine.

"You *wanted* this."

"No. The condom must have split or something . . ." Her hands reach toward me and it makes me think of waking in ICU, the panic and fear as those figures moved toward me, taking my blood, inflicting pain . . .

Then, there was no escape. But this is worse. "Fucking hell, Zoë. You have no idea what a disaster this is."

"It's not a disaster. It's a shock, yeah, but you'll get used to it—"

"No! I won't. I've *never* wanted children." The day the doctors told me my heart problem was probably inherited, I knew I couldn't inflict this on a kid.

She smiles indulgently. "All men feel like that to start with. But you'll make a great dad. You're kind and you're patient and —"

"You have no idea what I'm really like. Not a bloody clue. I'm damaged, all right?"

"I've seen damaged, Joel Greenaway, and you ain't it. I've seen things that would fry your rich boy brain, but this is a new life. Between us, we can give a kid the best childhood."

It's as though she's reading the script from her favorite soap. The hot anger inside me fights against the urgency of making her understand. "Zoë, stop! This is a daydream. We have to put a stop to it, OK? I'll come with you. I'll pay. Whatever you need. It doesn't mean you'll never be a mother, but you can't have *my* kid."

For the first time, she hears me. "You bastard. I thought you were different."

"I am. I wanted to help you, but this isn't the way."

Her expression turns defiant. "Fine. I'll do it alone. But don't think I won't get money, the Child Support Agency will take one look at your house and you won't get a choice."

I'm dizzy, disorientated. I need to end this farce. "They won't let you keep a baby, you realize that. With our history?"

"I've been clean for ages, even before we got together."

"Fuck's sake, Zoë. It's not all about you." I pull up my shirt. "See this?" I point at the bump of my ICD, still foreign and grotesque even though it's been a part of me for four years. "I've got a heart condition. Remember that night on the Level, when I first knew you? I died and this was all that brought me back."

Doubt crosses Zoë's face. "You had a fit."

"It wasn't a fit. My heart is fucked, OK? I could pass it on. *That's* why I don't ever want to be a dad."

Her hand touches her flat stomach. She's not acting now. "The baby could be sick?"

I nod. "There's a high chance I was born with whatever it is so a baby could be too."

"No! I bought a pregnancy magazine. Its heart is already beating. I'm taking vitamins, I know it'll be OK."

For a few moments, I try to imagine becoming a parent. I don't want to be "with" Zoë, but could we raise a kid together?

A kid with a heart that could fail at any time . . .

"I didn't get sick till I was seventeen years old, Zoë. But then I got *really* sick and now I don't *live,* I exist. It's why I'm still at home with my parents, why I've done drugs. Please, I'm begging you, don't inflict this curse on a child."

Her face crumples and she runs out of the guesthouse. I won't follow her because she needs time to accept this but I know I'm right, for her sake and my own.

Yet even as I neck beer after beer, I can't forget her expression as she finally understood that her dream of a happy family with me could never come true. I don't think I've ever hated myself as much as I do right now.

And there's only one thing I can think of that'll wipe away the memory.

29

Kerry

May 14, 2004

"This time next year, we'll be on your hen do," Mum says, as we walk back from town.

Marilyn slaps me on the back. "You've got stamina, Kerry, I'll give you that. Never thought it'd last."

We've been out for Mum's birthday, to a seafront club packed with wild people. We danced till they threw us out and now the Smith girls are tottering back, fueled by chips smothered in ketchup.

"It's lasted because Tim's a decent person."

Marilyn does an exaggerated yawn. "He fell on his feet with you. Money, sex, and a caregiver for his mother. She's getting sicker, isn't she?"

"No! She's fine," I lie. If even Marilyn has noticed, it must be bad.

It's past midnight but Brighton is buzzing: the Fringe is in full swing and I'm making the most of being out tonight, before I go back to studying for my A levels. A man whistles in our direction.

"Reckon he's after you, Kerry, unless he's got a fetish for pregnant women," Marilyn says. My first niece or nephew is due in

November. Not that it's stopped Marilyn dressing on trend: her Sienna Miller–style boho dress floats over the small bump and shows off her immaculately St. Tropezed legs.

"The joke's wearing very thin now."

"OK. But this just isn't what I imagined for my kid sister."

"Leave her alone, Marilyn." Mum links arms with me. "Nothing wrong with being the sensible one, Kerry!"

Marilyn pouts: she's not used to Mum taking my side. "This is love we're talking about. You should let your heart rule, not your head."

Mum reaches out to grab my sister and links arms with her too, to create an ungainly chain as we walk down the street. "What matters is that Tim loves Kerry and Kerry loves Tim. Right, sweetheart?"

"Right, Mum."

Except Tim seems distant lately, compared to how we were in India last summer. Obviously, the honeymoon period couldn't last forever, but we haven't even had the real honeymoon yet. I hope it'll be better after he gets his exam results, but what if it's not?

What would happen if I share what are probably normal doubts for a bride-to-be? Marilyn would try to persuade me to call off the engagement *right now,* and even if I refused, I bet she'd be straight in there at the wedding when the priest asks if there's any reason Tim and I shouldn't marry . . .

The thought makes me dizzy. Everything is mapped out: he'll qualify, I'll go to medical school, we will be the perfect doctor couple, and in five years' time, I'll be laughing about my silly last-minute nerves.

I work Saturday night and when I get home first thing Sunday, I climb straight into bed: I've been looking forward to this, to having the double bed to myself, starfishing and flinging off the covers without worrying about waking Tim, whose sleep is an elusive and delicate thing.

Tim's away at a public health conference in Leeds, giving a talk about our Indian experiences. Speaking at events will give him more kudos when he's applying for foundation training. I think when *I'm* a medical student, I'll aim to wow them with my clinical skills, but as Tim never stops telling me, it's different when you have to do it for real . . .

It's only once I'm lying there that I notice the envelope on the bedside table, my name on the front in his neat handwriting. (He jokes that he loses points in exams for never "mastering" the spidery scrawl of a true doctor.)

Has he suddenly developed a romantic streak, leaving me a note to make up for going away? I open the envelope.

There's no flowery card: just a folded sheet from the lined fools-cap pages he used for study notes. I unfold it. Half a page of dense writing:

Dear Kerry,

I know I'm a coward for doing it this way. More proof of why I don't deserve you. But I thought it would give you time to get used to what I'm about to say, so when I get back from Leeds you have any questions ready for me.

I close my eyes. The marriage is off. He can't do it. I file away the flutter of relief in my chest, even as my brain begins to list all the prebooked arrangements I'll have to cancel. But at least he's told me now: we should get most of the money back.

There's no easy way to say this. I've failed my exams. This isn't the fake panic everyone used to indulge in after we came out of an A level exam. It's stone-cold certainty. I messed up my last paper totally, and the other was—at best—borderline.

I should have told you last week, but like I say, I'm a coward. Which means every day we get closer to the result, I loathe my-self even more for being a liar as well as a failure. You've given up

so much to help me through medical school. The problem is me.
I wasn't as smart as I thought I was. I've screwed everything up.
You've every right to hate me.

I'll be home midmorning on Sunday. I'll try to answer any
questions you've got. As for what happens next, it's 100% up to
you.

With all my love, and all my apologies, but knowing none of it
will be enough.

Tim

It's as though someone's plunged me into an ice-cold bath.

I reread it three times. Each time I believe it less.

Tim *can't* have failed. There've been moments over the last four
years when I've wondered if he can really handle the *human* side of
medicine. But I've never doubted his academic ability, not since he
got straight As in his A levels.

There has to be more to this.

I get up, pull on my dressing gown, and begin to look for secrets,
starting with "his" drawers in the IKEA tallboy in the corner. The
loose bolts wobble as I open each drawer in turn, wincing at the
noise because the last thing I want to do is wake up Elaine.

I rifle through his underwear, his T-shirts, all neatly folded and
arranged in color order. I don't even know what I'm searching for.

Love letters, perhaps. What if he's still shagging Laura? But she's
engaged herself, now, to a handsome vascular surgeon.

Money, then?

He's had the same work desk since sixth form, a fifties rolltop,
ugly but solid, designed to withstand nuclear Armageddon. As I push
up the tambour lid, I know I'm crossing a line.

But I deserve answers.

Three piles of color-coded review cards sit to the right, along
with uni correspondence. I scan the letters: his exam results last year
weren't spectacular but he passed.

I roll the lid down again. What if it's all in his head? Burnout, a breakdown?

Underneath, there's a matching oak filing cabinet. As I unlock it with the key from his sock drawer, I let myself consider that he isn't lying. Resentment bubbles up, but I try to push it down. Surely he could resit in the autumn. Even if he had to repeat the year, it's not *that* much longer in the scheme of things.

Though I'm meant to be applying for medicine myself in September. It's *my* turn.

I pull out the hanging files. Medical: vaccination certificates, blood group card, a yellowed leaflet from the school nurse about exercises for flat feet. Credit cards: a couple of grand of debt I already knew about, but at my suggestion, he's been transferring the balance to lower-rate deals. I *am* surprised he's still using it to buy food and drink at the hospital, though. We take cash from our joint account each week to pay for everyday stuff. So what is he using the petty cash for?

As I put the statements back, my hand touches a pocket note-book I've never seen, hard-backed with a green cover. Inside, two columns: dates on the left, and on the right . . .

30
15
20

Pages and pages, nearly three years' worth, though with breaks, including a long gap from when we went to India in July, till late October. Is this column *money*? And if so, is it going out, or coming in?

The first date is September 28, 2002. Why is that familiar? I realize: the day of my sister's wedding. The day he came back from work and interrupted me and Joel kissing . . .

I refuse to think about Joel.

There's nowhere left to search. I put everything back where I found it, and read his letter again. *What aren't you telling me, Tim?*

I stare at my reflection in the wardrobe mirror. I look *wrecked*.

The wardrobe! I haul his big suitcase out from the densely packed clothes. He uses it to store the last clothes that haven't been eaten by moths—we had an attack last month that wiped out the hall carpet *and* our honeymoon fund by the time we'd paid the pest controller.

There's no paperwork, but his smart suit is in there, the one he wore to my sister's wedding. It says a lot about how mundane our lives are that he hasn't had to wear it since. There's a strong smell of mothballs, along with something else . . .

Weed.

Could that be it—a secret cannabis habit? No, this is the first time I've smelled it on his clothes.

As I lift out the suit, the smell gets stronger. Is there a joint in here? I rifle through the pockets of his trousers and jacket. Nothing.

I almost forget to check the inside pocket too, but when I do, my fingers touch plastic. I pull out a tiny bag, the resealable kind, only big enough for buttons and beads. And drugs.

The bag is empty. But it's enough to help me join the dots.

I sleepwalk through breakfast with Elaine as she speculates on how Tim's talk has gone and whether he and his doctor chums had a wild night out afterward.

We're in the living room when I hear the wheels of his case outside. As he walks up the path, I see the apprehension in his face, and I turn to Elaine.

"He looks pretty green," she says, sounding almost proud of him for having a hangover.

I let him say hello to her and, without meeting his eye, say, "Before we hear how you took them all by storm, I reckon you need a walk around the block."

Elaine smiles approvingly. "I hope you were celebrating a standing ovation!"

He grimaces.

We manage to get all the way to Dyke Road before I dare to look at him again. His eyes are hooded and his skin is lined from dehydration: a snapshot of the man he'll be when he grows old.

"You read it?" he asks, his voice dry as parchment.

I nod and keep walking. "How much of it is lies?"

He catches my arm. "None of it. I'm sorry. I know it must be a shock, but it's all the truth. I promise you."

I shrug him off. "Like you promised me it was going to be my turn next?"

The streets are busy with Sunday couples and their Labradors and their pushchairs. "Kerry, it will be. We'll find a way. If you even want to be with me anymore. I'd understand if you don't—"

I stop suddenly. "This is your last chance to tell me the truth, Tim. I can handle you failing, but not that you didn't tell me till now. So. Any other skeletons in the closet?" Or baggies in the jacket pocket?

Doubt flickers across his face.

I can't do it, I can't let him lie to me again.

"For fuck's sake, Tim. I found your notebook. And the little bag in your suit. You failed your exams because you're taking drugs!"

Please, please, please, let there be another reason.

What little color there was in his face drains away, like a movie special effect. He opens his mouth, but nothing comes out.

"Aren't you meant to deny it? Tell me you're all doing it, that medics pop pills like Smarties?"

He stares at me. "They do. But . . . probably not as often as I do."

The first honest answer he's given me. That's something. "What do you take?"

"Depends on what I need. I've struggled with the course, with the patient contact, with *everything*."

"*Everyone* struggles, Tim. That's medicine. If you'd talked to me, if you'd tried to get help then, none of this . . ." I stop, realizing how futile it is. "OK. You've got to tell me everything."

He turns his palms so they face me. "I'll try."

"Right. Number one, why did this kick off on my sister's wedding of all days? That's the first date in your bloody green book."

Tim sighs. "Because of Joel."

"You're blaming ancient history for ruining your career, my career, our entire *future*?"

"No." He looks up at the sky. "I'm blaming Joel because he was the first person to sell me drugs."

Joel

May 28, 2004

This time, I don't want to be saved.

Or even found.

I've been in a squat since I started using again and my parents threw me out.

"Joel! Joel, someone's here for you."

People coming to see me is always bad news, but I can't move. I don't remember what I've taken and I close my eyes, the way little kids do because they believe if they can't see anything, no one can see them.

"Joel?"

A wave of self-loathing spreads through me when I recognize her voice. "Go away." I still don't open my eyes.

"What the hell have you done?" She reaches out to grab me by the shoulder and I flinch. It's been days since anybody touched me.

I do open my eyes now. Kerry's rounded face and clean hair make her seem like an angel sent down on a mission to hell.

"Go away. I don't want your help."

And I definitely don't want her to see me like this: bloated *and* skinny, my skin permanently sore from not washing properly. My hair's been proving too much hassle, so I've shaved it off, badly.

"I didn't come to help you. I came to ask why the fuck you want to ruin *my* life as well as your own."

"What are you talking about?" But I *know* straightaway.

"I get that you're not happy with how your life turned out, but that's not our fault. So why are you so determined to drag Tim and me down with you?"

When I don't answer, she looks around her for the first time and I see the disgust on her face. This is no hippie squat, with sunflowers painted on the wall and a rota for cooking nut roast. It's a secret slum, hidden inside a sturdy red-brick house. I've got used to the smell, and to the obstacle course on the floor: sharps and bottles, takeaway trays, and coils of stained bedding, sometimes cocooning people, mostly impossible to tell.

I'm not a junkie-tourist anymore. I've gone *native*. What I did to Zoë proved what a waster I really am.

"Oh, Joel."

For the first time, she doesn't sound angry, but I prefer rage to pity. "Have a good look and then go, all right?"

"Do your parents know how you're living?"

"They've given up. How the hell did *you* find me?"

She looks shifty. "There are a few perks working for the ambulance service. Like having access to certain addresses we get called to a lot. This is the third shithole I've tried."

"I'm flattered."

"Don't be. Tim's failed his exams thanks to you."

Typical of that wanker, to blame someone else. "You believe him?"

Doubt crosses her face, then disappears. But it's enough to tell me she hasn't just come to berate me. She also doesn't know whether to trust Tim . . .

I could tell her my side of the story: that Tim started it. That if he hadn't asked for that first "favor," I'd never have met Zoë or the other junkies, would never have ended up like this.

The wound throbs where, during the worst trip of my life last week, I tried to gouge out the ICD. Two of the other squatters stopped me, but only just. I had wanted to die, but knew my defibrillator would fire over and over till the batteries ran out.

Kerry stares at me. "Of course I believe him; he's my fiancé. You've screwed us both over, by the way. It was meant to be my turn next."

"For what?"

"I always wanted to be a doctor, Joel. But you dumped me and I failed my A levels. In another universe, where we'd never met, I'd be almost qualified by now, a long way from you, from Tim, from all of this . . . mess."

She's close to tears. I can't bear it.

"If I'd known how it would turn out, I'd never have sold him drugs."

Kerry hesitates, but when she speaks, it's quiet and bitter and certain. "And if I'd known how you'd turn out, I'd have left you on the grass to die on New Year's Eve."

After she's gone, a hint of her perfume remains, a pocket of rose-scented air in the fetid stench of the squat, until that fades away too.

I suppose it's the last time I will see Kerry Smith.

Someone is grabbing my hand.

"Jesus Christ, mate, talk about in the nick of time. Come on. You're not staying here."

Ant. I want to hide under the nearest duvet because I've let him down too. After I paid for Zoë's abortion, and she slipped away from Brighton like a ghost, I stopped turning up for café shifts. Again.

"Leave me."

I've no strength, thanks to what I smoked after Kerry left. He slots his hands into my sweaty armpits to haul me up and a sudden jolt brings me upright. I think he had been expecting me to weigh so much more.

"Ugh, Bananaman, your clothes really stink."

I laugh in his face.

He recoils. "And you need some Tic Tacs. Your breath could spontaneously ignite, it's pure alcohol."

"Just mouthwash."

"Is any of this your stuff?" he asks, casting a disgusted look at the blankets and carrier bags that surround me.

I gesture at my big coat with all its pockets. "Most of what's mine is in here." There's a rucksack too but I don't plan to be alive by the time the weather turns cold enough to need the sleeping bag or army boots again.

He helps me toward the front door and out into the blinding day.

I groan.

"Are you hurt?" Ant asks.

"No, the sunshine—"

A Fiesta is parked outside the squat with its passenger door open, and it reminds me of something. *Someone.*

Kerry sits in the driver's seat of her mother's car, drumming her fingers on the steering wheel. The passenger seat has been covered in a bin bag, and the footwell too, like they're trying to get rid of a body.

It occurs to me that I'm the body.

When Kerry sees us, she gets out of the car and moves toward me. She doesn't say a word, but the two of them maneuver me into the passenger side and then pull the seatbelt across.

"Where are we going?"

"Somewhere safe," Ant says.

Somewhere safe turns out to be the second bedroom above the café. I don't know how Kerry's persuaded Ant to let me stay here, but it's this or the streets as no B and B would let me within five hundred meters without full decontamination.

This used to be Ant's bedroom before his parents went to Spain and he took over the Arsehole. The single mattress has been covered in a thick rubber fitted sheet and layers of fleece blankets, and they've covered the Smurfs roller blind with a black bin bag to cut out all the light. The other furniture's gone, though they've left his New Kids on the Block posters. There's a plastic bucket, a row of mineral water bottles, and a stack of old towels on the floor, plus a clock and a radio on the high shelf that I can't reach.

And there's a bolt on the outside of the door.

"This is an intervention, is it?" I say in a fake Californian accent, my sarcasm failing to disguise my terror.

"More like the last-chance saloon," Ant says.

"Isn't a last-chance saloon meant to have liquor?"

"Funny."

Kerry still hasn't said a word to me. But she stays in the room after Ant goes down to the café.

It begins. The beginning of the end or the end of the beginning.

Kerry sits with me during the days, and holds my hand and even embraces me when I shake. She takes away my puke, brings me cereal and toast, takes me to the toilet outside, though she lets me piss and shit alone so long as I don't lock the door. But she still doesn't speak, beyond asking me what I want.

It's Ant who talks to me in the dark. He tells stories I've forgotten from our childhood. First thing this morning, he started one and then put his hand to his mouth when he remembered that the memory was connected to football. Most of my best memories are.

"It's OK, Ant. They were the good times."

We play cards, talk about his dad's failing health, his mother's bitterness that the dreams she'd had of their retirement years have been replaced by the slow, lonely drudgery of stroke and vascular dementia.

But discussing anything else after my cardiac arrest is off-limits. *My* choice.

I'm too tired to fight. They bring in a private GP to prescribe something for my nausea, but apart from that it's the three of us, sweating together in the flat, as one hot day turns into another. I don't know what Kerry's told Tim to explain her absence, but maybe he's too scared to ask. She's still raging at both of us for screwing up her life.

"Why are you helping me, Kerry?"

It's day four—the shakes have stopped and I am waiting for the hallucinations—when I finally ask her a direct question. She seems to be weighing up whether to answer so I keep talking.

"I've ruined your life. You said so yourself. Are you trying to get made a saint?"

"Canonized," she says. "When you're made a saint, it's called *canonization*."

"Thanks. Of all the things that need fixing about me, my vocabulary has to be high up the list."

She can't stop the smile that twitches on her lips. "Well, well, a full sentence! Makes a change from the grunts and the moans. Does this mean you're feeling better?"

"For now."

"Hungry? I can ask Ant to make you whatever you like."

What I really want is for her to talk to me, but offering me a choice of food seems like a big leap forward. "I don't know what I like."

"How about scrambled eggs on toast?" she suggests. "That's what my mum always made me when I was feeling poorly."

"Sounds delicious." To my surprise, it does. I don't even like eggs, but knowing they'll be cooked for me by someone who cares, who hasn't written me off, despite all I've done, makes them sound like the most delicious meal ever.

She stands up. "Don't you dare go anywhere."

"I'm too much of a coward to risk your anger, Kerry."

She opens the door, then turns back. "To answer your question. It's because otherwise, what's been the point of any of it?"

"Huh?"

"The reason I've stuck around. It's because I am too stubborn to give up on either of you."

31

Kerry

The detox was the easy bit.

Now we've got to give him a reason to stay clean, and alive, or it was a total waste of time.

"He needs something to keep him distracted. How about ballroom dancing?" Ant says, keeping his voice down. We've sneaked downstairs after Joel has finally fallen asleep.

Weirdly, Joel has been glued to a new TV show where celebrities try ballroom dancing. "I doubt learning the fox-trot would be enough to keep him off the hard stuff."

"Some day trips, then?"

"Would riding the roller coasters at a theme park give him a greater sense of purpose?"

We're eight days past the "intervention" and beginning to make tentative plans for the rest of Joel's life.

Ant laughs. "I was thinking about something a bit more meaningful. A cemetery tour?"

"That would only work if he was afraid of dying."

Ant gets up, opens a couple of beers, and hands one to me. "You know, he went through a bad patch once before, last summer. Stopped turning up for his shifts, hung out with the wrong people."

"You've no idea why?"

Ant shakes his head. "It was like being on the shore and watching a boat get farther and farther away. I tried, but it was after Dad had another stroke, and I only had so much to give."

"I'm sorry about your father."

"Yeah. He's more stable now but not the man he was. Old age sucks. But if I lost Joel . . . He's been my best mate my whole life."

"I hope he's out of the woods."

"Thanks to you. I still don't get why you've done so much for him, Kerry. Unless you are an actual saint."

I take a swig of the beer. It's a question I keep asking myself. Why didn't I turn around and leave him in that squat? I'd gone there to shout at him, not rescue him.

The stink of the place comes back to me, so strong it turned even *my* stomach. And the moment the rags in the corner rearranged themselves into the shape of the first man I loved is one I will never forget.

"You saw that place, Ant. I don't think I'd have been able to live with myself if I'd left him there and he'd died. Even if he's no longer the Joel I knew."

Ant nods. "You two were close, once. I even thought you might end up . . . well, together."

I laugh a little too loudly. "I've never been his type."

"No. Sure."

"I ought to get back home, I'm behind on studying for my exams." I give Ant a quick hug. "But we've crossed one bridge, right? He's clean."

It's hot and busy as I walk along the seafront, still holding my beer bottle. I don't feel like rushing back to the bungalow. The atmosphere there is as oppressive as the weather: Elaine has no idea Tim has failed, but she's sensitive to the tension and keeps asking pointedly if anything's wrong.

Everything is wrong. Before, I always thought that whatever our ups and downs, at least I could *trust* Tim. Now I don't believe a word he says.

I should walk away from Tim *and* Joel. Marilyn would have told them both to piss off. So would my mother. But I don't have their confidence. While they loved the limelight, I stayed hidden—until that moment on the lawns when Joel needed me, when I suddenly felt I existed, like I was worth something.

Is that what I'm trying to get back, by being needed? The thought makes me want to escape, from them and myself.

The sun on my back reminds me of India. Could I run away right now? Sneak back into the bungalow for my passport and driving license, then get on the train to Gatwick and board the first plane south? I could be seeing the sunrise on a beach tomorrow morning. Alone.

But I won't do it. I have exams to take, my own future to plan. However mad it seems to everyone else, I have to see this through.

I have a rappel booked for the day after my last exam and, on instinct, I decide to drag Joel along with me. He puts up a token fight, but I think he's relieved to get out of the flat.

On the drive to Arundel Castle, he keeps checking his reflection in the wing mirror. "Shit, I look rough. Older than my dad."

He *is* pale, but since withdrawal, he's had a fortnight of wholesome food from the café and his body has lost the bloated look, while his face is a lot less gaunt.

"You looked way worse in the squat. Didn't you have mirrors?"

"A couple, but they were for snorting coke off." He gives me a sideways glance, as though he's still half-expecting to shock me.

"Amazed you could afford coke. Unless it was paid for from all the money you made selling drugs to Tim?"

He shakes his head. "Coke's cheaper than you think and I only ever charged Tim what I paid. It was him started me off selling stuff, did he tell you that?"

Tim has no idea I'm in touch with Joel. I don't bother to explain my long absences from home, though we've both told Elaine I'm doing a lot of overtime to pay for the wedding. The wedding I postponed last week.

I told Tim I couldn't go through with it, that I had some serious thinking to do about our future. He didn't try to change my mind, though he begged me not to tell Elaine until I've decided what I want.

Why didn't he try to persuade me I was wrong? He's ashamed of letting me down with the exams and the drugs, but it's less than a year since he told me he couldn't be the person he is without me.

Have we both given up too soon?

"So this thing today. Why the hell are you doing it again?"

"To raise money for a local hospice."

"What does shimmying down the side of a castle have to do with a hospice?"

"Nothing specifically. It's one of the things people sponsor me to do, in aid of different charities. I started doing this kind of stuff a couple of years ago, for fun. I've done a parachute jump, a bungee jump, a midwinter sea swim."

He exhales. "Whoa. You jumped out of a plane?"

For a fraction of a second, I'm back there: the noise vibrating through me, my heart rate soaring as the flimsy plane took off. Within seconds, we left the runway behind and the green fields became patchwork squares, the rivers the silver threads that stitched them together. "The jumping was fun. But the flying was better. From up there, everything is beautiful. Even the poor old pier. I mean, it looked like matchsticks, all stacked up in the turquoise sea."

"Was it hard to jump?"

"It was a tandem thing so I didn't have much choice. Though I'd do it again like a shot."

I remember clouds and cold brilliant air and my body at the mercy of gravity as we plummeted toward the beautiful curve of the earth . . . then the sudden kick as my buddy activated the parachute, and the feeling I had of wanting to be there forever.

Joel is shaking his head. "When did you turn into a full-on adrenaline junkie?"

"You're not the only one who's changed, Joel. I'm not the same nerdy girl I was at school."

Arundel Castle is ahead of us, on its own little hill, and the first butterflies flutter in my tummy. We park up and join the other rapellers in their purple tunics. As they chat nervously, I realize everyone but me has a personal connection to the hospice.

I am a fraud. Hospices do a brilliant job, but I'm here for the thrill, not the cause. It's become a standing joke at work. Hardly anyone sponsors me anymore because they've got so bored of "Krazy Kerry" and her latest stunt.

"How high is that?" Joel points upward.

"Just under two hundred feet. It doesn't compare to jumping out of a plane."

I volunteer to go up with the first group of fundraisers. We're fitted with harnesses and told what to do, though it's hard to concentrate, knowing Joel is watching. Tim never comes and I've never minded, because this is my secret vice.

With the others, I climb the stone steps up to the keep, where they've erected a scaffold structure to attach the harnesses to. I drink in the panoramic view—bright green fields, darker clusters of trees, red-brick houses grouped together to form communities, and, farthest away, the glistening blue band of the sea.

A middle-aged superhero couple push to the front—the wife is dressed as Wonder Woman, her husband as Superman. They're bickering till the moment the woman steps off. Her face is set in a grimace as she disappears over the edge.

"She had to go first to make sure I would go through with it," Superman says to me. "I'm bloody terrified of heights."

"Why are you doing it then?"

"Our daughter," he says, and I immediately regret asking because his eyes blur behind his tears. "Would have been unbearable if it hadn't been for the hospice."

"Come on, you big fat coward," Wonder Woman calls from below. "Get it over with so we can start on the brandy!"

Superman squeals in delighted panic all the way down.

My turn. I climb onto the scaffold plank, my harness connected to the rope. I hear the wind in my ears and I tune in to the thump of my heart in my chest. I love this sensation, it's the most alive I ever feel.

"Ready, sweetheart? Turn around, lean back . . . and off you go."

It lasts only seconds but oh, *what* seconds. Adrenaline and gravity and the whooshing view of Sussex over my shoulder as I accelerate, unable to take it steady.

"Kerry! Come on, Kerry!"

It's Joel: the only person who knows my name. As my feet hit solid ground, I want to run back up the stone steps and do it again. Joel appears from nowhere and he's grinning. "That took guts, mate, I'll give you that."

I blush. This still feels embarrassing, him witnessing my excitement. "You should try it."

"No one is ever going to let me do that with an ICD, are they?"

"They might." But I'm remembering the forms I had to fill in and the disclaimer I signed. They definitely wouldn't.

"Ah, fuck it, I never liked heights much anyway. But *you* do. You've got this wild look. Happy, though. No offense, but these last few weeks, I haven't seen you smile once. And now you can't stop. You do actually look like the *old* Kerry again."

"You make me sound like a right miserable bitch."

"Detox isn't a laugh a minute for anyone, is it?"

We're back to how we were back then, for a moment. All the justified anger on my part, all the self-loathing on his, is forgotten. It's not embarrassing for him to see how much I love this.

It's intimate.

The gap between us narrows—I can't tell if he's moving toward me or me him or both—and I look at his lips and remember how it felt to kiss them and oh how much do I want to feel that way again . . .

"Hooray!"

The cheers behind us snap me back.

"Right, back to Brighton before rush hour," I say, backing off and trying to remember where I parked the car. What the hell was that about? Joel broke my heart. And he's a junkie. I'd have to be a masochist to get involved again.

As I drive, he bombards me with questions about my other challenges, as though he's scared I might say something about what almost happened.

When I pull up outside the Girasol, he is still talking, fast, and it takes me a moment to tune into what he's saying.

". . . and I could do it too."

"Do what?"

"One of your mad sponsored things. I want to get fit again. I could raise something for your favorite charity."

"You really don't have to, Joel . . ."

"I'd like to. If you and Ant aren't going to let me die, I'd better find something to keep me occupied."

32

Joel

JUNE 22, 2004

"Promise me you've taken all your meds?" Kerry says.

We're alone by the beach on the first morning of triathlon training. It's too early for the rest of Brighton, the lazy sods. They're missing out on a trippy haze that makes the sea and sky blend into one.

"What are you, my mum?"

She tuts. "No. But the last thing I need is another arrhythmia on my watch."

"Sure. Sorry." I stretch out my quad, showing her what to do. My repertoire of stretches comes back to me easily, like the lyrics of an old song.

"What did they feel like?" she says, struggling to keep her balance. Clumsy *and* cute at the same time. Except I'm not allowed to think about her that way now.

"Huh?"

"The shocks?"

I've tried to block out my low points, but I can't forget how it feels to have nine hundred volts stopping my heart.

"Sickening. Like someone had detonated a bomb inside me."

Kerry looks at me closely, her blue-gray eyes as luminous as the sea in the morning light. "Yet you kept bringing them on. You must have been desperate, Joel."

I turn away from her. "Almost as desperate as you are right now. I know your game. You're asking me questions to put off the moment we start running. You're scared you'll be lapped by a junkie heart patient."

But I bet she's not as scared as I am. I've signed up to do a minitriathlon with her next month, in part as a thank-you for all she's done. But every time I've tried to run, in the cheap trainers and joggers they'd bought for me to wear as I detoxed, I've chickened out.

Part of it must be fear of another shock, I guess, even though I take my meds religiously now. But I'm scared, too, of feeling the same way I used to on the pitch, the pure joy of being fast. I've hurt everyone. I don't deserve anything good.

When I told Kerry I was struggling with training, she didn't interrogate me, she just arranged to come to the beach one morning, after a night shift.

I really don't deserve *her*.

But she's here, real, and she reaches for my hand and starts to run. I have to go with her.

She's not a natural runner—she overpronates, the right leg twisting in. I try to pick up the pace, but she's out of breath already.

Ha! Despite my crappy heart and my weak muscles, I am still Joel Greenaway. As soon as I realize that, and relax into the run, I begin to love it again.

Kerry is wrecked by the time we reach the beach huts at Hove, but if she wasn't here, I could keep going to Shoreham and back. Instead, we buy coffees from the Meeting Place and walk down to the water's edge. I take off my dodgy trainers and feel warm pebbles under my feet. It's unbelievable that a body I've tried to wreck, cell by cell, can bounce back like this.

"Not bad for a man who has died three times, eh?"

"I'm going to whup your ass at the swimming, though, Joel, don't worry about that," she says.

The trouble with recovery is it's not only stamina that's coming back.

My sex drive is back too.

I'm trying to train the desire out of myself, like a boot camp recruit. But it's *not working*. Every week that goes by, my feelings grow. Whenever I train with Kerry, we fall into a rhythm together that feels like a substitute for what I really want to do.

The only thing that stops me acting on it is knowing I couldn't live with myself if I hurt her again.

I don't think she notices. She's as focused as Coach Coley when we're working out. We talk about VO2 Max and muscle-building diets, and avoid anything about feelings or the past. She also barely mentions Tim, though she says he's hopeful he's done better in his medical resits. Which is good.

I mean, I still hate the prick, but I want her to be happy.

Though today I wonder if I'm getting the full picture. After five weeks of training, we're finally ready for the big event, a mini triathlon in Herefordshire, in the grounds of a stately home. We're staying over in a pub to save having to drive back tonight. When we check in, I offer to pay for her room at the same time as mine—my parents reinstated my allowance after I took a urine test to prove I'm clean. It makes me feel like a loser every time I take their money out of an ATM, but I will find a way to pay them back.

"You're all right," she insists. "Tim's already paid. As a treat. He . . . well, he thinks I'm here on my own."

"Oh. Right. Makes sense, I guess."

Except, does it? As I get ready to race, I wonder. Kerry lying to him isn't exactly healthy. And why hasn't he come to support her? If I were with Kerry, I'd always be waiting for her at the finishing line.

I pull on my wetsuit, glad it hides the ugly bump and scar of my ICD. What do I know about relationships?

We walk to the lake together, along with hundreds of other crazy people. We've agreed to do the race aiming for our own personal bests—so she won't hold back to humor me when she's swimming, and I won't hold back during the run.

But as I launch myself into the lake, she's there at my side.

"You . . . go . . . on . . ." I gasp, in between swallowing great gulps of cold water.

But she doesn't let me drop behind and with her next to me, I'm safe.

We clamber out on the other side. She's wearing a short wetsuit and her calves are mottled by the cold water, but she couldn't look more gorgeous. We laugh as we get on our bikes, and keep laughing as our legs burn going uphill.

When we start the final run, she tells me to go on ahead. But what kind of scumbag would do that?

We cross the finish line together. When we hug, our bodies sweaty and smelling of pondweed, the warmth of her gives me this rush of something that . . . Well, it feels like love. And lust too. I break away before she can notice.

"No offense, but you need a shower, Kerry!"

"Piss off. You stink way worse than I do."

As I shower, the water running over my body, I think of hers as she emerged from the lake. I think of her now, in the room next to mine. Imagine knocking on her door, kissing her, telling her how I feel. After the triathlon, anything seems possible.

No. I'm damaged goods.

She's waiting for me in the bar. She's never looked prettier, though I don't think she's wearing any makeup. It's just the euphoria, the happy chemicals she says exercise produces.

"What a rush!" Kerry says as she opens her quarter bottle of cava and takes a huge gulp.

"Here's to us. The mini-triathletes." I hold up my glass of Diet Coke—no booze for me and I don't need it when I'm with her—and we toast. "But we're going to ache tomorrow."

"Let's not talk about tomorrow!" Her eyes cloud suddenly.

"Did you call Tim?"

"Yeah. He was pleased for me."

"So why didn't he come up here? I'd want to support my fiancée if she was doing something so huge."

"I'm not his fiancée anymore, OK?" she snaps. "Look, there's a lot I haven't told you because it's private. But things have been difficult. I told him I needed time to myself this weekend. To think."

It takes my brain a few seconds to make sense of it, but my heart has already understood. "Do you want me to leave you alone too?"

She shakes her head. "No. You don't count."

"Charming."

The pause goes on too long.

Now we speak at the same time:

"Kerry, I need to tell you—"

"Joel, I wish—"

I smile. "You go first."

"I wish I could feel like this all the time. I'm so sick of life passing me by. At home, I feel about a hundred years old, but here, it's different." She takes another gulp of cava. "I think I might need something stronger. And steak. I need steak."

As I queue at the bar, I feel closer to her than ever. Images of us making love are running through my head. I want her so much—

STOP.

I don't want to be that man: the sleaze who takes advantage of someone who is having a tough time.

"Two steak and chips, please mate, on my tab. And a big glass of red."

"What do you want? We got merlot, shiraz, rioja —?"

I turn back to call across and ask Kerry which she prefers. She's staring out the window, frowning, and she looks exactly like that girl who once sat by my hospital bed, day after day, willing me to recover.

Now the images in my head show what our lives could have been like if I'd trusted her, instead of shutting her out, when the football club let me go.

She's not happy with Tim. What if that's because what we had—what we *could still* have—is the real thing? If what I thought was lust is something much more important?

"Give me the most expensive one." I only take my eyes off Kerry as he hands me the glass.

I stride back to the table and put the wine down.

"I love you, Kerry Smith."

She blinks. I try to read the look in her eyes. Hope soars. She's going to say it back . . .

"No you don't." She takes a huge swig of wine. "Sit down."

"I know how I feel," I say. But I sit down, understanding why she doesn't believe me.

"Joel, I care about you, a lot. You're doing your best to be kinder and braver. About time too. But you hurt me too badly for me ever to love you like I did."

"I was an idiot—"

"Yes. And what you're feeling right now? It's nostalgia, and the endorphins from finishing the race. Not love."

I want to tell her I've changed. But have I? Only a few months ago, I hurt Zoë by stringing her along, without caring how vulnerable she was. Even if she'd never got pregnant, or had an abortion, I was always going to hurt her because I always look after number one.

Maybe the part of my brain that died when my heart stopped means I will let people down over and over again.

"Plus, you're not the answer, Joel."

"The answer to what?"

"To all my cock-ups." Kerry laughs. "It's not just you that's made a mess of the last four years."

"It was my fault you went off on the rebound with Tim. He doesn't make you happy."

She raises her eyebrows. "And you did? That's not how I remember it."

"Could be that neither Tim nor me are good enough for you."

A group of people at the next table start laughing in response to a joke. Kerry sighs. "Life isn't a Disney film, Joel. There's no Prince Charming. Relationships take work."

"But they shouldn't make you miserable, should they?" My certainty that Tim is wrong for her makes me reckless. "And you don't lie to someone you really love."

She winces. "No? All I've ever wanted is to fix things. To make the people I care about happy, by doing the right thing. But I don't know what the right thing is anymore."

"Have you told him that? The truth?"

"The truth. It sounds so perfect, doesn't it? So simple. But sometimes we think the right thing is to lie. And then there's no way back." Kerry takes a swig of wine. "I've been lying to you too, Joel. For years."

"What about?"

"About what happened on Millennium Night. About who it was who saved you, or hurt you, or however you see it now. It was me who pounded up and down on your chest so hard you felt like your ribs were cracked. Me who did the CPR."

"No. It was Tim. He told me himself."

"All this time, you were blaming the wrong person. He froze for . . . well, it was less than ten minutes but it felt like years."

My brain can't process this. My imagined version of that night's events scrambles and I try to remake it but . . . "Why would you lie about something like that?"

She scoffs. "It was meant to protect Tim but it's all backfired. See? I've screwed everything up too."

I say nothing.

"I should have told you years ago and I'm sorry." When I still don't reply, she stands up. "Coming here with you, it was a mistake. It's dredged everything up again. But at least you know the truth, and now we can all move on."

When I say nothing, she mutters something about canceling the food order—like that matters—and I watch her leave.

I let my head drop onto the table. All those times I blamed Tim for my incomplete life, for losing football, for the bump in my flesh where the ICD sits . . . What would have been different if I'd known it was Kerry all along? She lied to me from the first moment I woke up. Thousands of lies, for *years*.

But I'm not angry. What must it have cost her to keep this hidden? She did what she thought was best. Can I ever say that about myself?

No. I've been self-obsessed and weak and full of hate for so long. No wonder I liked drugs so much. They stopped me remembering what a bad person I am.

And if I've ever needed something to take the edge off, it's now. Even here in the sticks, I bet I can spot the guy in this bar who'd know where to get hold of what I need. *Takes one to know one.*

Nothing too heavy. Some weed or . . .

But the sticky wood of the tabletop reminds me of the many floors I've passed out on. Compared to Zoë and Ham, I'm so bloody lucky. There has always been someone to pick me up when I fell: my parents, Ant. Kerry. The woman who saved my life.

I sit up. No. I don't want to relapse. I don't want to fill my body with shit so I can deny the damage I've done.

Move on, Kerry said. That's what she wants. If she won't love me back, I can do the next best thing. Stop feeling sorry for myself and start over.

Tim

33

JULY 25, 2004

Is it better or worse to be in genteel surroundings when you shatter the illusions of someone you love?

Taking Mum to the village of Alfriston seemed like the right idea this morning. But now I'm less sure. None of the gift shops are accessible and it's been raining, so the riverside is too boggy to navigate. As I wheel her chair into a café, the doilies and the cake stands and the teapots hem me in so much I want to smash my way out of here.

"Are you sure it's all homemade?" she demands of the poor waitress, "because this menu looks far too big for that to be probable."

I struggle to find small talk while we wait for our lunch, knowing time is running out. I'm certain Kerry will come home from her triathlon and tell me it's definitely over. I'd offered to go with her, but she insisted she needed time to *"do some serious thinking. And while I'm gone, please talk to your mum. Whatever we end up doing, the wedding is not going to happen next year. If she realizes we've been lying, she'll never forgive us."*

"But what will I tell her?"

"You can tell her as much or as little as you want."

Our jacket potatoes arrive, the size of cannonballs, and Mum stares disdainfully at her plate.

"Looks nice, doesn't it?" I say, for the waitress's sake. The first forkful burns my throat and tongue as I swallow. A laryngopharyngeal thermal injury, but not bad enough to get me out of telling her the truth.

I can't bear to do this to her, but this is one favor I can't expect Kerry to do for me. "Mum, I've got something to tell you and I'm sorry because I don't want you to be upset."

Her face doesn't change but she seems to lose another inch of height in her chair.

"It's about the wedding." I have rehearsed these words over and over in my head. Saying them out loud is different. "Kerry and me, we've decided to postpone it."

It's as if she's aging in front of me. Her sharp blue eyes fade to gray and the lines around her eyes deepen.

"Mum, did you hear me? We've postponed it. Kerry has got most of the money back, or a credit note in the case of the hotel . . ."

"Is it another woman? Have you been unfaithful?"

"Mum!"

"After everything she's done for you! You got it from your father. Bad genes. I am so ashamed of you, Tim. I can't bear it." In her rage, her accent has got stronger and her voice louder, and people are looking at us.

Down the years, I've trained myself to let her cruelties wash over me, but she's never said these things in public before. "That's not why. She's . . . we're . . . we're not sure anymore. About marriage."

"But you're *made* for each other. You always were."

"All done?" The waitress regrets her question as soon as she sees Mum's face, and snatches away our plates before scuttling back to the kitchen.

"Mum, I'm trying my hardest to make it better, but it might not be enough—"

"Trying your hardest? That's defeatist talk. You need to fight with all you've got."

"Sometimes you can fight and you can fight but it won't change someone's mind."

I never told her I heard the rows. She fought for my father. Cajoled and seduced and wept and raged and begged and it made no difference. That's how I learned that telling someone how you feel is not enough.

On the journey back, Mum's hostile silence seems bigger than the car. She maintains it all the way to Brighton. I park Kerry's mother's Fiesta in their driveway, but when I try to persuade my mother back into her wheelchair to get across the road, she shrugs me off and stumbles painfully back to the bungalow.

Kerry isn't due home till late. Mum pushes open the door to her bedroom, but I catch it before it slams behind her.

"I know you're upset but—"

"You're risking everything, Tim. What would you be without her? Nothing, that's what."

It's the kind of thing I heard her shout at my dad before he left. "Do you really mean that?"

Doubt crosses Mum's face, and shock at being challenged. "Maybe I'm too harsh, sometimes, Son. But it's always because I want you to be the best you can be. And I know you need Kerry a hell of a lot more than she needs you."

She waves me out of the way and closes the door.

In the kitchen I pour myself a shot of cooking brandy. It tastes disgusting but not as bad as knowing my own mother—who adores me more than any other person in the world—thinks I am doomed without Kerry.

I text Kerry to ask if we can meet before she comes back to the bungalow and I suggest the café at the top of Devil's Dyke. I walk there early, so I can gather my thoughts. It's close to the city but all you can see from here is dazzling green fields, countryside so lush that it makes you start humming "Jerusalem."

When she arrives, I see she's still in the hire car; a Golf GTI. Typical Kerry. I bet she put her foot down on the way to the triathlon, though I can't imagine she was in a hurry to come back. When she gets out, I'm afraid to look at her face, in case I can see her decision. The last of the daylight is fading and, with it, the warmth.

"Hey," she says. We hug, out of habit, but there's no kiss. Was that my choice or hers?

"Hey. Well done. For finishing." She texted me the time but I have no idea if it's good or bad. No wonder I'm going to lose her.

"Yeah. It was such a buzz."

"Did you get chance to think?"

She nods. Why isn't she saying what she's decided? It has to be bad.

Because I don't know what else to do, I start walking toward the trail, opening the gate. She steps through and I close it behind her, like some Victorian suitor. The shrubs and farmland give off an herbal scent as the air cools. This is what I will remember whenever I smell this again. The night I lost her.

"Tim —"

"I told Mum. And she said if I let you go, I'm finished. That I would be nothing without you."

Kerry turns. "Oh, Tim, that's not true."

"So are you ending it or not?" I brace myself.

"I just want us to be happy." She turns away again and walks slowly, pulling at the greenery along the lane. Now the air smells of wild garlic.

My head throbs and my mother's words come back to me: *you need to fight for her.*

"Please don't leave. Tell me what it'd take to make you happy."

As I wait for her to reply, a memory catches me unawares. The very first time I came to this spot was with her and her parents. I was nearly nine years old. We'd been to see the paragliders floating above the valley and all she could talk about was how she'd love to try it. I was more interested in getting home to look up thermal columns in the encyclopedia.

Afterward, her mum bought us hot chocolate and dinosaur cake with an entire spiky thagomizer made of icing, and I couldn't understand why I was getting a treat when it wasn't my birthday yet.

When I got home, Dad wasn't there. His coat and shoes by the door had gone, his briefcase, his tennis bag. That was, I realize now, the last outing where I'd feel like a kid, not a caregiver. I had become the head of the household.

Kerry has stopped at a turnstile. "I don't know. For you to feel OK?" She shakes her head. "But that's about you. I wish I knew what I wanted for me."

"Won't medicine be enough?"

"Like it's been enough for you?"

"I can't blame medicine for the mess I got myself into, but I'm doing my best to dig myself out." I help her over the turnstile. "I wasn't sure till now why I suggested coming here, but I just remembered. You and me, against the world. You probably don't remember but it was the day my dad left and—"

"I remember." She says it so tenderly that I want to cry. But I won't. It's not something I do. "It was shitty what he did. Abandoning you to look after your mum."

"No, it was fine, I wanted to look after her," I say automatically. Except, is that true? I had no choice in the matter.

"I know what your mum is like. More than anyone else, I've seen her at her worst."

"She can't help herself." My voice cracks. No. I am not going to cry. "She needs me."

Kerry hears my weakness. She reaches for my hand. "Being needed is addictive, isn't it? But what I'm realizing is that there's a time to help, and a time when you have to let people get on with it for themselves."

I want to ask her how am I meant to do that when my mother is so helpless?

But she's turning around to go back to the car. After we climb in, she waits before starting the engine.

"What I said about not leaving, Kerry. You mustn't stay because you feel sorry for me," I say, wanting her to deny it, to say we're together because she loves me. "I know it's my turn, now, to support you the way you've supported me. Let me do that. Please."

"I don't want you to be something you're not. That's not how love works."

Love. "Tell me what you do need, then."

"Right now what I need is more time."

At least she's not saying it's over.

As she reverses with a ferocious whoosh, I make a promise in my head, to her and to myself. Starting tonight, I will do everything I can to fix myself, and then fix us. Even if I fail, at least I will have tried.

34

Kerry

It's like someone flicked a switch: the secret one that turns Tim into the ideal partner.

On the hot August night after I get my A level results—the AA I needed four years ago—he takes me to the Regency on the front, buys us cava and a frightening seafood platter, and promises he won't give up till I'm a doctor.

He helps me with my med school applications, researching the best places for mature students, sending off for booklets about how to get in, adding the right buzzwords to each section of the form. Meanwhile, he's passed his resits for the exams he failed in May and is a model final-year student. He's even joined Narcotics Anonymous— his suggestion, though I can only imagine how painful he finds it sitting in a room talking to strangers about *feelings*.

He does more hands-on caring for Elaine, to give me space, yet he also refuses to do certain things when he believes she can do them herself. To my surprise—maybe his too—she cooperates more than before and becomes quite self-reliant.

Change is good.

But.

I don't know if it's enough to save our relationship.

We are trying our hardest and I don't want to rush into any decisions, at least not until after Tim's finals early next year.

Joel is out of the picture too. That night after the triathlon, I knew it was only euphoria that made him think he loved me. On the drive home, he was quiet, perhaps because he was embarrassed, or because of what I told him about me doing the CPR. Either way, he's kept his distance since then.

It makes things simpler for both of us.

Once I popped into the Girasol, which he's running while Ant tries to settle his parents back in Spain. Four months ago, Joel couldn't run a brush through his hair.

Would these things have happened to Tim or Joel without my help? I am not vain enough to take all the credit, and I am trying very hard not to be a control freak. Still, I pushed Tim *and* Joel in the right direction. Knowing that is almost as much of a buzz as jumping out of a plane.

But now it's time to put myself first.

Winter creeps up on me, but suddenly it's mid-December, season of flu and alcohol poisoning. At least being busy makes time go faster.

Tim's most of the way through his ob-gyn placement—thankfully, for both their sakes, he wasn't on duty when my sister gave birth to my gorgeous niece, Ava, a Bonfire Night baby. He's finding it tough juggling the placement and his finals review, but he's still pulling his weight. Whenever I get home from a twelve-hour shift, the house is immaculate, dinner is ready, and he's almost pathologically upbeat.

"Got plans tonight?" my colleague Mo asks as we mummify ourselves in fleece layers in the locker room, bracing ourselves for the hail we can hear ricocheting off the pavement outside.

"Seeing an old friend." The slightest charge goes through me when I say it. The same charge I felt when he called asking to meet.

Joel picks me up in Ant's van, and when I climb in, he leans over to give me a lightning-fast peck on the cheek. Yes, old friends, that's what we are.

As he drives along the front, the radio plays: Girls Aloud murdering "I'll Stand by You." Wind whips across from the sea and the string lights look as though they'll be torn free. I take surreptitious looks at him and am pleased with what I see. Joel looks even fitter than he did for the triathlon, and he sits upright in the driver's seat.

The van turns left up Old Steine and we head out of the center. "Where are you taking me?"

"Magical mystery tour, remember? Settle back and enjoy the ride."

We travel up the Lewes Road, then take a right and wind through the twisting roads of the estate. Joel parks outside a community hall that reminds me of the St. John's Ambulance Cadets HQ.

"Ready to find out what I've been up to?"

Joel pushes the wooden door open. Inside, a bearish man in a tracksuit is laying out gym mats, hoops, and skipping ropes on the worn parquet floor. When he looks up, I realize he has a ring of tinsel around his neck, like a dog collar.

"All right, Greenaway. How's your week going?"

Joel goes to the man, and they shake hands in a bloke-ish way before he calls me over. "Kerry, come and meet Steve. He's been keeping me out of trouble for a few months now."

Steve can't help crushing my fingers in his spade-size paw.

"Hi, I'm a friend of Joel's—" I start to say.

"I think you're more than that, aren't you, darling? Joel told me the whole story."

"Er, no—" What the hell has Joel been saying?

"I mean, you brought him back to life, didn't you? That makes you a lot more than a friend, in my eyes. A guardian angel, in fact."

Joel glances at me and smiles. He's forgiven me for lying to him about the CPR.

I need to change the subject. "So . . . what's happening here?"

"It's our rehab class," Steve says, laying out more pieces of equipment. "Joel's been coming for a few months now, haven't you, kid?"

Is this drugs rehab? But the people who're arriving behind us don't look like thrill seekers. Mostly they're portly men of my dad's age or older, except for one skeletal younger guy who seems barely able to take more than a few steps at a time. There's a Christmas theme: Santa hats, velour reindeer antlers, snowflake socks.

Joel is next to me. "Guessed yet?"

When I shake my head, he unzips his fleece—his T-shirt rides up, revealing his flat belly and the line of hair disappearing down past his waistline. I have to look away.

"Ta-da!" he says, pointing at the logo on the T-shirt fabric.

"Coast Along Heart Charity," I read aloud. "Oh! This is *cardiac* rehab." I smile, but it's not good news. Joel's confidence—or his health—must have taken a nosedive to be going for something this gentle after completing our triathlon: cardiac rehab is for heart patients who can barely climb the stairs.

"Starter's orders, guys and gals." Steve calls out and people take up stations in different parts of the gym. "Any hospital admissions in the last week, symptoms you need to report? Excellent job. Music, maestro, please!"

It's Joel who turns on the CD player and the urgent rhythm of "Another One Bites the Dust" blasts out of the speaker.

Joel walks over to Steve at the front, winks at me, and claps his hands in time to the music. "All right, let's warm up with a light march."

He's not participating in the class: he's *leading* it. What a relief.

He catches my eye and grins. "And that includes you, Kerry Smith! There are no shirkers here."

Joel encourages, cajoles, laughs, performs. He's good. *Very* good.

And as he demonstrates the exercises, he has his grace back. I haven't seen him move so effortlessly since 1999.

Joel and Steve take it in turns to lead different sections, making a great double act. CPR anthems keep popping up—"Stayin' Alive," "I Will Survive"—and I realize it's an in-joke, and that the gallows humor that keeps us sane in the ambulance control pit is important to these patients too.

After the class ends, Joel comes over, his face and body glowing. "Well?"

"I approve. What gave you the idea?"

"After the triathlon, I realized I'd been moping about for roughly four years too long. Decided I needed something else to do. I googled *heart* and *volunteering*."

"You're a natural." I've spent so long teasing and nagging him that paying a compliment feels awkward. "So, what now?"

"*Now* it's party time."

The Coasters, as they call themselves, are having a Christmas get-together in the Anchor nearby. Partners are invited along too, filling a big section of the snug.

"This your girlfriend, Joel?"

"You're punching above your weight, mate!"

I blush, but Joel is shaking his head. "Not my girlfriend, she's too good for me. But she was my lifesaver."

"Oh, come and sit with me, sweetheart," one of the women says, budging up and pouring me a glass of red. "We can swap war stories."

Her name is Ali, and she's married to Luke, the thin man who looks so much sicker than the others. "Most of the guys have only had *trivial* stuff like heart attacks or stents or quadruple bypasses. But Luke had a cardiac arrest, like Joel."

She tells me that her husband, fit as a fiddle and a big deal in the local tennis league, went to bed one night and she woke up to hear him gasping. She couldn't wake him and she called 999. "It felt like it was happening to someone else. They told me what to do and . . ."

Her eyes are huge and haunted as she remembers. It's the side we never see in the control room.

"He's OK, though, right?"

Ali glances up at Luke. "They say he's doing well. His memory is crap and he gets very tired. He's a teacher, and at the moment, I can't see how he'll be able to do that job again. I hope it'll get better . . ."

"And you?"

"Oh, I'm fine!" she says. "I mean, I don't sleep that well. I get nightmares about waking and finding him dead next to me in the morning—" She stops suddenly and I realize her husband is watching her closely, and she grins back, though it looks strained. "Really, we've been so lucky. And seeing how well Joel is, what, nearly five years after *his* arrest, gives us both hope. Did he recover quickly?"

The question stumps me. Physically, yes. But mentally—should I lie to reassure her?

I scan the room for Joel. He's in the center of the group standing by the bar, telling stories and laughing. When he sees me, he raises his bottle of Coke and winks. Happiness glows inside me, a football-size sensation of warmth and acceptance.

"Joel had his struggles, believe me. But hopefully he's on the right track again now."

"And what about you, Kerry? You gave him CPR too, didn't you? Are you OK?"

No one has asked me this before. I could tell her how hard it's been, that saving his life still affects mine to this day. But that doesn't have to be *her* story. It's better if she focuses on the positives.

"I'm fine. I'm just grateful I could help."

On the blustery drive home, we talk about the Coasters and Joel tells me he has plans. He's doing an online nutrition and personal training course—"Only a basic one, but I really enjoy it. And this is me, the kid who paid zero attention at school. I might apply for a full-time diploma, even a degree afterward."

"About time you got your shit together."

"Did you like them? The guys?"

I'm touched that my opinion matters to him. "Very much. And you're already helping people. That guy, Luke; it's early days for him but his wife says he's so encouraged by seeing how fit you are. Hey, you could even start playing football again."

He focuses on the road. "No. I'll never play again."

"What, not even a kickabout when you have a family?"

Another silence. "I'm never having kids. In case my faulty heart," he taps his chest—"is something I'd end up passing on. Plus, I'd be a shit dad."

We're getting closer to home and I wish the journey was longer. "Drop me on the main road, please." Tim still has no idea I'm in touch with Joel, never mind meeting him tonight.

He nods. "So, what shifts are you working over Christmas?"

"Christmas Eve to Boxing Day. Overnight shifts."

"Wow, you must really have pissed off your bosses."

"I volunteered. So many of my colleagues have kids and it's more important for them." Plus it means I have an excuse not to endure a full Smith Family Christmas, complete with my sister's relentless interrogation about the postponed wedding. "How about you?"

"Mum's ordered the slaughter of several poor organic farm animals to celebrate the return of the prodigal son from the edge of drug oblivion!"

"Way too harsh. They've been through hell with you, Joel."

"You're right. Remember that joke we had. *How are the jerks?* I'm the jerk, right?"

"I didn't see a jerk tonight, I saw . . ." I saw my first love. "I saw someone who is trying."

He turns up Hazelmere Crescent and pulls in, just out of sight of the bungalow. "Look, Kerry. There's something else. The full-time sports science courses I'm considering for next year, they're a long way from Brighton. I thought . . . after what we talked about after the triathlon, well, I could do with a fresh start."

No!

The reaction is immediate, visceral. My heart races, my stomach drops. I want to cry out: *stay, Joel.* But I told him after the triathlon that he didn't love me, that I could never love him again. He's made plans because of that; I should be pleased for him.

He leans in to hug me.

Don't go. I can't bear it if you go.

I drink in his smell, and his warm hands on my back, and it feels as though we're shipwrecked and clinging to each other to stay afloat.

When he disentangles himself, he's clearly expecting me to come out with some festive platitude. Good luck. *Goodbye.* Merry Christmas and a happy 2005. Have a good life.

Instead, I pull his face toward mine and I kiss him and I know I can't let him go.

35

Tim

I've never seen a patient who looks so scared.

"This is Zoë, aged twenty-five. She arrived in A & E shortly after midnight last night, with abdominal pain, query premature labor. No prenatal care recorded but obviously they sent her up to us. How are you feeling now, Zoë?"

The consultant directs his full-beam benevolent smile at the woman, who stares back, pupils dilated, afraid. Zoë's body is so slim she could be a child, except for the taut, distended belly that fixates us all. Her cheeks appear flushed but when I look more closely, I realize they are lesions, livid and sore against her otherwise pale face.

"I'm not in so much pain now, thank you." Her voice is a surprise; calm and unaccented. Her hands—one cannulated—lie on her lap.

"Let's keep it that way. We believe that Zoë is in her thirty-sixth week of pregnancy, although her . . . lifestyle means we can't completely rely on the size of the neonate to estimate gestation. Any thoughts on the treatment plan?"

Lifestyle? I am trying to interpret this when Laura raises her hand. The consultant nods at her, and she answers, "Corticosteroid injections. Attempt tocolysis to see if we can avoid premature delivery, but ensure medication isn't contraindicated in the case of a substance-abusing patient?"

The young woman looks at the floor. *Substance-abusing.* It's so obvious. The wasted appearance, the lesions, the lack of prenatal care.

The consultant nods. "So far the tocolysis appears to be working and we have a second corticosteroid due at around two P.M. Fetal heartbeat is normal but being monitored. We will review again tomorrow morning. You try your best to stay nice and relaxed, there, Zoë, OK? With luck, we can keep your baby safe and sound well into 2005."

We move out of the bay and out of earshot. The consultant stops and says, "Social services are aware. If her contractions start again, we'll probably allow labor to proceed: apart from anything else, there's space on the NICU at the moment, so that could work well as he— it's a boy, but she doesn't know—will almost certainly need treatment for neonatal abstinence syndrome. Either of you know the likely symptoms in the infant?"

Laura is on it again. "Tremors, uncontrollable crying and irritability. Sweating. Similar to the symptoms of adult withdrawal."

"But much more distressing to see, and hear, and it can last for several months." The consultant shakes his head. "Silly girl. If she'd sought help, we'd have popped her on buprenorphine to reduce the duration of the NAS."

I wonder if he'd feel as judgmental about my old habits, and any of his colleagues who might use drugs themselves to get through the day. But no, we're *different*: our self-medication is necessary, our stresses so extraordinary we can justify most things. It is amazing, the way doctors can place themselves above the rest of the human race when it suits them.

"Will she be allowed to keep the child?" I ask.

"They'll try with her and if she works hard, then perhaps. But would you leave an infant in the care of someone so patently unable to look after herself?" The consultant shakes his head. "I think it'd be a brave social worker who'd make that call."

I'd been dreading ob-gyn, but to my astonishment, I like obstetrics, because there's hope here, and moments of real joy. Babies don't judge. If you can work out their needs, and meet them, they respond with incredible speed. And laboring women are refreshingly direct.

Woolworth's helps. I've developed my own fail-safe method of overcoming my introversion when I start a new placement: I buy whichever chocolates are on special offer—one box of dark and one of milk—and take them straight to the nurses' station on day one. I also make it a priority to memorize the tea/coffee preferences of everyone I work with.

When the ward round is done, Laura follows me into the kitchen. "I can't believe that patient didn't try to detox once she realized she was pregnant," she says, as I line up seven mugs and add the requisite tea bags or spoonfuls of instant coffee granules. Laura had better not be angling to take the credit for them.

"How do you know she didn't?"

"You'd try properly, wouldn't you, if you were having a baby?"

Laura has hardened up since we started medical school. Everyone has, except me. I've gone the other way. Things that wouldn't have affected me at all, that I'd barely have noticed before, now lodge themselves inside my head. When I'm trying to remember symptoms or conditions, the words elude me. Instead, I see the faces of patients in pain, patients who died.

One of the midwives pops her head around the door. "Which one of you two needs a complex-needs for your project portfolio?"

Laura shrugs. "I've already got two written up."

"You then, Timmy? The girl in Bay 3 is threatening to leave. Sit with her and make sure she doesn't."

I look at the row of teas. "Is she nil by mouth?"

"No, a tea might shut her up for a bit."

I follow her out.

Zoë's voice echoes down the corridor. "Has anyone seen my shoes? Has some bastard nicked them?" She sounds a lot less well spoken than she did talking to the consultant.

I nudge my shoulder through the gap in the privacy curtains, holding a mug in each hand. "I'll go and look for your shoes in a minute, Zoë. But would you like a drink first? Coffee or tea? I've got one of each."

She looks suspicious. "Who are you?"

"I'm Tim. I'm a medical student."

"No way are you watching me push this baby out."

I shrug. "That's fair. The offer of a drink still stands, though."

"Tea. Then I'm off. Out of here."

I gesture at the chair next to her bed. "Can I hide with you in here for a bit? Otherwise the midwives will put me on bedpan duty."

"They look like total bitches."

"Actually, they're really nice to *patients*. But med students are the lowest in the pecking order in the whole hospital."

"Lower than junkie scum?"

I don't know how to reply: it's something they don't train you for. I sip my coffee and wonder how I'll write up this encounter. We're meant to keep a record of challenging cases and reflect on what we've learned from them.

Mostly, I learn that I can't do small talk. I look around the curtained-in space for inspiration. Usually, there's something on the bedside table: Get Well or Congratulations cards from family, a puzzle book to dip into.

Zoë has no belongings here. Her body offers the only obvious topics for conversation: how long ago did you start using heroin? Have you self-harmed lately? What the hell were you thinking, getting pregnant?

Even I know none of *that* counts as small talk.

"So what's the goriest thing you've seen since you started your doctor training?"

I smile: why do people always ask me this? "You really want to know?"

"I've got a strong stomach."

"I went to India last year, observed a few clinics. There was a man with gangrene in his leg. When the nurse moved the dressing aside, there were more maggots than flesh."

She looks unimpressed. "That all? I've seen that on the streets, it's no big deal. I was hoping for a crossbow through someone's chest. Or someone with a firework up their arse."

"Does a bicycle pump count?"

She laughs. "Did you try blowing it up?"

"It was tempting. Might have stopped him doing it again."

Zoë's face changes. "Have you delivered a baby, then?"

"Not on my own, but I've seen three births since I've been here."

Her hands are gripping the mug so hard her fingers have gone white. "And those births didn't count as the goriest thing?" Her eyes dart up to meet mine, then she looks away.

She's scared. Of course, she is.

"It can be messy but . . ." I try to think of a way to reassure her, without lying about what lies ahead. "It's a *productive* mess. Most things I've seen in hospital are where something's gone wrong. Birth is different. Human bodies—women's bodies—are designed for this."

Though it was having me that kicked off my mother's lupus: more than once, she's called me a parasite. Technically, she's right, though it's an odd way to think of your child.

"Hurts, though, right?"

"They won't let the pain get out of control."

She bites her lip. "Mate of mine said they don't give you anything if you're a user, because the baby's hooked enough as it is."

"Honestly? I don't know quite how it works. But they'll do what's best for you and for the baby."

"Don't know much, do you? When do you become a proper doctor?"

"I'll have my final exams in April, and if I pass those, they let me loose on the wards in August."

"That's fucking soon, considering you know nothing."

I laugh. "You took the words out of my mouth. What work do you do, Zoë?"

"Casual pub shifts. Not around here. I've been in the West Country for a bit. But when I got too big to stand up for hours, I came back to Brighton."

"Are you still with the baby's dad?"

She gawps at me and I hope she's not going to make a complaint about me asking inappropriate questions. "Yeah. He's popped out for champers and the biggest bunch of red roses you've *ever seen*," she says, putting on an accent like the Queen's.

Her voice is transformed and I smile. "Amazing. You sound like a member of the royal family."

"Yeah, I wanted to be an actress. I can do all different voices. I could play Scottish junkies, or Welsh junkies from the vaaalleys, American cheerleader junkies—" She stops abruptly and looks down at her body.

"Come on, Zoë. This could be a new beginning for you. I'm sure the hospital could help put you into a rehab program . . ."

"I don't want this. *Any of it.* I don't want to be having a baby!"

Instantly, she's on the edge of tears. I think back to my obstetrics lectures: she's on a hormonal roller coaster. Perhaps she needs me to hold her hand while she rides it. "Did you not mean to get pregnant then?"

She scowls: that's better than crying. "I didn't think it'd be like this."

Something about the way she says it makes me think that she *did* want this baby, once. "Tell me what happened, Zoë. If you want to, I mean."

To my surprise, she does. There was this guy she liked, a bit younger than her. Kinder and less messed up than most of the addicts she hung out with, or so she thought. So yes, maybe she wasn't too upset about getting pregnant at first. Maybe she even wanted it to happen.

"I was gobsmacked, after all the shit I've done to my body. I'd already stopped using when I fell pregnant and it gave me the best reason to stay clean. But then . . ."

I wait, not knowing whether she's stopped because of physical pain, or sadness. "What changed, Zoë?"

She sighs. "When I told the dad, he was so angry. He told me . . . well, stuff that made me realize the whole thing was fucking doomed. He even paid for an abortion, but I did a runner at the last minute. I was back on my own, thought I could manage, but I was too weak. Started using again. Smoking. Thought it might do less harm to the baby, no dirty needles, right?" She looks at the cannula in her hand. "I wanna get out of here . . ." Her face crumples.

She needs someone who loves her, not a tongue-tied student like me. But I'm all she's got right now. "Even if you don't want your baby now, you do want to do the best for him, don't you?" I remember that she doesn't know it's a boy. "For him or her?"

"I've already screwed it up. Poor little sod is going to come out disabled *and* addicted, all because of me."

"Disabled?"

She's becoming agitated again and the midwives will not be impressed if she rips out her cannula and does a runner while I'm meant to be calming her down.

"Look, I'm not a doctor yet. But you can tell me or ask me anything. I promise I'll be completely honest with you in return."

Her face is wary. "What if there was something wrong with the baby's father?"

"He was on drugs too?"

Zoë shakes her head. "No. He got clean. Cleaner than me, anyhow. I mean something in his blood. His genes?"

"Oh." I was reviewing genetic conditions last week. "Well, we can inherit illnesses or traits from either parent. But even the more serious conditions can be managed if we know early on, ideally from birth."

She says nothing.

"Is this what you're worried about? Talk to me, Zoë."

But I've lost her to her memories or her fears. She starts to claw at the bedding and when she lifts the sheet, her bed is saturated. Zoë looks at the clear liquid and begins to sob.

Looks like labor is on, despite our attempts to stop it. "It's all right, Zoë. It's only your waters breaking. I think things might be moving now. I'll just go and get the midwife."

She grabs my hand and holds on. "Don't leave me on my own!"

The midwife will be cross if I don't fetch her straightaway. But for once, I don't want to do the correct thing. I sit back down, gripping Zoë's hand back, and I push the call button. "I promise you, I'm not going anywhere."

There are times over the next nineteen hours when I regret making that promise to Zoë, but mostly I am focused on her and her pain.

She needs somebody. It could be anybody. But today it just happens to be me.

I get sworn at, and her fingers leave bruises on my arm. I reassure her she can do it, even when I have my doubts. I ask her every few hours whether she's certain there's no one I can call—a friend, a family member, her baby's father.

She swears some more.

Sometimes, when the door opens, we hear carols and Christmas songs coming from patients' TVs. The contrast between the sentimentality of "When a Child Is Born" and the messy reality of Zoë's labor makes me feel uncharacteristically feminist. Women are much stronger than men.

In the downtimes between contractions, we walk up and down outside the delivery suite, and I honor my other promise—to answer every question honestly. She uses it against me for her own amusement, as though we're playing a one-sided spin the bottle.

How many people have you had sex with?

Two.

Wow. How many times a week do you do it with your girlfriend now?

Once (this is not strictly true, not since Kerry found out about my exam screwup, but I justify it by telling myself I am averaging it out over our three and a bit years together).

Is she the love of your life?

Yes.

Are you the love of hers?

I hesitate. "You'd have to ask her that question."

Zoë nods. "Is she a doctor too?"

"No. Well, not yet. She works for the ambulance service but—"

"Arrrgh! Fucking hell. It's back again."

The midwife examines Zoë, but when she asks me if I'd like a look, it feels odd, as though I've crossed an invisible barrier from student observer to birth partner.

"Go on," Zoë says. "You might as well get something out of the beating you're taking from me."

"I'm no expert, but I think you're not far off," I say, looking to the midwife for confirmation.

She nods in agreement. "Yup. Now, Zoë, because Baby is coming a bit early, it might get quite crowded in here. Would you rather not have a student in the room?"

"Tim's not going anywhere. But now I need him up at my end."

The room does start to fill up, till I'm the only one still focused on Zoë's face. It's almost more frightening because I can't see how the delivery is advancing.

"We're very close to the baby arriving, Zoë, hold on to all your energy so you can give a great big push when I say so. All right?"

I hold Zoë's hand and I smile at her, not letting her look away, as she puts everything she has into pushing.

"You're amazing, Zoë," I whisper, and I mean it.

She screams, once, and the midwife says, "I can see Baby's head, so wait. . . . One last push, now, my love, come on . . . And that's it, Baby is here . . . It's a boy, Zoë, your little baby boy is here and he's a beauty."

We wait for the moment that means it's all OK: the moment when the baby takes in air and lets out his first howl. I don't break eye contact even now, though it's taking so very long . . .

"We've just cut the umbilical cord now, Zoë, and the team are checking on your baby. You've done so well!"

I hear the urgency in their voices and catch the odd word that I hope Zoë doesn't understand.

"Why isn't he crying?" Zoë's eyes are wide from the pain and the shock and the fear, and it takes everything I have not to let on that I am afraid for her baby too. "He should be crying."

The midwife says: "Zoë, your baby needs help with his breathing so they're using a machine to help, which means he can't cry yet. But we'll let you see him as soon as we can."

Zoë begins to sob, but I'm the only one comforting her. Everyone else is focused on the new life.

"I've killed him," she whispers to me, "haven't I? I've killed my baby before he was even born."

What do I say? Because she almost certainly *has* affected this baby's chance of survival by using drugs. "Zoë. The doctors are doing everything they can—"

A cry comes, not the angry protest of a healthy baby but a keening sound. Still, after that terrible silence, it is the most hopeful sound I've ever heard.

"He's alive," I say.

And the NICU team are placing him in a heated cot, but before they wheel him out, they pause so she can see him. He has an astonishing crop of dark hair, and his body, though small and skinny, is complete. The swollen eyes are shut tight.

"He's mine?" she asks numbly.

"You'll be able to see him properly later," the midwife says. "Right now, they're going to look after him and we're going to look after you."

I stay until she's delivered the placenta and has returned to the ward.

"You'll come back and see me?" Zoë asks.

"I'll try," I say, though I'm meant to have Christmas off. My spirit soars a little bit in anticipation of the surprises I've planned for Kerry, between her shifts. By the time I'm back at the hospital, Zoë will probably have been booted out, though her baby will be kept here for weeks. And even when he is ready to leave, I don't think he'll be going to his mother.

I walk all the way back to the bungalow, my breath condensing in the subzero air. A taxi slows down next to me, and I am so tempted to get in, but we're in full-on money-saving mode, putting everything away for September, when Kerry won't be earning and we're all trying to exist on my F1 salary.

As I walk along the sparkling pavements, the thought of climbing into the warm bed beside Kerry is all that gives me the energy to keep putting one foot in front of the other. But when I let myself into the dark bungalow, she's not there.

I must have got her shifts wrong.

The shock of the icy sheets is like a slap, and now my mind starts racing, with thoughts of what will happen to Zoë, what will happen to her baby.

I understand why she couldn't cope without something to take away the pain life has inflicted on her. I've had so many more advantages than her: a stable home, a loving fiancée, a supportive mother, the prospect of a rewarding career. Yet still I needed the uppers, the downers, the sleeping pills, the odd line.

Life is better now I'm clean. Even lying alone in this cold bed, there's a purity about my doubts and fears. Perhaps now, with the right help, Zoë will realize it too: that however tough things get, drugs just postpone the moment of reckoning, when you have to face your responsibilities.

Kerry helped me realize that love is stronger than addiction. Maybe Zoë's baby will help her feel the same way.

36

Joel

December 25, 2004

I'm in *Love Actually* overdrive, counting the hours till Kerry's overnight shift finishes.

My backpack is ready: a bottle of alcohol-free champagne, luxury crackers, plus festive lingonberry garlands my mum got in return for hosting an interiors photo shoot at Curlews in the summer. At the time, Dad and I were united in our mockery. Not anymore.

In the movie version of today, I'm going to present them to an earmuffed, rosy-cheeked Kerry as the snow falls photogenically on the seafront.

In reality, as I wait outside the ambulance control room, there's no snow, just mizzle, and the morning's still dank. But I get one bit right. At just after seven, Kerry steps out of the building with a colleague. She looks up, and when she sees me, her eyes widen and her cheeks turn the deepest pink.

She says something to the woman she's with, but her eyes don't leave my face and she runs toward me. We kiss as though it's been weeks, not less than twenty-four hours, since we last saw each other. In the nine days since I took her to the Coasters party, we've been meeting in secret whenever we can, making plans. It took me saying I might leave Brighton for her to realize she wanted to be with me.

"Hey, you two, get a room!" her colleague calls out, laughing. "Merry Christmas, Kerry. See you tonight if you can drag yourself away . . ."

Kerry ignores her colleague and kisses me. I don't know if it's for two minutes or ten or . . .

She draws away and my heart seems to stop. Fucking hell, she's beautiful.

"I don't want to go home," she says.

"Good, because you don't have to."

OK, she will have to, later. Tim is planning a "surprise" festive lunch: she saw the bottle of cheap fizzy wine and microwavable turkey dinners he'd hidden in the garage. Even though she's decided to leave Tim, she didn't want to do it before Christmas. *Too cruel.*

To me, it doesn't seem any less cruel to tell him on Boxing Day, but Kerry won't be swayed. The kiss in my car after I took her to the Coasters Christmas party broke through our pretense that we can live without each other. No more denial, no more lies.

Old lies don't count. I've considered telling Kerry about Zoë, but it's all in the past. I want to believe what happened was for the best, though sometimes I wonder. A baby was the last thing Zoë needed. Wasn't it?

"Why have you stopped?" she asks. "Can you kiss me again, please?"

"You've got to catch me first."

I start to run, and Kerry runs with me, grabbing hold of the ridiculous garland I've wrapped around my waist. We head for the seafront, as Brighton kids always do. On the beach, a group of sea swimmers gather at the shoreline, ready for the annual Christmas dip.

"Fancy it?" I ask her.

Kerry shakes her head. "No way. But . . ." She looks toward Palace Pier and nods.

"It's closed on Christmas Day."

"Even better." She runs past the shuttered hot dog stands and candy floss kiosk, toward the barricades. As I watch, she darts to the right-hand side. And now she's gone.

I walk toward the gates.

"Come on, you can sneak in through here . . ." She puts out her hand and helps me clamber through the narrow gap and over the roof of a stall. I've never seen the pier completely empty before, and she starts to dance up and down the boards. I chase her, lasso her with Mum's berry garland, and throw my arms around her. I kiss her with the sea smooth and green-gray between the planks under our feet. In the distance, the capped heads of the mad sea swimmers bob like balls.

I pour champagne into plastic flutes. We drink it looking out toward Shoreham, and beyond that, to the edge of the world. We are young, we can do anything, go anywhere. We've made mistakes. No, *I've* made mistakes, but I don't have to be punished for those forever.

"Kiss me again, please," she asks.

I turn her face toward me, and this time it's a movie kiss, tender and slow, one that justifies the changes it's going to set in motion.

"I should go," she says.

"Tomorrow, we start again."

She flinches, as though she's already playing out the scene in her mind. "It'll be messy, to pull apart, after all this time . . ."

"It'll be messier the longer you leave it."

"You're right." She takes my hand and we walk back to the pier turnstiles. She clambers back over the roof of the stall, and holds out her hand to help me through the gap. We're going back to real life, but only for another twenty-four hours.

We kiss one last time, leaning against the turquoise railings, then I watch her walk away.

Our happy ever after is in sight.

———

My phone rings as Mum is trying to force-feed me a second helping of brandy-free Christmas pudding. It's revolting.

I expect the display to read *Kerry Calling* but it says *Unknown Number* and the ringtone goes right through me, like a mini-shock.

My mother frowns.

"Probably Ant," I say. "Sorry, I won't be a minute."

I go into the hall. It's dark outside but lights twinkle on the ten-foot tree.

"Hello, is that Mr. Joel Greenaway?"

A woman's voice: stiff, officious.

"Yes."

"This is the hospital here."

Blood rushes to my head. My heart thumps. My parents are safe, so it has to be Kerry. "What's the matter? Tell me!"

In the background, I hear gulls and waves. It doesn't sound like a hospital.

"Ha, Joel, had you going there!" The laugh that follows is familiar and frightening.

"Zoë? Are you ill? Or is this a windup?"

"No, I'm not ill. I'm happy, happy, happy."

"You're on something."

"I'm on . . . *love*. And I've got some amazing Christmas news for you. Guess what? You're a daddy!"

The fairy lights are dazzlingly bright on the tree, and for a moment I can't breathe. "Look, Zoë, I know this time of year must be hard for you, but please don't make sick jokes like that."

She laughs again. "Not a joke. You're a daddy! He's a month early and he's got your eyes. But hopefully my heart, it's beating like a good 'un. Not that you ever had a heart anyway . . ."

I try again to breathe or speak, but nothing comes out.

"Don't you want to say congratulations?"

"You're serious?" My voice comes out as a whisper.

"Yes. Your son was born on December 23. Mother and baby doing well. Or at least, we're both alive."

"So you didn't . . ."

"Get rid of it? No. Went into the clinic, but had second thoughts when they gave me the consent form."

My brain can't process it. *I am a father.* "It's a boy? He's . . . OK? Genuinely?" Not that it means anything. I was OK for seventeen years before I died.

"Cries a lot. That's babies for you."

"Where are you? You sound high."

"Celebrating." But her voice cracks a little.

"Are you with him? A month early; that's bad, isn't it?"

"You don't get to pin this on me, you arsehole. Yeah, so I was using but can you blame me?"

I sit down on the marble step, close my eyes. "The baby was born addicted." It's not a question.

The squawking of the gulls is joined by a soft whimpering. I recognize the pitiful sound Zoë makes when she is crying.

"Zoë, are you in Brighton?"

"No."

"Where are you, then? I can come and get you."

"No. Too late. You won't ever get to see him. He's in the special care baby unit because he's a bit poorly on account of being early. They're gonna help me be a mum, right? And I'm gonna try, really try. But if something goes wrong, they won't ever give him to a pig like you. They've got loads of nice families who'd adopt." Her voice breaks. I know all she was trying to do was create a family of her own.

"Zoë—"

But she's cut me off.

The sharp edge of the step presses against the back of my legs. The smell of fig and pomegranate room fragrance nauseates me. I am a father. It changes everything.

Unless Zoë is right and it changes *nothing.* For the first time in years, I have a future, with Kerry. The chance of training for work I enjoy. Even my parents seem happy, now I'm clean.

And I believe Zoë when she says she will do everything she can to keep *her* child away from me. If she'd listened to me, he wouldn't even exist. And she has the ability to slip away, like a ghost, as she has many times before.

37

Kerry

Since I walked away from Joel yesterday, every minute has felt like an hour. Even the shift has dragged, despite the Boxing Day dramas that kept the lines busy: gravy burns and overdoses and now all the falls and broken bones that have arrived with the snow and ice.

Being at home was way worse than work, though. Christmas dinner for three was unendurable, my lips still tingling from kissing Joel. To make it worse, Tim and Elaine seemed to have made a pact to be as cheery as possible, pulling crackers and opening gifts with the hammy gusto you'd expect in a festive edition of *Friends*.

As I cleared the table after the meal, I couldn't imagine the bungalow without me.

But Tim and I have had three years to try to find a way to make each other happy. There've been times when we've managed it, but I've been kidding myself. Do I feel guilty about what I'm about to do? Totally. Is guilt a reason to do nothing?

Never.

"Almost there," says Mo, bringing me back to the present with a jolt. She hands me a coffee. "I plan to spend the next week in a Baileys and brandy butter coma. You?"

"Much the same."

I'm going to tell Tim this afternoon: I'll take him to the pub and buy us both doubles, to give me the courage to go through with it. There's no way of knowing how he'll respond.

I've texted Mum, saying I may want to stay over there tonight. What I really want is to go to Joel's straight after, but I can't do that after breaking Tim's heart.

There's no rush. Soon, Joel and I will have all the time we need to enjoy being together. The old me is back, but wiser, more grateful, more certain than I ever was then of what I want and need.

As Mo and I step outside the building, the cold wind makes my teeth hurt and my eyes water. We've just heard about the awful tsunami that has hit Thailand. They reckon hundreds might have died. Between that and the usual post-shift fatigue, we're feeling odd and fragile.

"Aye-aye," Mo says. "He's back again."

I look up to see Joel standing on the pavement, and warmth rushes through me, top to toe.

Except . . . his stance is different. Cowed. And his face doesn't change when he sees me. It's almost as if he's looking right through me.

Mo gives me a quick hug. "Happy New Year, love. See you in 2005!"

I don't move. Something is wrong. Even taking a step toward him will make the bad thing come sooner. "What are you doing here?"

"Kerry, I—"

"You've done it again, haven't you? Decided you don't love me after all."

He frowns. "No. Never. But I need to tell you something."

We don't touch, though I want to kiss him to stop him saying whatever it is that's going to break the spell.

"Let's get out of the cold," he says, and I follow him away from the sea and up an alleyway. He stops outside a dingy-looking pub. It's like the opposite of the TARDIS, smaller inside than out, decorated in blood shades, furnished with faux mahogany.

"Coffee, or something stronger?" he asks.

"Whatever you think I'm going to need."

He goes to the bar and I find a dark corner. He brings over a Coke for him and a glass of white wine for me. Even holding the cold glass makes me shiver. *Whatever it is, I don't want to know.*

"I had . . . strange news yesterday. It doesn't have to affect us, but we promised we'd be honest with each other, right?"

"It's that serious?" I take a gulp of wine. I *love* Joel, despite all his faults. I can't imagine anything that would turn this feeling on its head.

"I've just found out I have a child."

I stare at him. I must have misheard. "Sorry, you *what*?"

"A baby. I hoped it had been aborted but—" He picks up his glass and drinks, and for a moment I wonder if there is vodka in it. "No. *Hoped* is the wrong word." He frowns.

"You have a child you hoped was aborted?" I close my eyes, to block out his face and try to make sense of the words on their own. I open them again. "Start at the beginning. Who with?"

"One of the girls I used to hang out with. Zoë."

Something clicks into place. "Was she at the beach that time? When the pier burned down."

He nods.

I can vaguely picture her. A junkie: skinny and lost. Not the kind of mother I'd wish on any child, however much I understand about addiction now. "How old?"

Joel looks down. "The kid was born three days ago."

I want to stop the world before it closes in on me, but Joel's talking.

"Me and Zoë, it only lasted a couple of months. I'd got clean and so had she and it felt like we were enjoying life again. We always used a condom but . . . accidents happen, I guess."

I stare at him.

He exhales. "She was excited when she told me, like we were going to live happily ever after. I'd never talked about us having a future or anything. Hadn't even told her about my history, the ICD, anything."

I take a gulp of wine and it tastes off, like rotten egg. "How could she not know? You had sex with her!"

"Only a few times. I kept my T-shirt on. I didn't want her to know. It was meant to be a bit of fun . . ." He looks at me, his eyes appealing for understanding that I won't give. "When she told me she was pregnant, it was still early days. I explained about how I never want kids because of the risk of what I had being genetic."

"You don't know *what* caused it."

"No, but even the smallest chance of passing it on is too much. You see that, don't you, Kerry? I thought she agreed that ending the pregnancy was the right thing. I paid for the abortion, but now it turns out she changed her mind at the last minute."

I'm doing the calculations in my head. "So this was when? March? But if you were clean, how come I found you in a squat two months later?"

"It was April. And I spiraled down fast after that because I knew I'd hurt her, just like I'd hurt you. She was vulnerable and I took advantage."

I need a moment to process this. My urge to fix things is kicking in already. I didn't plan to become a stepmother, but if that's the deal, I love Joel too much to reject him for something he had no control over. "When did you find out?"

"She called me yesterday afternoon. She told me the baby had come four weeks early so he's in special care but it'll probably be OK. He, I mean. It's a boy."

Already I'm wondering what he looks like, the child of this man I love.

I recall my niece as a plump, rosy-cheeked newborn. Something tells me Zoë's baby is in altogether worse shape. "Have you seen him yet?"

He shakes his head. "No. She says she doesn't want me to know him and I guess it's easier that way, for all of us. It doesn't have to affect *our* relationship at all."

"You're not serious?"

"It doesn't change anything, Kerry. It was Zoë's choice, not mine, so I don't need to get involved. We have to focus on *our* plans, right?" He pulls out his phone. "I've been looking at rental flats, the last thing we want is to live in the guesthouse—"

I recoil. "You have a child, Joel. A *son*. Don't you want to know what he's like, how he is?"

Joel shrugs. "Why would I? Look, I'm only telling you now because I don't want us to have secrets from each other. He'll probably be adopted, and even if he's not, kids grow up without their dads in their lives all the time. Look at Tim . . ."

"You're bringing *Tim* into this?"

"Well, he's done OK."

But he hasn't. If his father hadn't left, he'd have been allowed to be a child for longer, instead of becoming sole caregiver for his own mother. Everything in his life might be different now.

"You don't know anything about Tim or what he's been through. You've always had parents with money who've bailed you out no matter what."

"All right. I'm sorry. I just think we should focus on *our* future. You and me, together, after all this time."

The future is not what I thought it would be.

Joel is not who I thought he was.

"You and me," I repeat.

"Oh come on, it's me that's in shock, Kerry. I don't even know where she had the kid. They could be in Blackpool or Llandudno or Timbuktu for all I know."

"And that lets you off the hook, does it? You get to walk away, leaving your child—who is premature—with a girl who can barely take care of herself. In what universe is that the right thing to do?"

"How am I meant to find him? I don't even know the kid's name." He lifts his Coke to his lips, then slams it down again on the table.

"Look, adoption will be for the best. Better he's with carefully chosen adoptive parents than a junkie and a former junkie with a heart problem."

I stare at him. "You've made your mind up?"

He frowns. "I made my mind up when I was seventeen. I don't want kids. Fuck, I need a proper drink."

"Yeah, because that'll really help. You don't deserve a kid." I push my chair back, unable to be in the same room as him anymore. "I thought you'd changed, Joel. I really thought you'd grown up, understood that there are bigger tragedies in the world than your poorly heart and your lost career. But no, you're worse than ever."

"Kerry, wait!"

My legs are stone-heavy as I walk toward the door. I turn when I realize I have one last thing to say. "In case you are in any doubt, I *never* want to hear from you again."

This time, I leave without looking back. I flinch at the cold and scurry up the street to hail a cab back to the bungalow and the good life I already have. Once I get through the front door, I pretend it's the bite of the wind that's made my eyes fill with tears.

Tim has pushed the boat out for New Year's Eve. He takes me to a dinner dance at the Metropole and everyone spills onto the pavement when the clock strikes midnight and he does look handsome in his tux and I kiss him because I love him in my way and he loves me in his. I have learned my lesson. Again.

A GUIDE TO THE CHAIN OF SURVIVAL:
PART THREE

Cardiac arrest is usually an electrical problem—and it takes electricity to fix it.

Giving CPR helps keep the brain and other organs alive. But the next step is to give the heart an electric shock. This stops it—like pressing a reset button—to try to get it to beat normally again.

You've seen this on TV too, usually on hospital shows. The pads go on, everyone *STANDS CLEAR,* and the patient jerks and everyone waits for that sound of a heartbeat. It's called defibrillation.

But you don't have to be a medic or in a hospital to use a defibrillator. These lifesaving machines are called automated external defibrillators (AEDs) and can now be found in thousands of public places: stations, shops, schools, even pubs. And they're automatic. The machine calculates if a shock is needed and tells you exactly what you need to do to help the patient.

The 999 call handler will tell you where the nearest device is. But you should send someone else to fetch it; you mustn't stop the CPR.

Link 3 means getting a defibrillator to the patient as soon as possible—whether that means operating one yourself, or the ambulance crew bringing theirs. Every minute still counts.

38

Joel

JANUARY 1, 2005

Today I am five years old.

It is five years since I was shocked back from eighteen minutes dead. Five years since the only woman I've ever loved pummeled my chest and breathed air into my empty lungs.

It is also my son's tenth day on the planet.

Why don't I feel what I *should* for this new person, my flesh and blood? Kerry looked at me as if I was a zombie when I told her I didn't want anything to do with the kid.

Perhaps that's what I am, an emotionless monster.

I get up off the sofa to grab a beer from the mini-fridge. Fuck it. I haven't had a drink since my detox in the summer, but I intend to get wasted—

I catch sight of myself in the mirror. *Do you really want to do this?*

I turn away.

Through the window of the guesthouse I can see my mother, at the bifold doors of the kitchen. Last night I couldn't face her epic New Year bash, and she's staring at me, her face twisted with worry.

That's what parenthood is like. I'm twenty-two years old and she's still scared about what I'll do next.

No wonder I don't want that.

My reflection is still there, in the mirror over the fridge. I step closer.

Does my son really have my eyes, like Zoë said?

The bottle is cold against my hand. The lid pops off with a hiss. I sit back down on the sofa and I can smell the yeastiness. It's only *beer*. Barely counts as alcohol.

Ten days old.

I don't even know how big he is or what he can and can't do.

Nothing to do with me.

I lift the beer up to my lips. The smell sickens me but the effect will make up for it.

Zoë took the choice away from me by having the kid. But should she also have the choice about whether he's allowed to have a dad? I know how hard her life has been, but that makes her even less able to make the right decisions on behalf of her son.

Our son.

I throw the bottle across the room, but it doesn't even smash, it just coats the timber wall in beer. What a mess I make of everything.

The last few days, I've been mourning my relationship with Kerry. I've considered calling her, telling her I'd try to find the baby if she'd reconsider. But even I know it would be a terrible reason to be in a child's life.

I wonder who is caring for him. If Zoë isn't allowed to be there, does he sense that the people around him are paid to be there?

Could I make a difference? It's something I've been wrestling with since talking to Kerry the day after Christmas. Being a dad terrifies me, but there's more at stake now than my own cowardice.

I know what Kerry would say: being afraid is not an excuse for me to let him down.

———

I get to the social services building just before 8:00 A.M. on the second of January. Their webpage told me they open at nine, so it means waiting another hour outside, but it's worth it to be first in the queue.

I've been up all night, thinking it through. Even though I never wanted a kid, knowing my son exists makes everything different. Five years ago, I came back to life and maybe *this* was why. I don't want to waste any more time. While I wait, I stamp my feet to stay warm, rehearsing what I am going to say in my head.

When they open the doors, the Christmas decorations still hang limply off the ceiling, and there's a faint smell of pine air freshener and candy cane. The two women behind reception are giggling as they catch up on festive gossip, and look faintly put out to be interrupted by a customer. Client. Whatever I am.

"Happy New Year," I say brightly. "I don't know if I'm in the right place, but I want to inquire about a baby."

The older one stops laughing: her red-framed glasses make her look a bit like a kids' TV presenter, but there's no warmth in her scowl. "What about a baby?"

"I think . . . A former partner of mine has had a baby and I want to meet him. His mum takes drugs, so I think social services will probably be involved."

She sighs. "What's the name of your ex-partner? I can't reveal anything personal but I might be able to make you an appointment with a member of staff who can advise."

"It's Zoë."

She looks up from the Post-it she's writing on and waits. "Zoë what?" she prompts, eventually.

"The thing is . . . it wasn't a surnames kind of relationship."

Her eyebrows rise. I've dressed carefully, to look more mature than I feel, but I know I must seem so bloody irresponsible.

The entrance door opens behind me and a teenage girl tries to maneuver her double buggy inside, as both her children cry out in protest. I want to help, but don't know where to begin.

"Date and place of birth?" the council official asks, her voice sharp.

I open my mouth, pleased that I can answer something in full. "August the tenth, 1982. Sussex Hospital."

This time, her sigh almost blows a pile of leaflets off the desk. "The child's not yours."

Shit. "Um, the twenty-third of December. Eleven days ago. It's a boy, but I don't know where she had him. Possibly Brighton, though."

"I don't suppose you're named on the birth certificate?"

"I don't know."

"This isn't the Number 1 Ladies' bloody Detective Agency. There's nothing I can do without a bit more to go on."

I take a deep breath. I need to get her on my side. "I'm sorry. I know I sound mad. But I didn't even know I was a dad till a few days ago, when my ex called. She's . . . vulnerable. Struggles to look after herself, never mind a baby."

A couple more customers have arrived by now. I have quite an audience, all women.

"I'm not saying I'd be any better than she would. But kids want to know who their parents are, don't they? I want to be there if he needs me."

The room is silent. Even the babies in the buggy have stopped grizzling.

"Look, love, it's not as simple as that . . ." Her voice is softer now, more maternal. "If your ex is going to struggle, then social work will decide what's best for the baby. But that wouldn't automatically be you."

I know this, from the research I've done online, but still, it feels more final coming from someone in authority. "I have to try. Don't I?"

"Go on, give him a break," the teenager behind me says. "Most dads don't give a shit about their kids."

The woman rummages in a drawer and holds up a leaflet about parental rights. "There's a number on the back there." She turns it over, circles something. "This is a helpline. They might be able to help you work on legal stuff. If it's something you really want to do?"

I nod.

"Have you got money? Or can you get hold of some?"

"I can try."

"You shouldn't need it, but . . . it might help. Either way, it's not going to be easy."

I take the leaflet. "Probably shouldn't be. Thanks."

As I turn to go, the girl with the buggy winks at me. "If you don't find your actual kid, you'd be welcome to play Daddy to these two."

I look down at them: a big kid and a little kid. I can't even guess their ages, never mind how you'd start to feed or soothe or play with them. What the *fuck* am I doing?

I smile weakly. "They're lovely."

She nods. "They can be. Good luck."

By the time I've walked home from the social services office, I've realized one thing: if I need cash to fight this, I have to tell my parents. Mum's poring over cookbooks deciding what to tell the caterers to cook for her next "casual" kitchen supper. Dad's holed up in his office, working on new ideas that will never get commissioned.

I ask them into the kitchen. As I make a big pot of tea, I try to imagine there's a child in the room with us, grubby fingers poking into power sockets, tiny hand reaching up toward the kettle cord. Can I really keep a small human safe?

My parents face me across the kitchen island. I used to think their marriage only survived because Mum went away so often. But I've changed my mind. Now I think the constant fighting for me—first, to get me to the top in football, and later, to stop me dying—has cemented them together in another, slightly healthier way. They seem happier lately, and I think Dad might even have got rid of his "secret" mobile phone, the one he always used to communicate with his latest fling.

Are they ready to be grandparents?

Here goes.

"This is going to be a shock and it was to me too. I'm a dad. I've got a kid. And I want to be a part of his life."

Dad inhales with a half whistle. Mum's mouth opens but she says nothing. Lynette Greenaway, who has never, ever gone blank on live TV, is lost for words.

"I only found out a few days ago. On Christmas Day, when I rushed out? That was his mother calling me. I don't know his name but he was born on the twenty-third of December."

"Jesus," my mother says.

"I didn't even know you had a girlfriend," Dad says.

Mum gives him a withering look as if to say, *That's how little notice you take.* Except she didn't know about Zoë either.

"Her name is Zoë and she wasn't really a girlfriend. More like someone I used to hang out with. When things were . . . difficult."

"She's a *junkie?*" my mother says.

I feel protective of Zoë, suddenly. "She has used drugs, off and on, like I did. But when we were together, when the baby was conceived, we were both clean."

"You knew she was pregnant?" Dad asks.

"Yes, but we agreed it wasn't the right time. Or at least, I thought we had. I gave her money for an abortion and I didn't hear from her again until she called me on Christmas Day."

My mother shakes her head. "We can all guess where *that* money went."

"Mum, you don't know her."

Her eyes widen with anger. "This is some girl who went ahead and had your baby without telling you. Yet you're defending her?"

But my father reaches across the marble countertop to touch her hand. "Lynette. Let him finish."

"What more is there to say? Our son got some druggie pregnant with our grandchild and this is the first we hear of it?"

"To be fair, it seems like it's the first he's heard of it too," Dad says. "Why did you originally decide to end the pregnancy?"

I tap the place where my ICD sits under my skin. "I was scared a baby might inherit whatever it was that made me need this."

Mum's face falls. "The baby is ill?"

I hear the change in her voice, and I love her for it. Why did it take her seconds to begin to care, when it took me days? I suppose it doesn't matter. What matters is that I do care now.

"I don't know for sure. He was premature, but only by a few weeks. It's possible that Zoë started using . . . stuff again after we broke up."

"What kind of a mother does that?" Mum says. But the disgust in her face makes me want to defend Zoë, despite what she's done.

"The kind of mother who is desperate. Zoë's a good person, at heart. Grew up in care, never knew her parents, never had any of the support you two have given me. But when she's on form, she's funny and sharp and full of life."

"That's what Zoë means," my mum says softly. "Life. I always liked the name."

Dad looks at me. "The child, *your* child. Where is he now?"

"I don't know where he was born. When she called me, I think it was because she wanted to hurt me. She said she wants to keep him, but if she's not allowed to, she'd rather he were adopted than come to me."

"What do you want?" Mum asks.

"At first I freaked out." I shake my head, remembering how I responded and how Kerry—rightly—disapproved. "But now I want to be in his life. Or at least, for him to know I cared enough to try."

Dad taps his fingers against the counter. "Are you sure? Adoption would be better than you getting involved and then changing your mind." His face is stern, testing me.

"I'm sure."

Mum and Dad glance at each other and I see, so briefly, a look of solidarity pass between them. "What do you think, Granny?" my father says, and I expect her to slap him, but instead she grips his hand and mine.

"OK, Grandpa." They smile at each other, almost shyly, and for the first time in days, I know I'm not alone. "Joel, what can we do?"

"I've been reading up on what it's going to involve. It might be expensive."

Mum looks around the room, with its designer appliances and its double-height glass atrium. "That's fine. We can handle expensive."

For a moment, their love takes my breath away. They never gave up on me, no matter what I did. I want my son to know how that feels too. "The other thing is, if it ends in some messy fight between me and Zoë, you might hear stuff about me that I'm really not proud of."

My mother's face doesn't change. "We love you, no matter what you've done. You'll understand this soon: we're your parents and we'll do whatever it takes."

It takes money, and determination, and still there are no guarantees.

First, Dad hires an iffy private detective from his investigative TV days to find out where Zoë gave birth.

While we wait, we plan for the next stage. Apart from when I was first sick, it's the only time I can remember us acting the way families do in the movies: cheerleading and urging each other on whenever one of us begins to doubt that this will work out.

It's a fortnight before the detective confirms that my boy exists and was actually born here in Brighton. While I was imagining some fairy-tale future with Kerry, my son was coming into the world only a couple of miles away.

It feels as though I should have *known* somehow.

But now I do, the world seems different.

The helpline tells me to do everything by the book: fill in the forms in my best block capitals, agree to the DNA test, wear a suit and a passive smile to all meetings, agree my past has been problematic, work to prove I deserve a role in his life.

As his mother, Zoë doesn't have to prove *that* to the social workers, but she's not making it easy for herself. Her decision to drop out of the system and not get any antenatal care has meant our child was born an addict. Edwina, my social worker, says she did well after the delivery, agreeing to rehab and even expressing milk for the baby. But now she keeps going AWOL and it's not looking quite so promising.

Meanwhile, I wait some more: for the results of the DNA test, for my assessment, for crumbs of news about my son's progress. He doesn't even have a name yet and Zoë can wait till the beginning of February to register his birth. I don't know if it's because she's waiting deliberately, or because her life is still chaos.

"We can't just call him *baby*," my mother says, "but a name feels wrong, because we'll get used to it and then it'll be weird when she calls him something else."

"Spud," Dad says. "That's what we called you before you were born. The baby could be Son of Spud."

"Spud will do for now," I tell them.

I have dreams of walking along rows and rows of plastic newborn cots, looking for *my* son. When I finally get to the last cot, there's no baby, but a redcurrant-sized heart, pumping madly on its own.

What if he's sick because of my faulty genes?

I try to focus on other things: my online nutrition course, my own fitness. One afternoon, I go to the big WHSmith at Churchill Square and buy every mother and baby magazine on the shelf.

Back in the guesthouse, I pore over their cheery advice about night feeds and colic remedies and milestones, even though the same magazines suggest I have no real role to play in my son's life. The soft-focus photos show mothers and babies; men, if they ever appear, are blurs in the background. When they're mentioned in the articles, it's because they're pestering for sex or jealous of the attention their baby is getting . . .

Apart from meeting my son, there's one other thing I am desperate to do: tell Kerry she was right and I was wrong and let her know she's stopped me making the worst mistake of my life. The only reason I haven't is because I am scared something could still go wrong. So I promise myself that as soon as I know I'm going to be allowed to be part of my son's life, I *will* tell her I came to my senses.

I want so much more: a reunion, forgiveness, a future. I lie awake in the guesthouse, imagining me and my son and Kerry coming together to create a family, as though all the trials we've endured have been leading up to our deserved happy ending.

"You've passed the checks so far," the lawyer says when she calls in early February, my parents with me, listening on speakerphone, "though you can expect some hard questions on your past drug use and future plans. Your ex is still trying too, though given her erratic behavior, I'd say she's got a bigger fight on her hands."

The lawyer expects me to be glad that Zoë is failing, because it might make it easier for me to succeed. But I'm not: I know how much she wants this, because I feel the same way. More than that, I want Spud to be loved.

At my next meeting with Edwina, she hands me a photograph, face down. I hesitate before I turn it over.

"Don't expect too much," she says. "His foster mum isn't exactly Annie Leibowitz."

She's right. The picture is blurry—perhaps on purpose—with the child's face turned away, his hair merging with the soft fleecy rug he lies on. Yet it affects me more than anything else has so far. I stare at him, fascinated but also terrified, because I don't yet recognize him or know if I can be what he needs.

"My little Spud."

"Oh!" Edwina smiles, and the lines around her eyes fan out like sunrays. "Ah, I have news about his name too."

"Tell me?" I hold my breath, preparing to pretend I don't care if my kid is called Pluto or Turnip or—

"Leo. Your son's given names are Leo Zachary."

Leo.

I don't have to pretend I like it. It sounds . . . right. So close to my own name, and to Zoë's too.

Did she do it consciously, wanting to give him a lasting connec-

tion to us both, however tenuous? I take my share of the responsibility. I treated her badly, tried to railroad her. We are both to blame for
the fact that our child was born in distress.

The delays nearly do my head in but today—March 3—is the day
I get to meet my boy.

Edwina is due to meet me outside the children's center. They
don't want me to have the foster parents' address, in case something
goes terribly wrong at the hearing. I pace the pavement, the photo of
Leo in my hand, the only thing I have of him so far.

"Joel!" Edwina scuttles across the street toward me. She has the
look of a woman who has seen it all. She gives me a cursory smile.
"Ready?"

Never. But I try to pretend. "Yeah. Been looking forward to this."
The words seem inadequate and I worry that I've already failed.

We climb the tiled steps. The building is a nondescript 1960s
block, but to me it's a fortress. It's brightly decorated inside, with
murals and wall stickers in primary colors. But the hospital-like smell—
disinfectant and hot-running radiators—brings back memories of my
worst times and with them, the girl who was always there at my side.

As Edwina heads off to check if everyone is ready, I sit on a plastic
chair, my hands under my thighs. I want to run. What do I know
about my son? Of his first months, or his pain? I have nothing to offer
him.

I remember the words Kerry hissed at me the last time we met.
You don't deserve a kid. She's the person who knows me best in the
world. What if she's right?

No. She doesn't know the new me, the one who has grown up
more in nine weeks than the previous twenty-two years. Kerry did
that, held a mirror up so I could see my selfishness and my cowardice.

I want to prove her wrong. And make sure she knows she made
it happen.

Yet as I sit here, trying to rehearse what I'll say to her, my words
start jumbling. It matters so much that I get this right.

Unless . . . it's her birthday tomorrow: I never forget. I could send her a card, with a copy of Leo's photo. The message could be simple, so that even if bloody Tim reads it, he wouldn't understand the significance.

But Kerry would.

Will it make her want to see me again? I can hope . . .

"Joel? We're all set." Edwina stands halfway down the corridor, beside a door.

I stand up and a horrible sensation starts at the bottom of my chest. Is this the v fib? Am I about to be shocked?

No. I smile when I realize the truth. It's not my heart misfiring, it's . . . butterflies.

The glass in the door is papered over with pages from superhero comics, so no one can see through. As Edwina grabs the handle, I see Batman.

And then I see Leo.

He is lying on a mat, with a baby gym arching over him. I can't see his face at first, but his body is solid, even chunkier than I expected, in a bright green onesie. His hips look disproportionally wide. Is there something wrong with his legs? *Why haven't they warned me?*

I realize it's probably the nappy underneath.

He has *so* much hair, loose brown curls covering his head.

A plump blond woman sits opposite him on the floor: his foster mother. She smiles at me, though it doesn't quite reach her eyes. She beckons me over.

As I approach, I am almost afraid to look at his face. I've been told that he is developmentally delayed: that the drugs may affect his behavior and his learning. What if I find him impossible to love?

I make myself look at his face.

I know you.

I am flooded by certainty. He looks like me in my own baby photos. If I'd passed him in the street, I would have known he was mine. People say it's a biological trick, to make babies resemble the dads more at this age, to reassure them the child is really theirs. It works.

Leo stares at me. He doesn't recognize *me*. I am nothing to him. Worse, a person who wished for him never to exist.

But he is here now. Eyes darting everywhere, hungry for what life has to offer. He can't raise his head yet so it's the eyes that move the most. As I lower myself onto the mat, he smells of vanilla. His hands poke out from the sleeves of the onesie. They are wonderful, chubby and perfect, and as for his fingernails, they are . . . well, miraculous.

"Hello, Leo," I say, testing the name out.

His smooth forehead wrinkles momentarily. I hold my breath, terrified he's about to cry. Instead, he blinks and his eyes seek out the familiarity of his foster mother's face.

I already know that proving I am fit to be his father is going to be the toughest thing I've ever done.

39

Tim

MARCH 4, 2005

"How have you been, mate?" one of the other NA regulars asks as we pull our orange chairs into position.

"Getting there," I say.

He nods. "Yeah. It gets easier, mate." From what he's said in meetings, he lived his twenties and thirties at double speed. He's fortyish now but looks a decade older, even though he's been clean a couple of years. Cellular damage, presumably.

I know everything about his downfall, his regrets, his recovery. But he knows nothing about mine. I barely say a word at these meetings.

But despite my silence, I keep coming back. The sessions help me stay off the pills, which is the only thing I seem to be getting right.

"Take a seat, guys. I'm Anya and I'm hosting today so let's get Friday started."

Anya runs through the rules—confidentiality, respect, nonjudgmental listening, all the usual—and asks if anyone is new. A handful of people raise their hands.

"There's no pressure to speak yet, just listen in and if you'd like to contribute later in the meeting, we'd love to hear from you." Anya has the Brighton yoga vibe to a T: wiry limbs draped in gray marl, matching hair, a soulful expression. You'd never guess she used to shoot up in the old sewer entrance under West Pier, among the puddles of piss and seawater.

Of the newcomers, one of the men looks high-functioning, which is how I'd have described myself when I first came. The other guy is further down the line to oblivion. If I'd have seen him in the waiting room in A & E, I'd have nudged a colleague to get him triaged sooner rather than later.

And then there's a woman with her back to me, spiky black hair cut into the nape of her neck, skinny legs crossed at the ankles.

"So, let's kick off," Anya says. "Friday already. How has this week been for everyone?"

I let my mind and my eyes wander: up to the stained foam tiles on the ceiling, down to the double-glazed windows and the rain lashing against the glass.

At least while I'm here, I don't have to put on a show. Finals are only weeks away and I pretend I am confident, but it's hard work. Mum is distant and cold. For a while, I thought it might be her lupus flaring up, but now I believe she simply can't forgive me for almost losing Kerry.

Some days I'm not even sure I haven't lost Kerry after all. She says the right things, encourages me, helps me with test questions, but when she doesn't think I'm watching, her smile drops and her posture slumps and she looks so *tired*.

I owe it to them both to qualify. But the idea of what comes next is suffocating.

". . . anything to share?"

I drag my eyes away from the window and back to Anya, who is smiling at me.

"Will they ever forgive me?" I say.

Anya looks as surprised as I am that I've spoken. "Who?"

Everyone gawps at me, albeit in an empathetic way. I don't want to share my innermost fears with these strangers. But who else am I meant to share them with?

"My girlfriend. My mother."

More silence. I know this is how it works: give the speaker the floor, let them take their time. "My girlfriend put everything on hold for my work and in return, I started using. Lying. Sometimes I think she must really hate me."

"Hate is a very strong word," Anya says. "What makes you think she feels that way?"

It's nothing she's done. At New Year, Kerry told me she was as determined as I am to try—*really* try—to make our relationship work and she surely wouldn't have promised me that if she hated me. Yet as I picture her face, all I can see is unhappiness. Nothing I do or say seems to reach her. Today is her birthday, and I have bought flowers and the ingredients to cook her favorite mushroom risotto when she gets home from her shift.

Yet already I know I will see something in her eyes that tells me it's not enough.

"Because nothing's turned out the way it was supposed to. We were meant to be high fliers, both of us. Instead, I'm a recovering addict and she's miserable."

"You're young," says the man who greeted me when I first arrived. "I don't mean to patronize you but if your relationship doesn't work out, there will be so many other chances."

Except I don't fantasize about other women. I fantasize about being alone, with no obligation to make anyone better.

There's coffee afterward.

I don't usually hang around, but talking about the situation at home has made me want to stay out a little longer.

"You were brave."

I turn toward the voice. It's the woman, the new one with the cropped black hair. I have never seen eyes like hers: they look black too, though I know it's an optical illusion, the merging of iris and pupil in this dark room, against the bright white of the sclera.

"You mean self-indulgent."

"No. I know what I meant. I could see, that did not come easily." Her voice is low, accented. Italian maybe? I heard it when she spoke in the session. She didn't say much: that she had moved to the city, was looking for a group.

"Did you find this morning useful?"

"Maybe." She shrugs, it's very Gallic, very *nonchalant,* so perhaps she's French. I can't stop looking at her eyes, which dominate her angular face. No one would ever describe her as pretty. But still, she's so striking that I feel she should be on a movie screen, not here, in real life.

"Will you come back?"

She smiles for the first time. "Will you?"

"I'm part of the furniture," I say.

She's older than me, I think, but not much. I have this sudden urge to know her story, what she struggles with and why she's here right now, ready to make a change.

But even *thinking* that feels like I'm being disloyal to Kerry.

"Well, until next time, maybe." She finishes her coffee, throws the cup in the bin, and walks out of the conference room.

I never asked her name, and I have no way of knowing if I'll ever see her again.

I am stirring the risotto and sipping wine—Kerry and I have agreed that alcohol is not off-limits for me—when I hear the snap of the letter box and the whisper of something landing on the mat.

It's another card, in a silvery envelope. The post came already this morning, a stack of birthday greetings ready for her to open when she gets home from work.

I pick up the card. No stamp, but properly addressed. I open the front door and see a figure sprinting off into the twilight, as though they've just lobbed a grenade into the bungalow.

When I recognize him, an irrational irritation takes hold and I step out of my house.

"Oi!" I call out. He doesn't look back so I ram the card into my pocket and run after him. "Oi, Joel Greenaway, wait!"

Where's it coming from, this roiling, acidic sensation in my abdomen? He's only sending a card to the person who helped save his life.

Isn't he?

The last time I saw him, the final time he sold me pills, he was so wrecked I wasn't sure he'd survive the summer.

I catch him up. Not only has he survived, he looks well. It's more than his clear skin and the heft of his chest under a show-off triathlon T-shirt. There is a certainty about him that I envy far more than his looks.

"What is this?" I hold up the card.

"A birthday card, that's all. It's today, right?"

My fingers burn where they're in contact with the envelope. It's heavier than a card should be and there is something about Joel's eyes as they dart from my face toward my hands and back again that makes me feel like it contains a threat.

I could open it now, in front of him. Or take it home and give it to Kerry at the end of her shift, watch her as she reads, ask her to show me whatever he's written.

"Look inside, if you don't believe me," he says.

It's not sealed. I can read it and put it back, and Kerry won't know. But *he'll* know I did that, and that would give him power over our relationship.

Except he's always had power, hasn't he? Since Millennium Night, Joel has come between Kerry and me.

And then there was Marilyn's wedding. But that was just a drunken kiss, before Kerry and I were even engaged. Wasn't it? My head tells me she wouldn't cheat, but my heart . . .

What do hearts know? Nothing. The brain is the processing

organ, and my brain can overcome this disproportionate response to such a trivial event. I take three deep breaths. Yes, they kissed, years ago. But it can't have meant anything, or she'd never have chosen me. Despite all the ways I let her down, she always came back.

"Nice of you to remember, after so long."

"Oh, you don't tend to forget that sort of thing. You both OK? And your mum?"

"Mum's fine. I'm almost at the end of med school but Kerry will be next. It was always the plan, I don't know if you recall, that we'd both get to be doctors? Well, it's finally happening." I'm blathering now. "How about you?"

He shrugs. "All right. Not a doctor or anything, obviously, but I'm taking a course to become a personal trainer."

"Ah, that explains the muscles. And the triathlon thing." I gesture at his T-shirt.

"She told you?" His voice is quiet.

I stare at him. "Told me what?"

Everything freezes: Joel, under the streetlamp, me in my stupid kitchen apron. Ridiculously, it makes me think of the moments before a duel. Are we fighting for Kerry?

He shrugs. "I bumped into her in town a while back, told her about my course. I thought she might have mentioned it. She was pleased, considering how I could have ended up. A vegetable. Worse." It's like he's deliberately putting himself down now.

"Hope it works out for you. I must go. Got something on the hob."

I turn back, jog toward the bungalow, through the door I left wide open. I place the card in the middle of the pile on the dining table. There's a smell of burned rice in the kitchen and I have to jab the wooden spoon against the bits of risotto that have stuck to the bottom of the pan.

An hour before Kerry gets home. Enough time for me to make the risotto again? Yes. I won't let some blast from the past spoil our celebration meal. I tip the congealed rice into the kitchen bin, fill the pan with soap and water, scrub away the remnants, and measure out another lot of ingredients.

Enough.

The new rice starts to bubble but it still doesn't feel right. Bloody Joel turning up like that has brought up all those bad feelings from the night on the lawns.

Well, I won't have it. I snatch the silver card from the pile and bury it in the burned risotto before taking the bag out to the wheelie bin outside, tying knot after knot in the top.

"Hello, my name is Dr. Palmer and I understand you are having some problems with your testicles."

Kerry allows herself a sly smile and stretches out on the sofa. She's in a better mood than she was last night, when we ate her birthday risotto in a heavy silence. Afterward, I watched her as she worked her way through the pile of cards, trying to see if she was disappointed not to get one from him.

"Oh, yes, Doctor. The most awful trouble with my crown jewels." Testing me with the worst scenarios I might get in my practical exams always cheers her up.

I give her a pained look. "Seriously, Kerry?"

She raises her eyebrows. "It's Mr. Plum to you." But her teasing is gentle.

"Doctor?" She nudges me. "I'm waiting and the throbbing is giving me so much grief."

"OK. I'll need to examine you, is that all right, Mr. Plum? And I am going to invite someone else to sit in the room for the examination."

"As you wish, Doctor." She reaches for the wineglass and takes a sip. Turns back into Kerry. "All right, we've got a chaperone with us to see Mr. Plum's gonads. What do you do now?"

As I describe the process I'd follow during examination, she tells me what I will find, based on the book of scenarios she's working from. I try to think about Mr. Plum's pretend symptoms instead of the birthday card that still sits in the bin outside, waiting for the rubbish collection tomorrow.

"So what you're going to see is testicles that look like a bag of worms. Which is nice. What's your diagnosis?"

I close my eyes, trying to imagine the picture from textbooks, as I've never seen this in real life. "If I ask you to lie down, does the appearance change?"

"Good call. It does. What else?"

"Um . . . How old are you, Mr. Plum?"

"I'm sixty-one."

I diagnose varicoceles and suggest that radiotherapy is likely to be the best treatment if confirmed.

Kerry nods. "Is that all?"

She looks at me steadily.

I close my eyes. What else could it be, at this age? *Cancer?* I try to picture the vessels and tracts and imagine what else might be lurking. "I think we'd also want to get him tests to rule out invasive renal cell carcinoma . . . ?" My voice rises uncertainly.

She closes the book and drops it onto the carpet. "You've passed."

"Thanks to you. You're going to be the top of the class once you get to medical school."

Her smile tightens, and for the first time, I notice black rings around her eyes. What am I not seeing? For diagnoses, we have these endless mnemonics—from DR GERM for abdominal exams to SOCRATES for evaluating pain.

If only there was one to diagnose the problem in an ailing relationship.

I daren't ask outright what's bothering her, in case she tells me the truth and the last solid plate of my life shifts and I fall through the gap.

"Tim?"

When I look up at Kerry, the blush the wine had given her cheeks seems to have disappeared.

"I need to tell you something," she says. "A decision I've made."

Is it about Joel? Was that unsettled feeling I had something I should have analyzed further?

"Yes?"

"I'm going to defer my med school application for the year. Well, I already have. It's nothing to worry about. I just think that with all the uncertainty around which part of the country you're going to, it might be easier for the three of us if we have an extra year to get ourselves organized, save up a bit of spare cash."

I stare at her. Of all the things I was expecting her to say, it wasn't this. "But you worked like crazy to get your A levels so you could start this September. I don't get it."

She stands up. "It makes perfect sense to me. Anyway, there's no point arguing. It's done. Another year is neither here nor there, really, is it?"

As she leaves the room, I am certain I am missing something. Maybe it's Joel, and his card and whatever secrets it contained. Or could she have lost her nerve about medicine? No. Not Kerry. What I do know is that if Kerry's decided not to tell me, I have no chance of working out *what* it is.

But if it was definitely over between us, she would have said so. I have to cling to that.

40

Kerry

Elaine sits in the waiting room in her wheelchair, her eyes staring straight ahead. She looks so different away from home, and I curse myself for not noticing the changes before. Slack, yellowing skin drapes over her cheeks and collarbones, as though her body underneath has shrunk in the wash.

We both know this is not going to end well.

"Elaine Palmer, please?"

A nurse leads us to the small office. The corridor is so narrow that it takes three tries to get Elaine's wheelchair through the doorway. The consultant has a flamboyant mane of sandy hair that surfs up from his forehead. As the nurse follows us into the room and leans against the consulting couch, my sense of doom grows.

"Mrs. Palmer, I'm Mr. Greer. Thank you for waiting. I've had the chance to look at the test results now from last week. We put you through the mill, rather, didn't we?"

Elaine nods. I know her: she wants facts.

"I'm afraid that the results do confirm what we suspected, that you have cancer of the pancreas. It's a very difficult cancer to detect early, and in your case, the tests we've done show that, unfortunately, we're beyond the stage where surgery is an option."

He leaves silence, for the information to sink in. It's not a surprise to me, not really. I might not be a doctor but I already knew enough from the extent of the tests and the expressions of the staff carrying them out to postpone my med school applications. At least that's one problem I could solve.

In the distance, I can hear a trolley rattling along, the faint nee-naw of a siren.

I reach out for her hand. She lets me hold it but doesn't grip back. *Oh, Elaine.*

"Is there any treatment?" Her voice is clear and free of self-pity.

The consultant doesn't flinch. "There is chemotherapy, which we will certainly recommend. This is palliative. By which I mean it is aimed more at controlling the growth and effect of the cancer both in the pancreas itself and elsewhere in the body. It is not a cure."

"This isn't a good one to get, is it?" she asks.

He shakes his head. "No. We've made some positive steps in recent years but still . . ."

"How long?"

"I am always unsure how to answer that one, Mrs. Palmer. But, um, we are talking in terms of months, rather than years. I'm really very sorry."

The journey to the cafeteria is long and complex, the warren of corridors and lifts hard to navigate, especially with a wheelchair.

Eventually, we sit down with our pot of tea and the scones neither of us feels like eating.

Elaine exhales. "Well, whatever I did in a past life, it must have been extreme to deserve this luck."

I think about how cruel she's been to Tim in *this* life, but that doesn't mean she deserves to suffer. "It's unfair, Elaine."

"At least I won't be hanging around for years." Her voice breaks slightly on *years,* but she picks up the knife and cuts her scone in half, focusing on spreading the jam evenly across the two halves. "That had always been my fear, that I'd become even more of a burden to Tim."

I've never realized Elaine has had any concept of how hard it's been for her son. "Oh, Tim loves you to bits."

"Yes, hen, but I'm still a burden. To both of you. This way . . . it'll be cleaner."

I think of the 999 calls I take from people with advanced cancer, and I know that "clean" is the last thing we can expect. The next months will be chaotic. *Merciless.* "We have to tell him now."

"Not yet."

"Elaine . . ."

"Not till after his finals. I've been tough on him because the world is a tough place. But he's so close now. We can't risk him falling at the last fence, can we, Kerry?"

"You're going to get a lot sicker before then."

She smiles. "Probably. But observation has never been one of Tim's strengths. The longer we can keep him in his bubble, the better his chances of passing. We've all worked too bloody hard to let him fall at the final hurdle."

Lying about this, and about my reasons for deferring university, turns out to be doable. As Elaine says, Tim is not a great observer.

Plus, it's not the first time I've kept huge things from him. He never knew what happened with Joel and me at Christmas, though he's seen the aftermath. In January and February I felt lost. If anything, the blackness that descended was worse than the first time Joel let me down, because I felt like such a fool.

Tim didn't push me. Instead, he was kind and he waited, and I see those qualities now for what they are: the mark of someone who is growing up and trying his hardest. However hard it is, I know I made the right decision to be with him. That rebounding between them, like a ball in a pinball machine, had to end.

The confirmation of Elaine's cancer has made me snap out of my self-obsession. Now I am all about the practicalities as we hunker down. I make lasagnas and soups on my days off and parcel them up so Tim can stick a portion in the microwave between study sessions, shoveling it down so fast I'm sure he doesn't notice what he's eating. The system works well for Elaine too, because I can reheat stuff for her when she isn't feeling nauseated.

Though those times are getting rarer. Her weekly chemo is beyond brutal. I go with her when I can, sitting in the overheated therapy room while she endures the poison entering her body, hoping it'll buy her precious extra months. The only thing she's made a fuss about is refusing a central line because she's scared Tim might notice it.

The weather is cold enough that she can hide her cannula under cardigans but they keep having to put in new ones when the blood vessels fail. The bruising makes me want to take her in my arms— she's almost light enough now—and carry her out of the hospital because this isn't going to cure her.

At most, she'll get a few extra months. But she endures it for Tim.

"Oh, I'm colder than the Grampians, Kerry."

"Shall I get a blanket?"

She shakes her head gently. "It's not my body, it's this bloody thing." She's got a cold cap, even though this drug isn't the worst for hair loss, but it's the one thing she knows Tim might notice. He's oblivious to the blue-black patches under her eyes, and the way she's getting smaller and smaller.

As she shrinks, the residual fear I have of her does too. I begin to forgive her what she's done to her son because I see she hasn't treated him any worse than she treats herself. Her response to her own sickness is self-critical to the point of brutality.

"You could take it off, Elaine, for a bit. It won't make a difference, I'm sure."

"No. Only two more weeks to go. I am going to see it through if it's the last thing I do!" She smiles at the irony.

The day after Tim's last exam, and five weeks after diagnosis, Elaine arranges afternoon tea.

We all travel together in Mum's car, with me driving. As Elaine climbs into the passenger seat, I notice how she winces when she pulls the belt across her sore, exhausted body.

"So where are we going?" Tim asks, clambering into the back. He's a little hungover, after going out with Wilcox and the others to celebrate last night.

"It's a surprise," Elaine says.

Not to me. She's treating us to the Grand. It's her money and her choice. Why shouldn't she enjoy every bloody moment that's left? But it does mean that every time Tim walks past this place in the future, he will surely remember the news he's about to hear.

"You're teasing me, Mum." He catches my eye in the rearview mirror as I reverse out of the drive, and smiles. He is as sure as he can be that he's passed, that all the work he's done has paid off.

He chats as we go, about the possibility of a holiday before he starts his first year as a foundation doctor in August. Our local hospitals are popular so can have their pick of the best students. Failing his exams in year four means he's got to accept a less popular location, at least a three-hour drive from here, double that in rush hour.

". . . we could get a last-minute deal self-catering somewhere," he's saying, "maybe near my new base."

I hate knowing that this is all about to be irrelevant.

A liveried porter opens the car door and helps Elaine out, seeming to sense instinctively that she needs to lean on him as she walks up the steps. Another one offers to park the car for me. I'm about to refuse, but Elaine turns and calls out, "Go on, be a devil, hen, it's all my treat. And you don't often hear a Scotswoman telling you that . . ."

The conservatory area is flooded with light: beautiful but exposing. As soon as we sit down, Elaine orders champagne teas, not even checking the price. I've only been here a couple of times in my life, but the smiley, unobtrusive service makes up for the slightly stuffy décor.

"I'm underdressed," Tim says, looking at the two men at the next table, three times his age, wearing smart suits and ties, with matching paisley handkerchiefs.

Two waiters bring the tea stands, laden with treats: triangular sandwiches, golden scones, cakes iced in pastel colors, and dishes of clotted cream and glossy strawberry jam. *Blood and bandages.*

I have zero appetite.

"Well, tuck in," Elaine says. I catch her eye, questioning.

There's no right time to tell Tim, no etiquette on whether you should share a terminal diagnosis before or after a meal. Tim and I practiced *breaking bad news* as a role-play a few times, so I know the basics—a warning shot to prepare someone for the worst, a euphemism-free statement of fact, an expression of sympathy, a question to confirm they've understood fully.

I chew a mouthful of cucumber sandwich, tasting nothing.

And now the pianist is playing "As Time Goes By" and our food is finished and the champagne flutes and teapots are empty and Elaine has still said nothing. I stare at her until she gives me the tiniest of nods.

"I wonder if it's too late for me to learn the piano," Tim is saying, "it's one of those skills that I always thought I might enjoy—"

"Son, I need to tell you something. I only kept it from you so as not to jeopardize your exams. And there's nothing you could have done."

Tim gawps at her. "Is this about Dad?"

She shakes her head. "That scumbag is still hale and hearty, as far as I know. Tim, it's me. I have . . . cancer."

I watch his face and I can see the exact moment that he really *looks* at his mother for the first time in months. "What kind?" he whispers.

"It's pancreatic cancer. I've been having chemo for a wee bit and they think they've put the brakes on but it's a tricksy thing and—"

He talks over her. "I know what pancreatic cancer is like, Mother. I'm a bloody doctor. I know what it does. I—" He stops. His face ages ten years as the glow from the afternoon champagne fades away.

He turns to me. "How long have you known?"

"Five weeks."

"Five—" He thinks for a moment. "So this was why you deferred medical school." His eyes close as though he can shut this out. When he opens them again, he looks furious at the betrayal. "How could you do this? Treating me like a child who can't be trusted . . ."

Seeing him so lost makes tears well up but I have to swallow them back. I touch his arm. "It wasn't like that. Elaine made the choice for your future. You couldn't have done anything to change the treatment. Or the prognosis." That last word was a mistake. Too soon to heap another dose of misery onto his shoulders.

Elaine takes over. "I don't have all that long, Tim. I'm sorry. But let's make the most of the time we do have. Starting today."

I keep my hand on his arm. What would the advice on *breaking bad news* suggest now? Empathy, then a confirmatory question.

Instead, I stand up and wrap my arms around him. After a moment's hesitation, he embraces me back and we stay like that for a few seconds. When he lets me go, I see steeliness in his eyes.

He takes his mum's hand and I see him flinch as he registers the thinness of the skin and the lightness of her bones.

"I did it because I love you, Tim," Elaine says.

He nods. "I know. You did what you thought was best."

That night, in bed, he reaches for me and I think he wants to make love, which hasn't happened since he failed his exams last year. I want to be close to him again, not only as a comfort.

But instead he turns on the bedside light and sits up.

"You've been there for her when I wasn't."

I sit up too. If he's angry, it's part of the process. "Your mum made the decision not to tell you, Tim."

"No, I mean for months. *Years.* It was easier for me to play the precious medical student while you paid the bills and helped Mum when she needed it. Just like it was easier to let people think I helped to save Joel Greenaway's life, when it was you on your own."

"That's a long time ago, Tim, and it doesn't matter—"

"It does. Let me finish, please. I know I can't stop her dying, or change how things have been. The mistakes I've made." He leans across and kisses me on the forehead. "But you and Mum are going to be all I think about this summer. We'll take her to the places she's missed out on. Maybe she wants to go to the Isle of Wight or on the Millennium Wheel in London."

He's speaking faster than usual and he's wired and wide-eyed, racing against the clock to put everything right.

"You do understand it's stage four, don't you, Tim?"

He looks at me and as I look back, I see him as he is now. Not the boy I grew up with, but a man who knows what he has to do.

When people ask how we met, I always say, *We grew up together.* Now I realize that the growing up is only just beginning.

"Yes, Kerry. And I understand it's time for me to make it up to both of you."

41

Joel

April 14, 2005

Leo is the first thing I think about when I wake up and the last thing before I fall asleep.

Leo knows nothing about all the ways I've failed people, though I know I'll have to tell him someday. We're almost at the end of our transition visits, ready for him to come home with me for good in thirteen days. Leo is changing and growing and so am I.

But the waiting is torture. Even though I now have Parental Responsibility, and Zoë gave up fighting before the final hearing, I am still struggling to sleep in case something dreadful happens.

"Penny for them?" Luke sits down next to me. We're in the pub after a Coasters workout session. I usually get a high from leading a class, but not today.

"Bit of family trouble," I say, the understatement of the century.

He grimaces. "I hear you."

Seeing Luke struggle to recover from his cardiac arrest has reminded me of how I felt. Except he seems to be turning the anger in on himself, whereas I lashed out. Neither approach is healthy.

I remember Kerry meeting Luke's wife, Ali, who confided in her that she couldn't sleep for months after his cardiac arrest.

Did Kerry have nightmares after saving me? I never asked.

I try to focus on the present, on Luke, on the flat planes of his face and the anxiety in his eyes. He's not forty yet but his slow recovery has given him the pallor and shadows of a man fifteen years older.

"It gets better."

He frowns. "Well, *you* came through it. You're an inspiration."

"No, mate, I'm a cautionary tale. How to screw everything up when the universe grants you a second chance."

Luke looks astonished. "You don't look like you've screwed it up. You're fit, you've got a lovely girlfriend. A future."

At Christmas, they all assumed Kerry was my girlfriend and I haven't told them what's happened since. I'm beginning to accept it was for the best. When I dropped her birthday card off, I still hoped it might be the start of something new. And when Tim confronted me, and mentioned the triathlon, I thought she'd told him everything.

But when I realized she hadn't, I saw the truth: he is better for her than I could ever be. All I'd ever done is drag her down, make things more complicated.

I hope he gave her the card with the photo of Leo inside, but I have heard nothing from her. Once my son is safely at home with me, I might try one last time. Not because I want to get her back, but to show her I did the right thing in the end.

"But I guess you must miss it," Luke continues, and when I don't reply, he adds, "football?"

I'm about to make some joke when I think about it properly. "Yes," I find myself saying, "I miss it more than almost anything."

"But you've never tried playing again? Not even at amateur level?"

"Couldn't see the point."

"What, there's no point playing unless you're a pro? Try telling that to the kids at my school."

"Or me," one of the other guys chips in. "I lived for my pub team, even though we hadn't scored a goal in two years."

Now they're all adding their football stories.

"We should set up our own team," Luke says, and everyone laughs.

Everyone except Steve, who raises an eyebrow at me.

"You lot laugh but we really could do it," he says, "and with Greenie here to coach us, we might even be half-decent."

I'm ready to tell them *exactly* why it's a dumb idea, but then I stop. They've never been this united. The excitement even starts to rub off on me and I'm agreeing to research grounds where we might be able to have a kickabout.

But it'll blow over. These things do.

When I turn up to the council pitch, I expect it to be me and Steve kicking a ball between the two of us for an hour. But instead, half of the cardiac rehab group shows up, enough for two six-a-side teams.

I've researched walking football, which seems a safe option, but after about twenty minutes of this, a surreal, slo-mo game, everyone demands we switch to the full-speed kind.

I try to stay on the sidelines, coaching them with tough love and affectionate abuse, channeling my old coach Coley.

But Steve won't have it.

"Come on, Greenaway. We wanna see what you're made of."

For the first few minutes, playing feels wrong, even frightening.

But when I take a corner and the ball goes exactly where I wanted it to, I realize how much I've missed this . . .

I lose myself in the game, caring about nothing but how my body and the ball connect. I even forget about the social workers and the paperwork and the suspicion that it could still be for nothing.

But when Steve blows the whistle, Leo is the first thing I think about.

For the first time, I let myself really believe he's going to live with me, and I picture myself teaching him how to play.

42

Tim

JULY 9, 2005

I keep wondering what the last few months would have been like if I hadn't been a doctor.

As Mum's illness has progressed, fast and slow at once, I have pushed for her when she's needed me to, but also fought for respite when the treatment threatens to do more damage than the disease.

Not that there's much more damaging than cancer of the pancreas, an organ so tricky it even gets its own punch line in advice to new surgeons: *eat when you can, sleep when you can, and don't fuck with the pancreas* . . .

"This really is a lovely space," Kerry says as she steps into the room where my mother is going to die. I wheel her in.

We've seen the hospice already, but not this room because until yesterday, it was someone else's haven. I don't know if they died, or went home. I don't *want* to know. Nothing matters except Mum: even the headlines about the bombs in London barely register. We are in a bubble.

Despite all the medical equipment surrounding it, the bed has been made with a sunshine yellow duvet cover. There's a big window with a view of the garden, full of ostentatious summer flowers. Yes, there's a high-backed hospital chair, but cushions disguise the wipeable surface. And instead of a standard-issue laminate locker at the bedside, the nightstand is made of honey pine, old-fashioned but reassuring.

"I will be very happy here," Mum says, and as I help her out of her wheelchair, I believe her.

Kerry and I tried to talk her into hospice at home, but she said she wanted to be "out of the way, so you can still start the next stage of your training without having to nurse me too."

It's true that, time-wise, this is the perfect storm. In twenty-four days, it'll be Black Wednesday, the day junior doctors start their very first job. I will be one of them.

"I'll unpack for you, Elaine, tell me where you want me to put everything." Kerry unzips the suitcase. The hospice people sent a list of what to bring, as though Mum was coming on holiday, albeit a holiday where you spend most of your time in pajamas. The giant paper bag of pills sits on top, but underneath there are books and Kerry's iPod, loaded with Mum's Beatles and Bay City Rollers CDs.

"Where shall we put this?"

Kerry holds up my mother's favorite photograph, of me and Kerry as children, in our St. John's uniforms, gripping our gold and silver medals.

Mum smiles at the picture. The steroids mean that from certain angles, her face has a healthy plumpness, so it looks better than when she "only" had lupus. Her spindly body tells a different story. "Next to me on my bedside table, please!"

I shift her empty suitcase into the bottom of the wardrobe and have a premonition of bringing it home again, packed with her belongings, but lighter without the meds that are maintaining her fragile grip on life.

At first, it's unfamiliar, the stinging behind my eyes. But now I recognize it. Tears. I am not, have never been, a crier, not even when Dad left.

"I could smell cake baking when I came in," I say, forcing myself to turn toward Mum and Kerry in the knowledge that I *can't* cry, not in front of them. "What flavor do you think it is?"

The emotional danger passes, as we speculate: carrot or chocolate or Victoria sponge.

"It's not a sponge," Mum corrects me, "it's Victoria *sandwich*. Don't they teach you the important stuff at medical school?"

She jokes now, sometimes. I don't remember her doing that before.

The nurse arrives to check on the medications and talk through Mum's routine. Kerry and I head for the garden and she links arms with me.

When we reconciled, I worried she was playacting for my mother's sake, but now it feels natural. We've even started making love, and it happens even more often than when we first got together as teenagers.

The closeness has created a kind of positive feedback loop: the more we are together, the better it feels. Oxytocin, maybe.

"I've been thinking . . ." Kerry says.

I turn to look at her. When did she have her hair cut? She's always been pretty, but today she looks beautiful.

"It's dangerous, thinking," I say.

"About your mum, and about us."

I have no idea what is coming, so I wait, eyes closed, braced. And in the moment of waiting, I remember a silver envelope on the doormat, a confrontation, a fear that I'd somehow missed something important.

Did I do the right thing?

"You're different now, Tim. This . . . it's changed you."

I search for words to puncture the seriousness I can hear in her voice. I am afraid of what she might be about to say to me.

"Don't interrupt," she says. How can she read me so well when I can't read her at all?

I bring my finger to my lips, signaling I'll stay silent. There's a bench next to the jasmine and she walks toward it. As I sit down next to her, I feel the warmth of the wood through the fabric of my jeans. The faint teak aroma reminds me of something . . .

Of India.

"I thought perhaps we could get married."

My body jerks. You'd have thought she'd just applied a defib. "Don't joke about things like that," I say.

"Not joking. I've researched how it could work. People can get married in hospices. It's usually patients, but if we do it here, your mum can be part of it."

I let myself imagine standing in this garden in a suit, Kerry in a beautiful dress, her hair pinned up, decorated with flowers. Usually, I have trouble picturing things that haven't happened, but right now it's so real: not only Kerry as a bride but Mum regal in her wheelchair . . . it's perfect, except for one thing.

"You don't have to, Kerry. Not if it's only because she's dying."

She takes a deep breath. "It's not that. I can see you more clearly than I have since we were kids. And what I see is a good man who gets better every day."

It takes ten days to make the arrangements.

The momentum gives the hospice a carnival atmosphere. The chef has created a menu with all Mum's favorites, and someone's ordered a crate of Irn-Bru to celebrate her Scottish heritage.

I emailed Wilcox but he can't get back from his holiday, so Kerry's dad is stepping into the best man role.

He takes me to Moss Bros. I am such an average size that it's no problem finding a suit to rent. As I try it on, it hits me that statistically, half the grooms who've worn this could already be divorced.

"Come on, Tim. Too late to change your mind now."

He hustles me out to a shop in the Lanes and persuades me to buy a silk pocket square and a matching cravat. The print shows an anatomical drawing of a heart, in the deep dark red of venous blood.

The wedding is tomorrow and though we're meant to spend tonight apart, Kerry and I are both at the hospice. The orange evening light falls onto the bed but doesn't add any color to Mum's face. It's clear from the changes she's needed in her meds, and her expression when she thinks I'm not looking, that she's getting sicker faster than we'd hoped.

A couple of times, I even doubted she'd survive till the wedding itself. Part of me wants to sleep alongside her tonight, just in case. But if Death taps her on the shoulder, I think she'll tell it to *piss right off*.

Something makes her wake up. She nods. "There you both are. Good. I need to talk to you, and it's serious."

We know her funeral plans down to the last flower. It's hard to imagine what could be left to discuss. "We're listening," Kerry says.

"What you've done for me is above and beyond." Mum's voice is soft and hoarse, but her Glaswegian accent becomes stronger when she's tired or medicated. "But I must know you're not only getting married for my sake."

"Mum . . ." I start, looking to Kerry for backup.

Silence.

"Kerry?" Mum breaks it. "Look, I have always wanted to see you together, that's no secret. But you mustn't go through with it unless you're quite sure Tim is the man for you. Or I promise I will haunt you forever."

I remember what my mother said that lunchtime in Alfriston, about me being nothing without Kerry. Does she still think I don't deserve her?

As the silence persists, dread coils through me, like smoke. "Mum, do you mind if we go out and talk alone, so—"

Kerry holds up her hand. "No, it's all right." Her gaze is fixed on my mother, so I can't read her eyes at all. "Elaine, you know Tim and I have had our struggles. Living in the same house, you can hardly have missed the bad times.

"We grew apart, but now we've grown together again. Love isn't about big dramas or declarations. It's what we do every day for each other, the little kindnesses. We trust each other. There are no bad surprises. Only good ones, like seeing how he's changed since you got ill."

Mum is still frowning. "He is a decent boy. Mostly. But I don't hear much passion, hen. Are you sure?"

Kerry shakes her head. "Tim and I both know from our work that nothing is ever a hundred percent certain. What's happened to you proves that too. But we are happier together than apart."

And that is it, isn't it? We love each other. I will be the best husband I can be.

My mother closes her eyes, and I wonder if she's fallen asleep. She opens them again with a jolt. "Is that enough?"

"It is for me." Kerry reaches out her hand to take mine. "That is if it's enough for Tim as well?"

I say yes.

I say yes again the next day and it's all exactly as I imagined it.

Better, because I know I am lucky it's happening at all.

Three days later, I sit at Mum's bedside as the lengths between her breaths grow and grow, and I tell her she can leave and I don't know if she hears me, but an hour or so after that, the wait for another breath goes on and on till I know there will never be another. She's gone.

I don't call anyone into the room for a while. Instead, I hold her hand.

"Thank you, Mum. For believing in me, even when you shouldn't have. And fighting for me. And fighting against me when you thought I was doing the wrong thing."

I forgive her too, but I can't speak those words out loud. *I forgive you for blaming me for making you ill and for Dad leaving. I forgive you for being angry so often. And for pushing me harder than I would ever have pushed myself.*

If she hadn't done that, I wouldn't be the man I am, the one who is becoming better.

The funeral is preorganized; all it takes is one call.

I let the tears come. I don't have to pretend to be brave now she is no longer here.

43

Joel

"Shall we interview you here?" the presenter suggests, "with the team warming up behind you?"

The team.

The football thing hasn't blown over. The opposite: six months down the line from that chat in the pub, the Unbeatables are preparing for their first competitive match.

"So, can you start by telling us about your rather unusual football squad?"

I've thought about exactly what to say in advance. Even though it's nearly five years ago, I haven't forgotten how badly my first TV appearance went.

"We're called the Unbeatables and we're a mixed bag of players, men and women, all ages, and a range of abilities. But we've got two things in common. One, we love football. Two, we've had heart problems and that's what brought us together. Four of us have actually died, technically—our hearts stopped—but we've come back from that. So whatever happens when we play our first matches next week, we're always going to be Unbeatable. That's how we got our name."

"And this is a subject that's literally close to your own heart, right? Tell me about that."

"I had a cardiac arrest in 2000 and it ended my football career. I'd played for the Dolphins under-twenty-threes and I dreamed of playing in the Premiership. So do most boys, but in my case, it was so, so close. And that was very disappointing."

The presenter nods off-camera but doesn't ask another question, expecting me to keep talking. And as the light shining in my face dazzles my eyes, I know my answer was glib and I get this mad urge to tell the truth.

"OK. More than disappointing. When my heart let me down, it was the end of everything. I couldn't see that I'd been given another chance, that I was lucky. Instead I felt like a dead man walking."

I'm not seeing the presenter and the cameraman and the sound-man anymore. Instead, I feel as though I'm talking to Kerry.

"People went out of their way to help me but I threw it back in their faces. Got into trouble. Hurt my friends, family members. I was selfish, and a lot of what I did was unforgivable.

"But the guys behind me . . . they're not like that. They're brave and strong and they've come together to create something amazing. Watch them play, see the joy it gives them. What doesn't kill you really does make you stronger. And I want to thank them for showing me how crazy I've been for turning my back on what was once my whole world. Being in this team has reminded me why I love football so much. It's more than a game. It's life."

The presenter nods. *There's your sound bite,* I think.

I am not telling the whole truth. Leo, not football, is my reason for living, but he's too precious to share. Being his dad is not only the toughest thing I've ever done, it's also the most important.

But football is allowed to come second.

The presenter calls next day. I know enough about TV to ask straightaway if they're dropping the piece.

"No, it's the opposite. When we viewed the rushes, we were blown away. We'd like to follow you guys all the way through your first season for our regional documentary slot."

I agree, because of the others. But when the camera crew comes back, I'm much more careful about what I say, because I want to protect Leo and myself.

Transmission is two days before Leo's birthday and four days before Christmas, so the program couldn't matter less to me. Mum has abandoned her sophisticated décor preferences and gone full tinsel, so the house looks like a cross between a Turkish bazaar and an infants' school hall.

Her love for Leo has helped me understand her more. What producers and directors have seen as stroppiness is really the fierce tenacity of someone who fought her way out of poverty, and will fight to keep her family above water, no matter what.

I hold my squirming son in my arms as he points at the red and green garlands. Suddenly I realize Leo will probably end up going to the same primary school as me. How weird and amazing it's going to feel to drop him off at the gates on his first day . . . I know he might struggle academically, but he's already doing better than we were told to expect.

I'm in the kitchen when the doorbell rings. Sounds like carol singers and Mum heads off to answer it. In her newfound grandmotherly mode, she'll probably bung them twenty quid to do an entire concert for Leo in our entrance hall.

But moments later, the kitchen is full of Unbeatables.

"Surprise!" Luke says, pushing a bottle of wine into my hand. He's made so much progress since we started playing, even going back to work part-time.

Mum has set up Dad's snug as a viewing room, pulling down the massive screen down like we're going to watch a movie. As we take our seats, I'm slightly irritated by the fuss. Yet as the title music plays, and she plonks Leo on my lap, the others seem so excited that it's started to rub off on me . . .

"Football is the beautiful game," the presenter says as she stands outside the entrance to the pitch where we train, "and it's usually played by beautiful people like Beckham: superfit young players who often model in their spare time.

"But in this ground, there are players who won't be getting any modeling contracts anytime soon. Some are old, some are carrying a few extra pounds, most are out of condition."

"Oi!" Steve shouts out. "That's plain rude."

". . . one thing in common. They've all cheated death. It's a feat more impressive than a hat trick. But as they prepare for their first ever season as a team, will the Unbeatables meet their match? Let's find out . . ."

Mum and I exchange a glance, raising our eyebrows at the cheesiness of the script. No one else seems to mind: they cheer as the shot changes to reveal all of us, in our full out-of-condition glory.

"But they do have a secret weapon," the voice-over says, as the camera zooms in on me. *Ugh*.

When the presenter introduces me, my teammates cheer and I feel like a fraud. I swig my alcohol-free beer, wishing it was the real thing.

In my lap, Leo has stopped wriggling. He faces the screen, and as the shot lingers on me, his arm rises and he points a chubby finger.

"Dadda!" he says and turns his head back toward me and does a double take straight out of a comedy film. "Dadda!" He sounds confused and I hold my breath, in case he starts sobbing in that inconsolable way that always breaks my heart.

But as he repeats the action—looking at the screen, then me—I hear the best sound in the world.

Leo starts to laugh and I join in and so does everyone else and it was *almost* worth all the filming for the joy and love in this moment.

I have missed knowing I belong.

On Leo's first birthday, I text Zoë but it comes back as undeliverable.

He has a brilliant day, and a terrible day, and a boring day, and a sleepy day: all normal for him and us.

When I finally put him to bed, I watch him. It is the calm after the storm, his perfect skin lit by the night-light, his eyelids flickering as he dreams. This love is bigger than anything I've ever felt or can imagine feeling.

This time last year . . . No, don't go there. Don't punish yourself by thinking what might have been, if you'd only played things differently.

I don't want Kerry back. Bollocks, that's a lie. I do, I probably always will, but she's made her choice. Yes, there were times over the summer when I was so tempted to drive around there, talk to her in person this time, even introduce her to Leo. Then my mother heard from someone in the shop that Tim's mum had died of cancer and I knew it was time to move on.

I lean in close to kiss Leo's forehead and his breath warms my face. If Kerry hadn't pushed me, I might have thought the love I shared with her was the only kind there is.

But what I feel for my son has made realize *this* is the love that I needed to give and receive. This is the love that has healed my dys-functional heart.

$-\Lambda\Lambda$ 44

Kerry

Parachute jumps are easy.

For real terror so bad you end up with *actual* shooting pains, nothing beats med school interviews.

"Sorry we're running a bit late, but you're up next," the uni administrator tells me, and I smile, even though what I want to do is run away.

I don't remember it being this bad when I was seventeen and believed that with enough hard work, I could make life go exactly according to plan.

Now I'm older but not much wiser. The waiting room is full of sixth formers: only six years between me and them, but it might as well be sixty. They look so fresh and hopeful and I can't imagine how the panel will be able to judge which might grow up to be decent doctors, and which should never be let within five hundred yards of a patient.

The "kids" have all been chatting about their applications and aptitude test scores and though they haven't deliberately excluded me, I've kept quiet. Even though I have the right grades at last, one of my four choices didn't call me for an interview. I'm still waiting to hear if the two entrance panels I *did* attend liked me enough to choose me over a malleable teen.

Today is my last chance.

"Kerry Smith, please?"

As I stand up, the room seems to sway, but I take a breath to center myself before I follow the assistant into the corridor, toward the interview room.

Come on, Kerry, I tell myself, *you've saved people's lives, this should be a doddle.*

I open the door and see the panel sitting in front of me, silhouetted against the bright sun streaming through the window. Here goes.

Afterward, I try to call Tim but it goes to voicemail and I leave a message.

> Hi. I guess you might be delving into someone's small bowel, but call me when you get a chance. It went all right, I think. A bit more old school than the other two interviews, but nothing I couldn't handle. Except we've got some hideous tea break chat ordeal to get through now, bet I end up spilling boiling liquid over someone. Speak later.

Tim hasn't been back home for a fortnight and I miss him. He's halfway through his second rotation, in GI surgery, and the hours are so insane that he's now staying in digs when he's rostered on for several days. Driving home would be too dangerous.

Is that why I still don't feel married? Elaine dying only days after our wedding meant we spent our honeymoon period waiting for her funeral. The day after, Tim started his training while I went back to work.

At least I've found a kind of peace alone in the bungalow, sorting

Elaine's meager things into piles: keep, charity shop, rubbish. Tim hasn't had enough time to mourn her—doctor foundation training cannot accommodate personal tragedies—and when we do spend time together, he behaves oddly. Sometimes he's distant, almost dreamy. Other days, he's hyper. But he's still going to NA and surely that has to mean he's not back on the pills . . .

"Miss Smith!"

I turn toward the voice, already knowing it belongs to Mr. New-combe, the patrician surgeon who chaired the panel. My smile falters as he looks pointedly at my ring finger.

"Though, if I'm not mistaken, this suggests you're not a Miss at all?"

I nod. "Well spotted! I got married last July. My husband has just started his first foundation year in the Marine health region."

"Can't win 'em all, eh?" he says, and I can't tell whether he's referring to my marriage or the fact that Tim's training placement is seen as a backwater. "What can I get you?"

I ask for a black coffee, wondering if I should have offered to serve *him* instead. Behind him, I see the other candidates gathering, ready for their turns to impress him.

He hands me my coffee. He's probably in his mid-fifties but has a silver fox aura about him, well-groomed hands and an expensive suit that makes him look slimmer than he is. He hasn't shared his specialty but I can imagine he'd make a mint privately in gynecology. "So, is Smith your name or your husband's?"

"Mine. I am quite attached to it, as I've lived with it my whole life."

"How long have you and your husband been together?"

My smile falters but I can't think of a polite way to tell him it's none of his bloody business. "We were always friends but it turned into more in the last few years."

"How sweet," he says. "And children?"

I shake my head. "No."

His expression doesn't change. I guess he must have decades of practice, whether he's breaking the best or the worst news. "Of course, you'll be in your early thirties by the time you make it into your foundation years if you start medicine this September, won't you?"

I did arithmetic at school, so funnily enough, I have worked that out. "I'll be just thirty, actually."

"Your early thirties, as I said. There are plenty of happy medic couples, though mostly they started out at the same time, so by the time that biological clock starts ticking, the female should be on track to finish her GP training or whatever tedious family-friendly area she's picked also. You're taking it to the wire!" He laughs, as though we're sharing this joke.

I have no idea how to respond. It would have been illegal to raise this in the interview itself, but this chat is deniable, his word against mine.

Do I lie and tell him I'm infertile? "I don't want kids. I'm happy staying an auntie."

As I say the words, it occurs to me they might well be true.

"Good for you, Miss Smith. And your husband feels the same way?"

"He's incredibly supportive. As I have been of him throughout his training. It's my turn now."

Mr. Newcombe says nothing, and before I can change the subject, a couple of the sixth formers launch themselves at him. The coffee tastes stale. I have a sense that my wedding ring has made whatever I said in my interview utterly pointless.

I am down to two chances of getting what I want.

On the train home, my anger at the way the surgeon dismissed me festers.

Even though I loathe his blatant sexism, it's made me wonder why Tim and I have never discussed having kids. During his training, he even enjoyed obstetrics, but it never led to a discussion about us having a family one day.

I can't imagine Tim as a father. It seems too messy, too risky, too full of uncertainties to be something he'd want to do. And although I don't blame him for his struggles with empathy, could I make up for that lack if we had a child?

I let myself into the bungalow, still half-expecting to hear the trill of Elaine's *hello there, hen*. I bend down to pick up the post: bills and more bills. We should sell up, clear the debts, buy a smaller flat, but there's no point till we know if I've got a place at med school, and where.

As I rifle through the envelopes, the last one is addressed to me. It has an NHS frank, and for a moment, I am convinced that somehow today's interview panel have conspired to get my rejection to me even faster than I could travel back.

My mood plummets even further when I realize it must have come from one of my other two interviews. The envelope isn't thick enough for it to be good news. Still, I open it.

Dear Miss Smith, Thank you for attending our interview day. I'm sorry to inform you . . .

Disappointment feels like a wave of physical pain. On paper, I have everything they're asking for. I have worked *so bloody hard*. The first time I failed, I knew that my exam results weren't *me*, they were a result of what I'd done or hadn't done.

The years between then and now were tough, but there was still the promise of something better ahead. I had, as all the teachers said, all the time in the world.

But life moves on. Miss has become Mrs. Tim is Dr. Palmer. Everything has changed. Maybe I've been fooling myself by believing I might ever become a doctor.

45

Tim

FEBRUARY 6, 2006

Grief has peeled away the thick skin that used to protect me from the world.

So many things now have the potential to floor me: a patient being unexpectedly kind, a memory sparked by the smell of apple crumble in the canteen. It's over six months since Mum died, but the emotional ups and downs are still way more dramatic than any I have induced pharmacologically.

"OK, and Beds 4 and 6 are stable?"

I nod at Debbie, the doctor who is taking over for the night shift. "Yeah, though after the day we've had, you might want to keep your fingers crossed at all times."

Two patients have died today, one expected, one not. The latter was a guy in his fifties whose liver cancer had stripped away everything but his charm. I liked him a lot.

"You look shattered, Tim."

I shrug. It's not done to show weakness on the ward. My childhood was the perfect training for this.

"It's been a long day but it's nothing a pint won't fix," I tell my colleague, though I rarely drink now because that releases my feelings in an unstoppable tide.

Outside, the darkness welcomes me, after the unremitting brightness of the ward lights.

I check my phone and my heart sinks when I see four missed calls from Kerry. It was her last interview today. On the voicemail, she sounds downhearted and I have to steel myself to call her. I *want* to be supportive, but even at stable times, I am better at practicality than empathy.

And now is not a stable time.

"Bad shift?" she asks when she picks up.

"Ah, same old. Busy. Sorry not to call sooner. How did it go?" I cross the road, into the estate.

As she tells me about some old fart of a surgeon giving her the third degree about being married, it startles me. I can't quite believe Kerry is my wife, though it's one of the things patients and nurses always ask about. Being married seems to make me a little more attractive to the women I encounter.

Guilt makes me flinch. *Must try harder.*

"What was his problem?"

"Kids. He was implying that it'd be a waste of time training me because I'd only run off and have kids."

I wait for her to scoff but she doesn't. I've always assumed she thinks the same way as me, that kids are for other people.

Except I'm not sure about that anymore. My first placement down here was in pediatrics. Maybe it was because Mum had been so sick, but it was a revelation to see how kids bounced back so fast. It was even more surprising to discover that I *liked* spending time with them. That children are people too.

So much has changed since last August.

Kerry is waiting for me to say something.

"You don't want to train at a school that endorses that level of outdated prejudice," I say, though in reality, dinosaurs exist in every hospital and she'll probably have to face far worse.

"I want to train *somewhere*. I'm running out of options."

I make a soothing noise. "It'll happen. You were born to be a doctor."

She says nothing for a while.

"You are coming home at the weekend, aren't you, Tim? It's lonely in the bungalow without you."

Her vulnerability feels like another demand on my limited resources. "Of course. Look, we'll find a way to sort this out between us, we always do."

I say this more because I know it's expected than because I really believe it's true.

My landlady is out, which is a relief. She talks too much. My room is the cheapest one I could find, coffin-size and shared with a suspended skeleton. My landlady's not a medic, and I haven't dared to ask why she owns one in case the answer makes it even harder to sleep.

I open a cider—one of the local habits I've been happy to embrace—and wait for the alcohol to perfuse. But even after I've finished the bottle, I can't shake this feeling that I've missed something important.

Is it because I'm worried about Kerry? She deserves a place at med school, but that doesn't mean it'll happen. The number of places on offer is finite and some people have to apply several times. Yet I fear she won't apply again; the rejection will be too much for her.

Still I'm unsettled. Why? The deaths on the ward shook me, but for once, I don't feel like crying. I take out the notebook I use to reflect on my practice.

As I write, I go through my usual list of prompts. *What did I do well, what could I improve upon?* Most days, I can list half a dozen answers to the second question, but my errors are never serious or irreversible. Next, I ask myself, *What would a good doctor have done?* This question challenges me more. The pragmatist in me knows one day I might end up competent, but I can't ever see myself being *good*.

Even as I put away the notebook, something still gnaws at me. But I'm too knackered to let it keep me awake . . .

I come to in an instant, my body knowing it's very early before my brain does.

The bleep. Shit shit *shit*.

I leap out of bed expecting to feel smooth hospital lino under my feet, but instead, it's carpet, followed by the rattle of bones as my ankle hits my landlady's skeleton.

What the fuck am I doing at home? If it's a crash call, I'll never get there in time and—

My phone vibrates on the floor. It's not the bleep, it's someone ringing me.

I'm not on call, *it's OK*.

Except it's a private number, which usually means the hospital and it's not even 6:00 A.M. and—

Just fucking answer it.

"Hello. Dr. Palmer speaking."

"Hi, Tim. Listen it's Fred Dornan."

My consultant is really sound. He hasn't forgotten what it's like to be a junior, though I've never heard him sound so stern.

"I need you to come in before your shift, ideally now."

I sit up. "What's happened, is it an accident or—"

He coughs. "It's one of our patients. Mrs. Lomas."

I can't picture her. "What's wrong?"

"OK, so she's gone into anaphylactic shock and it looks like a prescribing error. We need to get your statement before you come on duty."

I blink. *Prescribing error.* "Is she all right?"

A long, long pause, during which I do remember her: a woman in her late thirties, who'd had a cholecystectomy. Routine stuff. I can picture her children too, being told off by the head nurse for running up and down the corridor.

"Don't panic, Tim. But I do need you to come in as soon as you can."

This is real.

Mrs. Lomas is allergic to the penicillin I prescribed for a wound infection at her operation site. I didn't know about the allergy, but I didn't check for it either. It would have been there, somewhere in her notes.

And because I didn't check, she's now in ICU and there is a significant risk she will never wake up.

I describe the steps I took and everything I can remember about her treatment. The human resources woman tapes my statement so there can be no comeback later.

There is a protocol for this.

Fred Dornan's voice is calm again, but he won't quite meet my eye, and I am asked if I am prepared to take today as leave. I then have five scheduled days off till I'm due on shift again next week.

By that time, we may have a clearer picture of what's what.

The words sound as though they're coming from a long way away.

I go to the mess and remove everything from my locker. Debbie, my night shift opposite number, comes in. I brace myself for an outburst because I know the other foundation doctors will have to take up the slack while I'm away.

But instead, she puts her hand on the locker door. "Hey, I'm sure it'll be all right."

She knows already. They will all know by the end of today.

"How can you be sure, Debbie? I don't think anyone knows what's going to happen to Mrs. Lomas."

She sighs. "It's shit. But human beings make mistakes. Mostly they get picked up but this time you were unlucky."

"Not as unlucky as my patient."

"Look. They say every doctor will have one, a patient we'll never forget. There but for the grace of God or whoever the patron saint of junior doctors is."

There is no grace, no God. Somehow I've always known this moment would come and now it has, I am numb, for the first time in six months.

I manage a half smile, for Debbie's sake, and I carry my box of stuff down in the lift and along the corridor and out the back, the same route I took on my way home eleven hours ago. At that exact moment, Mrs. Lomas must have been receiving the drug her body would reject with an attack that could take out her own organs as collateral damage.

When I get back to my digs, it's still not quite light and my landlady's bedroom curtains are closed. I tiptoe into the flat and grab my bag, leaving a note for her, and take a taxi to the station.

I should call Kerry now. I take my phone out, ready to dial.

But I can't do it.

I can't bear to hear her voice when she realizes how badly I've screwed up this time.

The only consolation is that my mother will never find out.

As I board the train to Brighton, I send a text. The reply comes back immediately:

COME OVER. WHATEVER IT IS, IT CAN BE FIXED xxx

46

Kerry

I wake up feeling sick, remembering what happened at my interview yesterday.

I wait for the nausea to pass, but instead it keeps building and I rush into the bathroom to throw up.

It doesn't make me feel any better.

The nausea comes again and this time I am sick for way, way longer. I stand up, dig around in the bathroom cabinet for a sachet of rehydration salts. I tip the contents into the tooth mug, suddenly too knackered to go to the kitchen for a fresh glass, and I try to force down the salty-sweet liquid.

When I catch sight of my reflection in the mirror, for a moment, I hardly recognize myself, my eyes wide and my complexion deathly pale.

But there's something else that's different about me.

I can't catch my breath.

Because I must have realized it subconsciously but not been able to admit to myself until now.

I board the train, knowing I can't wait till the weekend to talk to Tim. I tried to call him but his mobile was switched off, and the phone is no good for this kind of news either. He's smarter now. Thanks to the work we've done together to help him read emotions, he can usually locate the most appropriate thing to say in the majority of situations. But his *face* can't lie and I need to be with him to know how he really feels about us having a baby.

A baby.

Even as I peed on the test stick I bought from the pharmacy at Seven Dials, it felt like a cliché from a soap opera. The feckless woman, the unwanted pregnancy.

Except I'm not feckless. I'm on the pill, though there were times last year when I wondered why, because Tim and I pretty much stopped having sex.

The last time we made love was New Year's Eve. We celebrated surviving the year, as individuals and as newlyweds. As the fireworks went off over the city, he clung to me and I clung to him. Our love-making was noisy, because we don't have to keep quiet anymore.

I was drunk too, a rare thing for me. Did I forget my pill? No, that's not something I'd do. My stomach was upset for a day or two over Christmas, because of all the comfort food we ate, but could that really have stopped the pill working? I sigh: looking back is pointless now. It's the future that's the bigger issue . . .

The train isn't that busy but there is a mother with a small baby, sitting diagonally across the aisle. I stare at them now with the same intensity Marilyn had when she was trying to get pregnant.

But I'm not coveting the baby, I'm studying his mother. She looks tired, yes, but not out of her depth. The paraphernalia she's brought seems manageable and she still looks capable of conversation.

Perhaps letting this happen wouldn't be the worst thing, especially if I'm not going to be a doctor. I could stay with the ambulance service, go part-time, share childcare with Marilyn, who has baby

Alfie now as well as Ava. Being a *younger* mum isn't all bad either. You bounce back sooner, don't you?

The train pulls into a station and the woman gets off. There are another twenty or so stops before I get to Tim.

That's when it'll feel real. When I see his face, it'll tell me if this is something we can do together.

Even though, I guess, it's something we've already done.

The hospital is a fraction of the size of the Sussex, yet I can't find my husband.

"He's meant to be on shift," I tell the nurse once I get to the gastroenterology ward.

She shakes her head. "I don't know about that."

Behind her, a junior doctor looks up from tapping into the computer. He meets my eye for a moment, before hurriedly returning to whatever it is he's doing.

"What's going on?"

No one replies.

The unsettled feeling in my belly tells me something's up. "Is he sick? You have to tell me because right now I'm fearing the worst."

Back on drugs? Surely not after everything he put me through . . .

The nurse sighs. "The relatives' room is over there. I'll see if I can find the registrar."

The room is nicer than they usually are. The little potted rose is coming into bloom, the magazines are new, and I can just about see treetops through the high window. I crave cities, but I'd hoped a quieter deanery might be the perfect space for Tim to develop his skills. It feels safe.

Felt safe. Now it feels anything but. Has he been attacked? Or caught stealing drugs? My chest tightens, pain spreading across my shoulders.

Tim's boss steps into the room. Young, balding, so tall that the room suddenly feels half the size. He introduces himself. His name is Fred but I don't register his surname because I'm more worried about the fact he's the consultant, the *boss*. This is bad.

I try to read his body language—warm handshake, anxious eyes.

"Tim hasn't called you?"

I shake my head.

"There's been an . . . incident. He's taken leave for a few days, I assumed he'd gone home. Brighton, isn't it?"

At least Tim's not sick or off his head on something. "What sort of incident?"

"I can't go into detail but it involves a patient. It would be better if he could tell you himself."

"Yes it bloody would, but he's not fucking here, is he?" I regret the words as soon as I've said them. "Sorry. I'm sorry, I'm just . . ." Tears are welling up.

Hormones. *Pregnancy* hormones, already? Everything is out of control.

"Oh, Mrs. Palmer—"

"My name's Kerry and you don't need to mollycoddle me. I'm in the ambulance service. I know there's no way you'd give a foundation year doctor leave unless it was serious."

He nods and sits down next to me. "You're right. It's serious, though we've . . . contained things. The patient involved is showing some early signs of a recovery. I don't want to preempt the process but every junior doctor makes mistakes and with the right training and attitude, it doesn't have to mean the end for Tim."

"Does *he* know that?" I shake my head. "Sorry. Stupid. You can't know the answer to that without being a mind reader, and even if you were, Tim's mind would be *very* difficult to read."

"The thing is—" His bleep goes off, and as he stands up, I half-expect him to bang his head on the ceiling. "Is there a family member or friend he might have gone to see? To talk it through, lick his wounds?"

He doesn't have time to wait for an answer but there isn't one anyway.

Now Elaine has gone, Tim only has me.

I call him again as I walk toward his digs. It goes straight to voicemail, like before.

"Where the hell are you, Tim? Whatever's happened, we can fix it."

My bloody mantra: let's fix this, let's put things right. My mending mania, the compulsion that means I am always there when I am needed, so I can get that buzz when it all works out . . .

His landlady tells me she hasn't seen him face-to-face since last Wednesday. "But he woke me up this morning, because he slammed the door behind him, like he was in a temper or a rush?"

I search his room methodically, revolted at myself but also hating him for turning me into a paranoid, snooping wife who is searching for . . .

What? Infidelity? Not the Tim I know. But this brings back memories of when I had to do this two years ago, turning the bungalow upside down to find out why he *really* failed his exams.

St. Kerry swung into action then. Rescuing *him* wasn't enough: while I was at it, I had Joel locked up above Ant's café, "fixing" him too. I never doubted my own magic. After all, I'd brought someone back to life. Everything else is easy compared to that . . .

My head and shoulders throb and my belly churns, as though the tiny life inside me is already reminding me it has a heartbeat too.

For the first time, I let myself consider that Tim might have taken his own life.

No. He couldn't do that to me.

Unless he felt there was no other way to escape.

There is nothing left for me to do here, so I walk back toward the station, the cold air making my chest hurt even more. I board the train home and try another call. This time, the voicemail doesn't kick in straightaway. As his number rings and rings,

It's Tim here. Or, to be exact, not here. Please leave a message.

You have to tell me what's going on. You can't run away from me, from whatever this is.

I watch my phone for the whole journey but no message appears. At Brighton, I catch a bus from the station to the hospital and go looking for Laura. She's the only person I can think of who Tim still sees or talks to. If she doesn't know anything, I have no other ideas.

I find her in the diabetes clinic. When I tell her what's happened, she looks shifty.

"You knew?" I try to read her face. "Are you . . . the two of you? You're not *together* again, are you?"

"No! I'm very happily engaged, OK?" She scoffs. "Bloody Tim, I can't believe he's put me in this position."

"If you know where he is, please tell me. I have to talk to him."

She exhales. "All right. Let me get a pen."

Six years of taking 999 calls has given me a complete mental A–Z of the city. The address Laura gives me is under a mile away but I'm so exhausted that I get a taxi.

The flat is in a nondescript modern block behind Preston Park. When I buzz the intercom, a woman answers.

"Hello?"

"My name is Kerry Smith. I've been told this might be where my husband is staying."

The connection goes dead. Is this real? Part of me wants to go home, curl up under the duvet, pretend it's yesterday.

The lock buzzes. "Third floor."

As I climb the stairs, the weariness of the six-hour round trip makes me light-headed.

A woman answers the door. Angular, but attractive, with dark, oval eyes that bore into mine. "I'm Maria."

I want to ask: are you my husband's lover? Instead, I manage, "He's here?"

"Come through." She has an accent—Spanish or Italian.

Tim stands by the window, his face dark and strained against the brightness of the winter light.

I step forward and, without planning to, slap him hard across the cheek. My fingers sting. He flinches but says nothing.

"How *dare* you run away, after everything?"

His eyes dart about, settling on anything except me. Behind us, the living room door closes softly. This room is nothing like the bungalow: it's sparsely but tastefully furnished from charity shops. Neat piles of books serve as lamp tables. No TV.

Perhaps they're too busy talking—or screwing—to need distractions.

Stars appear at the edge of my vision. "I need to sit down."

That startles him out of his self-pity and he grabs my arm, steering me toward the sofa, just in time to stop me falling. "Kerry. It's OK, I've got you."

I try to will myself not to faint. I need answers. Now. But there are so many unknowns that my head spins trying to work out where to begin.

"What have you done, Tim? The hospital . . . there was a patient . . . your consultant said . . ." The words come but in the wrong order and the harder I try, the more stars I see and even though I've never fainted in my life before, I know the blackness is coming and a part of me welcomes it.

47

Tim

The call handler recognizes her name.

"*Our* Kerry Smith?"

My Kerry Smith. Did I do this to her?

"Yes. She collapsed and I've got her on the floor, in recovery position, but I think . . . I think she's going into shock. She's border-line tachycardic at ninety but her BP has been dropping and she's in and out of consciousness."

"We've got a vehicle on route. Is there external bleeding? Vaginal, anal?"

I look down at her groin. No sign of discharge. I should remove her trousers to make sure but doing that here, in Maria's living room, seems indecent.

Get a grip, you stupid bastard. I begin to fumble with her belt . . .

"Tim—" Kerry's mouth goldfishes and I lean in.

"The ambulance is coming, Kerry, it's going to be OK."

"I came here . . . went there . . . to tell you . . ."

"It can wait. Don't try to talk, focus on breathing."

"No! Listen to me!" She grimaces from the effort.

"Where is the pain? Show me."

As she gestures up toward her shoulder, I try to think what it could mean. "Just that side?"

She nods.

Shit. Her vital signs tell me this has to be more than a muscle injury. Referred pain, then? It suggests internal bleeding, but where and why? *Think.*

"I'm . . . pregnant."

At least, I think that's what she says. I repeat. "Pregnant?"

The call handler repeats it back to me. "Kerry's pregnant? OK. How many weeks?"

"It's what I needed to . . . why I came," Kerry says breathlessly.

I close my eyes. I think about the last time we had sex. "New Year?"

She nods.

"Early," I tell the operator, "no more than five weeks."

There is a long pause and I think the call handler must reach the same conclusion as me at the very same moment.

"They'll be with you very soon. I'll let them know what to expect . . ."

The surgeon steps into the room. "Is Mr. Smith here?"

"That's me. Kind of."

Miss Eliades does a double take. "Shit, it's Tim, isn't it? I'm so sorry but I've forgotten your surname."

"Palmer. Don't worry, it's been two years since I did my rotation with you. Kerry is my wife. Is she . . . has it gone OK?"

"Yes." She nods, though there is caution in her eyes. "Let's sit down. The abdominal bleed was significant, but she's had three units and she's otherwise healthy so I would expect her to make a full recovery. Except, well, as I'm sure you know, unfortunately, there was no way an ectopic pregnancy could progress so . . . I'm sorry, she's lost the baby."

The "baby" I didn't even know about until three hours ago.

I don't say that. "It was very early, wasn't it?"

"Around five weeks. Her left fallopian tube has been too badly damaged to repair, but as you know, with monitoring, she should be able to have a normal pregnancy in the future."

"Right."

"Would you like me to take you to recovery now?"

As we walk down these familiar corridors, I wonder if Kerry will refuse to see me, because of what I've done. But her folks and sister are on holiday in the Canaries so it's me or no one, though I guess she'll have a steady stream of work friends once she's on the ward.

The nurse steps aside as I approach the bed. Kerry's makeup-free face reminds me of the first time I saw her, the day after we moved into the bungalow, and her sister drenched us with a hose before Kerry dried us off and we ate four packets of Wagon Wheels to make us feel better.

"Hey." I kiss her forehead. She smells of disinfectant, but underneath that, I can almost taste Tropical Sun coconut tanning oil and the warm PVC of the Smiths' paddling pool . . .

"I went all the way to your hospital to tell you about the baby," she says, her voice hoarse from intubation. "As soon as I realized, I came."

"Don't worry. It's all going to be all right, you—"

"Who is Maria?"

"We shouldn't do this now. You've only just come around."

Her eyes fix onto mine. "I'm not that woozy. And it's not like I'm going to forget."

I get closer so people can't overhear us. "Maria is a friend from NA."

"I didn't think you had any friends except me."

Ouch. I don't respond.

Kerry winces, though I don't think she can be feeling physical pain. "She looked like a lot more than a friend. Do you love her, Tim?"

I don't have time to invent a lie. "I don't know."

Kerry closes her eyes and I hope she's drifted into sleep again. But when she opens her eyes again, they're full of reproach.

"I . . . I haven't cheated on you, Kerry, I promise. We're close but nothing like that has happened."

Yet.

When Maria first showed up at NA last March, I tried so hard to keep my distance. And when we did start talking properly, after a few months, I told myself that our connection was about our shared commitment to staying clean, nothing more than that. I convinced myself we only swapped numbers so we could keep each other on track if our resolve weakened.

But some things you cannot ignore. Like the fact that when we're together—or even when we've talked for hours on the phone—everything feels crisp and sharp, in a way even Wilcox and Joel's supplies never achieved.

With her I feel—possibly for the first time ever—it's all right to be me.

"Why did you go to her after things went wrong, and not come home to me?"

"Please, Kerry."

"Don't you dare fob off a sick woman, Tim."

"I went to Maria's because I didn't want to disappoint you again," I say, tentatively, watching her face. When she stays silent, I add, "When I see your expression after yet another one of my failures, I feel terrible."

"But Maria loves you as you are, is that it?" she says sarcastically.

"I don't know about love but . . . she knew *me* before she ever knew or cared about me being a doctor."

"That's unfair. So did I. I've only ever wanted to help you be what *you* wanted, Tim."

She's right. But till Maria, I've never had the guts to tell anyone outright that I didn't want a life of patients and crises and gossipy doctors' messes. That I don't want to be a doctor at all.

The porter comes through the double doors, ready to move her onto the ward. He coughs. "Ready to rumble? Heigh-ho, it's off to gynecology we go!"

The nurse gets the drip and monitors ready to move, and I prepare to walk with them.

"Go home, Tim. You look knackered and I need sleep. Come tomorrow. I'll need you then."

I consider arguing but I can see from Kerry's face there's no point. I lean in to kiss her lips and she moves her head so my lips graze her cheek instead.

Home hasn't felt like home since Mum died, not really, and as I unlock the front door into the hallway full of pictures, I long for the minimalism of Maria's place. I hang up my coat and see that the 2005 Scottish Lochs and Castles calendar still shows a misty photograph from last July because neither Kerry nor I have noticed it needed changing.

I take a shower and pour myself a large brandy, knocking it back fast so that the roughness doesn't linger too long on my throat. I run a bath with Mum's favorite Fenjal bath oil because there's a part of me that wants to trigger memories and let all the emotion and guilt spill out, now that I am alone.

I've messed up so many times, starting that bloody night on the lawns. My failed exams. My disgusting drug use. Mrs. Lomas, who I almost killed with my stupid mistake. My career. My future.

Our marriage.

Our baby.

Why has it taken me this long to realize that my mother got it wrong? She believed I was meant to be great, but I never had it in me.

The house wakes me up with its familiar sounds. The heating creaks on, the post whispers through the letter box. I call the ward: Kerry had a comfortable night. I call her parents and update them before I text her to say *good morning*. When I don't get a reply, I remember I brought her phone home with me to recharge. When it turns back on, the screen lights up with worried messages from her colleagues. News travels fast.

I start packing a bag for her: a pot of Nivea face cream, the book on her bedside table. Something to replace the nasty hospital night-gown? I pull out the drawers and look for old clothes she won't mind throwing away afterward.

The red T-shirt at the bottom is good quality: that would be soft on her body. I unfold it. The logo on the front looks familiar. I turn it over. *Lyonshall Manor Mini-Triathlon, July 2004.*

Instantly, I know why it looks familiar. I picture Joel, at the top end of Hazelmere Crescent, his broad chest filling out an identical T-shirt.

He was there with her. The weekend she was deciding whether to leave me.

I sink down onto the bed.

Maybe I always knew it. Even someone as dense as me couldn't completely ignore the fizz and buzz whenever they were together, like an unstable current. I almost allowed myself to acknowledge it last year, when he delivered that card and I sensed there was some-thing more.

But I chose to ignore my gut.

Was she unfaithful? I want to believe she wasn't. But even if they didn't have sex, I know now that you can be unfaithful just by hold-ing hands.

I get up, tear around the house, put the washing on, clear up the kitchen. Anything to stop the noise. But it doesn't work, my brain speeds up, recalibrating our shared history. Me, Kerry, Joel, locked together, since the last minutes of 1999.

I should hate him, and her. Instead, I think of Maria. Before I met her, I was utterly skeptical about the idea of fate, or the idea that there was The One. I wouldn't say I am now a believer, but I am open to the possibility that some things were meant to be.

Maria and me.

Joel and Kerry?

Should I call him? He would want to know she's sick because . . . well, you do want to know when you love someone.

I pick up my phone and stare at it for five long minutes before I start to type.

> Joel. Kerry is in hospital. She's OK. She had a small operation, but it went fine. She didn't ask me to tell you and I don't know if you're even in touch these days but I thought you should know. Brunswick Ward. She'll be in a few more days, I should think. Tim.

A message pings back almost instantly.

> Thank you.

Still, I'm waiting for the anger to kick in. I walk into the hall and retrieve the post. There is a letter for me from my boss, asking me to call HR at my earliest convenience to organize the disciplinary.

I don't think I am ever going back.

Under the junk, there are two letters for Kerry, both with NHS franking. The first comes from the hospital she visited two days ago—is it that recent? It feels like months—and the thinness of the white envelope makes me certain it's a rejection, just as she predicted.

That can wait.

But the other is in a brown A4 envelope and has heft, the kind that comes from accommodation forms and health questionnaires and . . . it has a London postcode.

Some things are meant to be.

I push on my trainers, check I have my keys, and launch myself out of the house. Outside it's cold and misty and I almost turn back to grab my coat, but instead, I begin to run toward the hospital because I don't want Kerry to have to wait a single second longer than necessary to find out she's finally getting what she's always wanted . . .

48

Joel

My cardiologist once told me that when your heart goes into ventricular fibrillation, it quivers like jelly, moving this way and that but unable to do anything useful.

That's how my whole body feels, after the text from Tim.

My father finds me, pacing the kitchen, not knowing what I should do next, while Leo gurgles happily in his high chair.

"All right, J?"

"No. It's Kerry. She's in hospital and I don't know whether to go in, or whether that'll make it worse, and I can't think of what the hell to do, Dad, I—"

Dad rears back slightly. "OK, we can fix this, slow down."

"We can't fix it. I want to see her but she might not want to see me, I could make everything even worse."

"Flowers," he says. "Flowers fix most things." He walks into the hall and calls up the stairs. "Lynette! We need you for grandmotherly duties."

Before I can argue, Dad's bustling me into his four-by-four and heading toward Seven Dials. He stops outside the florist. "What do you want to say? Get well soon? Sorry? I love you?" He laughs at the last comment.

"I don't want balloons."

He shakes his head. "No, the florist can tailor what she puts in the bouquets depending on the message you want to get across."

I wonder how many it-was-fun-while-it-lasted bunches he's sent to his mistresses over the years. "I want her to know she means a lot to me, and I'm sorry."

"Right. Won't be a tic."

He disappears into the shop and emerges with an arrangement bigger than his head. No balloon, at least. There isn't one for *Sorry you're ill and I am such a loser.*

"Bloody hell, Dad, how much did that cost?"

"Money's no object for the woman who saved your life, right?" He gets into the car and hands the bunch to me. There are roses and tulips and lily of the valley. The scent of the flowers is so intense that they don't seem real.

"Do you know what's happened to her?"

"No. Just a brief text from her fiancé. Tim, you remember? The one who was there at the same time."

"Oh, Tedious Tim! That's a shocker, that they're getting hitched. I always thought she had more about her. Didn't you two have a thing for a while?"

I shrug. "Nothing serious."

"When did you last see her?" Dad asks.

"A year or so ago. We've mostly lost touch because . . ." I don't know how to finish the sentence. *Because I was a coward who wasn't good enough for her.*

"You know, you can't blame yourself for getting it wrong, sometimes."

I can't see his expression because the flowers are in the way.

"After the *thing* happened . . ." Dad has never been comfortable with the words *cardiac arrest,* unlike Mum, who has reveled in the whole my-son-was-dead-for-eighteen-minutes business. "You were different. I don't know if you were even that aware of it yourself but I looked it up. When your brain has been deprived of oxygen, it's a bit like after someone's had a head injury."

"I was a monster," I say, quietly.

"No. No, you were never that. Well, OK, there were times when you did display monster-*like* characteristics, but that was never you. The old Joel could be self-centered, but only when it came to football. And you jumped in with both feet sometimes, but again it was instinct, and yours was usually right."

As he indicates left to head east, I don't know how to respond. Dad doesn't go in for speeches and that's probably the longest I've heard him talk uninterrupted—well, ever.

I suppose it helps that he can't see my face either.

"But after your *event*, you were Joel on steroids. Selfish, with an insanely short fuse. But the worst bit was seeing you turn all this anger on yourself. I even called a helpline . . . well, several different ones. Turned into a bit of a habit. A guilty one, mind."

"Did they say there was no hope for me?"

He scoffs. "No, they mostly said to give you time. Though managing that was the hardest thing we've ever done, me and your mum. You were in self-destruct mode and we could do nothing but watch. One day, when Leo starts going out in the world on his own, you'll find out what that's like. Though hopefully he won't go nearly as far as you did."

I can't ever imagine letting him out alone. "I worry I lost the nice bits of myself when I had my cardiac arrest."

"Well, if you did, you found them again."

Dad reaches out to push the bouquet aside so he can look at my face. "Just because we're not the most demonstrative family doesn't mean me and your mother aren't proud of what you've become. How you handled the Leo situation in the end . . . how you're working to get trained as a P.T. The Unbeatables. It was close at times but—"

"The lights have changed, Dad."

He puts his foot down quickly before anyone can insult his masculinity by honking, and we're almost outside the hospital.

"Never too late to fight for her. If she's what you want, you—"

I open the car door. "Yeah, thanks, Dad."

As I walk along the last bit of pavement toward the weathered Georgian entrance, I repeat the words in my head. *Never too late, never too late.*

Before I have second thoughts, I walk quickly into the hospital lobby, to the reception desk, where a white-haired man frowns at me.

"I'm looking for Brunswick Ward. What do they treat there?"

"It's Gynecology. Eleventh floor of the tower block. But you're not allowed to bring flowers onto the ward. Not since 1996."

"Oh."

"Infection risk."

I go back outside, wondering what the hell I am supposed to do with the bouquet. This hitch has rattled me and I need a second opinion about whether I should go through with this visit. I cross the road, head toward the sea, and get my phone out to call Ant.

Even though I can hear the familiar sounds of café breakfast chaos in the background, he doesn't sound stressed or pissed off to hear from me. He's become the best surrogate uncle to Leo and has proposed to his girlfriend, Ellie, partly because Leo makes him so broody.

"Whassup, Bananaman?"

I tell him where I am, and why.

"Poor Kerry. Great that she called you, though, I thought you'd lost touch."

Ant doesn't know how close we came to getting together the Christmas before last.

"We fell out over something quite big and . . . she said she never wanted to hear from me again. I've written to her since and she hasn't responded."

"Ah. I won't ask. So how come you're at the hospital?"

"Tim texted me, so it must be quite major. I'm worried about her. But I don't want to upset her either."

I hear him thump the coffee into the machine, followed by the hiss of steam. It's cold here on the seafront. I crave the warmth and the feeling of belonging I get whenever I go to the Girasol.

"I'd say . . . yeah, two quid, mate, cheers . . . Joel, I'd say go for it. Nothing to lose, so long as you're prepared she might tell you to leave. What if she does that, Joel? How would you feel?"

"At least I'd know I'd tried. Thanks. I needed that." I'm already retracing my steps toward the lobby. A weary-looking woman is walking her sea-wet spaniel up the street and as I pass her, I say, "Could you give these a home?" and I hand the bouquet to her without pausing to see her reaction.

The man from reception taps his blazer when I walk back in again and I think it's some old-man sign of respect until I look down to see pollen and leaves stuck to my fleece, along with some of Leo's banana porridge breakfast.

The route to the tower block lifts is familiar and I select Floor 11. This building is the story of my life. On the top floor, Zoë gave birth to Leo. I wish I knew how she was doing now. I paid private detectives to look for her, and they sent me the address of a hostel in a Somerset seaside town. It was a relief she was still alive, at least, and I wrote an offering to let her see Leo, to pay for any help she needed. I didn't hear back.

On the ninth floor, I lay in a coma and woke to Kerry's face. On the seventh, I recovered from my surgery—and returned more than once when I tried to die.

Floor Eleven, doors opening.

I go right, following the signs to Brunswick, but as I turn the corner, I see something—someone—that makes me freeze. It's Tim, a few meters ahead of me. I hold back as he buzzes the intercom to get past the ward doors.

It's never too late . . . *except when it is.*

A nurse turns the corner and swipes her entry card, so I slip in behind her, in time to see Tim heading into the bay on the left.

And now I see Kerry, sitting up in bed. Her face is too far

away to read but I'd recognize her thick chestnut hair and her posture anywhere. They don't kiss when he walks in but he's holding something—an envelope—and she tears it open and it's obviously a big deal because I hear a squeal and *now* they are embracing and kissing and—

"Can I help you?"

The nurse I sneaked in with stands behind me. She has that don't-fuck-with-me stance they must learn in training.

"Oh, I came to see a patient. Kerry Smith." I move backward, behind a trolley, so Kerry won't see me if she looks up.

The nurse narrows her eyes. "It's not visiting hours, so only immediate family are allowed in."

Immediate family. Does that mean they're married already?

I can just about hear Kerry's voice from here, the excitement in it, though not the precise words, and I know whatever it is Tim has told her, this is not the time to interrupt.

I got what I came for: I know she's OK. To push for more would disrespect her decision to make it work with Tim.

Sometimes it really is too late.

49

Kerry

SEPTEMBER 14, 2006

I stand outside the students' union building, waiting for someone to call me out as an impostor.

But as the minutes pass, I realize no one is taking any notice of me. I'm not being judged, I am being ignored.

Bloody Marilyn. I knew Freshers' Week would be a waste of time and it's her fault I am going through this. When she called to see how I was settling into the halls of residence, I told her I was going to get an early night so I'd be the one hangover-free person on the first morning of real lectures.

She scoffed. "That'd be the worst mistake you've ever made. And you've made some stinkers, let's face it."

"I'm not in the mood for socializing."

"You've just lost the habit. Setting up home with Tedious Tim before you were even out of your teens, no wonder you've forgotten how to have fun. Grab it, now, Sis. You're twenty-four, not seventy-four."

I let her talk me round, so here I am, in jeans and T-shirt, nothing that suggests trying too hard. But right now, I almost wish I was back in the bungalow in Brighton.

"Hey, what are you doing here?"

I turn to see a group of four students, two girls, two boys, all bright-eyed and bushy-tailed. I recognize them from the day one pep talk, when the dean told us, basically, that all nonmedic students are pissing about and we are the best thing since sliced bread, the Future and the Crème de la Crème.

I loathe that attitude, the idea that doctors are gods, but I hadn't realized it started so early. My experiences in the ambulance service, watching Elaine die, and being in hospital myself have made me determined I will always put patients first.

They must have recognized me too. They look so young, but we're in this together.

"You were at the lecture," a dark-haired girl says.

"I was, yes. Hi." I give them an awkward half wave. *I can do this.*

"Are you here to keep an eye on us?" the boy says. "We are going to behave, you know."

It takes me a second or two to realize what he means. *They think I'm one of the lecturers.*

"I . . . I'm not on the staff. I'm a student, like you."

"Oh." The girl looks embarrassed. "Sorry. We knew we recognized you but we thought you were a lecturer because you were . . ."

"Older?" I suggest.

"No, not at all. OK. Maybe a bit. Not that being older is a bad thing."

"Right."

They shuffle a little before heading into the bar, and as the doors close, I hear a burst of laughter. Perhaps they're laughing at me.

I don't judge them. They've arrived thinking that the world is theirs now, that their straight As, their impeccable work experience, their Duke of Edinburgh's Gold Awards will protect them from the suffering they're going to encounter. But I know that's not true, that we are all a heartbeat from disaster. And that's why I don't belong with them.

As I trudge back to my halls, I try to remember: did I feel that level of certainty at eighteen? Because now I am spikier than I'd like to be. Even a divorce where both parties agree takes its toll and I am missing Tim: not as a husband but as a best friend.

The one thing I do know is that once studying begins, I won't have time to feel lonely.

Our first lecture feels like déjà vu.

"There are as many different ways to think about the body as there are medical schools or lecturers. But we are going to teach you to look at the body as a set of eleven main *systems,* functioning—or not—simultaneously."

There's nothing mystical behind the sense of having been here before. I *have* seen and heard all of this before, helping Tim with his assignments and his exam prep. Twice.

I sit at the back and take sparse notes. After a few minutes, I realize someone is staring at me. I look up to see one of the girls from outside the union bar. Striking, Southeast Asian, with a glossy fringe that makes me think of Edna from *The Incredibles*. She's covered several A4 pages already, and a pile of shiny new books sits at her elbow.

I focus pointedly at the lecturer as he drones on—"and the endocrine system influences the body's functions through hormones, while the exocrine system"—and she takes the hint.

Later, I'm making a coffee in the communal kitchen in halls when the same girl walks into the room.

"You must have a photographic memory. You hardly wrote anything down during that lecture."

She's only being nice, but if I were to tell her why I know most of it already, that would raise way too many other questions.

"I do have a good memory, yeah."

"I'm Hanna," she says, holding out her hand. Her nails are French-manicured. *Who has time for that?*

"Kerry." The kettle's boiled so I let go of her hand and pour the water into my mug, a gift from Ant with the slogan KEEP CALM AND CARRY ON, I'M A MED STUDENT.

He's a good mate now: we bonded when we were helping Joel get clean, and I often call into the café when I'm near the seafront. There's never an agenda with Ant, and as I no longer have Joel or Tim in my life, I sometimes welcome a male point of view to go with my cappuccino.

The one thing we *never* discuss is the old days.

When I turn back, she's still looking at me. The lines that criss-cross her forehead remind me of Marilyn's daughter, Ava, when she's puzzled by something. "Have I done something to upset you?"

"No." Maybe I sound blunt, but I am still smarting from the encounter outside the union.

"So you're just rude then? Useful to know, before I waste any more time being friendly."

Not quite the dormouse I thought she was. I follow her out into the corridor. Funny how someone playing hard to get makes me keener: another Kerry habit to break. "Sorry. Hanna. You're right. I'm not used to this."

She stops. "Look, you're obviously older and wiser, blah blah blah." Her voice is softer but still forthright. "But maybe consider the fact that we're going to be neighbors for a year and studying along-side each other for five, before you write me off simply for being friendly."

Touché.

She seems to change in front of me: her wide eyes now look sharper, and those neat nails epitomize the good grooming we've been encouraged to adopt, to give patients confidence in our "fitness to practice."

"Was it that obvious?" I say, pulling a face.

"Er, yes."

I proffer my cup. "Can I offer you a coffee as an apology?"

"It'd be a start," she says, taking it and carrying it to her room. I wait for the door to shut behind her but instead she smiles. "You coming in, or what?"

"You're a cougar. I've never slept with a cougar before."

I have brought a man home. Technically he's a man.

"I'm only five years older than you," I say, and we kiss again, staggering toward my single bed.

Five years, though. Five years ago, my cute second-year geology student was *fourteen*. While I was earning money to keep two other adults afloat, he was at school in the Welsh town where he picked up his sexy accent, drinking dodgy cider and snogging girls on geography field trips . . .

"Come on," he says and pulls my T-shirt up over my head. "I was messing you about. You don't look a day over thirty!"

I laugh. This boy—Craig or Cam—is only the third person I've ever slept with. I almost didn't let this happen, but somewhere between my third and fourth cider with Hanna and the others, I decided I had some catching up to do.

It feels . . . new. The first new thing I've experienced in so long.

Strange too. Exposing. I am turned on enough—and drunk enough—to ignore my nervousness but not so drunk that my body doesn't register the heat as he kisses me from my collarbone and begins to move down my breasts . . .

Enough thinking, Kerry Smith. You're not a medical student now. You're a woman.

"Is this OK?" he asks and the eyes are unfamiliar but the desire in them is not.

"Yes. Yes."

After we've finished—a physical challenge in my tiny, monastic study bedroom—he falls asleep and I lie there, trying not to think too much but unable to turn the thinking off.

I'm warm and sated. It wasn't the best sex ever—

Do not think about the best sex ever.

But it was fun. And everyone from my sister to my co-workers insisted that I had to "get back in the saddle" after the divorce.

My foot's getting pins and needles from lying at the wrong angle in my single bed. I want to sleep. On my own.

"Er . . ." I say, trying to find a way of waking him without him realizing I'm not sure about his name. I touch his arm with my finger and draw back as though I've been burned.

He wakes, startled. "Huh?"

"Would you mind going home? Only I don't think either of us will get a decent night's sleep."

"Oh. Right, yeah." I shift aside so he can climb over me. "Wanna swap numbers?"

No one told me the right way to handle this. I look away as he starts to dress, his unfamiliar body suddenly all wrong in this space.

Never mind the game play of one-night stands. Do I want to see him again?

He's sweet and thoughtful, despite the drink. We could have fun together, date even, if that's what the nineteen-year-olds call it now. I certainly don't want to hurt his feelings or his pride or—

But what do I want? Do I want to see him again?

No.

"Let's leave it," I say. "I mean, it's been great, but we've only just started term."

After he's gone, I enjoy having my space back more than I enjoyed the sex. This is a new world for me. One where I can learn to be selfish, to ask for what I want.

As I lie in bed, I make up rules to see me through the next five years: no sex with anyone from the medical school. Fun, yes. Kindness, yes. But no serious relationships with anyone. Nothing to take my eyes off the prize.

They keep us away from patients till well into 2007, when they bus us out on our first hospital placements. The others chatter, trying to cover up their fear of actual humans. I sit with Hanna near the front, and even she looks travel sick.

But I am at home the minute I arrive. This is my world. We're split into tutorial groups to tour different departments, and the F1 foundation doctor who leads our small huddle has hollow cheeks and haunted eyes, but perks up when he starts to describe the grimness of life on the wards. "We call this ward *The Walking Dead,*" he whispers, before he buzzes us through into the Senior Care Ward. "It's not even that accurate; most of them can't walk."

Grim humor is a survival mechanism, but as we go from bay to bay, his attitude riles me. This hospital isn't the flagship one where the medical school is based, it's out in the sticks, neglected, and the patients in this ward are probably more neglected than most.

"Now I've got to take blood from this patient," says our tour guide, drawing the curtains around the bed. "You don't mind if these students watch, do you, Mrs. Marshall? We need to see how your body is responding to the nasty bugs that have been causing so much trouble."

His patronizing tone gets my back up, but Mrs. Marshall does her best to look cheerful.

"More the merrier, Doctor." She wears a bright pink dressing gown and has applied full makeup this morning, which makes her look much healthier than the women in the other beds. But it's clear she's not relishing the prospect any more than the doctor is. Her withered arm is polka-dotted with bruising in different shades at the wrist and the crease of her elbow. I'm sure I can see her veins shrink back under the thin skin of the antecubital fossa as the F1 moves the kidney dish toward her.

We all watch as he screws it up. Twice. Both he and Mrs. Marshall stare mournfully at the newly blooming marks.

"I'll give it one last go before asking the phlebotomist," the F1 says brightly, even though the patient's mascara is running because he's made her cry.

Our uni has a thing about learning by doing and, having taken blood from each other several times last week, we're all more competent than he is. But no one here would dare to challenge this kid because hospital hierarchies are strictly respected. He might be a minnow here in the ward, but we're not even amoebas.

Mrs. Marshall's eyes rest on me and I can see her pleading.

"Could I have a look?" I ask the F1 and instantly regret it.

Maybe it's because I am older than him, or shock at being asked, but he shrugs and lets me step closer. Her outstretched arm looks so exposed and I place my hand across hers. Her fingers are red, because of the band he's applied above the elbow to make the veins stand out.

"I'm Kerry."

"Florence."

I let my hand rest on Florence's for a few seconds, ignoring the huffing F1 and the stares of my peers. I make my breathing slow, and wait for her to match me. Above her bed, there's a child's drawing, with GET WELL SOOON NANNY written below a blue sky with a bright sun beating down.

"Who did the picture?" I ask.

"My oldest grandson," she says, "he's only six and look at his handwriting . . ."

As she tells me about him, I look at the crease in her elbow. There must be a vein that could work. *There.*

I look up at the F1. "That's the basilic, right?"

"It's not going to work," he says. "Don't you start getting ideas!"

But Mrs. Marshall is looking at me hopefully. "Let her have a go, Doctor. In for a penny."

"You have no authorization," he says. Yet I can tell the last thing he wants is to try again. This was the part Tim hated most too.

"I won't tell," Mrs. Marshall says, her voice desperate *and* determined. She reminds me of Elaine.

I start to pull on blue gloves before I prep the collection tube. My pulse speeds up. I could probably be booted off the course for this. Why I am taking this risk?

Mrs. Marshall is why.

Hanna shakes her head slightly when I look up and I ignore her. The vein is pale but I can see where the needle has to go. "Sharp scratch," I say to my patient and the point of the needle touches the faint line of blue and . . .

Blood begins to fill the Vacutainer. Mrs. Marshall and the F1 exhale simultaneously. The liquid is defiantly crimson, the color of life.

"All yours," I say to the F1 as I place the filled vial back in the dish. "Beginner's luck, eh?"

Now I feel it: that buzz. Knowing I made a difference to this patient. In this small way, I relieved suffering.

"Not a word to anyone," he says, gaining everyone's silent assent.

As I tape cotton wool to the inside of Mrs. Marshall's elbow, she touches my fingers with her other hand. "Beginner's luck my arse, love. You can come back."

No one says anything about it for the rest of the day, though on the coach home, someone starts singing "Bleeding Love."

And next day, Hanna informs me I have acquired a nickname: Dr. Vampire.

50

Joel

By the time I come round from the operation to replace my ICD, I've had over four hundred get-well messages, and my YouTube subscribers have trebled to almost twelve thousand.

"You're trending too," Mum says.

It wasn't part of my grand plan. I almost didn't post anything at all, but I wasn't sure how long I'd be offline and I knew some of my younger followers might worry.

So last night, I did a little video talking about my "magic gadget"—showing the relative sizes of the one that was inside me and the one that was going to replace it, using a pack of cards for my old one and a matchbox for the new, supercharged version.

The videos were Dad's idea, a way to grow my training business after I finished my sports science degree. I only agreed to it to help *him*. He's run out of chances in mainstream TV, so has rebranded himself as a digital talent agent, and needed to show his skills because, according to him, people nattering inanely on YouTube is the future of broadcasting.

He started off filming me doing simple routines, and I'd chat as I did them, about anything that came into my head. Eating well, getting fit after illness, how to exercise in crap weather.

The numbers were tiny at first, but then they began to grow. The Americans seem to love my accent, the Brits my sarcasm. Dad's camera angles and edits flatter me. I've developed a tough-love charm, taking the piss out of myself, sending the whole thing up.

Last night, though, I felt different.

The fear was part of it. I decided to record it with my webcam, instead of asking Dad to do it.

I started off talking about why I needed the surgery, and what defibrillation means, but soon I found myself going further than I'd planned to, talking to the camera as though there was only one person at the other end. Perhaps a boy or girl like I was, all those years ago when I couldn't decide whether to let them implant this machine in my body. I told my imaginary viewer how my life had been turned upside down by cardiac arrest. How many times the defib had shocked me back from the brink, even though to begin with I wasn't sure I wanted it to . . .

And I found myself talking about deeper stuff. I confided in the unblinking webcam that I'd never known real fear till I had my son, and now the terror of leaving him was greater than I could have imagined.

"This is my story, not his," I said. "He is entitled to his privacy so I won't tell you any more about him except to say he's taught me so much with his sweetness and his curiosity and even his insane small boy rages.

"Without him, I don't think I'd ever have graduated, I'd never have been the best man at my best mate's wedding.

"Honestly? I think he healed me. I was toxic before him. Full of self-pity, only ever thinking about poor me. But having a kid means you have to put them first.

"And I am so glad I went through with having the box put in all those years ago because, without the box, there would never have been him. It is the best thing that could have happened to me."

"Twelve thousand, three hundred followers now," my mum tells me.

Leo sits on the hospital chair, playing Super Mario on the Nintendo I bought for his sixth birthday. He seems completely unfazed by seeing me here. Which is a good thing, in case he ever needs treatment himself . . .

No. Don't go there. He's been fine so far.

So were you at his age.

"I can literally see the subscribers going up when I refresh your channel on my iPhone," Mum says.

I laugh it off. "They're only watching me as relief from all the stuff about what Kate Middleton's wedding dress will be like."

Dad raises his eyebrows. "I think you're in for a surprise."

The offers start coming before I'm even out of hospital.

I'm not on the superstar blogger scale, but TV producers chasing the elusive youth audience begin to phone Dad and, together, we pick and choose a few smaller-scale hosting gigs, to see if I like it.

I do a tryout on the same regional documentary program that made the film about the Unbeatables, and I enjoy every minute. Interviewing people about their experiences—whether it's gnome collecting or foreign aid missions—intrigues me. The producer tells me I'm a natural.

Another thing I thank Leo for: it's like he regenerated the part of my brain that makes me able to care.

51

Kerry

The rules I made in my first week at med school help me graduate top of my class five years later.

"And I'm delighted to award the Davis Medal for the highest mark in the clinical exam to . . ." The dean hams it up, as though this is Best Movie at the Oscars. ". . . Dr. Kerry Smith!"

My parents, my sister, Ant, and Tim are here, and they applaud and whoop, along with Hanna, who is graduating too.

Afterward, we go to a restaurant overlooking the Thames: the city has never looked so stunning and full of promise. When the Olympics comes next year, I plan to volunteer at Stratford. Be part of something. Belong.

Dad orders champagne. I offer to pay but he waves me away.

"It'll barely make a dent in what we had set aside for your wedding."

At long last, they've stopped hoping I might get married again. I am twenty-nine and happy to stay a spinster, though not celibate. I've kept my self-imposed rules when it comes to my sex life: no men with any connection to medicine, and no getting involved. I've not allowed anyone to distract me from the finish line.

"You're going to make a brilliant doctor, Kerry," Tim says.

"I know."

He laughs. "I like the new Kerry. She takes no prisoners."

Marilyn can't believe I invited Tim, but five years is a long, long time, and he kept his promise to support my studies. He lets out the bungalow and has sent me half the rent and it's kept me going during training. He lives in Barcelona with Maria now, doing some swanky research job. He even invited me to his wedding last summer, though I couldn't quite face that. But I've seen the photos: he looks far better in the bespoke suit than he did in the one he wore for our wedding. Tim will be thirty in October: being a proper grown-up suits him.

Ant sits down next to me. "You did it, Dr. Smith." He's married now, with twin baby girls. I didn't go to his wedding either but he understood. We got close when we were nursing Joel through his rehab, and if he's wondered, or guessed, why we fell out, he's never demanded the full story. I told him I'd prefer it if we didn't talk about Joel and he accepted it unquestioningly. That's Ant's style, easy come, easy go.

"Looks that way," I say.

"I always knew you were born for this, right from when you did that kiss of life business on the lawns."

I smile. Remembering that night doesn't hurt anymore. Or at least, the pain is so distant that I don't know if it's real or a residual warning from my neurons to steer clear of what caused the pain. Our bodies do this for self-preservation.

And if, occasionally, my survival instincts make me seem standoffish, well, it's better than, I dunno, bursting into tears because a patient hasn't made it. If you let the floodgates open, you can't control what comes out.

"What next, Nerdy Girl?" Ant asks.

"I'm staying in London; it's the best place in the world for what I want to do."

My results mean I got the pick of hospitals for my two foundation years, so I applied to the one attached to the medical school that turned me down five years ago. I have to admit there's an element of putting two fingers up to that paternalistic consultant who dismissed me at interview because he thought I'd end up subfertile and sobbing as my time ran out. Up yours, mate. I have a niece, a nephew, and a job I love. I am too busy to be broody.

Hanna is already quite drunk. "I'm going to miss you, grumpy Kerry." She's off to Birmingham, hoping to become a pediatrician, though we both have ten more years of training ahead before we lose the "junior doctor" label. I'll still be a junior when I'm forty.

"I'll miss you too. Who else is going to remind me not to be rude to the senior doctors?"

"You know it's for your own good."

"Ugh." I hate the sycophantic side of medicine. It's partly why I've got my eye on emergency medicine as a specialty, because status doesn't matter so much in A & E. It's all hands to the pump—and the defib—when a patient is on the brink.

"Don't think of it as creeping, think of it as . . . an investment in your future." She tops up her glass. "Here's to you, Dr. Smith."

"Back atcha, Dr. Chang."

My sister stands up, evidently fed up of me being in the limelight. "I still can't believe that my clumsy, awkward little sister is going to be let loose on *real* people."

Tim stands up too and turns to face her. There's a smile on his face to soften his words, but no mistaking the steel in his voice as he comes to my defense. "Your sister has never been awkward or clumsy. She just pushes herself further and harder than anyone else I've ever met. No wonder she occasionally gets herself into scrapes."

"Occasionally gets herself into scrapes," I repeat. "I think I'd rather like that as my epitaph." And I smile at Tim, the person who knows me best in the world.

Everything is going to be OK.

52

Joel

"Are you nervous?" I turn to my cohost as the floor manager counts down.

"I can't bloody wait," Mum replies.

My mother's first TV job in three years has come about because the BBC realized she was the only person in the world qualified for this particular role. We're being featured as a mother-and-son duo, and it really matters to both of us.

I'm aware that most presenters would kill for a guest slot reporting live on *Hospital Live*. If this works out, I might become a regular.

I'm nervous but in a good way. This year has been incredible for me—I've done behind-the-scenes reporting gigs at the Olympics and Paralympics, plus stuff on the *Titanic* centenary and the Queen's Diamond Jubilee. The TV industry is full of people my age and we have a laugh, though sometimes they make me do stupid things on camera. And when the recreational drugs come out after hours, being a dad gives me the perfect excuse to leave. I'm a total lightweight and I love it. Coke could never compare with hanging out with Leo.

He still loves seeing me on screen, just like the very first time he saw me in the Unbeatables documentary. I close my eyes and imagine his face as he sits at home with my father in the viewing room, with homemade popcorn and the sugar-free cola Granny insists he drinks.

So long as I focus on the patients' stories, I can distract myself from my nerves . . .

In my earpiece, I hear the opening titles and the voices of the two main presenters as they introduce the twenty-four-hour New Year special from the Royal Bloomsbury Hospital.

"And to see 2013 in with some class, we also have a couple of new presenters. One you might recognize from many New Years gone by. But the other . . . Well, there's an excellent reason we're kicking off in the kids' accident and emergency department. Over to you, Lynette Greenaway."

The light on top of the main camera turns red and Mum turns on her own full-beam smile. She's wearing a Scandi jumper and she looks in her element. "That's right. Over here in the children's casualty, it's a family affair—and we're no exception. Because my cohost for the next week is someone I know rather well . . ."

"Hello, I'm Joel," I read from the Autocue. "I'm a personal trainer, I make funny videos about staying fit—and I also happen to be Lynette's son. I've had a few mishaps, but Mum's always been there for me."

"Yes, this lad has given me many sleepless nights over the years, but somehow we made it through in one piece. Right now, we're going to meet another young man who has been in the wars . . ."

The camera tracks along as we head toward our first patient, a boy of Leo's age who fell off the new bike he got for Christmas. There are questions on the Autocue but my mother veers gently off-script and I try doing the same. It feels risky, after all this time working with anxious directors who literally put words into my mouth. But broadcasting live means the people in the gallery have no real control over what we say.

"When Joel was your age, he was always in such a hurry, we

wanted him to wear a crash helmet *in* the house, never mind on his bike."

"Yes, Mum, but you are the only one in our house to break a bone while icing a cake."

We tease each other and it relaxes the boy and his mother so much that they're soon joking around too.

In my earpiece, the director in the gallery counts us out of our segment and the other presenter back in, but I actually want the cameras to stay on us because this is . . . well, fun.

No, more than that: it's *almost* as much of a buzz as football was. As the red light goes off and we thank the boy and sign his cast, I exchange a glance with my mother.

Suddenly I understand completely what she loves about live TV and I realize it might run in the family.

I am on my way back to the broadcast van when I see her.

She's standing with her back to me outside the convenience store in the lobby, staring at sandwiches in a fridge. Her hair is short, her body swathed in green scrubs, but I know.

Kerry.

She shouldn't be here. I checked with Ant, because I know they keep in touch. He's always a bit cagey—I even wonder if she's told him not to tell me anything—but he did say she'd almost qualified, and gave me the name of her hospital. It was a big relief when I discovered it wasn't this one.

But he was wrong.

I am fighting two mutually exclusive instincts: to run toward her, or to run away. While I wait to see what my body decides, I'm staying still enough not to be noticed.

Except she's turning around. She's holding a sandwich in her hand—her fingers are ringless, but then, I know they can't wear jewelry in theater.

She's sensed someone is watching her.

I'm walking toward her.

She's exactly the same, except for a few faint lines on her forehead and the way her cropped hair curls around the bottom of her ears. When she sees me, too, her lips part in surprise and even after all this time, the thing I really want to do is kiss her and . . .

"You're wearing *makeup,*" she says, incredulous.

I put my hand to my forehead and feel the odd smoothness of the powder.

"For TV. I'm here for work."

She shakes her head and laughter lines appear at the edges of her eyes, deeper than before but still mischievous. God, I've missed her. "That's your story and you're sticking to it, right, Joel?"

"It's the truth. It's good to see you."

Around us, staff and patients chatter and stride, but they're a blur because all that matters is her and me. How do I tell her that?

She's frowning. Why is she frowning? It occurs to me that she might think I took this job on purpose. "I didn't know you worked here too or I would never have . . ."

Kerry nods. "Don't worry, it's fine. How are you keeping?"

"Oh, you know. Same old. I had a new ICD fitted which is much smaller and I haven't had any more arrhythmias . . ." I stop, because she's stopped looking at me and has pulled her phone out of her trouser pocket.

"I'm sorry, but I need to get back to the surgical ward."

"Surgery. Wow. What's that like?"

"Intense. And rare. I don't get many chances to assist in theater; mostly I'm on the wards. But it's all good." Her eyes are bright.

"You look completely at home. I can't believe you did it, you really are a doctor now."

"Better late than never." She blinks and it's as though she's already back in work mode. There's a sudden wariness in her eyes. "Sorry, we're on a skeleton staff over New Year, so I really do have to go—"

"Are you happy?" I don't even know why I ask her, but I know immediately it was the wrong thing.

"Why wouldn't I be?"

"No reason."

"Happy New Year, Joel." She turns away.

"Kerry!" I can't resist one last attempt at reconnecting with the people we were, the people we must still be, underneath. "How are the jerks?"

She frowns. "Sorry?"

"Don't you remember, when I was in the ICU? You'd ask about the jerks and I'd answer like you meant the doctors and . . ." I stop.

This time when her eyes narrow, she looks like the Kerry I knew: amused, not impatient. She's remembered. "Twelve years," she says. I think she's about to say something else, but she blinks and the moment has passed. "It's nice to see you looking so well. Happy New Year, Joel. Give my best to your parents."

She moves past me, still holding her sandwich.

"We could grab a coffee," I say, trying to walk alongside her toward the lifts. "I'm working here overnight but I could hang around, till you finish—"

"Joel, I'm sorry but I've no idea when my shift will finish and anyway . . ." Kerry reaches out as though she's going to touch my arm, but instead, she's pressing the lift call button, "I'm glad you're doing well, let's leave it there."

The doors open, and she steps inside. It's only as they close again that I realize she was so desperate to get away that she didn't even pay for her sandwich.

As I return to the van, I'm unsettled. I wouldn't have expected Kerry to greet me like the long-lost love of her life, but she seemed *too* different and distant. While they're broadcasting a video item, I find the researcher who'd been responsible for "casting" the doctors we should follow for the show.

"Did you happen to chat to anyone called Kerry? A junior

doctor, pretty. Kerry Palmer. Or she might be known as Smith, her maiden name. Probably working in surgery."

The researcher shakes her head. "No one on our hotlist, but let me check my notes . . . Yes, I've got a Dr. Smith." She holds up a photocopy of an ID badge: in the mug shot, Kerry is unsmiling. "Here we are, she's in her second foundation year."

Her maiden name? I try not to read too much into it.

"That's the one. Did you chat to her?"

The researcher pulls a face. "Yeah. Apparently, she's very bright. But she said no straightaway. Told me she didn't agree with cameras in the hospital, no offense, but it was a waste of resources. When I mentioned it to her consultant later, she wasn't surprised. Apparently Dr. Smith doesn't really suffer fools. And there's even some doubt about whether she'll pass this year."

"Why?"

She takes back the printout. "She's had a few run-ins with management. Not the best idea when you're at the bottom of the doctor pile."

"All right, reset everyone," the floor manager calls out. "Ready for the slot on not to make a nuisance of yourself in A & E on New Year's Eve. That's with you, Joel, all right?"

I position myself in front of the camera, shake the consultant's hand, and wait for the countdown from the director. Why has Kerry changed so much? I hate the idea that she's struggling. She was always there for me.

The set is quiet except for the director in my ear. Fixing Kerry will have to wait.

"Coming to you in five, four, three, two . . . cue Joel!"

"In a couple of minutes, Mum will be leading a group of hospital volunteers in a Gangnam Style K-pop dance routine. But first, as fantastic as the casualty teams are, the very last place any of us want to be as the clock strikes midnight is here. So how can you avoid being a party pooper? Let's hear it from the doctor in charge . . ."

THE FINAL LINK IN THE CHAIN OF SURVIVAL

You've done all you can: the experts will take it from here.

OK, so this is where it gets personal.

It can take many shocks from a defibrillator for the heart to start again. In my case, it took two. The medics call it "return of spontaneous circulation."

This is a huge step forward, but the patient isn't out of the woods yet. They may still need help with breathing, and until doctors can work out why the heart stopped, it could happen again at any moment.

Your job as a first aider is done now—the paramedics or emergency doctors need to get the patient stable and transfer him or her to a specialist center, to diagnose and treat whatever has gone wrong.

I spent thirty-six hours in a medically induced coma. A gadget was implanted into my body to shock my heart automatically, so I don't have to depend on a lifesaver being in the right place at the right time again. I was so lucky that someone knew what they were doing.

But I didn't see myself as lucky straightaway. Recovery isn't simple. My body didn't work the same way and my brain definitely didn't. It's taken years of support and patience to feel like myself again. Even now, I'm not quite the same Joel as I was before.

What many people don't realize is that everyone involved can be deeply affected too. Resuscitation is shocking in *so* many ways.

Link 4 is about getting the patient access to the medics, nurses, physios, and others who will continue treatment in hospital, and beyond.

But without lifesavers like you, it couldn't happen at all. I said in my first video that ordinary people make the difference—but I was saved by an *extraordinary* person. I will never, ever stop being grateful to her. And never forget that it didn't just change my history. It changed hers too. I was "down" for eighteen minutes. Those must have seemed like eighteen lifetimes to her, yet she kept going.

So—eighteen years too late—I want to say thank you, from the bottom of my misbehaving heart.

53

Kerry

February 28, 2013

"I think we should stop. Does everyone agree?"

Around me, my colleagues nod. As deaths go, it's not unexpected. The patient is in her eighties and there is probably a do-not-attempt-resuscitation order somewhere in the system, but there wasn't time to locate that when she arrested halfway through the paramedics' handover.

Act first, ask questions later.

The bay empties, and a nurse begins to clear away the detritus that goes with trying to shock someone back to life. After all the noise, there's a stillness now in the space bordered by the curtains, though beyond the fabric, the hum of A & E continues as though nothing has happened.

"Is there any family I need to talk to?" I ask the nurse. Sophie. Stephanie? Something like that. I should probably remember by now, I've been working with her for almost a month.

"She came in alone, by ambulance."

"Good, I need a coffee."

. The nurse frowns and leaves the room. Did I sound cruel? I should probably follow her and explain, but there are patients who're approaching the four-hour waiting time limit. There are *always* more patients.

Not that I mind. Now I'm an F2, I've finally started my emergency medicine rotation, and it's everything I hoped for: the bright, noisy chaos, the complete unpredictability, the constant challenge, the shifts that go by in a flash . . .

As I head off to check who is next, I overhear my colleagues talking about plans for tonight. It's one of the other junior doctors' birthdays, but I won't go, and they have no idea it's *my* birthday in four days. There's nothing in my job description saying I have to bond over tears or tea or G & Ts in the pub around the corner.

I prefer a glass of wine alone; that way, if I get mopey, I don't inflict it on anyone else.

My current low mood is just a phase. I did complete the PHQ-9 depression questionnaire, out of curiosity, and my scores were a tad high, but it's not actual depression. I don't cry or anything. OK, there are days when I feel like I'm going through the motions, but there are other days when this job makes my heart soar.

Though when was the last time I had a day like that?

I shake my head to rid myself of my thoughts—too much introspection is a bad thing, I tell myself—and go to find that coffee.

"They're knocking the bungalow down!"

I don't come home often so I never even saw the For Sale sign. I haven't seen the builders move in, or the barriers erected.

"Does it feel sad?" Mum says, standing behind me as we look through the lounge window at the shell of the building, the windows removed, and Elaine's favorite toile de Jouy wallpaper just visible through the hole left behind.

This is dangerous territory, but I check myself. I feel nothing. "No. Though we had some good times there."

When Tim asked about selling, so he and Maria can buy a permanent place now they're going through the adoption process, I didn't mind. He insisted on giving me a percentage, even though I never thought of the place as mine.

"You do know you can talk to me about anything, don't you, Kerry?"

I spin around to face my mum. "Why do you say that?"

She shrugs. "Well, I worry. It's a mother's prerogative."

"Do you worry about Marilyn?"

"She's an open book."

"And I'm a closed one. Doesn't mean there's anything sinister buried in my pages, does it?"

"Sorry. I'll button it again now." She mimes it, pressing her lips together.

"Mum, I'm fine."

"Auntie Kerry, come through, we're doing karaoke," Ava calls from the family room. She's my sister's Mini-Me, but all the qualities that drove me mad in Marilyn when we were kids—the preciousness, the demands to be the center of attention at all times—seem utterly adorable in my niece.

She's already loading "Crazy in Love" onto the Wii. I told my parents I didn't want any fuss for my birthday, but I'll forgive Ava. She loves parties and I missed her "epic eighth birthday do" last November, along with most of her previous ones, Mum and Dad's thirty-fifth wedding anniversary extravaganza, and countless other dos. My family have stopped giving me a hard time about it, though I'm sure Marilyn thinks I do it on purpose.

Maybe I do . . .

It's not only the unpredictable hours that separate me from "normal" people. Sometimes I feel like a soldier coming back from the war, unable to explain what I've seen and incapable of taking pleasure in the everyday routines of the Smith family. How can I tell them that as lovely as it is being at home, it seems monochrome compared to the work I was born to do?

I *could* try to tell my family some of the day-to-day details: wounds debrided, X-rays read, bleeding located, clots busted, mysteries solved. They'd laugh at what we've called the "*Fifty Shades* effect": the increase in chafing injuries each weekend, caused by patients trying to improvise handcuffs from household supplies.

With a little more effort I might even be able to remember some of the people behind the symptoms. The drunk man, younger than my father, whose swaying turned out to be not the alcohol but the subtle pressure of a tumor inside his brain. The woman my age who had chosen the wrong pills for her cry for help and was sent to ICU to see if they could keep her comfortable while her organs failed, one by one.

It was a deliberate choice not to let emotions cloud my judgment, but even I never thought it would be this effective. It's now given rise to my latest nickname: instead of Dr. Vampire, I'm Robodoc. I pretended for a while that it was affectionate, but who am I kidding?

Sticks and stones can break my bones but words will never hurt me.

"Crazy in love!"

"Crazy in love!"

But as Ava and I build to a tuneless finale, I glance back at the bungalow when the wrecking ball takes away the corner in a powerful blow. It reveals the garden behind the house, with the swing Tim's dad erected a few months before he buggered off, leaving his son as Elaine's sole caregiver and emotional punchbag.

And I experience the unfamiliar pang of something lost. Tears are building behind my eyes and I have to cover the break in my voice with a yelp.

Turns out I can feel something after all.

Before I leave, Mum gives me a pile of post to read on the train back to London. I've moved digs half a dozen times in the last few years, so all the important stuff goes to Brighton, along with the increasing pile of medic-related junk mail.

Once I've settled on the train, one envelope stands out: A4, with my name handwritten on the front. I'm curious enough to open it now, but it's just another brochure. I'm about to add it to the recycling pile, when I see that the letter paper-clipped to it is personalized.

Dear Kerry,

Happy birthday!
   Do NOT throw this away. Because this is not a circular, it's a once-in-a-lifetime opportunity to learn to fly.

I shake my head in irritation at the sales bullshit. But I read on, just in case.

   You have been gifted 3 one-to-one flying lessons in a Piper PA-28 aircraft by a benefactor who wants to stay anonymous.
   This is your chance to take to the air. Many of our trial students have gone on to get their licenses—some even make their living now as commercial pilots.
   Your voucher is valid for six months so do NOT delay. We look forward to helping you make the most of this amazing gift.

I call Mum straightaway. "This is so lovely of you. But why didn't you give it to me in person?"

She plays dumb and when I read out the letter, she insists they had nothing to do with it. "We couldn't afford anything like that. It must have cost hundreds. You got a secret admirer?"

"I doubt it very much."

"A grateful patient, then? It beats a box of Milk Tray."

"They wouldn't have my address, plus I'm not really *that* kind of doctor."

"What's that meant to mean?"

"I'm too junior." And too stony-faced for anyone to give me presents. "I can't accept."

"Bollocks, Kerry. You used to love doing madcap stunts."

I'm transported from the sweaty carriage to somewhere high above, remembering how much I loved the flight for my parachute jump. How amazing would it feel to sit in the *pilot's* seat this time? "It might be cool."

"Well, then. All work and no play has made Kerry a dull girl. And if you don't go, I'll go myself!"

I think about my mother's driving. "It's my duty to the people of southern England to make sure that doesn't happen."

It's another fortnight before I get back down to Sussex again to take my first lesson. I try to persuade my instructor, Des, to spill the beans on who paid for my gift, but he tells me that only the office would know, "and they're more secretive than Al Qaeda."

As I climb into the cockpit alongside him, my body tingles, as though my blood is starting to carbonate. I went on some white-knuckle flights after my elective in Africa, but this is different. This is *good* scary.

Pure.

As Des taxis, he talks me through the controls, but I'm struggling to focus on his commentary. I just want to be up in the cold and the blue. The plane speeds up and I'm aware of our weight and that of the metal fuselage. Even though I understand the basic laws of aerodynamics, it seems impossible that we are about to leave the tarmac and take off . . .

But now we do, and it feels so right.

Des is still gabbling about lift and drag, and of course, it matters if I am ever to do this myself—and I want to. Yet there's something almost sacrilegious about interrupting this moment.

"Please, can I just . . ."

"You're here to learn and—"

Finally, he does fall silent. The engines roar, but apart from that, this moment is perfect.

So perfect I can't believe it.

Who gave this to me? Maybe this does come from a stranger whose life I saved after all. Except how would a stranger know that *this* would be my idea of heaven?

In the distance, I can see Brighton. The poor old pier keeps shrinking as the waves bite into her skeleton. Just inland, the turquoise roofs of the beach huts form one stripe, and the bright green lawns another.

I try to dismiss the name that comes into my head. Ridiculous.

He seemed as shocked as I was when I saw him again at New Year. Is this an apology, or thank you, or—

"Am I allowed to speak again yet?" Des asks.

"Yes. Sorry. It was because . . ." I don't have the words to describe why this is so faultless. Perhaps it's that no one can get to me here. There are no expectations. No demands. Just sky and land and—off to the left—sea. And us in between.

"Special, isn't it?" Des says.

"You've no idea how amazing it makes me feel."

After the flight, I meet Ant for coffee at the Girasol. He's rebranded it as The Dizzy Sunflower and it's gone upmarket, everything organic and fair-traded and the rest. His wife, Ellie, bakes incredible cakes, and they have three-year-old twins, Lola and Mia, who look like they've walked straight out of the Boden catalogue.

"How was it?" he asks.

"Sensational. The perspective it gives you is incredible."

"Where's your selfie?"

I shake my head. "Ugh, what is it with this selfie stuff? I don't need a photo because I'm never going to forget how that felt." I look up at the sky and decide it's now or never. "Ant, do you think it could have been Joel who arranged it?"

He frowns. "He hasn't said anything to me."

"Fair enough. Silly idea." I know that Ant and Joel must meet up regularly but I've never talked to Ant about it. Now that I have, I have this urge to ask one more question. "Does he . . . does he ever mention me?"

Ant looks surprised. "You told me you didn't want to talk about him."

"I don't. Not really, but maybe being up there, seeing the beach and the lawns . . . it brought back memories."

"Well, he doesn't really mention those days either, and the few times he has, I've steered him away. I thought you'd probably prefer that? But he's doing well. The TV stuff has taken off and he picks projects that don't take him away from home too often, for Leo's sake."

"Leo?"

Ant stares at me. "His son."

"Oh." *He always said he didn't want kids.* That's why he abandoned that girl when she got pregnant. Why we split up. Sadness engulfs me and I have to work hard not to show it. "How lovely. Is the mum in TV too?"

"Joel's raising him alone. He has nothing to do with the mum; she was a bit of a mess. But Leo turned eight at Christmas and he doesn't miss out at all, he's a great kid . . ."

Eight years old at Christmas . . . for a split second, I am back in a dingy pub, crushed by disappointment that Joel was not the man I thought he was.

Leo must be the child he wanted to forget about. Realizing Joel did the right thing in the end should be a relief and yet it stings horribly.

No. It *burns.*

"Is he happy?"

Ant smiles. "Yeah! Loves being a dad. The kid has a few issues because the mum was taking drugs. But he's done very well." He shakes his head. "I'm amazed you didn't know. Your mum's nose for gossip must have failed her."

"She probably knew. But she also knows I don't like talking about the past."

"Ah." He points at the wedge of walnut cake still on my plate. "Ellie's going to have the hump if you don't finish that."

"It's lovely but . . ." But my throat is dry. "The flying, you know. My tummy's still full of butterflies."

He transfers it onto his own plate and pats his round belly, the middle-aged spread arriving early. "Maintaining this takes dedication, but customers never trust a thin café owner, right?" He takes a bite. "What about you, Kerry? Are *you* happy?"

"Medicine is great. Everything I hoped for."

"That's not what I asked."

I summon up a smile, even though the news about Joel has made me want to hit the bottle. "I'm getting there."

"OK. Well, I have a fail-safe plan to speed things up. Let me get you a bag of Ellie's salted caramel brownies to take away; they never fail to induce happiness."

54

Joel

MARCH 25, 2013

I am running out of hope when I meet Olivia.

The other two producers are people I wouldn't trust to make a cup of tea, never mind make a program that could change everything for me and Leo.

"Look, you know how it goes, Joel. If you go on the journey yourself, we're talking peak time potential. Without that, you'll struggle to get a daytime slot."

She pulls a face. Olivia is already well beyond making daytime TV. She's only a couple of years older than me, but she's getting a name for making tender but intelligent documentaries.

Her face must help her convince interviewees to open their hearts. Those giant gray eyes convey sympathy and there's a promise of a smile you want to work hard to see. She dresses in muted shades that conceal what looks like a great figure.

"So are you not interested in working with me?" I ask. "I'd rather know now, save both of us time and energy."

I wait as she thinks. The braying of the other media types bounces off the glass-and-blond-wood walls of the private members' club my dad chose for these meetings. The documentary was his idea: to explore the issues involved with genetic testing while going through the screening process with Leo, something I've been considering for years.

Things have moved on since my cardiac arrest thirteen years ago. Back then, they called it "idiopathic"—it had no known cause. But now scientists have identified more faulty genes that might be to blame. If they find one of those in my DNA, they can also tell if I've passed it on to Leo.

The proposal appealed because I have been looking for a project with meaning, alongside the fluffier work that pays my brand-new mortgage. But there is one big issue. If it goes ahead, I'll have to try to talk to Zoë. I already post her new photos of Leo every few months, with a note on what he's doing and learning. I always end with an offer to arrange a meeting, but she's only replied to me once, saying *one day, when I'm in a better place.*

Instead she sends him Christmas and birthday cards, signed, *Mummy, who loves you and thinks of you every day.* I agonized over whether it'd confuse him to see the cards, but in the end, it's better for him to know she's thinking about him. I try to make sure he isn't missing out. Work lets me be there for everything that matters: concerts and hospital appointments and sports days in the same playground where I used to kick a ball around.

"Be honest with me, Joel," Olivia says at last. "Is this about your career or about the message?"

"That makes a difference to you?"

She frowns. "Yes, because you don't need this. You're good on-screen, I hear you're not a diva. You're going somewhere already. This program would mean exposing your personal life, and your son."

"Which is why I need a get-out, if the news is unbearable."

She ignores that. "They're molding you for peak time. Magazine shows. Working with me would take you in a different direction, toward more serious programming. Not as well paid either. If I'm to take this on, it has to be because it's close to your . . ." She blushes when she realizes what she was about to say.

"To my heart?" I laugh. "It certainly is. But I can't promise how I'll respond if the results are bad for Leo."

"You've seen my work? I don't sugarcoat things to make my contributors look better."

"I don't need babying. I need someone to trust. Is that you?"

She leans down and takes a large Black n' Red ring-bound notebook out of her messenger bag. I see her write something on the first page.

"Does that mean we're on, Olivia?"

At long last, she gives me a half smile, and I wonder what the full beam might look like. "Joel, I never waste a notebook. And you can call me Liv."

Liv wangles a commission despite the uncertainties—she's like a very posh terrier. She also cuts through all the hospital red tape, from the NHS PR people to the steely consultants. Liv reminds me of my mother, and when the two of them meet, they bond immediately.

"That's exactly the kind of woman you need," Mum says after Olivia drives off. "Someone strong who doesn't put up with any of your crap."

"As a producer?"

Mum winks at me. "We'll see."

Leo is always the toughest to win over. I'll never know whether his shyness is due to the drugs Zoë took or just his personality. But even he succumbs to Olivia's charm offensive in the end.

We start filming in early May. Today, I'm interviewing my consultant about genetic testing.

"Can we chat here, before you go in?" Liv asks.

We're in a little park alongside the Thames. London is lovely today but I couldn't live here. Leo is a real water baby and I'd never tear him away from the seaside, or his grandparents, his friends, the life we both love.

I sit facing Liv on a bench and she lifts the camera onto her shoulder. "Rolling . . . Tell me why we're here, Joel."

"The consultant we're seeing today is one of the world experts in—"

She interrupts before I've even finished my sentence. "You're going into piece-to-camera mode. Stop thinking like a host and try to tell me how it feels to be Joel the dad . . ."

"Do I have to?" Suddenly I feel exposed.

"If you want to reach viewers, you've got to be a human being."

I close my eyes as I breathe in. I can smell spring flowers. I don't have a clue what they are, but they remind me of something.

A time.

A person.

"OK, Joel, tell me about the testing process. What could it mean to you and your son?"

"So, Leo means the world to me. I'd do anything to protect him from harm. I have to decide to find out if he's got a gene that could kill him."

That smell again. I look down and see the white bells of lily of the valley in the flower bed, and I remember the bouquet my dad bought for me when I found out Kerry was in hospital.

I wonder if she enjoyed the flying lessons. Whether they've made her any happier.

I blink: those are not feelings the viewers want to know about.

"Talk to me about how you'll make your decision about the tests, Joel."

"It seems like a no-brainer. Finding a faulty gene could mean Leo getting the right medication, or even his own 'magic gadget'—that's what Leo and I call my internal defibrillator.

"But . . ." I hesitate, trying to find exactly the right words. "What if I'd had the test, as a kid? If we'd known I might drop dead, I'd have been wrapped up in cotton wool by my parents. I would never have found football, never been allowed to train and play in those few precious matches that made me feel alive . . ."

Liv stays silent but nods, urging me to keep pushing myself.

"I'm trying to weigh up quality of life against *quantity* of life. I got lucky, I see that now. I got to discover what I was born to do but I also got my second chance.

"Kids like Leo, don't they deserve to grow up without fear? Genes aren't destiny."

"So are you having second thoughts?"

"And third thoughts and fourth and fifth. I believe in people having the right to be tested. But it's a horrible choice when you have to make it for your own son."

She nods and reaches up to turn off the camera. "That's more like it," she says, with a smile.

"Glad my trauma is giving you good footage," I say.

She doesn't rise to the bait. Instead, she puts the camera down and smiles. "I wouldn't push unless I thought it'd be good for you too."

It takes a month to get the results. We've been following another family who discovered their girls were carrying a "bad" gene, so I walk into the consultant's office feeling like the condemned man.

"OK, Joel, in our first tests, we had identified the genetic variation we believe caused your cardiac arrest. It seems to have appeared spontaneously, so your parents didn't pass it on. We've now completed sequencing on Leo, and I'm pleased to tell you that we have not detected the same variant. Which means . . ."

"He's clear." I whisper the words, unable to believe them.

The consultant nods, smiling. "Yes. Leo is clear. Which doesn't mean any future children would be clear too, but . . ."

I don't hear the rest. It's Zoë whose face I see now, Zoë, who gave Leo the *good* version of the gene that literally broke my heart. I wish she was sitting here right now, could celebrate with me.

But I will write to her again. She deserves to know our boy is perfect, because of her . . .

I look up and catch Liv's eye. She raises her eyebrows, offering to stop filming. It's only now I realize I'm crying.

Afterward, Liv repacks the kit in the boot of her car while I phone my parents.

She offers to drive me back to Brighton. "You probably don't fancy the train."

"You sure that's not because you want to film me seeing Leo for the first time after getting the good news?"

Liv looks hurt. "Is that really what you think of me?"

"I—No, sorry. I'm being an idiot. You don't have to give me a lift."

"True. I don't. But after what just happened, I'd like to."

We don't speak on the journey back, as the sun ahead softens from harsh white to deep orange. She drives fast but carefully.

Who is Olivia, really? She knows everything about me but I know scarcely anything about her.

She pulls up outside my parents' house, but not on the drive. "In case you still think I'm going to whip the camera out behind your back."

"Thank you. For driving me back and for being with me on this. I couldn't—wouldn't have done it without you."

When Liv turns toward me, I go to hug her, something we haven't done before, but after today, it feels right.

And when her lips touch mine, I can't say if it's her or me who initiates the kiss. But I do know it doesn't matter because that feels *right* too.

55

Tim

When the waiter turns up with my thali, I wonder if I have accidentally signed up for an extreme eating challenge.

Kerry laughs. "I did warn you about the portion sizes."

We're in her local. Decent Indian food is one of the few things I miss in Spain, so it's top of my list while I'm staying with her in London. But right now I don't feel hungry.

Before I flew over, I had my speech planned out. This trip is about resolving unfinished business, starting with telling Kerry that I knew she got closer to Joel than she's ever admitted. The counseling I've had to prepare for adoption has made me see I prefer everything out in the open. Except right now, I'm less sure if it's the right thing for her too.

I approach the eight circular pots of curry in a clockwise direction, starting with dal. The taste is so reminiscent of our time together in India, and I close my eyes to let it overwhelm me.

When I open my eyes, she's looking at me closely.

"It's ten years since we went to India," I say.

She nods. "I was thinking the same. You haven't changed a bit."

But *she* has. When she picked me up at Heathrow yesterday, I almost didn't recognize her. Maria teases me about my lack of observational skills, but even I can tell that Kerry's too thin, and there are gray hairs peppering her parting. Though as I am exhibiting clear signs of male pattern baldness, so I shouldn't draw conclusions from our respective scalps alone.

"Well, you haven't lost your reckless streak," I say. She's been telling me about the various scrapes she's got herself into during her F2 year. It's her usual fools-rush-in tendency, but what's new is the feverish way she talks, like a comedian trying to squeeze too many jokes into his set.

She's off again, with a story about a woman with a headache who turned out to have cerebral venous thrombosis. I try to eat, but I've lost my appetite.

"What's the team like?"

"Really cliquey."

I wait till there's a brief pause while she chews on some chapatti. "There must be some decent people. You need allies to make the job bearable."

Kerry sighs. "I guess. I'm not the easiest to work with either, to be honest, though I've been trying to be less snappy. But sometimes it's so overwhelming that I struggle to be *nice*."

"You're always nice."

"I don't know if I am anymore. I feel I've hardened. Like . . ." She looks up. I know that expression of hers, it's the one she gets when she's trying to come up with a way to explain deep feelings to me. "OK. There was this guy in his thirties came in a couple of weeks ago. Sweaty, skin blue-white with intermittent flank pain."

I look up from the second pot of curry—a cauliflower and tomato dish. "Renal colic?"

She nods. "The X-ray, honestly. His kidney looked like a hailstorm, with one really big stone blocking the ureter. That's how I feel. Like I'm calcifying inside and all the emotions are blocked up. I don't feel anything except adrenaline rushes."

I haven't seen her this vulnerable since her ectopic pregnancy. "I know you're tough as old boots, but that sounds a lot like burnout."

"*Burnout?* Since when was that a real thing?"

"Since I had it."

She shakes her head. "That was different."

"It looks pretty similar from where *I'm* sitting, Kerry."

"You were in the wrong job."

"And this is your dream, I know. But that doesn't mean you can't ask for help. Talk to your mentor. Ask his advice."

"Ha. I did already and he told me there's no *u* in *team* but there is a *u* in *cunt.*"

It makes me laugh, but upsets me too. This isn't the Kerry I know. "You need to make time to switch off. Have you tried yoga?"

She laughs so hard that curry almost comes out of her nose. "No, but I'm starting anesthetics in a fortnight, perfect for *chillaxing.* Unconscious patients, regular theater hours."

"You'll be bored."

"Yeah. I'm actually thinking I might do a sabbatical after this year's over. Go back to South Africa, maybe?"

"Please God, no." When Kerry was doing her elective in a trauma department in Johannesburg, I worried about her the entire month, imagining she'd get caught up in one of the incidents that makes the city the ideal place for learning how to handle gunshot wounds. "There must be some other way to get your adrenaline fix."

"Syria?"

I shake my head. "There's no talking sense to you, is there?"

"You're the one who had to move countries to find true happiness. Do you miss Blighty? Apart from the curries?"

Arriving into London yesterday was like visiting a foreign country. The newspaper front pages were plastered with pictures of the new royal baby, as though that's more important than what's happening in the Middle East. Even if Maria wasn't Spanish, I don't know that I'd have wanted to raise a child in England.

"I miss Marks and Spencer ready meals. And a halfway efficient civil service. Visiting Islington Register Office this morning was a reminder of what makes Britain the best bureaucracy in the world. Spain's adoption process is like wading through shark-infested dulce de leche."

"I really admire you two for going down this route."

"Don't admire us. We're just . . . stubborn. We like to do things our way."

It's taken the two of us a long time to work through our issues, but the decision to adopt was mutual. Neither Maria nor I have any emotional attachment to the idea that blood is thicker than water. We agree: there are children who need parents and we can offer complementary kinds of love. Maria's version is the more demonstrative kind, while I can offer the dependability I never had, that reassurance that I will be there for a kid, through thick and thin.

"We're going to have to get a doggy bag," Kerry says. She can tell I'm already struggling with curry number four, a lurid spinach and beetroot combination. We pay up and they give us foil trays full of leftovers. When I put them in her fridge back at the flat, the shelves are almost empty.

"You're not eating enough."

"I'm fine. It's different when you live on your own. Not that you'd know."

She's right that I've never been alone, even though I'd see myself as a loner at heart. "And there's no one on the horizon?"

"I happen to *like* having a double bed to myself, and not having to pick up someone else's socks. Naming no names."

I've known her so long, yet I can't tell what's truth and what's bluster. But I do know I want her to be happy.

I say so.

Kerry steps forward and puts her arms around me. "Yeah, I'll get there in the end," she says.

She's my best friend. Which is why I need to tell her I know everything. I disentangle myself and sit on her futon. "Listen, I have to talk to you about something."

"That sounds ominous." When I don't respond, she sits down next to me, pouring herself a glass of the cava I brought over to celebrate finishing her two foundation years.

Do I have to do this? It won't change anything. Yet I promised myself I would set things straight this time, because I hate knowing I haven't been completely honest, even now.

"It's about Joel Greenaway."

She winces. "What about him?"

"There's something I never told you that's been playing on my mind. He came to the house once, to bring you a birthday card."

"Huh? When?" She sounds impatient and I get a sense of what it might be like to work with her now.

"The year Mum died. Though it was before we knew she was sick." I shake my head. "Before I knew, anyway."

She smiles sadly. "Eight years ago? Why are you telling me about this now?"

"We had a bit of a discussion."

"What about?"

"What he was up to, what we were up to. He said he was doing a course to be a personal trainer." I picture his triathlon T-shirt and stop talking to give her a chance to tell me the truth.

I know it shouldn't matter all these years later, but it does. Maybe because there's always an edge in Kerry's voice when she talks about Maria, as though she's somehow to blame for what went wrong. Or my brain needs the exact order of events. I am not comfortable with uncertainty.

Kerry shrugs. "Is that all?"

"No. I never gave you the card, I threw it away, even though I got the sense that it was . . . important."

She looks away. Eventually, she says, "Joel has a son. Did you know that?"

"I think I saw a photo in a magazine." I know I did because I immediately turned the page.

"He's eight now," she says and for a second I wonder if it could somehow be her baby, but eight years ago, we were living together and even with the distraction of my finals, I would have noticed if she'd carried a baby to term. "What a long time ago it all seems, doesn't it? We were kids ourselves."

Were we? I don't ever remember feeling like a kid. "Anyway, I'm sorry."

Her eyes meet mine. Can she see what I need from her in return?

"For not giving me a card? Come on. I did my share of crappy things back then. For intelligent people, it took us a bloody long time to work out we were destined to be best friends instead of husband and wife. Right?"

"I suppose it did." But I won't break eye contact.

When she does speak, it's a whisper. "But, you know, I'm sorry too."

I realize I've been holding my breath. When I exhale, I feel lighter than I have since I arrived back in England.

Kerry lifts her glass to her lips and finishes her cava and yawns ostentatiously. "I need some kip. And so do you, you have to be on your toes tomorrow."

It's almost disappointing, how little he's changed.

Physically, of course, he's different: he's lost a couple of inches in height already and is completely bald. But emotionally . . .

He has booked lunch at his "absolute favorite," an oak-lined dining room where even the dessert menu features animal parts. From the moment he shakes hands I know this meeting won't give me what I hoped for.

Which is not the same as thinking it's a mistake.

My father talks about himself all the way through: his partnership, his sailing club, his new family—two daughters, who have already given him three grandchildren. I've never met them, or his second wife, and have no real desire to.

He remembers to add in a few references to how tough it was financially when they were small, perhaps to justify his actions toward me and Mum, but I see no struggle. A couple of times, when he's talking about playing with his grandson, the twinkle in his eyes does remind me of those rare occasions when he was a fun, romp-round-the-back-garden dad.

He brushes over anything awkward—the fact I asked him not to come to Mum's funeral, my own failure to finish my medical training. He has a house near Kingston upon Thames now, "so we both live by water, eh, it must be in our DNA."

I realize before they bring the starters that I won't go through with the showdown I've been rehearsing in my head since he left us. He is impermeable and the only person it would damage is me.

"Keep in touch," he says, after paying the bill with a flourish, and leaving no tip. "Who knows, one of these days I might even pop over to Barcelona!"

The air outside is charged with the storm due any minute. I watch him hail a cab and decide to walk back to Kerry's flat, even though it's over four miles.

When it starts to rain, I begin to laugh. Instead of nipping into a shop, I let it drench me, ruining the suit I only ever wear to funerals or meetings with long-lost and disappointing relatives.

Tomorrow I fly home, to Maria, to the work that makes a difference, and to start creating the family I know we can build together, despite my father, not because of him.

56

Kerry

MARCH 17, 2014

I am home. Back in my own city, my old street, my old bed.

When I started the anesthesia rotation last summer, I tried so hard to lose my "difficult" reputation. But once you've got a bad name, it's almost impossible to live it down. I did relaxation tapes and read books on assertive behavior. Even bit the bullet and tried *yoga,* though the stress of trying not to fart canceled out any meditative benefits.

Ninety-five percent of the time I was the perfect specialty trainee. But my previous record meant even a frown would cause eyebrows to rise above the theater masks. Conversations would stop when I stepped into the locker room, and resume as whispers when I left. It hurt.

When I went to my consultant, he pretty much told me I'd made my bed so I'd have to lie in it. To my utter horror, my eyes began to fill with tears. We were both so desperate to stop them spilling out that he offered to pull some strings, and a week later, he announced there was the option to transfer for my second specialty rotation.

My "fresh start" would mean ending up back where it all began. Actually, the last six weeks have been better than I feared. Brighton is a village pretending to be a city, so I keep running into old ambulance colleagues, school friends, neighbors, both on the streets and in the hospital corridors.

I pin the smile on my face as I pass the ambulances in the car park and walk through the automatic doors into A & E. A plume of cigarette smoke wafts toward me and for a fraction of a second, I picture Joel's father, in this same spot on Millennium Night, before we knew if his son would live or die.

Forget it. These flashbacks are inevitable, but luckily they happen rarely. One of these days, I'm bound to run into Joel for real and that'll be harder. I couldn't even watch his documentary last month, though I did read his piece in *The Times* about genetic testing. I'm glad his little boy is in the clear. I tried not to spend too long analyzing the fact he didn't mention a partner . . .

"I made St. Patrick's Day cupcakes," I say, plonking the Tupperware box down on the Emergency Department counter. "The green coloring is 99 percent natural, though I can't vouch for the last one percent."

The baking skills I honed playing housewife with Tim and Elaine are coming in handy again. Any suspicions my colleagues might have about my shameless attempt to bribe them generally disappear after their first bite.

"I need these," the registrar says, "it's been an insane day and I guess we'll be getting our share of leprechauns later but it seems qu—" He stops himself saying the Q word, to avoid jinxing me. "We're still busy but manageable."

Busy suits me. As he starts the handover, the list of patients and their presentations gives me something solid to latch on to.

"See you in the morning," I say as he trudges back to the locker room.

My first guy tonight is homeless. I can smell him even before I pull the curtain aside. Colleagues with more sensitive dispositions, or noses, rub Vicks inside their nostrils, but I've learned to breathe in through my mouth.

It's a her, not a him. She looks more like a pile of rags than a person. Another pile, this time of bags stuffed with belongings, is balanced precariously next to her bed. I see from the notes that she's not been here long. Under an hour.

"So, Miss . . ." I look at my sheet, "Allsop, I'm Dr. Smith. Can you tell me in your own words what the problem is?"

She looks up and I think: *I know you.* It's the eyes. They're clearer and younger than the rest of her. I check the DOB on her records. She's only thirty-four.

"I'm dying."

Her speech is slurred. I think she's drunk, but it could be gas or spice or whatever else she might use to make life on the streets tolerable.

Though that doesn't mean she's *not* dying. Sometimes patients suss it out long before medics do. And rough sleepers die at twenty-five times the rate of the rest of us.

"Let's try to get you sorted. You told the triage nurse you had pain in your tummy and back, so let's start there. Why don't you lie down so I can examine you."

She gives me a warning look when I try to lift up the layers of clothing, and does it herself instead. The smell gets stronger. Even though I'm still breathing through my mouth, I can almost taste its zoo-like pungency. Her skin, what I can see of it, is deep brown, from dirt.

Do I recognize her because I've seen her in A & E before? There's not much on her notes, but she's probably come in under a false name. Plenty do, to try to get hold of opioids.

As I palpate, she cringes. "Tell me where it hurts most if you can . . ."

But she doesn't seem to be able to articulate it. "Have you been bleeding when you go to the toilet? Or from your vagina?"

"No."

She's still chatting to me but I stop hearing her because I feel something pulsing under my fingers and my heart beats faster.

I try to find other possible explanations, because I want to be wrong. But my gut tells me what we're looking for.

I pull the curtain to one side to call out to my colleagues. "I think this one needs to come to resus ASAP. Query ruptured AAA. We need a CT and can we bleep the on-call vascular consultant *now*."

There's a grim satisfaction in her smile. "I am dying, aren't I?"

Most patients with a ruptured abdominal aortic aneurysm die during or after surgery. "We need to get you a scan now, but if this is what I think it is, you'll have to have an emergency operation. It is very serious, I'm afraid. Is there someone we can call?"

She reaches for my hand. "No. You'll stay with me, though, won't you, Kerry?"

I freeze. *I was right.* We've met before. She hasn't just read my name badge, she knows me.

"I can't promise that, but you will be looked after, Miss Allsop." I look at her notes, for her first name, because the surname feels too distant for someone who is facing death alone. "Zoë."

And now I know who she is.

When they take her off for her CT, I stay behind the cubicle curtains, to give myself a minute to work out what to do.

Zoë is Joel's ex. Leo's mother. If she wanted me to call Joel, she would have asked.

Yet surely there can't be anything worse than dying alone. Do I follow the regulations, or follow my heart? Breaching her confidentiality would be a grave disciplinary offense, and I arrived here with a shady record as it is.

I could be sacked.

But sometimes medicine isn't about the rules, it's about what's right. I already know what I have to do.

I go into the corridor to call Ant on my mobile. "Is Joel in Brighton at the moment?"

In the background, I can hear the twins screaming for more of something. A bedtime story, maybe. "Think so. Why?"

"His ex is here, in hospital. Zoë, Leo's mum. It's *serious,* she may not have long to live. She recognized me and so she must know I know Joel, but she hasn't asked me to call him. Would he want to know? She's got nobody else."

"Shit. *Shit.* Poor Leo. Yes, I do think Joel would want to know. Let me call him now."

"Thanks. Tell him to go straight to the gastro ward, Zoë's going to theater, so she's not my patient anymore. And it'll probably complicate things if we see each other."

"Even now?" Ant asks, and I wonder what he knows, or suspects.

I hesitate. Whatever happens tonight, this will be tough on Joel. "All right. Tell him . . . tell him, I'm here if he needs me."

It's past midnight when my skin prickles and I know he's behind me.

I've finished with a patient who sprained her ankle in the middle of a drunken jig and it's been a struggle to keep my patience with her mates and their chorus of "Danny Boy."

When I turn, Joel has that untethered look family and friends get when the worst happens to the people they love.

But he also looks well. Healthy, especially without that silly TV makeup. My pulse still quickens at the sight of him, but I don't step toward him to embrace or shake his hand.

"Hey, Joel. You've been to the ward, I guess. How is she?"

"In surgery." His eyes focus on mine, as though they're asking the question he daren't articulate: *is she going to die?*

I check my list, tell the charge nurse I need two minutes to talk to a relative, and take Joel into the family room. It's been refurbed since I waited here with Tim and Ant fourteen years ago, but sometimes—now—I do remember exactly how terrifying it felt.

"The doctors have explained what's wrong with her?"

"Something's burst in the blood vessel coming out of her heart?"

I nod. "Yes. The surgery is to try to repair it. But the level of bleeding means there's a very big risk she won't make it. I'm really sorry."

Joel shakes his head. "How did it happen?"

"It's rare in someone her age but family history or smoking could be a factor. There may not have been many symptoms. By the time she came to us, the aneurysm had already burst."

He doesn't move. "I didn't even know she was back in Brighton. I've been writing to her, sending her photos of Leo at different addresses. Weston-super-Mare. Hartlepool. She likes to be near the sea."

"I'm so sorry, Joel."

"The last time I saw her was just after she'd told me she was going to end her pregnancy." He stops. "I don't know what to do about Leo."

I wait for him to say more. The second hand on the clock does a full circle before he speaks.

"Leo hasn't had any contact with his mother since he was a tiny baby. This might be his last chance."

I nod. "How old is he now?"

"He just turned nine."

Nine years since it ended between us. How can it feel like a decade *and* yesterday at the same time?

"Do you want to tell me what you're thinking, Joel?"

"I . . . it changes second by second. But mostly I'm thinking, shouldn't he have the chance to meet her? What if he grows up and thinks I kept him from her?"

I take a deep breath. I've seen children dragged from their beds in the middle of the night to say goodbye to parents or grandparents. Who knows if it helps them, or not, in the years that follow?

"You know, Zoë may not even make it out of theater. Is he OK with hospitals?"

Joel nods. "Yeah. He's had checkups because of the neonatal abstinence syndrome. And he took it in his stride after I had my ICD replaced. But . . . he doesn't *know* his mum. Will she be in a bad way? I mean, I know she will, but to look at, when she comes around?"

The patient I saw was smelly and dirty and lost. She'll have been cleaned up a bit for surgery but still . . . "She's been living on the streets, I think. She looked quite neglected."

"Kerry . . ." He holds up his hand and I want to grasp it. "What would you do?"

It's the question we're not meant to answer. But am I a clinician, now, or a friend? I stare at the blue-gray floor. "This isn't a medical opinion, Joel. But I personally would wait until the morning, when we'll know more. Bear in mind she didn't even ask me to call you. Maybe if she comes around, you can ask her yourself what she wants?"

He nods. "That's what Liv said too."

Liv.

I hate the name even before I am sure of the role of the person it belongs to.

"Liv?" I make my voice casual.

But he looks up sharply. *Guiltily?* "My . . . well, *girlfriend* seems wrong at our age. We met at work. It's still quite a recent thing."

"It's important you have someone there. To talk to."

Joel nods. "I ought to go back to the ward."

I smile. "Yeah. I've got patients waiting. But take a minute in here, if you need to be on your own. And the surgeons are excellent. With her being so young, it might be OK . . ."

As I turn around to go, he touches my arm, and all the sensations he used to make me feel rush through me, like a time machine back to my teens.

"Before you go, there's something else. I need to thank you, Kerry."

"For what?"

"For telling me what a piece of shit I was not to find Leo.

Without that, I would have missed out on so much. I did try to tell
you, not long after we broke up, but—"

"Kerry! We need you in resus!"

Joel lets go. "Off to save another life?"

"More likely something involving bodily fluids."

And I leave the room before I can say anything stupid.

57

Joel

MARCH 18, 2014

There've been sleepless nights with Leo, dozens of them. He was a grumpy baby, and as he's grown, we've been through night terrors and terrible twos and incidents when he threw up like a zombie from one of my teen horror movies.

But this sleepless night is different. Every minute seems stuffed with dread and memories and missed chances.

As I wait for news, a nurse offers me leftover green cake, and I remember: it was St. Patrick's Day 2004 when Zoë got in touch to tell me she'd got clean. If I'd ignored her text, there would never have been a Leo.

I should have done more for Zoë. I might have *saved* her. If she makes it through this, I'm not going to take no for an answer. I'll be her stalker. Send her letters and messages and photos of our son, to convince her that life *is* worth living.

Except—

It didn't work when people tried to do that to me. I ignored them all: the doctors, nurses, paramedics, friends, my parents . . .

Kerry.

Is she happy now? She seemed calmer than last time I met her, during my first live outside broadcast. But she was being professional, putting my feelings first.

Like she always did.

"Mr. Greenaway?"

A woman in scrubs comes into the waiting room. "Is she alive? Is Zoë alive?"

"Yes. The surgeon will be along later but we wanted you to know she's come through the operation, though she's lost a lot of blood. We're moving her to ICU and once she's settled, you should be able to see her, though she will be sedated."

Dawn is almost here by the time they let me into the same unit where I came back to life.

Is that a sign? Miracles do happen.

"Oh, *Zoë.*"

She's breathing but unconscious. Probably good, because I'm crying at the sight of her. Not because of the machines and the monitors but because of what she's become: wizened, old before her time.

When I was using, people used to pass me on the street or the beach and you could see the disgust at what I'd *done to myself,* the loss of dignity. Yet it was different for me. Even at my lowest ebb, I could have gone home, asked my parents to help me.

But Zoë was rejected and left to fend for herself, right from when she was a baby. She survived on cheek and cunning and that amazing gift for mimicry.

There's still a tube in her throat to help her breathe and I want to wrench it out so I can hear one of her accents when—if—she comes around: her cheeky Cockney, her Spanish cabaret singer, even the hospital official she pretended to be when she called all those Christmases ago to tell me I was a dad . . .

I swallow the lump in my throat. "Hey, Zoë. I didn't know you were back in town. You should have called. There's someone who would really, really love to meet you."

She doesn't respond.

"She may well be able to hear you," the ICU nurse tells me.

"Really?" I didn't hear a thing when I was in my coma, but that doesn't mean Zoë won't.

The nurse beckons me to step away from the bed and when she speaks again, it's in a whisper. "It's one of the last senses to go."

I let this sink in. "Does that mean she's dying?" My own voice stays low, so there's no risk of Zoë hearing the question.

The nurse looks at me steadily. "The surgeon told you the risks? Shock is the main concern, but also organ failure from when she was bleeding before we operated. We are managing it all as aggressively as possible but that comes with its own dangers."

"Right." I get a chair and go back to Zoë. It's past 6:00 A.M. but something about the lighting around the bed reminds me of telling Leo a story every night, before he grew out of it. I reach to touch a part of her arm that's visible between wires and tubes and the hospital nightgown. It surprises me that she's warm, though it shouldn't. She's alive, still.

"Let me tell you about your son, Zoë. About the amazing little boy you made. Number one thing about him, he's *fearless*. We call him Lion King, because of the name you gave him, but really, he's the Lion Heart. He knows there are things to be scared of, he's seen me in hospital and he's worried about global warming and tsunamis, but what he's most worried about is he won't grow up fast enough to fix them."

The nurse glances at me, then looks away.

"Second thing, he's a hell of a mimic, like you. Listen." I take out my iPhone and I find my favorite video of him, as he pretends to be Pharrell Williams, singing and dancing through "Happy," his arms and legs flung this way and that, voice copying that American twang.

His face is scrunched up in concentration as he tries to remember all the words, and he misses the odd step, but it's like the song's been written for him personally.

"That's what he is, Zoë. That's the third thing. He's happy. I think he was born that way, despite everything. I'm moody, as you know, so he must have got that from you. Imagine if you'd had parents who'd given you what you deserved, you'd have been like him too . . ." I stop because I don't know if this is stuff she should be hearing. It's no use to her right now.

"Leo is perfect. He can heal you, like he's healed me, and as soon as you're well enough, I can bring him to meet you and—"

The alarm sounds and though I can hear it's coming from one of her monitors, I try to convince myself it's another patient crashing, not her.

Not her.

Even as the staff come rushing over to her bed and one of them moves me out of the way, I tell myself she still has a chance.

But deep down, I know that's not true.

58

Kerry

MARCH 19, 2014

I go via ICU when I turn up for my last shift of the week and they tell me Zoë arrested a few hours after surgery and they couldn't get her back.

I don't feel anything. My shift is uneventful, though I do three abdominal exams and each time, half-expect to feel that same out-of-place pulse that spells catastrophe.

"What are you up to on your days off?" the reg asks when I hand over next morning.

"Flying."

He laughs. "Our very own Amelia Earhart."

"I hope not. She disappeared midflight."

"Yeah, that's a point. Who would cover your shifts at the weekend?"

As I get changed, I'm exhausted and it feels as if it goes even deeper than usual after a run of nights. The idea of being back here at the weekend, and for days, weeks, months, years after that makes me feel almost faint.

But after a decent sleep, I am ready for my flight. Inland, the sky is gray but as I take off, the coastline has a luminescence that draws me. I steer that way.

The numbness I've experienced since I learned of Zoë's death has been different from the usual detachment we were trained to adopt, to protect ourselves from distress at our patients' prognoses.

Right now, I feel as though I've been anesthetized. My hand on the yoke seems to belong to someone else.

I've been flying solo since last year, as often as I can afford it. That's been the one positive thing about living at home—I have more spare cash for flying hours. It's the beauty and the peace I usually seek up here, but today I am not soothed by either. The hum of the engine and the rush of the air outside fade away and instead I hear the echo of voices: Zoë's and Joel's and my own. Up here, all the infinitesimal outcomes of other decisions I might have made rush past like clouds.

Joel's resuscitation replays vividly in my head, the feeling of his body, the violence of it. For all these years, I've remembered it as a triumph.

Now I can only remember the fear.

I try to put that out of my mind, but now other patients come back to me, all the people I didn't think I remembered. The countless times I'd congratulated myself on locking the bad stuff away, when really they were waiting for their moment to ambush me with the feelings I should have processed at the time.

I even see Elaine and everything she went through . . .

A bank of nimbostratus obstructs my view and I'm discombobulated. I want to cry but I have to keep it together because *I am flying a fucking plane.*

A break in the cloud lets through a blinding flash of sunlight. It grows and glows, like water bursting through a dam.

I can't hold back anymore.

"Shoreham Control, Piper PA-28 Dougal requesting clearance to land."

"Piper PA-28 Douglas, Shoreham Control, is there a problem?"

Nothing is wrong with the plane, everything is wrong with me.

"Shoreham Control, Piper PA-28 Dougal, negative, but requesting clearance."

As they give me permission, I can't hold back the tears or the terror that I am disintegrating, piece by tiny piece.

I manage to land before I fall apart completely. I taxi back to the parking zone in tears, knowing it's going to take someone else to put me back together.

My counselor's name is Earl and he's the same age as me, and multiply pierced. The room where we meet is as alt-Brighton as he is, with tie-dye cushions and a miasma of joss sticks.

I sit in an IKEA chair that's identical to one in my second London bedsit. When Earl smiles, the stud in his cheek twitches and I think of how many infected piercings I've had to treat over the years.

Half an hour ago, I was in control. All the patients who I'd treated during my shift were still breathing, and no one had gone beyond the target waiting time. Now . . .

"How does this work?" I ask him.

"However you want it to."

Is that it? I am paying forty-five pounds per fifty-minute session, money I could be putting toward flying hours or even a deposit on a flat, and this so-called expert is pushing all the responsibility back onto me?

"How long does it usually take?"

The smile doesn't falter. "There is no usual. Everyone is unique. It could be a few sessions, or months. Even years."

I close my eyes. Certainty is what I want: a clear prognosis, an aggressive treatment plan.

"People often start by telling me what brought them here."

I open my eyes again. There's a window facing my chair and a tree beyond that, silhouetted against a blue sky. It is a beautiful day and I'd rather be anywhere but here . . . I am about to say so, when it comes back, the wave of disintegration I experienced in the Piper.

I want to find the words to tell him about it but instead, I start to cry, and the tears flow so violently that I don't know if fifty minutes will be long enough to let them all out.

59

Joel

No one argues with Olivia Coombs. It's one of the qualities that make her such a brilliant producer-director.

It also makes her bloody awkward as a life partner.

"You have to be willing to take a risk, Joel. Otherwise, what's the point of us being together?"

I close the doors to the terrace, so our neighbors won't hear. I've got a hunch this is gonna get heated, and even though I'm sub-Z-list on the celebrity scale, there's no guarantee someone won't post our arguments on social media.

"Liv, I'm not saying never. But I'm not ready now. Not yet."

"The genetic odds aren't going to improve, are they? And my fertility is declining year on year. It's logical to start trying now. Unless you don't want kids with me."

The honest answer is *I'm not sure I want any more kids with anyone.*

Trouble is, I love her. I want her to be happy because she's made *me* happy, and Leo adores her. After Zoë died last year, the guilt was overwhelming, but Liv made me see that in the end, Zoë made choices that no one else could have changed . . .

And that Leo needed me to keep it together even more than before.

"You know it's not that simple for me, Liv."

"Well, here's simple. We've been together a year, which is enough time to know one way or another. Meanwhile, I want a child, and I'm thirty-five, and if you don't want one too, I probably need to look for someone who does." Her voice is calm but as she turns to leave the flat, I see her face is flushed with frustration.

I should tell her to wait, so we can talk it through some more. Except where do we go from here? This isn't about me wanting a beach holiday and Liv wanting a city break. We've had exactly that scenario already and ended up in Stockholm, because she talked me around, as she generally does.

I open the folding doors again and look over the balcony, watching her stomp away down Gardner Street, before she disappears. She'll be heading for the sea, where she'll drink a double espresso in her favorite café, curse me under her breath, skim a few stones with frightening accuracy, and head back feeling calmer . . .

Could we try counseling? There aren't many counselors who'd be a match for Liv's bossiness. Ant sometimes tells me I'm henpecked. I prefer *directed*: Liv and I work together quite often, so it's natural that she falls into calling the shots at home as well as on location. But despite the teasing, Ant thinks it'd be grounding for me to have another kid. And his little girls love babies.

It's so seductive, the idea of doing an even better job this time: being there when Liv does the pregnancy test, for the scans and the shopping and decorating the nursery. Our penthouse has a lift for a pushchair and the terrace for naps, and we could always sell it to move to Hove.

I can actually picture Liv cocooned in the hanging chair across from where I am standing now, feeding our baby—a girl, I think— with Leo proud to be a big brother.

Yet I can't set aside the fear. It was one thing Zoë giving birth to a child I never expected. It's very different to try to conceive, knowing there's a huge chance the new person we create might be blighted by a life-threatening disease. Just because I didn't pass the faulty gene on to Leo doesn't make it any less likely I'd pass it on to another child. And going down the embryo screening route isn't an option: the abnormality they found is so rare that it hasn't been authorized for in-vitro testing yet.

But I'm afraid of losing Liv too. We work together, live together, love together, and I am happier than I ever expected, in our unconventional family. I don't want anything to change.

Which scares me more? Being without Liv, or taking a risk that could bring bliss and pain in equal amounts?

When I'm stuck, I sometimes imagine Kerry is here, trying to talk some sense into me.

I think she'd tell me that life is never risk-free . . .

"Do you think there's something different about baby-making sex?" Liv whispers in my ear after we've got our breath back.

I laugh. "No condoms?"

"Not just that, idiot. It feels . . . reckless. After all these years trying *not* to get pregnant, I'm getting an added frisson from playing baby roulette."

"It's nature's way of giving us something to look back on when we're new parents and sex is a distant memory."

"Bullshit. I will *never* be able to share a bed with you without wanting to shag you, Joel Greenaway. Even when we're in our nineties, I will still be harassing you for sex."

"Poor me." I kiss her, the idea of growing old with Liv adding to the afterglow. Of course she got her way about trying for a baby. Right now, I'm completely on board with the plan and I want to hold on to this warmth and—

"Dad! Livvy! Time to get up!"

Leo bounds into the room, jumping into the center of the bed, even though at ten years old, and growing rapidly, he could easily do serious damage to us or the bed frame.

"Yeah, all right, Lion King, we're allowed a lie-in occasionally," Liv says, winking at me. "Dad will get you breakfast, then how about the beach?"

I grab my boxers from the floor and pull them on as I usher Leo into the kitchen. Sun pours through the folding doors and I feel as if we're in an advert for something wholesome—bioyogurt, maybe—because this is what life's best moments should feel like. I start to make Leo's favorite eggy bread, which was my favorite too when I was his age.

Liv comes through in her dressing gown, smelling of the shower gel she uses that reminds me of our first holiday together, and I'm already looking forward to Leo's playdate this afternoon because we'll get more time to try to make a baby . . .

I interviewed a positivity guru for the *Secrets of Well-being* show I do and he said that we often only realize we *were* happy in retrospect after things go wrong. That part of the key to contentment is to take the time to notice the present moment, and to be grateful.

So I say it in my head: *This is happiness.*

60

Kerry

July 31, 2015

"You really think I'm ready to leave?"

"What do *you* think, Kerry? It's your decision to make."

As always, Earl, my counselor, throws the most difficult question back to me.

"Our relationship has lasted about the same time as my marriage. I'm scared of what it'll be like not to have you as my safety net."

"What is there that I can do that you can't do alone now?"

I look out the window, at the leaves rustling on the trees. It's my second summer of watching them from this bloody IKEA chair. In the first summer, when I was falling apart, they were mostly a green blur because after so many years refusing to cry, I suddenly couldn't seem to stop. We talked about how alone I felt, how I couldn't imagine admitting these feelings to anyone: not Tim, not Ant, not even Hanna from med school days.

By autumn, the leaves turned red as my tearfulness turned into deep gloom. This was when I went to my GP. She wanted to sign me off for a fortnight with depression, to give the SSRIs she prescribed a chance to kick in. We compromised on seven days, and there was no mention of depression on my sick note. I hadn't worked my balls off for nine years to destroy my career with doubts about my mental health.

Earl told me my response meant I was still in the bargaining stage of grief. But what had I lost?

By winter, the trees were bare and the antidepressants were keeping me afloat while I began to understand. Earl and I worked backward. I'd been in denial about my losses: Elaine's death, my ectopic pregnancy, the divorce. Yet I couldn't blame those recent events entirely. When we mapped it, I'd been having my "funks" as I called them—weeks when my life faded to gray—since my late teens.

Becoming a doctor was meant to heal me. Instead, I shut down my emotions in an attempt at self-preservation. But what did I need preserving *from*?

It came to me this spring, when pink buds grew from dead branches, and I finally talked about Millennium Night: those eighteen minutes of pummeling life into someone and the five mind-altering months that followed it. Euphoria, love, rejection, failure. I've been cycling through that same sequence ever since.

Until the counseling forced me to admit that I can't save everyone. That sometimes even the doctor's basic law, *first do no harm,* is an almost insurmountable challenge.

"Kerry?"

"Sorry. I was thinking about your question."

"And?"

"I . . ." I am about to bottle it, tell him I still need him, when I remember a patient from the weekend. "There was this woman on Saturday. Younger than me. She'd been knocked off her bike. She arrested in the ambulance; we took over resus. Kept going for a very long time because you could see she was fit, capable of surviving most things.

"But it didn't work. When we removed her helmet, we could see why she was never going to make it—her whole head . . . Well, her injuries were not compatible with life.

"For the first time I can remember, I knew there was nothing more I could have done. We had a debrief, and when I took the newest member of the team into a side room—it was his first resuscitation—I held him and I told him it was OK to cry. And I meant it."

Earl nods.

I expect to cry again now, but it doesn't happen. "I'm done."

It's the first Saturday in August and Tim is over for a conference: he's been the main attraction, talking about what developing countries can teach other nations about maternal health.

I doubt the delegates would recognize the Tim who has just danced nonstop to the Human League. We're at Pride with a couple of doctor friends from A & E. Laughing gas canisters—a.k.a. hippie crack—are scattered like bullets all over the park, and I feel sorry for colleagues who'll be dealing with the aftermath later.

"Keynote speaker *and* you've got the moves, Tim," I say when the others go to get more beer.

"Yep. Who's the daddy?"

"*You're* the daddy."

And he is. He and Maria finally become parents last September, when they adopted three-year-old Julia and her baby brother, Andreas. It's his first overnight away from them. He got the early flight into London this morning and is heading home first thing tomorrow.

"I've got the wrinkles to show for it." He grins at me. "Whereas you are all zen and glowing, like you walked off the set of *Grey's Anatomy*."

"Ha. Hardly. But I do feel better."

"The counseling has helped?"

"Massively. My only problem these days is that I'm about to start a stint in ICU, which I know will be a deadly combination of dull *and* scary."

Tim laughs. "I meant to mention, I've found you the *perfect* specialty."

"I'll be fine once I get back to the blood and gore in A & E."

"What if you could have blood, gore, *and* helicopters?"

"Nah, I looked at the air ambulance years ago; you have to be a grizzled old consultant or army medic to do that."

He shakes his head. "It's changed. I read it in the BMJ mag. Pre-Hospital Emergency Medicine is becoming a specialty in its own right. Adrenaline, zero hierarchy. No long-term relationships with patients. Your dream job."

I google it on my phone. He's right. As I read the person specification, my mind is already whirring with the things I'd have to work on to get my application to stand out: my physical stamina and strength, my portfolio, my commitment to the specialty.

There are only a handful of places available each year, and I don't tick all the boxes.

Yet.

Even though the new, improved Robodoc is more touchy-feely, she's still bloody-minded. As soon as I'm home I'll start a list of what I must do to become the *inevitable* candidate.

I work hard, but start to play hard too. I meet Marek the following spring, on a team night out—something I'd have endured, not enjoyed, before counseling. It's a light and sound show in the woods, *very* Brighton. The installations are hidden among the trees—giant birds with ethereal voices, a harp that plays itself, the strings being pressed by invisible fingers.

"Someone fancies Kerry . . ." one of the nurses says in a singsong voice that's loud enough to be heard all the way back to the hospital.

"Bullshit."

But I look up and . . . she might be right. That guy *is* staring at me, and I don't *think* he's an ex-patient I've sewn up wrong.

The man is too pretty for me, with an Edward from *Twilight* vibe, tall with very dark hair and skin so pale in the blue lights that I'd be getting X-rays for TB if he'd just walked into the department.

He walks over before I have time to hide behind an exhibit. "Do you like the show?"

"It's fun," I say. "You?"

"Fun. Yes. I think it would be more fun if I could walk around with you? I'm Marek."

I am about to say a polite no—I'm with work people, after all. But instead I say, "Kerry. Yes, tag along."

As we walk through the glades, he tells me he's Polish and he's in Brighton for a week looking for somewhere to live, before he takes up a position in the Archaeology Department at the university.

"Permanent?"

"Two academic years only."

I'm relieved. Whatever this is—and I know already that it is *something*—mustn't distract me from my work. I imagine Earl leaning back in his IKEA counseling chair and wagging his finger at me. I laugh.

"What is the joke?"

"I was thinking that it's perfect if you're only here for two years maximum because that way we can't get serious . . ." I laugh even more. "I am laughing at myself because we haven't even kissed yet."

Marek frowns. "So, that I can fix right now."

He leans in and we kiss on the edge of a magical pond, where frog princes dance on the water and music made by moon-powered wind chimes means the same melody will never be played twice.

I lose my colleagues in the woods. I ask Marek where he's staying tonight and he tells me the name of the hotel and I suggest I join him.

"Too soon, Kerry. As an archaeologist, I believe the best things take time to develop."

I relax into the lightest relationship I have ever had.

I do the coupled-up stuff I used to do with Tim, the stuff I was too young for at twenty, but feels right now that I'm thirty-three. At dinner parties, Marek charms my sister and her husband, and jokes with Ant and his wife. He plays with everyone's children, but afterward, we agree that it's a relief to hand them back.

He's often away on digs, but separation and anticipation are part of the pleasure. I let myself go in bed, in a way I haven't felt able to since Joel. Then, I was wild and open because I didn't know how bad it felt to be hurt. Now I know hurting is part of life, and survivable.

Time is the hidden element that makes it work between Marek and me. It's been almost a year now, but there are two countdowns that give us boundaries. I start my PHEM training in August and he goes back to Poland next spring. Every time we meet, we know we are simply having fun.

Nothing—even the coins and dishes Marek digs up—lasts forever.

61

Joel

FEBRUARY 11, 2017

We move into our "forever home" the weekend before Valentine's Day.

Liv and I have mocked this kind of house for years: an adorable terrace in the quiet neighborhood of Poet's Corner. It has Victorian features, a sunny garden, and three bedrooms—one for us, one for Leo, and one that will make a perfect nursery.

"All we need is a Labradoodle and our lives will be complete," Liv says as we collapse onto the giant beanbag that's serving as a sofa till the bespoke velvet one she's ordered arrives from Italy.

A Labradoodle *and a baby*: the thing we don't mention, the elephant in our new living room.

When she fell in love with this house in September—and I fell into line—maybe we secretly thought that conception would follow, because we've made a space for a baby. I'm still working on the BBC Two well-being show, and a decluttering expert I chatted to insisted that the things you really want only come when you make room for them.

Yet here we are, two failed transactions and five months later, and the duckling wallpaper in the nursery the previous occupants chose makes me queasy. Instead of baby stuff, the room is full of the boxes we don't yet have a home for.

Why isn't this happening?

There's a bottle of sparkling grape juice in the fridge and I get up to grab it. Liv went teetotal as part of an organic, raw regime designed to promote conception. But when the holistic stuff failed, we went down the medical route too. Our joint infertility is "unexplained." The next step is IVF, not because there's any scientific reason why lab technicians should succeed where we've failed, but because our consultant says, "It often works."

The cork pops gently, which is good because Leo has only just fallen asleep after spending hours getting his new room exactly how he wants it: installing the Darth Vader mood light, lining up his many pairs of trainers in the *right* order.

"Cheers. Here's to us," I say, filling her glass and mine.

"Here's to me and you at number twenty-two."

After we've toasted, she picks up the local events calendar the previous family left for us. Month by month, it details the community activities our new neighborhood is famous for. With a big red pen, she begins to circle the things we're going to go to: street parties and park barbies and the annual Paddle Round the Pier beach festival in July. Might she be expecting by then?

We've talked about the other ways we're going to make room for a final member of our family. Work-life balance is going to be our motto, though that doesn't quite match the mortgage we've had to take out on this place—or the fact Liv has accepted a series director contract for season two of *Into the Fire,* the fire service documentary she won a BAFTA for.

She hands me the calendar and I realize we're never going to have a free weekend ever again.

"This is where things are going to happen for us, Joel. You wait and see. This is the beginning of the rest of our lives."

I hope the Fates are listening because my Liv is not a woman to be ignored. I kiss her and she responds and we make mad, teenager-style love on the Farrow-and-Ball painted floorboards.

Let's start as we mean to go on . . .

The pain comes from nowhere.

So immediate and sharp that I yell, closing my eyes to block out everything else. It feels as though there's a knife sticking into my chest.

We're on the beach, watching surfers and paddleboarders and swimmers dressed as Vikings race around the old pier.

It's a beautiful day to die.

"Liv! I'm falling . . ."

Her arms hold me up and I open my eyes as she leads me toward a bench. Gravity makes me drop down heavily; she's not strong enough to stop it.

The pain is still there.

A shock from my defib?

No. That feeling is unmistakable and brutal, but it's always over in an instant. This horrible stabbing pain seems to be getting worse.

Instinctively I try to breathe more shallowly and the agony lessens slightly. Leo is staring at me, and the terror in his eyes is unbearable.

"Leo. It's OK. Hold my hand."

He takes it and I am aware of how warm his skin is compared to mine and I can feel sweat breaking out all over my body and even though I am fighting it, my eyes are closing as I hear Liv shouting down her mobile:

"Ambulance. I need an ambulance for my partner, we're at the Paddle Round the Pier and I think he's having a cardiac arrest . . ."

I can't count this as one of my deaths because even though it's life-threatening, my heart hasn't stopped.

"All right, so it seems that one of your ICD leads has perforated the muscles of your heart and that needs fixing now before it does more damage."

"Perforation? How did that happen out of nowhere?" Liv is in terrier mode, as though this is something the poor junior doctor is personally responsible for.

"Liv, we can work that all out later, OK?" My voice sounds pathetic, though I try to smile for Leo's sake. My parents are on their way back from seeing friends in London to pick him up, but I know the longer he has to see me like this, the worse it'll be for both of us.

I beckon him forward. His Fred Flintstone costume is the only thing capable of making me smile right now. "Leo, mate, it's going to be all right. Just a bit of wiring bent the wrong way, right, Doctor?"

The doctor nods uncertainly. "It's a bit more serious than that—"

I give him a warning look. *Take the hint.* "Leo, could you and Liv go and find the hospital shop and get me a chocolate bar for later?"

"A Lion bar!"

"Yes, one for each of us. And one for the doctor too. Give me a quick kiss first, though."

As he leans in, I want to pull him onto the trolley with me, to hold him till the last moment when they put the mask over my face. But I'm not that selfish.

"Love you, Lion."

"Love you too, Dad."

Liv leans in to kiss me too. "Trust you to spoil our first Saturday off in weeks. Troublemaker."

I'd like to think she says it fondly. But if I'm honest, there's the tiniest edge to her voice.

She takes my son's hand and they disappear, back to the normal world beyond the curtain.

"We'll get you down to the theater pronto. You get the VIP treatment: we can't be seen to kill off one of the stars of *Hospital Live*."

Kill me off? It's meant as a joke but the words bounce around my head as I try to stay completely still, fearing even a too-deep breath might make the wires stab me right in my heart.

Apart from the kit tracking my pulse and respiration and God knows what else, I am alone for the first time in hours. Alone with my memories of this place: waking up from my coma, being readmitted after all my suicide missions. *Watching Zoë die.*

Fear is normal. I get that. But I'm more afraid tonight than I've been since I first got sick, and the only person I can imagine taking the fear away is Kerry Smith.

She might even be in this building, on duty, right now. If she is, she'll be busy saving someone else's life, so instead, I try to summon up the Kerry I knew when I was first sick, that girl who sneaked me out of the ward and bought me chips. The only other person on the planet who gets our joke about the jerks.

If only we could be back there again, in 2000, with all those years ahead. I would do it all differently . . .

Stop this maudlin bollocks right now, Joel Greenaway.

You have Leo and Liv, who remind you daily what you have to live for. They are enough.

I will come through this surgery and when I wake up, I will make sure I never forget how lucky I am.

62

Kerry

I'd never admit this to civilians because it sounds in bad taste, but within hours of starting my air ambulance training, I experience something like peace.

It's crazy soon. Our trainers haven't even finished outlining the curriculum, but I know in my bones that Tim was right: this will fit me like an XS latex glove.

"We aim to get you competent to deal with whatever might be thrown at you. But even if you do this for ten, twenty years, there will still be a patient or a scenario where you feel utterly unprepared, or afraid, or out of control.

"This year, PHEM doctors—and their colleagues—have faced some of the most challenging incidents in decades, at Westminster, London Bridge, and the Manchester Arena. You can never be ready for something like that.

"But we chose you guys for the program because we think you have the qualities to help those who need it, even in the most extreme circumstances. In the field, it's just you and the team and your training and your instincts. Transcending fear to make a difference is an incredible privilege."

It rings so true. These are *my* people. This is where I am meant to be.

After a month of drinking in every bit of knowledge, every skill set, I'm sent back to my air ambulance base. To begin with, I'm literally excess baggage on the helicopter, traveling alongside the crews but unable to do anything except the most basic tasks.

I make friends with the pilots first; I can talk aerodynamics with them and purr over the controls.

Next, I win the paramedics over with my willingness to clean up the mess that fills the helicopter after we've handed over a patient. Plus, they realize quickly that I can cannulate or intubate in my sleep.

Gwen the consultant is the hardest nut to crack but still, she's nowhere near as frightening as the average ward manager. Plus, she's awesome. If I ever get to be half as good a doctor as she is, I will be happy.

Life at base is about being prepared, like grown-up Girl Guides or St. John's cadets: stocking, restocking, counting, waiting. But when the red phone rings, the change is instantaneous. The first few times it happens, my response is physical—dry mouth, goosebumps, mild tachycardia. My body readies itself for the unknown and we board the helicopter.

"RTC, Dorking Bypass. One lorry, three cars."

On the way, I always try to build a mental model of what we're going to face. As we approach the crash, the pilot navigates the hazards of power cables and rows of houses to land in a playing field.

Gwen deplanes with Lars, her favorite paramedic, and I jump out behind them. My instinct to run first and think later is probably my biggest weakness, but I'm trying to learn from Gwen as she holds back, assesses the scene, establishes who is in charge.

"Hi, what have we got?" she asks the fire officer.

"Car versus lorry. Couple of other cars shunted behind. The occupants of the Honda have come off worse. Two females, passenger looks worse *and* she's pregnant."

I've spent four years dealing with the consequences of these David and Goliath accidents in the hospital setting. But as we approach, it seems miraculous that anyone might have survived inside the warped remains of the little blue hatchback.

The passenger's belly and the airbag have the same cushiony roundness, but everything else is harsh and sharp, the angles of the car helter-skelter.

Gwen leans in. "All right, love, my name's Gwen. I'm a doctor and we'll have you out of here very soon and off to hospital. Where does it hurt?"

As Gwen works, I am making my own assessment and soon she turns to me. "All right, Doctor, what would you do now?"

"Her pulse and O2 sats look OK but even so, we need to watch for bleeding when the fire service start cutting. And she needs analgesia. Ket. It's OK for a pregnant woman. Right?"

"So don't just stand there, go and get what we need."

Gwen and I work together to get the ketamine administered as the fire service begin to slice into the car, cutting off the roof and rolling the dashboard away. It's enough to stop our patient worrying about pain. Instead, she's babbling happily and telling Gwen she *really, really* loves her.

It's over an hour before our patient is on her way to the trauma center by road, with Gwen ready to step in if she needs treatment en route. I fly back to base with Lars and Carrot, our pilot. As we take off, the scene turns back into a model village: other people's lives in miniature.

"Sound work there, Kerry," Lars says. "She's warming to you."

"I don't see much sign of that."

When she gets back, Gwen asks me if I could stay behind after the shift. We only just fit into the cramped admin office: the air ambulance is a charity, so the facilities are even shabbier than the NHS.

"So, Kerry. Baptism of fire, right?"

"It's challenging, but I love every minute."

She laughs and her face softens. "This isn't an interview."

"What is it then?"

"It's . . . a small apology. Apparently, I've been quite hard on you."

I stare at her, genuinely lost for words.

"Lars has pointed out that most of our medics are consultants by the time they come to us, so it's hardly surprising you're not quite as competent yet. And, what you lack in experience, you're starting to make up for in enthusiasm. A little too much enthusiasm at times, so do keep a check on your tendency to rush in. But overall, I like you."

"*Really?* I thought you'd asked me here to tell me I should go back to hospital medicine."

Gwen peers over her glasses. "I don't think so, dear. We're spending a fortune training you, and it's nice to have another female around, especially a competent one. But that's not my main concern."

"Oh?"

"I need you to speed up. Prove you're up to the job and, specifically, for covering my shifts in December. Because otherwise I'm going to have to cancel my birthday trek in Myanmar and that will piss me *right* off."

So December is when the real baptism of fire begins.

I learn more than I have in the previous four years. I'm OK at this. And I am going to be *really, really* OK.

Marek is going home for Christmas so I take him to Gatwick first thing on the twenty-fourth, before my shift starts. We live together now. He moved into my flat six months ago, after he left the uni postgrad accommodation. It works well, though part of me is looking forward to having the space to myself while he's away.

We sit in the drop-off area, as the security men eye us, trying to work out if we're up to anything more sinister than saying goodbye.

Marek looks extra-handsome in his suit, worn to please his mother, who'll be waiting at arrivals.

"They will be so angry I have not brought you with me as their Christmas present."

I met Marek's parents when we went to Warsaw for the weekend in October. They were kind, but clearly unsure of what to make of me, or of our passionate-but-not-serious relationship.

They're not the only ones. I *do* care about him but I would choose my career over our relationship. I think he's the same about ruins. Or is he?

"A Polish Christmas sounds wonderful."

"Next year," he says. Is it a slip of the tongue or a test? We don't talk more than a month or two ahead. We never made it an official rule; it's how things have developed.

I let the idea of *next year* settle. It sounds . . . nice. And he's well-thought-of in his department, so they'd probably extend his stay. The only thing that's nonnegotiable is my training: I won't let anyone get in the way of that.

The security guard taps on my window. "No waiting," he says when I wind it down.

Marek leans across to kiss me. As he pulls away again, I hold on, though I can't explain why.

"Hey," Marek says. "You OK?"

"Yeah," I lie. I am not superstitious but I suddenly have this fear we will never see each other again.

I shake it away. I'm tired, that's all.

"Back soon, zabka." *My little frog.* "Missing ya already!"

"I bet you say that to all the girls."

There's a festive atmosphere at base—I've brought in some home-made mince pies, and we only get one call out in the morning, a walker found having a seizure on the downs. We transport her to hospital by air because the Christmas Eve traffic would take an ambu-lance three times as long.

Dusk comes just before four and we're all hoping that'll be it for the day. It's much harder to navigate and land in the dark, and today the rain is relentless.

When the red phone rings, I freeze, convinced suddenly that even *thinking* it might have caused trouble.

"Train derailment, near Haywards Heath." Stacey, our scheduler, repeats the details. The temperature in the shed seems to plummet ten degrees.

"I thought the bloody trains had stopped running by now," Lars whispers. "I'll hold on for the coordinates."

Carrot and I are already on the helicopter, headsets on, as more information begins to come in. Four carriages of the London train have derailed twenty miles north of Brighton.

"It's big," Carrot says.

Can I do this?

"You're ready," he says, answering my unspoken question.

Lars climbs into the front, pulls on the headphones, and Carrot prepares for take-off. "They're struggling to get access. We might be the first to get to some of the carriages." He turns around. "Talk it through with me."

"Primary assessment, triage using the CABCDE checklist. We don't treat anyone until we're sure the scene is safe and everyone has been assessed."

"It can be bloody hard not to jump in and help, Kerry. But stick to the drill. It really is the only way to keep control of a major incident."

From the air, the ground looks so Christmassy: yellow garlands crisscross wildly, the cars on the motorway and the A roads blinking like fairy lights, blurred by the heavy rain. Carrot's been flying on instruments, but as we get closer, there's a cluster of blue lights show-ing the way. *Not nearly enough people on scene.*

Lars and Carrot discuss the safest place to land, so I focus on trying to make sense of what I'm seeing. Whatever has made the train derail, it's happened in the worst possible place, bordering farm-land and several ditches or streams. The rear two carriages look only slightly off-kilter, as though they've been indulging in a little mulled wine, and I can see movement down there—walking wounded. But the front two carriages hang down the banks, twisted like a child's toy train.

The rain is still pouring down, and most of the emergency vehicles—two fire engines, three ambulances—seem to be stranded at the other end of a field.

We are easily the closest.

Carrot lands and Lars and I prepare to deplane. "We stick together, all right, Kerry?"

The adrenaline washes away my nerves. There are tens, maybe hundreds of people who need me. I have been building up to this moment for eleven years.

Maybe all my life.

63

Joel

DECEMBER 24, 2017

We're at my parents' for one of Mum's show-off shindigs and the folk band my mother has hired is about to start.

I am so tired I want to go to my guesthouse—alone—and sleep till 2018.

"All right?" Liv asks, handing me a glass of sparkling grape juice.

"Yeah. Don't think it'll be a late one, though."

She smiles tightly. She's not a natural nurse, and we're both sick of me being sick. The first perforation knocked me for six, and then I had another scare in November, on Bonfire Night. This morning, I realized I'm getting a cold.

I probably shouldn't have gone to the torchlit Burning of the Clocks procession that marks the winter solstice, but Leo had made his own lantern in the shape of a sports car and I didn't want to miss it . . .

A cold is no big deal, except I'm on edge every time I cough, in case the movement in my chest knocks out one of my ICD leads again. It makes me feel like an old man.

The band begins with "Fairytale of New York." They're raucous and loud, but still, we all hear Liv's phone when it rings at max volume.

She leaves the room to answer it, which pisses me off. *It's Christmas Eve.* Channel 4, or whoever it is, can surely wait.

She comes back in, eyes wide, cheeks flushed, and instantly I feel guilty. "What's happened?"

Her dad is older than mine and had a fall in the summer that almost finished him off. We live in fear of another phone call like that, and I prepare myself for a dash to Hereford.

"There's been a crash," she says.

"Shit. Is he OK?"

She shakes her head. "Not Dad. That was fire control. It's a train crash, at Haywards Heath. Major incident. Several people dead."

The look on her face wasn't shock; it was anticipation.

She doesn't have to tell me she's going, I already know she can't not. Season 2 of *Into the Fire* has just started filming. This could make the whole series, and the fact it's Christmas Eve will make it an even more powerful story.

Already Liv is heading for the door. "Will you apologize to your folks for me?"

"They know the score."

"Cheers." She's already in work mode. "How the hell am I going to get hold of anyone else tonight?"

"I could come with you to do sound?"

I say it without thinking, but once the words are out, I know it's the right thing. Leo is surrounded by his mates. It was his thirteenth birthday yesterday and he's grown into a popular kid, laid-back and funny. Later they're all going to watch a bootleg copy of *The Last Jedi* in Dad's viewing room, so he won't notice if we both go. This could be what Liv and I need to bring us closer again.

"Are you sure?" She gestures toward my chest. "You said you were tired and—"

"The adrenaline will kick in."

She smiles, and this time it's genuine. "Fuck, yes, please."

I drive while she calls around for reinforcements. Her self-shooting producers and assistant producers have scattered to the four corners of the British Isles for family reunions. The three local free-lancers she sometimes uses are at the same wrap party in Brighton too drunk to drive.

She gets hold of one crew from London, but after she ends the call, she says, "Can't see him being there much before ten. So it's you and me, Joel, like the olden days."

Can we resurrect the *olden days,* when we were together twenty-four-seven and still couldn't get enough of each other? These days, we no longer work as a pair, and even our time at home seems focused on keeping Leo happy. Anything but admit to the mess we're in.

It wasn't *just* the cardiac perforation. Two years of trying for a baby would put any couple under pressure, but my prevarication about agreeing to IVF hasn't helped. Liv found out we could even apply to have my problem gene added to the permitted screening list, which would mean our embryos could be checked. But still I've resisted.

I drive in silence now, while she sits the camera on her lap, prepping it for a night shoot. How do I explain my reluctance? I've tried to make sense of it. Maybe I want one thing in my life to exist *without* medical intervention. But that's not a reason to deprive Liv of the child she desperately wants.

Leo is enough for me. I can't imagine loving another baby as much as I love him. Yet if I don't love Liv enough to make this happen, perhaps we shouldn't be together.

I glance to my left. She's looking at me too but immediately pretends to fiddle with a camera setting. Sometimes I wonder if she's only waiting till I'm completely well before she dumps me for good. I wouldn't blame her.

But it would break Leo's heart.

The satnav skirts the queues on the motorway and gets us close to the site in under forty minutes.

"How far now?"

But the lights ahead answer her question. Liv is usually unshock-able, but even she's speechless at the number of vehicles and emer-gency staff on-site as we pull up. The field is already a bog where people have trooped through in heavy boots, and it wears me out just following her to the nearest fire engine. She's trying to locate one of the crews she's been filming for *Into the Fire*.

"They're by the track," she says. "Look, it's going to be grim. You don't have to come."

"You think I can't handle it?"

Liv sighs. "This isn't about how macho you are, Joel. You've been ill. And even if you can handle it physically, the last thing you need is another trauma to give you nightmares."

"What makes you think I get nightmares—"

"This isn't the time." She's already striding off, chasing the story. "Do what you want. You always do."

I *do* get nightmares. They started before Leo came to live with me and they still mostly revolve around him. But I've never told Liv. Has she seen me thrashing around in bed? Is this another thing we can't discuss?

I *do* follow, because whatever happens in the future, she needs me now.

I've spent plenty of time filming in hospitals, but I haven't been on the scene of a major incident before. It's Liv who craves drama, which means I stick to science and lifestyle stuff so I can be there for Leo, though now that he's at secondary school, he needs me much less. Liv is the one with her overnight bag always packed, her camera batteries permanently on charge.

The scene is suddenly extremely crowded, despite the remoteness of the field. The paramedics, police, and firefighters move with pur-pose, but the walking wounded dawdle and stop. Some wear winter coats but most have on only indoor clothes, as though they've been dropped here from their offices or kitchens.

I begin to notice their injuries: a girl in a party dress with her wrist doubled back on itself. A man sits on a camping chair, and in the dim light, I think he's wearing odd socks till I realize the green one is a sock but the red one is his bare foot, soaked with blood.

How Liv keeps filming I don't know. At least I can look away when I need to, whereas she must focus on the viewfinder. The firefighters are rescuing an elderly casualty, slicing through the wreckage, and his distress is unbearable.

I admire Liv for her resolve, yet being here makes me deeply uncomfortable. The casualties were in the wrong place at the wrong time. The emergency personnel have a job to do.

But us? What purpose are Liv and I serving, really?

OK, I've used the arguments myself when I've been talking to program contributors: the educational benefits of TV, the myth busting, and most of all the chance to tell an important story.

But where does education end and voyeurism begin?

Maybe I'm more uncomfortable because of the wrapped Christmas gifts that are scattered about, or the festive bottle of champagne leaking onto the carriage floor. But it feels like Liv is crossing the line tonight.

The casualty is taken away the instant the space is large enough to access—he was talking but now he seems to have stopped.

As we follow them toward the ambulance, I look back. The carriage has been cut down the middle and glitters under the emergency lights, like a fish that's been filleted.

64

Kerry

I see Joel before he sees me.

I've just got back from our first transfer, a casualty with a cata-strophic hemorrhage. We took him to St. George's in London, rather than Brighton, and now that we're back, the scene is more organized than when we first arrived.

Hundreds of people are here with one purpose—to preserve life. In the midst of all the pain, that thought gives me energy.

But then I see Joel. He has headphones on, like the ones we wear in the helicopter, but his are connected to a microphone, a ridicu-lously large thing covered in gray fake fur.

He's following a woman with a camera, who films a patient being extracted by a fire crew. She's getting so close to him that it's almost obscene.

I want to stomp over, to ask the two of them what the fuck they think they're doing, getting in the way of rescues, filming people who are in no state to consent.

No. It's a waste of energy, that's not what I am here to do. I turn away and head back toward the second carriage. Carrot has to go back to base because his flying hours are so strictly controlled, but Lars and I are staying on. There's no way either of us could leave.

The sounds are different now. Instead of moans and cries, the field hums with generators and engines and communications equipment. It's neither chaos nor order, but the systems are adapting to the scale of this particular catastrophe.

I find it harder to adapt to the magnitude of what *I've* had to do: I've never wanted to play God, but tonight I had no choice, picking my way between patients to find the ones who needed help first. *Disregarding those that were past helping . . .*

The Priority 1 and 2 casualties have all been transferred out, so Lars and I are going to meet in the area where they're treating the walking wounded. The regional trauma centers are closed to everything but the most seriously injured, so helping people here in the field will mean fewer patients swamping the walk-in clinics. Plus, we need to keep an eye on the Priority 3s, to make sure they've been classified correctly and nothing more serious has been missed.

What was that?

The high-pitched cry is almost inaudible underneath the other noises. Did I imagine it?

It's probably a farm animal: the bleat of a sheep whose territory has been invaded. After the things I've seen here, I wouldn't be surprised if my hypervigilance is making me hear danger where there is none . . .

Except there it is again.

Is it human? A phone or music player discarded by a passenger?

I'm getting farther from the train and from the floodlights that define the casualty area. I am about to turn back when I hear what I *know* is a voice.

"Grandma? Mummy?"

I stop, trying to locate the sound. I edge carefully toward a boggy area alongside the railway line.

"Hello?" I call out. "Is someone down there?"

"I want Mummy!"

My head torch shines into the face of a small girl. Five or six, not bleeding from anywhere that I can see, but very pale.

She begins to cry properly now.

"OK, sweetie, don't cry. I'm here." I edge toward her. Seeing me will reassure her, plus I can do a quick visual assessment before I radio for help. "We'll soon get you out . . ."

One moment my feet are on the ground and the next I'm slipping, falling forward, toward the ditch . . .

I brace myself.

My shoulder hits the sodden earth first and I tumble as white-hot pain flashes through me. The exact same pain as when I fell out of the tree in Tim's back garden.

It takes a second or two for the shock to subside, so I can make sense of what's happened. OK: I am in freezing water up to my waist. As I move my arm, my eyes fill with tears. A fracture as well as a dislocation.

I reach down with my good arm, through the water, to pull out my radio. The display is dead. It can't be. These are meant to be waterproof. Has it been damaged by the fall?

For a few seconds, I wait for a light: red, orange, green. Anything. But no. It's gone.

My phone, then. It's in the other pocket. Except as I twist to push my fingers between the folds of the fabric, there's nothing there. Disbelief makes me try twice, three times, before I can accept it's not there.

Think. The first thing I need to do is get to the girl. Someone up there will be looking for her. *For us.*

My head lamp doesn't give me any real sense of how far away she is and my useless arm is starting to hamper my progress, so I steel myself to try to get my shoulder back in joint. Dark pain swims over me and I howl involuntarily.

The girl whimpers. At least I know she's close.

"Shhh, it's all right. I'm here. Tell me what you were doing today."

I begin to crawl toward her voice and become aware for the first time that my ankle hurts too.

"We've been . . . shopping . . . on the train."

I don't like the sound of her breathing.

"Lovely. I'm nearly with you, it's just this mud is so sticky. Tell me your name, sweetheart."

"Emily . . ."

"And where do you live, Emily?"

She tries to tell me her full address but I don't catch all the words. I am almost alongside her, biting my lip as I crawl.

"See, I'm here now, Emily. Let's hold hands, I bet you're chilly."

As she places her hand in mine, I check her radial pulse. High, though her skin is cold and clammy. Is that from the water or something more serious?

I want to get her onto my lap to warm her up but first I try to work through the CABCDE checklist. It's hard to angle the head lamp to see much, so my ears and sense of touch have to substitute for my eyes. Even off-duty, I automatically assess everyone I meet, in queues or at the pub: eyes, complexion, gait can tell me so much. But now I am literally in the dark.

The sequence will keep me focused. Catastrophic bleed? Nothing external, as far as I can tell . . . but as I touch her abdomen, Emily screams.

"Emily, where does it hurt? Show me, with your hand."

I hold on as she runs her hand over her body: her left ankle, left hip . . . "It hurts the most here," she says, and her fist tightens around mine over her lower rib, on the left.

Ruptured spleen? If I'm right, she needs surgery to stop the bleeding before she goes into hypovolemic shock—unless she has already. But I can hardly operate in a ditch. All I can do is try to keep her stable until someone comes.

"I'm going to put my arms around you for a nice cuddle, OK, Emily? So we can keep each other nice and warm." It hurts my shoulder but she stays silent, so I guess it doesn't hurt her. "What happened, Emily?"

"The train . . . went all wonky . . . I was with Grandma and . . ." She starts to cry.

"Don't cry, sweetheart. You're safe now." *And crying makes her breathing worse.* "Tell me how you ended up falling over."

"There was a hole in the train . . . I climbed through it but it was all dark . . . and my glasses got broke . . . grown-ups were shouting . . . it was scary so I was running and it looked like people . . . but I . . . slipped."

"How long ago?"

She doesn't respond.

"Stay awake, Emily. How long do you think it's been since you fell?"

"I don't know." She sounds close to tears again. I don't want her to waste energy.

"What songs do you know, Emily?"

She tells me a few titles I don't recognize. My interest in music stopped the year I started med school. I try to remember songs Marilyn's children like, and as I picture Ava, fear seeps through me, as chilling as the water.

Don't be such a flake, I tell myself. *Of course you'll see them again.* My career might be DOA because I've been such an irresponsible fucking idiot, but I will make it out of this ditch, and so will Emily.

"What about 'Happy'?" I suggest. Emily begins to hum. I join in, as loudly as I can, trying to throw my voice up beyond the ditch.

Someone has to hear us soon.

We've run out of songs. "Let's start again, from the beginning."

But Emily's struggling to breathe and she's getting colder. "Where's . . . Mummy?"

"She'll be here soon. We just have to stay brave for a bit longer." She doesn't respond. I need to keep her awake.

"How about I teach you a song instead? One for Granny."

"A funny song?" she says, through the tears.

I haven't even thought of one, but it comes to me in a flash. The song I learned with Tim all those years ago at the St. John's Ambulance meetings: a children's song with the perfect rhythm for carrying out CPR.

"Do you know 'Nellie the Elephant'?"

"No . . ."

"Your grandma will know it. It's about an elephant who runs away."

"From where?"

"From the circus."

"African . . . or Indian?"

"I don't know. Which do you prefer?"

"Indian ones. They've got bigger ears."

"OK, let's say she's the Indian kind. Shall I teach you the words?"

Emily doesn't respond so I start anyway.

"It starts . . . 'Nellie the elephant packed her trunk' . . ."

65

Joel

"I can't do this anymore, Liv."

I've waited till she's got enough video material for a complete sequence about the casualty we've followed.

"Are you struggling?"

Yes. But it's not about my health, it's about what we're doing to make this situation even more horrible.

"I'm not in pain but I need to sit in the car for a while. Your freelance can't be far away now, can he?"

"Shall I come with you?" She is only offering because she feels she should, and I shake my head.

"I'll be fine. You carry on."

I lose her in the sea of hi-vis jackets. As I walk back toward the car, I admit to myself I *do* have some pain, though nothing like the piercing agony in July, when the loose lead nearly punctured my heart.

It's still raining, but shock has turned some people into human statues who don't seem to notice they're getting drenched. I wonder if I could fetch blankets or guide people toward the shelters. Anything to be useful.

A woman tugs at my coat. She's wearing a light-colored mac but her hair and face are saturated, and her eye makeup has run down her cheeks. "I can't find my granddaughter."

"Would you like me to help? I think they're organizing transport from the tent thing over there. I bet she's waiting or they've taken her to hospital."

"I've been there already, checked all the lists. Something's wrong."

"When did you last see her?"

"After the crash. She wasn't hurt. A bruise or two, same as me. We tumbled a bit when the train crashed because we were standing up, ready to get off at the next station, but it was so packed, we were cushioned by everyone else." She shakes her head. "Emily? *Emily,* where are you?"

As she calls out, I hear the panic and want to calm her down. "How old is Emily?"

"Six."

I try to imagine losing Leo. Even though he's twice this child's age, I'd be frantic. "Listen, I'm positive someone will be looking after her, but we'll make sure. I'm Joel."

"Barbara," she says, and her cold hand in mine feels like a contract.

Together, we head back toward the casualty area, under a tarpaulin roof. I explain we're looking for a child, and though I say nothing to Barbara, there's a fast chain reaction as different emergency staff check and double-check if anyone has found a little girl.

"I don't know what's happened to her," Barbara is saying, "after the crash, I kept calling for her but I think she got out of the carriage first . . ."

Behind her, I spot Liv coming under the tarpaulin and I realize someone must have tipped her off that a kid is missing. The last thing Barbara needs is to have a camera pointed in her face.

"Let's find her, eh?"

I nudge Barbara out the other way, so Liv won't see her, or me. We start walking. The rain is getting heavier.

As she scans the darkness, Barbara stops suddenly. "There."

My heart speeds up. "What is it?" I ask her.

As my eyes adjust, I can make out the white legs of horses in a field beyond the ditch. "We ride, both of us, sometimes. She's obsessed with horses. What if she went to find me there?"

It doesn't seem likely to me, but at least this keeps Barbara out of Liv's clutches. We walk with arms linked, so we don't slip. She leads, pulling me gently in the opposite direction to where the police are headed. I know this is futile, there's no reason a kid would have wandered off that far. But if I'd lost Leo, I would want everywhere to be checked.

"Can you hear something?" she says.

I strain but there's nothing but wishful thinking on Barbara's part. My phone's torch is feeble, but it helps us both avoid boggy puddles and the scattered debris underfoot. The farther we get from the emergency vehicles, the less light and noise there is . . .

"There," Barbara says again. There seems to be nothing to the right except for darkness.

And two voices.

Nellie the Elephant packed her trunk . . .

No one sings that song anymore; it's something my parents would have known when *they* were kids.

"Emily?" Barbara tries to pull me forward. I move my phone torch across the ground like a searchlight, in an arc. The singing seems to fade away as we walk.

". . . I can't." Definitely a little girl's voice now.

"You can, Emily. Nice and loud, come on—"

"Kerry?" My own voice is swallowed up by the black emptiness and the sound of rain. It can't be her. I'm hearing things.

Yet she is on-site somewhere. "Kerry, is that you?"

"Joel?"

"Yes. It's me. Tell me where you are."

"Down here. But it's slippery and steep, I fell. Don't come any closer. Can you get help? My radio is dead."

"I've got my phone, I'm already dialing," I say, swiping to call Liv, "but are you all right?"

"I'll survive. But tell them the little girl in here is P2, tell them that."

Liv answers. "This better be good, Joel! I'm with the crew look-ing for some kid—"

"We've found her. Next to the field where the horses are. There's a doctor with them and she says the child is a P2. They're going to need a vehicle to get them out, it's boggy and treacherous . . ."

I hear Liv calling out to tell someone, before she tells me, "Joel, I'm handing you over now to one of the firefighters, stay on the line, we won't be long."

"All right, mate, where do we find you?"

As I try to describe our location, Barbara is telling her grand-daughter how Santa will get through the chimney later.

Every cell in my body is telling me to climb down and get Kerry to safety—but I know I shouldn't make the situation worse, force the rescuers to have to haul three people out instead of two. So instead I kneel, feeling the thick, cold mud sinking instantly through my stupid three-hundred-pound jeans, and—passing my phone to Barbara— I lower my chest onto the ground.

Kerry has started singing again, but I can't hear the little girl join-ing in anymore. I shimmy along the wet earth, till suddenly there is no earth. My head and neck are facing down, into the ditch. My chest aches. My heart thunders.

A halo of a torch illuminates the girl's face and the torso of the person holding her.

"Kerry?"

"Joel? Are you real?"

I laugh, despite the situation. "Yup. Are you all right?"

"I'm fine. But we need help down here."

"They're on their way."

"Hear that, Emily?" Kerry says. "I told you the singing would work. Up there is Joel, a very, very old friend of mine."

I try to shift my arm from my side, through the mud, to the edge of the ditch, so I can wave. It's hard work at this angle. "Hello, Emily. I liked your singing."

She barely responds and her breathing sounds shallow and *wrong*.

"Come on, Emily, stay awake for me now," Kerry says. "Do you know, I can fly a plane? And that's because of Joel. He paid for me to learn." She looks up. "It was you, wasn't it?"

I smile. "Did they tell you or did you guess?"

"I guessed . . ." I see her hand stroking the girl's head. "Keep your eyes open, Emily. Are they nearly here?"

I twist my head around. "Barbara?"

"I can see them. Car headlights. People with torches," she says. "Hurry, please," she shouts down the phone.

"What are you doing here, Joel?"

I could tell her about Liv, and the filming. But I don't think that's the question she's asking. The rumble of emergency vehicles gets louder, but they still sound much too far away.

I move my other arm from my side up over my head, and begin to claw through the mud to propel myself forward, like I'm doing a front crawl in the swimming pool. All I want is to take Kerry's hand, hang on till she's safe.

Ugh.

Something stabs, near my heart. Has one of those leads worked loose again?

Not now. She needs *me* this time.

My brain and body scream at me to stop moving. But I won't give in. As my hands grasp for something solid in the mud, I inch forward and the pain stops. It must have been a branch or piece of debris digging in, nothing more. My fingers close around a root ball and I pull myself nearer to the edge. "I'm here."

Kerry's head lamp shines into my eyes and her hand reaches up. I shimmy farther, despite the pain as my ICD grinds against another dead branch.

Our fingers touch. She is so cold. I inch forward just enough to be able to wrap my fingers around hers, and she squeezes back. "Why *you*, Joel?"

"Because you were there for me."

66

Kerry

I wake to a dark winter morning, and Joel is there: a mud-covered scarecrow.

"Merry Christmas, Kerry Smith."

"Merry Christmas, Joel Greenaway."

"How are you feeling?"

"Pretty out of it. Did you sleep here? You didn't have to stay."

"I did and I did." He smiles. "But I ought to go now that you've woken up; Leo might be thirteen, but he still likes his dad there for present opening."

I smile. "Who doesn't?"

But I don't want him to go. I don't ever want to let him out of my sight again.

"Is there any news?"

"I checked on Emily," he says. "She had a good night."

The little girl *had* ruptured her spleen in the accident, but the shock took a while to kick in, enough time for her to get lost. She'll be too poorly to celebrate Christmas, but her family are with her on the ward, and Santa will no doubt make a special trip when she's feeling better.

I was right about my own fractured shoulder too—it'll probably need surgery—but I missed my matching dislocated ankle, which has earned me a night on the orthopedic ward, to keep an eye on the circulation. My parents dropped in last night, with Marilyn, and they got cross with each other over nothing when, underneath, they were furious with *me*.

Not as angry as I am with myself. I cringe thinking about what I did. In the context of a major incident that claimed four lives, my injuries could have diverted attention from more serious cases. Walking off like that was a major breach of protocol. There will be consequences at work.

Joel leans over to kiss me on the cheek, and the sheet turns gray from the dirt and grime on his hair and skin. "Do you want me to come back later?"

"Yes. Oh yes."

After breakfast, volunteers come around, wearing Santa hats, handing out shoeboxes lined with Christmas paper and filled with lavender soaps and hand cream.

I thank them. Yesterday's tragedy has made me appreciate every kindness.

Every brief moment.

Yet as I lie in bed, my shoulder and ankle start to throb because I'm due more analgesia. Everything seems to darken as the pain deepens.

It's over with Marek. The moment I heard Joel's voice as I lay in that ditch I understood why I've never committed to anyone else. I texted Marek on my sister's phone last night saying I'd been hurt at work, but not badly enough for him to cut his holiday short. When he's home, I'll try to explain. I care about him but he's not Joel.

It has always been Joel.

Except what if it's not, even now? What if he's *with* someone?

The thought is worse than the pain in my shoulder. When Zoë died, he said he'd met a woman, but that was over three years ago. I close my eyes. *Please let him be free after all this time . . .*

"Dr. Smith."

My eyes snap open. *Shit.* It's the director of the air ambulance charity, sitting by my bed. How long has he been there? I've only met him twice before, and from the expression on his face, he's not delivering a Christmas present.

"Mr. Sawyer. Hi. I hope you didn't make a special trip." My mouth is dry and the words come out thick and unclear.

"This has been a busy night on duty for all of us," he says. "Are you in pain, Kerry?"

"The meds are keeping it under control."

"Good. Well, in any case, I'll be leaving you a letter in case your memory is affected. I'm afraid I'm here to tell you that you're temporarily suspended. It's slightly academic, given your injuries, but we will be aiming to investigate and adjudicate as quickly as possible."

Gwen and the paramedics always say he's a stickler for the rules, but I don't blame him for sounding pissed off.

"I'm really sorry," I say. "I know it was the wrong thing to do, I should have got help immediately."

"Or not gone walkabout in the first place. The regulations are there for a reason, as you discovered. And now that you're plastered all over the news as some hero, it makes us all look like bloody idiots. Hence the disrepute clause in the letter."

"Sorry, what?"

"You really haven't seen it yet? Ah, yes, I remember. You wrecked your walkie-talkie *and* your phone due to your rash actions." He drops his iPhone into the tray table as though it's contaminated. "Go on, search for yourself."

As I type my name in, one-handed, Google is completing my search with the name *Joel Greenaway*.

The top result takes me to a YouTube video, which buffers for-

ever. I go back, to a report posted by BBC Online. The image pix-
elates, but the voice-over is clear.

"In the midst of the terrible scenes at the Sussex train derailment
last night, there was a moving fragment of hope. Air Ambulance
Doctor Kerry Smith located a young child who'd fallen into a dan-
gerously swollen brook after being separated from her grandmother
in the chaos."

The video keeps freezing, but I can make out enough to realize
that it's switched from aerial footage to something closer up.

I recognize myself, holding Emily's hand as she's being moved
onto a spinal board, ready to be lifted out.

How the hell did they get this?

"Dr. Smith fell down the bank and sustained fractures that left her
unable to climb out and raise the alarm. But in an uplifting twist, it
was TV presenter Joel Greenaway—there filming a documentary
about the fire service—who first located Dr. Smith and her young
patient.

"This remarkable footage shows the rescue, as Dr. Smith supported the little girl, despite her own injuries."

I look at Sawyer. "But I didn't know anyone was *filming* . . ."

He shakes his head.

The images change again and I force myself to keep watching.

"And as soon as the video was posted on social media, viewers
spotted another connection between Dr. Smith and Mr. Greenaway,
who presents *Secrets of Well-being* on BBC Two. Eighteen years ago,
the two hit the headlines as teenagers, when Joel suffered a cardiac
arrest in his hometown of Brighton, and Dr. Smith, then studying
for her A levels, saved his life."

I cringe as they play a terrible clip from that daytime TV show.
The item ends with a trailer for Joel's forthcoming show, and it's all I
can do not to throw the phone across the ward.

How *dare* he turn a tragedy into a PR opportunity? There was
true heroism yesterday, I'm sure, but it definitely didn't involve me.

This was why he was at the scene of the disaster, wasn't it? There was no mystical completion of the circle of life. No debt repaid. Instead, he got the kind of self-promotion that will boost his career—and might cost me mine.

"Mr. Sawyer, all I can say is sorry."

He takes his phone back. "It is *highly* unfortunate. Bad enough that you disregarded health and safety, but to have that misjudgment turn into a media circus will make us a laughingstock across the PHEM world. The charge of disrepute allows for termination of contract, and I have to tell you I will be recommending that." He stands up. "Get well soon, Doctor."

I won't cry. My situation is trivial compared to the suffering of the families of the train passengers who died. Instead I am angry. I wish . . . I wish I had never loved Joel, never trusted him. I wish I had never saved his fucking life.

67

Joel

I race home from the hospital, even though my chest and arms ache and my eyes are sore from not sleeping.

"Merry Christmas!" I say to everyone I pass. "Have a wonderful day."

This was *fate*. I don't even believe in fate, but what the hell else could it have been?

As I walk, my brain turns over what would have happened if I hadn't gone to the crash site, or if I hadn't decided to stop helping Liv when she went too far.

Liv.

Yes, I feel guilty. But really, will she be heartbroken by our relationship ending? We haven't been happy in months, if not years. The fertility issues became all that was holding us together. And I'm too shallow to focus on her for long because my head is full of ideas about what my life with Kerry is going to be like.

I click open the gate to my parents' house and walk up the drive. The door opens. But instead of Leo, impatient to open his presents, it's my father, his expression grim.

Fear makes my heart race. *Not Kerry.* Not now.

"Did the hospital call? Has she deteriorated?"

He shakes his head. "No. No, I'm sure Kerry's fine. It's Liv. Have you spoken to her?"

"No. We've been texting each other; she stayed at the accident scene all night, didn't she?"

He tuts. "I think you'll find she's been to the edit suite too. Come and see what she's done."

I call Liv after I've watched the video. "What the fuck do you think you're playing at?"

"Yeah, Season's Greetings to you too, Joel. Have you left your sweetheart's bedside especially to call me?"

Any doubt that she hadn't known what she was doing disappears. "You did this . . . *why?*"

In the background, I hear someone call her name: she's back at the crash site.

"People want hope at times like this, Joel. I don't think it's going to do your career any harm, nor my series. A little thank-you for your help last night. The sound is ropy but your actions during the rescue *more* than make up for it."

"You've no idea what you've done."

"Haven't I, Joel?"

Before I can think how to respond, she says, "The whole world adores a Christmas love story. Don't worry, if anyone comes to me, I'll lie. Tell them we'd already split up, that I wish you both well."

For a moment, I don't know what to say. "Liv, I—"

"You've never been able to love me completely. I thought it was because of your heart stopping. Or that junkie who almost messed up poor Leo.

"But it wasn't any of that. Funny, a camera viewfinder helps you focus, cuts out all the extraneous shit, and I've always had an instinct for knowing how to compose the shot.

"I saw it. You love her. Maybe you loved me a bit, in your own way. You're not a nasty person. But the way you looked at her when she was being brought out. You've never looked at me like that."

When she stops, I'm not angry anymore. I've no right to be. The way I feel about Kerry has been the big constant in my life since I was seventeen years old. Every time I've tried to ignore it, it's damaged her and me and other people: Zoë, and now Liv too. Love has consequences.

"Liv. I didn't realize how I felt until last night. If I had—"

"I'll try to remember that when I am in the IVF last-chance saloon. I only ask for one thing."

"If it's the house, we can work it all out. I don't want you to be worse off because this isn't your fault."

"I don't care about the house. Just promise me I don't have to say goodbye to Leo?"

I know that splitting up from Liv is the right thing for me, but Leo can't be allowed to lose someone he loves, the closest he's had to a mum.

"You can see him whenever you want." I think of him, still waiting to unwrap his presents. He comes first.

I wait till Leo is engrossed in his new *Legend of Zelda* game before I return to see Kerry. I park on the street opposite the hospital: it's the one day of the year when Brighton's traffic wardens aren't on the rampage.

The hospital looks benign and safe as I walk toward it.

Kerry will be pissed off about the video, but perhaps we can spin it to help raise money for the air ambulance or something? Surely what matters after all this time is that we've found each other again.

The burning sensation in my stomach is excitement, not fear. *Isn't it?*

When I go into her bay, the curtains are drawn.

"Kerry? Are you decent?"

I picture her naked. Imagine how it'll feel when we make love again, after so long.

Silence.

"Kerry?"

I know she's there, I can hear her breathing. Mine too.

I reach out to move the curtain aside a few centimeters. She looks up at me, her face contorted.

"Oh God, are you in pain, can I do something, get a nurse?"

"Yeah. I'm in fucking pain but you've already done enough. Your cute video? It's going to get me the sack. I bet you never thought of that when you were trying to keep your fans happy."

"It wasn't me, I swear. But why would you get the sack?"

"Because what I did when I found that girl was reckless and dangerous. Not heroic. Not smart."

"But you saved her."

She scoffs. "Go away or I will call the nurse."

I step inside the curtain. "No, hang on—"

Kerry holds the call button in her good hand. "I'll count to three. One . . ."

"This can be fixed."

". . . . two . . ."

"Please, Kerry."

"Please, Kerry," she mimics. "No. Not this time, Joel. It might have taken me eighteen years, but I have *finally* realized that you're poison. Goodbye."

And she presses the button.

At home, I act the part with Leo and my parents, playing *Zelda* till I want to hurl the console through the window, and forcing down my Christmas dinner. Shit, I wish I still drank booze.

The next day, I leave him playing while I go to see Ant. If anyone can fix this, it's him. His mum is over from Spain, and they're serving

Boxing Day brunch in the café to people already driven stir-crazy by their families.

"You can have him for twenty minutes, maximum," Ellie says, "but only if you take the girls out from under my feet too."

So we cross the road and go down the steps to the beach, and I pay for Lola and Mia to ride the carousel.

Ant's already seen the video, but I tell him how it's got Kerry into big trouble. "Sounds crazy that they'd sack her for being a hero, but she's never been someone to exaggerate and now she never wants to see me again."

"Bloody hell, you're still a trouble magnet, aren't you, Bananaman?"

"I need to fix this."

"Maybe you can't."

"If *you're* saying that, Ant, I really am in the shit."

The girls spin by on their gold-painted horses and the jaunty carousel melody sounds to me like something out of a horror film.

"You don't have any control over what Liv put out there. You don't have any control over whether Kerry's bosses throw the book at her. And you certainly can't change her mind if she believes you care more about your career than about her."

I nod. "Now you've put it like that, I guess I really am fucked."

"Uncle Joel, can we go again?"

I pay for them to repeat the ride. The sun is freakishly warm but I feel shivery and disorientated. What happens now?

"You know, sometimes I do wonder if it would have been much better for everyone if Kerry had never resuscitated me . . ."

Ant gives me a strange look. "Don't be so self-indulgent. It would have been a lot worse if she'd tried and failed."

"What can I do, Ant?"

The carousel is slowing and the girls are clambering off. "Wish I knew. It's not like you can take that video down now, is it? The whole thing's gone viral. You just have to wait till the next sensation comes along to knock yours off the top slot. So unless you can find yourself a skateboarding duck or a dog that sings like Rihanna, you'll have to be patient."

I don't move. His words swirl.

The girls swamp him with hugs and he stands up. "I'd better get back to the caff. You coming for a coffee? Joel?"

I stare at him, something else clicking into place. "You're a genius. I think I might know what to do."

68

Kerry

DECEMBER 31, 2017

After I'm discharged, I go back to the flat alone.

My parents come around with Christmas leftovers and I put on the best act I can. They try to talk me into going to the Players' New Year bash—this year the theme is *Stranger Things* so they've dug original 1980s tracksuits out of the loft—but they give up without too much of a fight.

After Mum and Dad leave, I sit by the window and watch as the sky turns gray, then deep blue, then black. The wind picks up.

I start a text to Marek on the replacement handset my sister got me. I find it hard to picture his face, even though he's the man I've woken up next to for the last six months.

Hey. I'm going back to bed early tonight. Have a wonderful night and I'll see you in 2018.

I usually add "xxx" without hesitation, but this afternoon it feels dishonest. I end it with "Kerry" and no kisses.

I half-expect a call but instead, I get a message back.

I will call tomorrow. Happy new year, zabka Mx

I hobble to the kitchen and pour a generous double of the fla-vored gin Marilyn got me for Christmas. There's no tonic, so I drink it neat. Hibiscus? More like Hibiscrub hand cleanser.

I'm pouring another when my mobile rings. An international number. Do they not give scammers New Year's Eve off? I answer, partly because I wouldn't mind swearing at someone. "Hi?"

"Is that Kerry?"

"Gwen?" Now I really wish I hadn't answered and brace myself for the telling-off of my life. She must be apoplectic if she's calling from Myanmar.

"Now, listen, Sawyer's been bombarding me with emails and links though I can't click on any of them halfway up Mount Phongun."

"I messed up. I'm sorry."

"Yes, you did. Worse than that, you managed to get yourself filmed doing it. First rule, don't get caught. I've had messages from the others. Lars is especially cross with you."

When Lars called me, he was sympathetic but there was a hard edge to his voice. If your own colleagues aren't backing you, you're screwed. "I'm angry with myself too."

"Righto. This call is costing me about a fiver per minute, so cut-ting to the chase. You've screwed up royally, Kerry, but in purely financial terms, I've no intention of letting stuffy Sawyer chuck you out and waste the money we've invested so far. I am *certain* we can work out a way of putting this right, and that Joel chap has suggested a few things—"

"Joel called you?"

"Nice boy. Don't know how he got through, but these TV people have their ways, don't they? Anyway, he was suggesting how we could turn this to our advantage. So consider yourself told off but don't worry. We won't be throwing you out of the helicopter just yet. OK?"

"Er. Yes. Yes, OK. Thank you."

"You will be making up for it, don't you worry. Happy New Year, Kerry. Oh. Nearly forgot. Joel asked me to tell you he's put something on his video channel, to try to divert people from the footage of you in the ditch."

"What?"

"No idea. No bandwidth here. Must dash, back on the twelfth. And avoid camera crews, will you, Kerry, for pity's sake."

I finish pouring the second shot of gin. It tastes slightly better now. I turn on my laptop, though I don't know that I can bear to watch anything Joel has made.

His YouTube channel has 1.3 million subscribers. I don't know if that's good or bad. I don't usually get time to waste watching stuff online. I click on the Latest tab, bracing myself to see the horrible rescue footage or his face.

Except there's nothing from the crash. In fact, there are only four new videos posted in the last month—yesterday, in fact. They each have only a big white number on a black background as the thumbnail.

The playlist title says:

How to Save a Life—Watch in Order but Please Watch Them Today

I click "Part 1," despite my reservations.

When Joel's face appears, I catch my breath. He looks exhausted. Even when I close my eyes, I see his face when they pulled me out of the stream.

He begins to talk to the camera:

Imagine a room with a hundred people in it: a packed pub, maybe, full of people you know and care about.

One by one, without warning, your friends and family

members begin falling to the floor. Eventually, only six or seven are left standing.

That's the truth about cardiac arrest. Without immediate help, fewer than one in ten people will survive.

It can happen to anyone, anywhere.

And the moment it does, the clock starts ticking. The heart no longer pumps blood to the brain and the body, starving them of oxygen.

But with the help of someone like you, many more patients could survive. Imagine thirty of those people you care about standing back up and dusting themselves down, alive and ready for their second chance.

It's ordinary people like us, not doctors, who are most likely to be there when the worst happens. At work, in the park, at home, even in the pub.

A person's chance of recovery depends on what happens next—starting with you.

I watch all four videos twice over. It must be the tiredness, or the gin, but I cry before the first one is done, reliving what I did and all that's happened since.

And though he never uses my name, in the last one it feels as if he's speaking to me directly. I replay it:

I said in my first video that ordinary people make the difference—but I was saved by an *extraordinary* person. I will never, ever stop being grateful to her. And never forget that it didn't just change my history. It changed hers too. I was "down" for eighteen minutes. Those must have seemed like eighteen lifetimes to her, yet she kept going.

So—eighteen years too late—I want to say thank you, from the bottom of my misbehaving heart.

I hit pause and look at his face, my own breathing uneven. It takes me a minute before I am together enough to scroll down. Already over two million people have viewed the videos and new comments appear when I refresh: *I never realized how bad the odds were from the telly,* one says, *you're a miracle.*

Others have written their own stories of their rebirths, or when they did CPR on someone who made it, or didn't.

Another writes simply: *Now I know what to do.*

I know what I *want* to do and that's call him. But I won't, because I'm drunk and emotional and I will see things more clearly tomorrow.

Still, I've been cooped up in the flat for too long and it's nearly midnight.

The flat is close to the seafront and I decide that I can make it that far, with my crutches. The gin has lessened the pain in my shoulder and foot, but when I step out of the communal door, I feel like Dorothy in the middle of the tornado. Takeaway cartons dance along the pavement. Even the gulls stay close to the ground, as though they're scared they too could be swept up and dropped back down in Oz.

More pieces of the West Pier will be lost to the waves tonight and the i360 observation tower with its donut-shaped platform is closed. But on Hove Lawns, a group of kids play football under the Victorian lampposts. They have to dodge the debris left by beach huts that haven't survived the storms.

If I narrow my eyes, I can imagine that one of the players is Joel, though none of them have his elegance or style.

I stand where I stood with Tim on that Millennium Night and I feel fond of the girl I was, as she waited for the millennium and the life to come.

I saved Joel; he saved me. We're even steven.

The childhood phrase makes me laugh. Life can't be put in columns and the score totted up. Cruelty and suffering come undeserved. We're at the mercy of the gods, or fate, or plain crappy luck.

The wind blows through me with only the crutches to keep me upright.

I check my watch. Five minutes till midnight. The beach beckons. I get as far as the rusty barriers before I remember pebbles and crutches don't go together. I look up. The clouds are racing past the stars a few millennia above them.

Two minutes left.

I hear a loud noise and turn as a large piece of beach hut timber skates across the tarmac of the prom.

A boy crosses the lawns. He's so like Joel that I catch my breath, my body primed to do what I did eighteen years ago if he falls to earth again.

A man falls into step beside the boy and they throw the football between them. The man looks up and his gaze locks onto mine.

It holds me.

The man hugs the boy, whispers something to him, and the kid kicks the ball against the back of the beach changing huts, while the man walks toward me. I feel texts buzzing on the phone in my pocket. Fireworks begin to go off all over the city.

He's next to me now.

"Do you come here often?"

"Oh, roughly once every eighteen years."

"Funny that. Eighteen years ago tonight I died," he says. "For eighteen minutes."

"Eighteen years ago tonight, I helped to bring someone back to life," I whisper.

"Was it worth it?"

"I think it was, in the end." I reach out for his hand, but instead, I touch his wrist, feeling for his radial pulse, steady and strong. "But ask me in another eighteen years, just to make sure."

69

Joel

JANUARY 1, 2018

Today is my eighteenth re-birthday, though I am also thirty-five.

I have a metal box in my chest and next year I will need my batteries replaced again. The leads that connect it all up have a habit of stabbing me in the heart when I least expect it. I have mild hypoxic brain damage that messed up my concentration so I'll never win *Mastermind* and I have to take pills for the rest of my life.

I am so bloody lucky.

I can't know when my heart will beat for the last time. No one can.

But looking at the girl who didn't give up on me makes me feel like a teenager again.

So I kiss her.

Author's Note

You, too, could save a life . . . here's how.

This book is inspired by the night I helped to save a life: Halloween 2013.

The chain of survival worked perfectly. It began with the 999 call taker who realized CPR was needed and told me what to do. It continued with the dispatch of five paramedics and emergency medical technicians from the South East Coast Ambulance Service. They arrived just after midnight and did CPR for twenty-six long minutes before restarting my partner's heart. And it finished at the Royal Sussex County Hospital in Brighton, where the medical staff stabilized him, cooled his body to protect the brain, and waited and hoped and celebrated with us when the induced coma ended and he woke up.

They are my heroes.

How to Save a Life is also about the rocky road to recovery: the shock, exhilaration, and hard work that follows a life-altering event. Treatment is geared toward healing the body, but for both patients and first responders, the mind takes longer to mend.

I did a first-aid course at work in 2002, but I never dreamed I would need it. I am usually pretty uncoordinated, but I was able to give good enough CPR. Which means I know you could too.

Please visit evacarter.net today for more information—it'll only take a few minutes to learn the basics of hands-only CPR *and* discover follow-up first-aid courses in your area.

Acknowledgments and Further Reading

This book has been a labor of love as well as a research-hungry monster. As a result, I am bound to forget someone. Huge apologies in advance.

On the research front, I especially want to thank Dr. Tom and Leigh Keeble, Kate Kennedy, Carli Poxon, Cath Quinn, Dr. Harriet Sanders, Chris Solomons, Pete Sortwell, Dr. Stuart Strachan, Mark Wendruff, and members of the Sudden Cardiac Arrest UK Facebook group, set up by the amazing Paul Swindell. I recommend their site as an invaluable source of information and support: suddencardiacarrestuk.org. Any errors that have slipped through are down to me!

If you want to know more about how medics and other first responders are affected by their work, I really recommend *Also Human* by Caroline Elton, *Direct Red* by Gabriel Weston, and *Seven Signs of Life* by Aoife Abbey.

I want to thank my many creative allies, especially Angela Clarke, Julie Cohen, Rowan Coleman, Miranda Dickinson, Araminta Hall, Stephanie Lam, Jane Lythell, Jill Mansell, Janie Millman, Tamsyn Murray, Sarah Rayner, Cally Taylor, Phil Viner, Araminta Whitley, Laura Wilkinson, Andrew Wille, and Mickey Wilson.

Huge thanks to Hellie Ogden and Allison Hunter at Janklow and Nesbit for the brilliant editorial input and cheerleading. Also shout-outs to Kate Longman and Rebecca Carter, Ellis Hazelgrove, Kirsty Gordon, Zoe Nelson, and Emma Winter.

I have been thrilled to work with the wonderful Hilary Teeman at Ballantine, who had so much love for the book and insights into how to make it better: Right from the first transatlantic call, I knew she was The One. Also thank you to everyone who has worked on the book at Ballantine, especially the meticulous and creative Caroline Weishuhn, and the sharp-eyed copy editor Susan Brown. I must also mention Sam Humphreys, my fabulous UK editor at Mantle/ Pan Macmillan.

Now to the hands-on research I'd rather not have done. Two friends dropped everything when the worst happened, despite new jobs and impossibly long dark drives: Geri and Jenny, you are life-savers.

Big love to my sister, Toni, and my dad, Michael.

All the love to Richard, for proving that two birthdays a year are much better than one.

My mum died shortly before I finished this book. But its origins lie in the gleeful stories she told about life as a trauma nurse from the 1960s onward, and her passion for reading. We sent *How to Save a Life* out to publishers on the date of her birthday. I think she would have enjoyed the serendipity of that.

Finally to you: thank you so much for reading. You can find out more about the true story behind this novel at evacarter.net or say hi on Twitter, Instagram, or YouTube, where I'm @katewritesbooks— I'd love to hear from you. You can even find out why I have two names . . .

Eva (and Kate)

How to Save

a Life

Eva Carter

Random
House
Book Club

Because
Stories Are
Better Shared

TM

A Book Club Guide

Questions and Topics for Discussion

1. In the opening chapters of the novel, we see Kerry and Tim work together to save Joel's life on New Year's Eve, and their actions that night change the course of all three of their lives. Have you ever had a moment like that in your life? Were you aware of its significance at the time, or did you only become aware of it in hindsight?

2. Kerry chooses not to tell Joel that she was the one who primarily gave him CPR on New Year's Eve. Do you think it was fair of her to keep that from him and allow him to be mad at Tim instead? Why or why not?

3. What do you think of Joel's motivations for breaking up with Kerry? Is he being selfless or selfish—why?

4. Joel's outlook on life changes for the worse after he loses his place on the soccer team. Do you think this was an overreaction, or can you relate to this if you think about your own experiences as a young adult?

5. How do you feel about Tim's choice to continue with medical school, despite not really enjoying patient care? Have you ever continued on a certain path simply because you felt like you were expected to and had no other choice? Did you see it through, or did you change course at some point? Why or why not?

6. Throughout much of the novel, Kerry focuses on helping and supporting Tim or Joel instead of focusing on herself. Do you think she makes the right choice in doing so? Can you relate to that desire to help others before yourself?

7. At the end of the novel, Joel, Kerry, and Tim are leading very different lives than the ones they'd imagined at the beginning, and they all seem to be happier for it. What about you? Did your life turn out differently than you imagined when you were eighteen—and have your ideas about happiness and success changed too?

8. One of the book's themes is how emergency responders and medics are affected by dealing with extreme situations, even though the public often expect them to stay heroic and not show distress. Was that surprising to you? Have you had experiences that resonate?

9. Has the book inspired you to learn how to save a life or help in emergencies? (You can find more resources at evacarter.net.)

The *How to Save a Life* Playlist

"How to Save a Life" by The Fray

"1999" by Prince

"Millennium" by Robbie Williams

"Stayin' Alive" by Bee Gees

"Breathe (2 AM)" by Anna Nalick

"(We Dance) So Close to the Fire" by Thomas Faragher

"I'm Never Gonna Give You Up" by Frank Stallone and Cynthia Rhodes

"Nellie the Elephant" by Mandy Miller

"Life Is Beautiful" by Vega4

"Chasing Cars" by Snow Patrol

"Someone Like You" by Adele

"The Story Never Ends" by Lauv

"Music of My Heart" by *NSYNC and Gloria Estefan

"Groovejet (If This Ain't Love)" by Sophie Ellis-Bextor

"Toxic" by Britney Spears

"Mr. Brightside" by The Killers

"Stronger (What Doesn't Kill You)" by Kelly Clarkson

"Fallin'" by Alicia Keys

"Breathe" by Blu Cantrell

"Mad Love" by Sean Paul, David Guetta, and Becky G

"Live While We're Young" by One Direction

"Happy" by Pharrell Williams

"All of Me" by John Legend

"Counting Stars" by OneRepublic

"Bad Romance" by Lady Gaga

"Break Your Heart" by Taio Cruz and Ludacris

EVA CARTER was inspired to write *How to Save a Life* by her own experience of giving CPR to her partner, who was successfully resuscitated, as well as her mother's stories of work as a trauma nurse. Eva worked as a BBC reporter before becoming an author, and she lives in Brighton on the south coast of England. She loves *Grey's Anatomy,* walking her dog, and running very slowly on the seafront. Read about the story behind the book at evacarter.net.